Crash Course

Nick smiled wickedly, and leaned Kate up against the Ladies' cubicle. He then rapidly lifted up her panties, easing one finger inside.

'Wet,' he whispered in her ear, 'you're dripping wet.' His finger slid along the moist lips of her sex, stroking gently along their length, and ended up at the front, just below her dark triangle of pubic hair, caressing and stimulating her clit. Hot arrows of sensation pierced Kate and her legs felt weak and shaky: she smothered a moan of need.

'Oh God,' Kate burst out, 'stop teasing, Nick. I want to feel you inside me. Now.'

Crash Course

JULIET HASTINGS

BLACK
lace

Black Lace novels contain sexual fantasies.
In real life, make sure you practise safe sex.

First published in 1995 by
Black Lace
Thames Wharf Studios,
Rainville Road, London W6 9HA

Reprinted 2000

Copyright © Juliet Hastings

The right of Juliet Hastings to be identified as the
Author of this Work has been asserted in accordance
with the Copyright, Designs and Patents Act 1988.

Typeset by SetSystems Ltd, Saffron Walden, Essex
Printed and bound by Mackays of Chatham PLC

ISBN 0 352 33018 X

Chapter One

'All right,' Kate said, trying to conceal the tiredness in her voice. 'I'll be there on Monday week for the planning meeting. Looking forward to seeing you then.' She replaced the telephone on the cradle and said to it, 'I lied. I'm not looking forward to seeing you then at all.'

Outside her office the sun was setting. The glare shone through the windows and reflected off her computer's monitor. Beastly thing, she thought peevishly. No wonder I get headaches. I suppose I ought to pull the blinds, but it seems such a shame to shut the sun out. Kate's small, modern office room faced north-west and the sun only crept into it at the very end of each day, as if to tell her that it was time to think about going home, a celestial alarm call. Now, prompted by the sun, she sighed and pushed aside the report she was reviewing. Her brain had had enough: it felt as if someone had hung up a little sign saying, *Full. No vacancies.* Friday evening, Kate thought. No use trying to go on when I'm this tired, I'll have to go home soon.

As she leant over to turn off her machine it beeped at her, three slow beeps. She switched quickly through to

1

her email. As she expected there was a little highlighted message at the bottom of the screen: *MAIL*.

I wish it said *MALE*, Kate thought. She did not want to read the email. It would be somebody else asking her to do something that she didn't have time for. She looked at her desk and sighed. Three reports sat there waiting for her final comments, accusing her. She flicked idly through them, looking at the titles.

A report for a large firm of lawyers on 'Practice Development Skills' – in other words how good their staff were at selling and what they could do about it. This one, headed 'Executive Remuneration', was fairly dull, she remembered: a routine report for a privatised utility on top executive salaries, giving them some grounds to justify further massive increases in pay for their board of directors. Both of these two were there for Kate's opinion on style and presentation; she had not been involved in the actual work. But the last report was one that her team had produced under her management, a long document advising a blue chip company on how to design and introduce assessment centres for its senior managers – courses at which the managers would be put through a number of tests and appraised by trained observers so that the company had an independent opinion on those managers' skills and abilities. It was a really interesting piece of consultancy work and had involved the whole of Kate's team for more than a month, and it carried a big fee tag too, but last thing on a Friday evening Kate could not summon up any enthusiasm to read it again.

On the top of each of the reports was a pink sticky note. Most people use yellow sticky notes and pink ones were bad news in Kate's office. They meant *A Message From Bryony*. Bryony, Kate's boss, had made it quite clear in recent weeks that she was looking for Kate to take on more and more client projects, as if she hadn't already got more work than one person could handle. When Kate had protested Bryony had said sharply in her quick prim Welsh voice, 'Client work brings in fees. If you haven't got enough time, cut down on the training you do for our staff. Nobody pays us for that,' and it had been no use protesting that the internal training work was interesting and satisfying in a way that client work never was. Not just reports, not just recommendations, but real action, real practice, things that made a difference to individual people. Kate was a natural teacher and coach and she loved the chance that training gave her to help people change themselves for the better.

She knew what the sticky notes would say without looking at them. They would be things like, *Let's get this out tomorrow*, and *Why did I have to wait three days to see this report?* It was all too much. Too much pressure, not enough thanks. The money was good, but it wasn't worth it.

She sat back in her chair, ignoring the stack of reports, and pulled the appointments pages of *The Times* out of her desk drawer. She had glanced at it on Thursday when it was printed and there were a couple of posts that looked very interesting. She had circled them with red ink and now looked at them again. Director of Training and Development, said one. Blue-chip Company. Competitive Salary and Executive Benefits. Top Level Car. Share Option Scheme. Call outside office hours on 0171 . . .

That's what I'd like, thought Kate. Tell other people what to do for once. Who wants to be a consultant? I've done it for seven years and I know. People only ask you for help when the problem's got so far it's insoluble, and then they blame you when you can't solve it either. Get into one company and concentrate on sorting it out, why not. Take on a new challenge.

She looked at the advertisement a little longer. Her full lips were folded tight in thought and her feathery dark eyebrows were drawn down over her greenish-grey eyes in a straight, direct frown. This was how her staff often saw her, absorbed and concentrating, her hand pushing unconsciously through the dark hair which was twisted up behind her head into a simple French pleat and secured with a big tortoiseshell comb. It was always smooth when she put it up, but by the time she had been concentrating for an hour little wisps would have been pulled out of it, making her look wind-blown and ruffled. The slanting sunlight gleamed on her shining hair and touched the line of her rounded cheek with gold. The weather had been good in recent weeks and Kate's naturally white skin had a slight tan, the fruit of some gentle nude sunbathing on the secluded roof-garden of her apartment, alone, alas.

Kate folded the paper and laid it on her desk as a thought struck her. She went to the door of her office, which stood a little ajar, and stood looking out into the open-plan office outside. It was late, but one of her staff was still working. She hesitated with her hand on the door, catching her lower lip in her teeth as she looked speculatively at the dark young man who sat poring over a computer screen. His hands were pushing through his hair as he tussled with something, and Kate took a long breath then left her door and walked over to him, saying, 'Problem, Alex?'

He jumped and looked up at her. 'No, no, it's OK.' He had dark lashes and sparkling hazel eyes behind his round glasses and very pale skin: his chin was blue with stubble. His rolled-up sleeves revealed well-muscled forearms dusted with fine dark hairs and his collar was a little open, showing his pale throat. He was a junior member of the team, only twenty-four, more than five years younger than Kate, and she found him so desirable that the hairs prickled on the back of her neck. 'Honestly, I'm fine,' he was saying, and she blinked. 'I've nearly cracked it.' He pointed to the screen, where a little flowchart glowed. 'This performance matrix,' he said, 'they want the world, clients always do, and some of the things are mutually exclusive. But try telling them! I think I'm almost there, though.'

4

'You're a paragon,' Kate said. 'The client always comes first, eh?' This was a sort of catch phrase among the team, always good for a laugh, and now Alex chuckled as she had known he would. She could smell the last faint overtones of some sharp fragrance, Xcess or Fahrenheit, she wasn't sure, mingling with the musky lingering scent of his warm skin. She swallowed. 'But don't stay too late. Tina will be expecting you.'

'Oh, she's used to it,' said Alex. Kate smiled at him, then hesitated. Ask him if he'd like to go for a drink, she told herself. Ask him! How often are you alone in the office with him? Ask him, dammit!

'By the way, Kate.' Alex turned and leant on the back of his chair, looking up at her over the top of his little spectacles, and Kate barely prevented herself from jumping. 'I've been meaning to ask. Are you all right? We've noticed, the team have noticed, recently, that you seem a bit, well, under pressure.'

'Me?' Kate tried to sound surprised and lighthearted. 'Well, there's a lot on, you know, Alex. And Bryony's been turning the screws, too.'

Alex glanced over at the closed door of the big office that dominated the floor. 'Has she?' he asked in a low voice. 'God, she is a cow. She's so task-focused she makes Margaret Thatcher look like Mother Teresa. What she needs is a good seeing to.'

Tell him that what you need is a good seeing to, said the voice in Kate's mind. Tell him that he's the man to do it. But she just laughed and said, 'Are you volunteering, Alex?'

'Me? God, no!' Alex shook his dark head earnestly. 'I mean, she's good-looking enough, but it would be like trying to fuck an ice cube. None of us would go near her.' He looked up again and his hazel eyes glittered. For a moment Kate thought he was going to say, 'Not like you, Kate. All of us would love to try it with you.' But he didn't. All he said was, 'Well, if there's anything I can do to help . . .'

Come back into my office with me and make love to me, said Kate's inner voice. She sighed, then said, 'No, Alex, it's OK. I just need a weekend, that's all.' She put her hand briefly on his shoulder, then went back into her office and closed the door.

Her hand was tingling. Every time she saw him it did the same thing to her: she could feel that between her legs she was wet, already aroused and ready for a man. And that was just when he was wearing office clothes. She had taken all her people out recently for a night ten-pin bowling, innocent enough, God knows, and Alex had turned up in the most unexpected gear. At work he dressed conservatively, but then he had worn jeans so tight you could tell he had nothing underneath them and a loose white T-shirt and a biker's leather jacket. Christ, she thought, it was close that night: I could have been on the front page of *The Sun*. She could see the headline now: Voracious female boss gropes junior!

But why did she never tell him how attractive she found him? Why stand over him, breathing in his wonderful smell, and never say a word? She spent half her time teaching people how to be assertive, how to negotiate, how to say what they wanted simply and directly, and where Alex was concerned she might as well be a tongue-tied teenager. It made her angry with herself.

She leant against the door, tipping back her head and closing her eyes. Her hand felt for the key and turned it in the lock. She went back to her desk and settled herself comfortably in her chair, leaning back, and pulled the comb out of her glossy dark hair so that it swung loose to her shoulders. If she couldn't have the real thing, she would make do with her imagination.

She touched her nipples gently through the fabric of her silk T-shirt. Last time she had done this, masturbated in the office, it had been early in the morning. She had been sure she was safe at 7 a.m., but when she had rubbed herself to a frantic orgasm and straightened her clothing and got up she had turned to see the window cleaner's cradle descending at speed away from her window, leaving tell tale white splashes on the glass where the watching cleaner had spurted his come against it and fled without time to wipe it off. Well, there were no window cleaners working now: she was alone with her thoughts. She spread her legs and ran her hand down her body.

Her brain supplied a tentative knock on the door and a crystal-clear image of Alex leaning his dark tousled head around it. He seemed disturbed and he was even paler than usual. 'Kate, are you busy? Can you spare me a moment?'

'Sure, of course. Come in, sit down.' She got up and went over to close the door. 'You look upset, Alex. Are you all right?'

'Well, I – ' He hesitated awkwardly. 'I – '

'Look, don't worry.' She turned the key in the lock and came and sat down next to him, not wanting to put the desk between him and her. 'What's the matter?'

'It's stupid,' he said, not looking at her. 'I can't talk about it outside, the guys would make my life a misery. It's Tina. She says – ' He looked up at Kate with anxious eyes. 'She says this job is killing our relationship. She says I don't want her any more.'

'Don't you?' Kate asked directly.

'Of course I do, it's just that – it's just that things at work sometimes take over, you know what I mean. I find I think about things at work more than I should, even when I'm at home.'

'What things?' Kate asked softly. She was leaning forward a little: the scoop neck of her silk top dipped to reveal her full white breasts, mounded in the shallow cups of a lace bra. 'What do you think about?'

Alex's lips were parted and dry. He put out his tongue nervously to moisten them and Kate saw that the tip was quite sharply pointed, pink and glistening. She would like to feel that pointed pink tongue licking her.

7

He swallowed as if it was hard for him to speak. At last he said hoarsely, 'I can't – '

'You have to tell me,' Kate said, leaning forward further. She let her tongue show between her teeth. 'I'm your boss. I need to know if you've got a problem. I might be able to do something about it.'

'I doubt it,' Alex managed to say. 'It's you.'

His hands were twitching in his lap, twisting nervously over each other as if they were cold. Kate looked at him very calmly, though her heart was pounding with excitement, and asked evenly, 'Me? All right. Is it something that I'm doing that's wrong?'

Alex shook his head and swallowed again. A hectic flush was beginning to colour the white skin of his cheekbones. 'You don't do anything wrong,' he muttered, looking down. 'Nothing. Nothing. It's just that – ' He lifted his head: his mouth looked dry and desperate. Words seemed to be forced from him. 'It's just that whenever I see you I think about – I – ' At last it came out in a rush. 'I want you, that's all. I want you.'

He was sitting with his arms crossed, defensive, anxious body language. Kate felt a surge of satisfaction and pleasure and desire. She reached forward and caught hold of his right hand in hers and lifted it towards her body. He looked at his hand and then at her with an expression of total disbelief. 'That's not a problem,' she said with a small smile. 'That's an opportunity.' She drew his hand closer towards her and put it on her breast and Alex gasped and looked wildly behind him at the door.

'It's locked,' she said, 'don't worry.' She pressed his hand down on her breast. 'Feel it,' she said, 'feel it, my nipples are hard. Alex, tell me what you think about.'

Suddenly Alex's hand squeezed her breast, strong and possessive. His eyes were very bright and he was frowning almost as if he were angry. 'I think about you,' he told her. 'I think about how I would like to – ' He

8

stopped, staring first at her face, then at her hand. His lips were trembling.

'I think,' Kate said steadily, feeling her nipple swelling and aching beneath the pressure of his palm, 'I think that I would like you to go down on me, Alex, right now. I would like you to use your mouth on me. I think you have a beautiful mouth, I want to feel it. Then you can do whatever it is you would like to do.'

There was a little silence: Alex stared at her. Then, without another word, he slid off his chair and knelt in front of her. He reached out and took hold of her silk T-shirt and lifted it over her head, then he pushed up her long full skirt and slid his hands up her thighs, over the tops of her stockings and on to the naked flesh. He came closer, closer between her parted legs, and with his fingers delicately pulled down the cups of her bra to show her swollen nipples. He touched them, first gently, then harder, pinching them so that she gasped and winced. She wanted to feel his mouth between her legs and she put her hands on his soft dark hair and pushed his head downwards and slithered forward until she was sitting on the edge of the chair and he could pull her panties down easily over her white thighs so that she was naked above her stockings. 'You're beautiful,' he whispered. 'You're lovely, you're so soft, your skin is so soft.'

'Lick me,' Kate whimpered. 'Lick me.' For a moment nothing happened, but then he breathed on her, a long cold breath almost like a whistle, so that she cried out with the coldness of it on her wet warm flesh. She felt his fingers on her legs, on the soft fullness of her thighs where they joined her body, and she moaned with the urgent need to feel him touching her. Then he licked her, one long stroke with that pointed tongue from the bottom of her slit to the top all in one movement.

'Oh,' she cried, 'oh God.' Alex laughed, and she could feel his warm breath stirring the crisp fur around her vulva. His strong white hands were holding her hips, denting the flesh of her thighs and backside. He said softly, 'Be quiet, they'll hear you,' and then he lowered his mouth on to her, the whole of his warm wet mouth wrapped around her wet sex. She whined with anticipation. Her clitoris was throbbing, aching, waiting for him to touch it, and the muscles of her vagina were tightening in helpless desire. He moved his mouth, sucking gently, and she whimpered again and lifted her hands to her breasts, squeezing them, pinching at her nipples. Then he touched the hard swelling bud of her clitoris with his pointed tongue and she gave a great shudder. Her head rolled back against the chair and her lips parted softly and she writhed as he lapped and lapped at the little button that was the epicentre of her feelings. His tongue was as sensitive, as imaginative as she had dreamed it might be: sometimes only its stiff pointed tip caressed her, sometimes the whole length of his tongue swirled over her, sometimes he caught the quivering flesh of her labia between his lips and dragged at it so that she groaned with the ecstasy of waiting. She fondled her breasts harder and harder, heaving her hips up towards Alex's flickering tongue and crying out rhythmically as her orgasm approached. She could feel it starting at her feet and beginning to sweep up towards her aching, gaping sex. But before she could come he stopped licking her clitoris and instead thrust his tongue deep inside her, exploring the silken walls of her body. She moaned with frustration as the sensation faded and he drew back a little and said softly, 'Wait. I want to taste you. Wait.'

'Please,' Kate moaned as he thrust his tongue into her again, 'please.' He gave his long tongue a final twist within her then took his right hand from her thigh and put his index finger deliberately on to the bead of her engorged clitoris, pressing it gently. She groaned with pleasure and her moist tunnel spasmed, wanting to be filled. As if he sensed her need his finger slid down the slippery soft lips of her sex and hesitated at the entrance and then slowly, delicately pushed inside her. She gasped and writhed and squirmed on his penetrating finger: involuntarily she clenched her muscles, gripping him tightly, and he gave another gentle laugh and very slowly lowered his mouth towards her straining bud of pleasure and touched it with his tongue. As he did so he put another finger inside her and then another. The sensation was incredible, like being taken by a very short but very thick cock, and as he slid his fingers in and out of her, faster and faster, he sucked on her clitoris as if it were a nipple, drawing it into his mouth and flickering the tip of his tongue against it.

'Christ,' she moaned, 'oh yes, Alex, yes.' Her head was rolling from side to side and her fingers were feverishly pinching and pulling her nipples. 'Yes,' she cried, 'don't stop, don't stop.' This time he did not stop: he lapped harder and harder and thrust his fingers deeper and deeper up into her streaming flesh until she gave a great cry and seized his head with her hands and held him there with his mouth on her as she came, waves of pleasure shuddering through her.

He pushed off her hands and lifted his head while she still shuddered with the aftershock of her orgasm. Her juices were gleaming around his mouth, and he smiled at her and licked his lips. 'Now,' he said, 'my turn.' He put his hands to his fly and unfastened it. Kate shook her head to clear it and looked down, suddenly curious to know what he wore under his well-cut suit. She leant forward and caught hold of his trousers and pulled them down then smiled with pleasure as she saw his neat tight backside revealed by a black close-fitting thong. His penis was hard and erect: the glossy purple dome at the top of its strong shaft stuck out of the front of his briefs. There was a drop of fluid glistening on it and she gave a little gasp and leant forward to touch it with her lips.

She pushed down his underwear and his cock sprang free. It was lovely, taut and eager, hot and smooth and dry under her fingers. The soft hairy pouch of his balls

11

was drawn up tight with the swelling of his cock. She wanted it to be wet with her own moisture, she wanted to taste it. She opened her mouth to take him in but he caught hold of her hair and pulled her back. 'No,' he said, 'no, I want to have you.'

'I want you to have me too,' she said, leaning back in the chair and spreading her legs wider. 'I want you to.'

'Not like that,' Alex said. He pulled her up from the chair. Her legs were like rubber and she leant against him, feeling the heat of his eager cock through her clothes. 'Not like that. I want you on the desk, on your desk, I always have done.' With one arm he swept the desk clear: papers and memos and pens tumbled to the floor. 'Clear desk policy,' he muttered. Then he made her lie back on the hard wooden surface, her legs hanging off the end of the desk, thighs parted, waiting for him.

'Oh God, I've wanted this since the day I joined,' he whispered. He was leaning over her now, lowering his mouth towards hers. Their lips met and she felt his agile tongue slipping into her open mouth, exploring it, teasing and tantalising. He tasted of salt, of sex, of her own fingers when she had masturbated. His hands were on her breasts, his square white nails gently scratching at her nipples. She was overcome with desire for him, she wanted to feel his body inside hers, penetrating her: but now he seemed to want to take his time. His hand slid down her body to the ruckled mess of her skirt and up between her legs. 'You're so wet,' he whispered. 'So wet. Say you want me.'

'I want you,' she replied obediently, heaving up her hips towards his waiting erection. 'I want you. Alex, take me, please.'

'I will take you,' he whispered, and she felt the head of his cock nestling between the lips of her aching empty pussy, hot as fire, satin-smooth. 'Oh, Kate, I will fuck you.' His voice was thick with lust and she quivered with anticipation, feeling his desperate eagerness inflaming her. His hands went beneath her bottom, clutching it tightly, holding her still, ready for him: then in one smooth movement he drove his hard shaft into her, all the way up her, stretching her and filling her so that she felt the softness of his balls pressed against the cleft of her bottom and she cried out with the delicious agony of it. He groaned and his flanks tautened and hollowed as he pulled all the way out and then thrust in again, penetrating her, possessing her.

'Oh God,' he gasped. His eyes were shut, as if he was overcome with the amazement and delight of having her at last. 'Oh God, it's really happening, I'm inside you, I'm inside you at last. Oh God, Kate, Kate.'

Kate arched her back and groaned as she felt his smooth hot shaft sliding in and out of her, in and out, again and again, his body meeting hers with a soft slap each time he forced himself into her. She opened her eyes to look at him as he took her. His face was transfigured with lust and achieved desire, she had never seen anything so beautiful. Pleasure flooded through her in waves, building and building as he moved inside her. 'I'm coming,' she gasped, staring up at his face, 'I'm coming. Please don't stop.' He thrust into her, harder and harder, until she felt her orgasm swell and overwhelm her and she shuddered helplessly beneath him and the feeling of her coming drove him over the top, so that he came too with a shout and she felt him trembling and quivering deep within her spasming body.

Kate squirmed on her chair, writhing as she rubbed her clitoris faster and faster with the middle finger of her right hand and slipped two fingers of the other hand in and out of her wet vagina. She was gasping, turning her head from side to side, the skin of her thighs and stomach fluttering as her orgasm approached. She imagined Alex's taut maleness moving in and out of her, imagined over and over again that blissful moment when he first slipped the broad shelving head of his hot dry shaft between the lips of her vulva and thrust and penetrated her, and at last she came, her whole body stiffening and shuddering.

After a moment she gave a great sigh and straightened in her chair. Nobody had knocked on the door, nobody was at the window; it seemed a bit of an anticlimax after her consuming erotic vision. She licked her fingers, savouring the musky taste of her own arousal, and then wiped them on the inside of her thighs. Fantasy! And what had she ever done to make it a reality? Nothing. Perhaps, she thought to herself, perhaps after next week I might actually do something about him, if I can get up the nerve. He can't be that tied to Tina that there would be nothing to spare for me.

The door handle depressed, lifted and jerked as someone shook at the door. 'Kate?' said a female voice outside. 'Kate, are you there?'

'Christ!' Kate exclaimed. She pulled her skirt down, hastily rearranging and tidying herself, and hurried across the room. Above the low neck of her silk T-shirt her skin was flushed with arousal and she put her hand protectively across it as she unlocked the door.

Bryony stood outside, holding a piece of paper and a thick envelope and looking thunderous. She was a petite pretty woman, no more than five feet two inches tall: Kate was only five foot five, but she looked down into Bryony's face despite her boss's high heels. Bryony was quintessentially Celtic-looking, fair-skinned and red-haired, and despite her small size she was very, very determined. Kate often thought that she was like a weasel, a tiny slender package of utter ferocity, afraid of absolutely nothing. 'Why was the door locked?' Bryony demanded.

'Working on staff reviews,' Kate said smoothly. 'I knew Alex was outside and I didn't want him wandering in.'

'Take them home if you want to do them in privacy,' said Bryony sharply. 'Now look at this.'

14

She held up the paper and Kate took it, feeling her heart still thumping under her hand. It was an internal memo. The name on the top made Kate purse her lips and whistle: a very, very senior director indeed, Bryony's boss's boss.

'There's an influencing skills course next week,' said Bryony. 'Their tutor has dropped out and they were going to have to cancel. Bob wrote to me because he knew you'd tutored the course several times. I want you to do it.'

'Next week?' Kate repeated. She handed the memo back to Bryony, feeling rebellious. 'Bryony, only yesterday you told me that you want me to do less of the internal training and concentrate on client business. Now you want me just to drop everything and go and manage an internal course?'

'Bob has asked particularly for you,' said Bryony, slowly and patiently as if Kate were stupid, pointing with her immaculately manicured finger at the signature on the memo. 'The senior director of our division, Kate. He's got his protégé on this course, some MBA smart alec or other. Do you want to upset him? I'm sure I don't.'

'I've got a lot on,' Kate said, truthfully.

'Never mind. Someone will cover for you. I'll make sure of that.' Bryony folded her lips sternly and thrust the brown envelope into Kate's hands. 'There,' she said, 'participant details and joining instructions. I'll call Bob now and tell him that you'll be pleased to do it.' She began to turn away, then looked around, frowning. 'You look flushed,' she said accusingly. 'What's been going on?'

'Nothing,' Kate said, trying to look innocent. Bryony frowned at her, then turned and stalked away.

Across the office Bryony's door swung shut with a crash. Kate looked at the brown envelope between her fingers and her lips mouthed silent obscenities.

Alex looked up from his desk. 'Well,' he said, 'that

sounds like an opportunity that's just too good to miss.' His hazel eyes glinted at her. 'Are you going to enjoy rearranging everything just to do Mrs T. a favour?'

'Very funny,' said Kate. 'It's just what I need. Three projects at the report stage and another just starting and I have to drop everything to go and cosset the director's pet lap dog.'

'You'll enjoy it,' Alex told her. 'You're bound to. It has to be better than this place, anyway. You might like the director's lap dog.'

'I suppose so.' Kate shook her head and swung the thick brown envelope to and fro, feeling gloomy. With sudden boldness she asked, 'What about you? Will you survive without me?'

'I don't know,' Alex said, smiling. 'I don't know about that.'

For a moment he sounded as if he meant it. She hesitated, wanting to tell him that she thought he was infernally distracting and she wanted him to come into her office and sit on her knee and take dictation. But her nerve failed; it always did.

'You'll cope,' she said at last. She retreated again into her office, wondering if Bryony had detected the slight but definite odour of her own arousal on the cool air.

Tonight, she thought, I need company. She frowned for a moment in thought, then lifted the phone from the hook and pressed an autodial button. Quick bleeps were followed by a ringing tone and then the click of an answering machine.

'Damn,' Kate said. The answering machine said, 'Hi. I'm sorry I can't get to the phone. Leave a message after the beep and I'll get back to you when I can.'

'David,' Kate said, hearing her voice dispirited and flat in her own ears, 'It's Kate. I'm sorry I missed you. I – '

'Kate!' She jumped and looked at the receiver. It was David's voice, warm and cheerful, not the least bit embarrassed. 'Hey, how are you? Caught me call-screening again!'

'David, I am glad you're in. Listen.' Now she had him on the telephone Kate felt a little foolish, but she pressed on. 'Listen, I've had a bloody awful day at work and I was wondering if you would mind if I came over for a bite of dinner. I just don't want to go home and fester. If you're busy, just say – '

'Hey, no, fine!' David sounded genuinely enthusiastic and Kate felt a happy warmth beginning to glow in her stomach. 'It would be great to see you. I've got the proofs for the new show, you can tell me what you think. When will you be here?'

'I don't know. Half an hour? I could drive straight over. Shall I stop by the takeaway and get us something to eat?'

'No, no, I wouldn't hear of it. I'll nip to the deli and get something in, no problem.'

Kate smiled. It must be wonderful, she thought, to have a job that left you with enough energy for cooking on a Friday night. 'That sounds marvellous,' she said. 'I'll see you soon.'

'Looking forward to it. *Ciao, bella*.'

Kate put down the phone, feeling better. She reached for her jacket and her bag and pushed the brown envelope of instructions into the back compartment with a resigned sigh. She started towards the door, then hesitated. Moving with quick decisiveness she returned to her desk, opened it and pulled out the copy of *The Times*. She shoved the main portion of the newspaper into her waste bin and pushed the appointments page into her bag.

'Good-night,' Alex called as she shut the door of her office and headed for the lift. Kate paused in her step, trying to get up the nerve to tell him that when she came back she really wanted to take him out to lunch. As always, she shook her head and sighed and said simply, 'Good-night. Have a good weekend.'

Chapter Two

Kate suspected that David might cook something exotic for their dinner. When they lived together he had always prided himself on providing cordon bleu surprises and now they had gone their own ways he was if anything more inclined to go over the top to impress. She wanted to look as if she had made an effort, so on the way to Docklands she pulled in by a City wine shop which she knew kept good champagne ready chilled for just these occasions.

'Good evening,' said the manager, who knew her fairly well. 'Champagne as usual? What would you like this evening?'

'I think I'll go for Perrier-Jouet tonight,' Kate said. 'Two bottles, please, chilled. And if you could wrap them so they don't warm in the car.'

The manager went to the chiller cabinet for the bottles and Kate sighed and looked at herself in the window. She looked tired and drawn: the pressure of work was beginning to prey on her. She tucked her straight smooth hair behind one ear and turned her face upwards, examining herself critically beneath the shop's harsh neon lights. At least, she thought, she was wearing the sort of clothes that David liked. He was so bohemian himself that he had always found Kate's office dress irresistibly prudish. Today's outfit, a cream silk T-shirt under a black Ralph Lauren suit with a fitted jacket and full skirt, would be sure to please him.

'Do you mind?' Kate asked, fishing out her handbag mirror and a little tube of mascara. She looked into the mirror and saw her eyes frowning back at her. They were interesting eyes, deep set and bright, changing colour from green to grey depending on the light and her mood. This evening, predictably, they were grey. She touched up the mascara on her long lashes and moistened her lips with her tongue.

'Going somewhere special?' asked the manager, handing over the wrapped bottles and accepting Kate's credit card in return.

'No, nowhere in particular. Just visiting an old friend.'

'Very relaxing. Enjoy the evening: see you again.'

She drove the rest of the way rather too fast, risking speed traps, playing *Don Giovanni* on the car's CD. The magnificent, threatening chords of the overture suited her gloomy mood. Just before 9 p.m. she pulled into the visitors' space outside the tall Victorian warehouse where David lived. The security guard smiled at her as she went to the lift and said, 'Shall I let him know you're on your way up?'

'Please,' said Kate. The lift doors slid shut and as she went up the six tall floors to David's penthouse she reminisced about the time when this flat was her home as well as David's. It hadn't worked out in the end because their lifestyles were too different: she was office-bound, tied to hours and meetings and appointments, while he worked when he felt like it with other people whose sense of time was equally vague. Not that she minded having a place of her own – it was fine to be independent and in many ways she was much more suited to a single life – but whenever she came back to Docklands she remembered how much both of them had enjoyed their six months together.

No regrets, she told herself. The lift arrived and the doors opened. Beyond the lobby the wide white-painted door into the penthouse was ajar and she pushed it open and went through, calling out, 'Honey, I'm home!'

The wide expanse of the living area was empty. The bare brick walls were hung with David's own photographs and with modern paintings: Kate had taken her modest collection of Victorian watercolours with her when she left. The blinds were open and through the huge window lay the River Thames, glowing in the summer twilight, and beyond it the constellation of lights that was the City. Kate glanced up to the bedroom gallery: also empty. 'David?' she called.

'In the kitchen!' replied David's voice.

Kate put her briefcase and computer down on the tiled floor, then staggered theatrically past the big trellis covered in green plants to the big bright kitchen. David smiled at her from behind the marble-topped island where he was busily chopping something, dressed in his blue-and-gold towelling bathrobe. David was a thickset man, not more than five feet ten. When Kate had first met him she hadn't thought of him as her type at all; normally she preferred her men tall and dark and slender rather than broad. She would never have imagined herself falling for someone with shoulders like an American footballer and curly hair the tawny colour of a lion's mane. David had lots of hair: the hair on his head was long enough to take back into a little ponytail when he was working, which to Kate always looked charmingly eighteenth-century, and his chest and stomach and groin were also heavily furred. In sunlight the fur glowed golden, making him look like a hairy angel. It was hard for her now to remember the time when she didn't find David attractive, because whenever she looked at him her body told her how much pleasure he had given her and her brain told her how kind he was, how imaginative, how humorous, how fond they were of each other.

She was staring, and David was grinning at her. 'Want

a better look?' he asked, pulling his dressing gown off one shoulder in a parody of a stripper's bump and grind. 'Gorgeous, eh? Just you wait. I'm busy right now.' He gestured towards the food on the counter top. 'Asparagus,' he said, 'and lobster. Lobster's ready. Friday only happens once a week for you nine to five types. I don't suppose you happened to bring any champagne, did you?'

'I know you well enough for that,' Kate said, putting the bag of wine carefully down on the work surface.

David cocked a sandy eyebrow at her as he took the first bottle from the wrappings and dealt with the cork. He was expert, and the bottle gave a barely audible hiss. The sound was accompanied by a glorious smell of toasty, lemon bubbles. He took a couple of flutes down from the tall cabinet and poured the wine, sniffing appreciatively. 'There,' he said, 'that'll do the trick. Nice day at the orifice, dear? You sounded rough when you rang.'

'Ghastly,' Kate said, taking a long gulp of the ice-cold nectar. 'Well, frustrating. After everything she said to me over the last two weeks Bryony dumped another damned influencing skills course next week. I'm bored to the back teeth of them. I have to think of something different, or I'll get incredibly stale. I need a new job. I'm going to resign.'

'Frustrating?' David was always quick to pick up on the sexual overtones of anything she said. 'How so? Lusting after your staff again?'

'You know me, Moriarty. Still failing to get up the nerve to tell Alex I think that he's sex on legs.'

'You should take lessons from me,' David said with a lazy smile, returning to his preparation of the asparagus. 'I never miss an opportunity.'

'Physician, heal thyself,' Kate said. 'I can tell other people what to do, I just can't do it myself. I don't want to talk about it, David. Take my mind off it, tell me what you've been up to. Didn't you say that you had the proofs for the new show?'

'I certainly have. Here.' David pulled out a thick glossy heap of papers from beneath the counter top and put them down by Kate's glass. 'Have a look. I think you'll like some of them.'

Kate took another deep draught of the delicious champagne and began slowly to turn the pages. 'They're lovely, David,' she said. 'I like black and white, I think it brings out the best in you. Some of these are like those wonderful old Hollywood portraits or something from *film noir*. You'll have every actor and actress in the country queuing up to have you take their picture.'

'Well, it pays the bills,' said David, abandoning the asparagus for a moment to lean over her shoulder. 'But look, look at the fifth section, the one called *Narcissism*. They're the best pictures in the show.'

His breath was warm on Kate's ear. She could feel him behind her, his big body warm and hard under the soft towelling of the bathrobe. She knew the smell of him, the feel of him, so well; it felt safe and reassuring to have him with her. If she turned to him now and pushed her hands below the thick robe she knew how he would react, how his muscular body would tense and quiver beneath her fingers, how his eyes would close in ecstasy. No rush, though. She turned back to the proofs and flicked through them until she found the fifth section.

'David,' she breathed, 'these are wonderful. Who is this model? I haven't seen her before. She looks just like Lee Miller.'

'Her name's Natalie. Isn't she great? All bones and profile: wonderful, can't take a bad picture of her. I've done portrait work of her before, but these are something special.'

Kate traced her fingers across one of the glossy pages. On it a lovely slender model lay on a couch in front of a gilded mirror, elegant and attenuated as an art deco figurine, almost boyish in the naked perfection of her slight body. Her face was turned away from the camera, visible to the viewer only as a reflection in the long mirror. The pose was not provocative, but something about the model's narrow face breathed erotic allure: heavy eyelids, half closed, bright red lips glossy and parted, an expression of smouldering yearning. 'She looks as though she can see her lover,' Kate said softly, tracing the line of the model's shallow breasts with her fingertip.

'She can,' David said. 'Her lover is herself. Narcissism: I couldn't have chosen a better model for it. Natalie is more self-obsessed than anyone I've ever met. She's convinced she is the most beautiful woman on the planet.'

'Was it easy to take the pictures?' asked Kate. The model's sensual, languorous face was making her feel uncomfortable, warm and wet between her legs.

'I wouldn't say it was easy. She worked hard, we both did.'

'And you helped her?' Kate turned from the book and looked into David's tawny eyes. 'You inspired her? How did you do that, David?'

'She didn't need me,' David said with a smile. 'A man's just another prop to her. She turns herself on.'

'So she was turned on.' Kate looked again at the face, those parted lips and shadowed eyes. 'I thought so.'

'It was a good pose,' David said thoughtfully. 'I liked it, the lighting was great, but she was shiny on her forehead and here.' He reached out briefly and touched Kate on her collarbone above the edge of her top. 'Shine would have ruined it so I got the old powder puff and went over to dust her down.'

'You just wanted an excuse to touch her tits,' Kate said accusingly.

'No,' protested David, 'no, we were working. How was I to know she was so hot? Anyway, there I was with the powder puff, and she said there wasn't any point.'

'Why not?'

'What she said was, "If you try to cool me off I'll just get sweated up again." ' David smiled at Kate, a lopsided amused smile that made her stomach turn over. 'When have you known me turn down a hint like that? So I said, "I'll just give it one try," and I took the powder puff and brushed it over her front and then I moved it down and touched her nipples, just very gently. She's got no more breast than a saucer, but don't you think her nipples are amazing?' He put his finger on the page. 'Really long and hard, like the tip of your little finger. Very photogenic. I didn't know whether they would be sensitive, but they were: when I touched them they hardened even more and she sighed, a really long sigh, and the whole of her body undulated like a rippling scarf.'

He was still standing behind Kate and she could feel beneath his bathrobe his body stirring as he spoke. She looked down at the picture, imagining David's big capable hands touching those long nipples, imagining the model's sharp intake of breath. 'What then?' she asked softly.

'I looked up at her and she wasn't looking at me, her head was turned, she was watching herself in the mirror, watching what I was doing to her. She didn't care about me, but she thought that the image in the mirror was the most wonderful thing she had ever seen. Her eyes were just slits, green slits, like a cat's, and her lips were apart and they had that loose soft look that means someone is really aroused. You know me, I'm used to naked women, but I could feel myself getting hard just looking at her watching me touching her breasts in the mirror. She looked so self-possessed, so sensual. It was hot under the lights and I could feel myself beginning to sweat and tense as my bollocks filled up and tightened. I carried on touching her nipples with the powder puff and after a moment she began to moan; then I got down on my knees beside her and leant forward and just took one nipple into my mouth and sucked on it like a baby and

24

she moaned even louder. I could look up and see myself in the mirror with my mouth on her breast and my hand touching her other breast, and she was watching me watching her. '

'Don't stop,' Kate whispered. She pulled off her jacket and slung it over a stool then pushed up her top and thrust her hands inside her bra, swirling her fingers over her nipples. She put her fingers to her mouth and licked them and returned them to her breasts so that the tight pink tips stiffened and ached with the delightful chill of her wet spittle on them. 'Go on.'

David's hands were on either side of her, leaning on the counter top. She tilted her head back against him, caressing her breasts as his soft voice murmured in her ear. 'I stayed there for ages, sucking and sucking at her breast, and I actually thought she would come, she moaned and writhed so much. It really got to her when I pushed my tongue into the tiny slit at the tip of her nipple, splitting it apart as if I wanted my tongue to go right inside her breast. I could feel she was desperate to come, her hands were opening and closing in fists and she was moving her hips as if she wanted to feel something inside her, but all the time she was staring at herself in the mirror, staring at me worshipping her breasts. She wasn't going to do anything to make herself come. So I took my hand from her breast and put it down between her legs and she was soaking wet, soaking. She spread her legs wide so that you could see her in the mirror. You see she's very fair and she's got hardly any hair there, her sex is almost naked, and it was pink and gleaming with juice like an open fig. I could see the head of her clitoris in the mirror at the top of her slit, protruding like a little fragment of stem. I slid my fingers into her and they were soaked with juice, then I just put one finger on her button, just one finger, and I gave it a little rub and she cried out as if I had stabbed her: so I touched her again and when I touched her I sucked at her nipple and pushed my tongue into the little crease

25

and she came just like that. Her back arched and she cried out suddenly, quite suddenly, and then she was jerking all over. I think it surprised her too, how quickly it happened.'

'What then?' whispered Kate. She reached behind her and took hold of David's hand and lifted her crumpled skirt and put his hand on her bare thigh, pushing back against him, still stroking her breasts with her hands. 'What then?'

David smiled. His hand slipped up Kate's thigh and inside her panties and his fingers slid experimentally over her soft vulva. 'Christ, you're wet,' he said in surprise. 'How'd you get so wet so soon? Masturbating at work again?'

'Got it in one, Holmes,' said Kate, pushing herself against his searching fingers. 'Tell all, don't stop. I want to hear what happened next.' And she gave a little gasp as he slipped one finger deep into her and began to move it in and out, in and out.

'Well, now,' David murmured, 'all right. She was lazy, really languid, and that mirror had all her attention. She didn't want to do anything that would mean she couldn't look at herself in the mirror. I actually asked her what she would do for me and she said anything as long as she didn't have to move! Well, I could have come up between her legs and just had her, but that would have been dull. So I took my clothes off, and she didn't even look at me.' There was a tinge of offence in David's voice: he knew he had a good body and he liked it to be admired. 'She didn't look once, not once. So I climbed up with my knees on either side of her shoulders and I said, "Look, you, there's something here that needs your attention," and I took her head in my hands and put my prick up to her mouth. I really needed it by then, I felt huge, my balls were so tight and full they were aching. She had come, after all, and not me, and it wasn't fair. She looked a bit startled but her lips were apart and I hung on to her head and just pushed my prick into her mouth as far as I could. I could feel her gagging to start with, then she seemed to get the feel of it and she began to suck me and swirl her tongue over the head and up under the glans, you know, where it really gets me: and I was so desperate I was holding her hair in my fingers and thrusting into her mouth as if it was her slit, really giving it to her.'

Kate fixed her eyes on the picture and imagined the beautiful slender girl with David kneeling above her on the couch, his hairy muscular legs straddling her face, his thick stubby cock sliding deep into her soft mouth. Her fingers pinched and pulled at her nipples and she squirmed on David's exploring finger. 'Go on,' she whispered.

'If you can believe it,' David said, 'when I looked down I could see that she had her eyes to one side, looking at herself. There she was in the mirror, her eyes wide open, watching my wet prick moving in and out between her lips. It looked beautiful, my thick shaft fucking her red mouth, I wished I had the camera ready for a picture, but another time. She was moaning again now, every time the head of my prick touched the back of her mouth. I wanted to hold her down, I wanted to have her head underneath me so that I could thrust into her mouth with all the weight of my body, I wanted to choke her with my prick and make her watch while I did it. But I wanted it to last too. When I knew I was going to come I pulled out of her mouth and knelt there for a moment, gasping, and she put her pink tongue out and licked my cock from the root to the tip. For a moment I let her do it, then I said, "Anything as long as you don't have to move?" and I slid down her body and picked up her legs and put them over my shoulders and then I leant forward, really far forward, all the way down towards her. She was flexible: when I folded her up she didn't flinch, just let me push her, and in the mirror I could see her pink slit opening up, waiting for me to fill it. I pushed her up on the couch so her head fell back

27

over the edge: I love to see a woman's throat when she's being fucked, I love the way they move their heads from side to side and their white necks twist and they moan and sigh. I saw her eyes in the mirror glued to my prick just waiting at the entrance to her tunnel and I pushed into her until all the head was inside her and then I just waited. I wanted her to respond, I wanted her to ask for it. So I leant forward and kissed her neck, then I bit her, my teeth in her white neck, and she moaned and shuddered but she didn't say anything. So I waited.'

'You bastard,' Kate whispered, writhing as she slid up and down on David's penetrating finger. 'You bastard.'

'She loved it,' David said. His penis was poking out through the front of his bathrobe, fully erect, thick as Kate's wrist, asking for her attention. She could not resist it: she lifted her hand and wrapped it around the thick shaft, gently stroking the velvety skin up and down. 'She loved it. She just wanted to see my prick there, waiting to enter her. In the end I couldn't wait any longer and I began to thrust into her and her eyes opened very wide as she watched me disappearing inside her, right up inside her in one thrust. I impaled her, she couldn't escape, I drove my tool right home into her. Then I withdrew and we both watched in the mirror as my glistening prick appeared and the pink lips of her sex clung to it as if they didn't want to let it go. I bit her again and she gasped and heaved up against me and I began to shaft her. I had my teeth in her neck and my hands on her little shallow tits and my cock deep up inside her and I knew I would come soon. I didn't know whether she would but she did, before I did even; she went stiff and groaned and I could feel her spasming round me and I thrust even harder until I came. But even then she didn't stop looking at herself in that damned mirror. She watched herself coming, I swear it.'

Kate sighed and gasped as David continued to move his finger inside her. Her nipples were swollen and turgid and she could feel her orgasm waiting tensely in

28

the base of her abdomen, aching with readiness. 'David,' she whispered, 'make me come.' David pressed closer to her and lifted her chin, twisting her face around so that he could kiss her. His lips hovered over hers and at last his tongue slipped into her mouth and he kissed her hard, his tongue moving in and out of her mouth as his finger slid in and out of her sex, and with his broad sensitive thumb he caressed the eager bud of her clitoris. Kate squeezed her breasts and her body jerked with the sharpness of the pleasure. She began to cry out rhythmically although his tongue was in her mouth. He wrapped his hand in her hair and pulled back her head and kissed her throat and found her rhythm, his fingers thrusting into her and his thumb rubbing at her, and she cried, 'Oh yes, yes, yes, I'm coming, I'm coming,' and then she was there, falling against him, helpless, consumed with pleasure.

David withdrew his fingers, licking them approvingly. 'Wait right there,' he said, and he turned to the stove and picked up the pan of asparagus and hurled the contents into the sink and turned on the cold tap. 'I've always wanted to try this, ever since we saw 9½ Weeks on video.' Kate gasped and sat down suddenly on the floor: her legs would not hold her up. 'Open your legs,' David said, and she obeyed, closing her eyes. Then she cried out in surprise as he took a piece of the thick soft white asparagus and thrust it up inside her: she could feel it burning hot and cold on the outside where the water had hit it.

'God,' David said, pulling out the stem and tasting it, 'better than anything, better than Sauce Hollandaise, that's all I want on my asparagus. Was it hot?'

'Yes,' Kate whimpered, and David reached up for his glass of champagne and took a mouthful and then leant down and placed his lips over her sex and forced the ice-cold liquid up into the depths of her. She squealed and without drawing breath he sucked, draining her, using his tongue. Then he returned to the asparagus. He ate

29

piece after piece, dipping the succulent vegetable into her juices and then sliding it into his mouth. He let her taste some of the thick stems, salty and sweet with the taste of her own arousal. When he had eaten enough he sat between her open thighs and said, 'Kate, what about me?'

Kate sat up: she felt in control again. 'Why should I do anything for you?' she teased. 'You probably already had sex with someone today.'

'Because I need you,' said David, pulling open his robe. His naked body was muscular and strong, with tawny hairs curling around his nipples and down the ridge of his flat belly into the dark thatch of curls in his groin. His thick sturdy cock stood up hard and proud from the soft nest of his balls. 'I want you.'

'You took advantage of Natalie,' Kate said reprovingly. 'I think that counts as sexual harassment. You ought to be punished for it.'

'Whatever you want,' David said, arching his back. 'Whatever you want.'

'Do as I say then,' Kate told him. She reached out and stroked her hand down the length of his hard muscular penis, feeling it swell and throb as she touched it. She ringed it with her fingers, teasing at the little bridge of skin beneath the dark head, and David closed his eyes, his breath whispering out from between his closed teeth. 'Do as I say.' She got quickly to her feet and unfastened her skirt and threw it away and stripped her top over her head. She pulled down her stockings and held them in one hand, and with the other she caught a handful of David's thick, light brown, curly hair and pulled him over to the table. It was a heavy marble table with iron legs, set for their lobster and champagne supper with silver and crystal and candles. She quickly pulled her stockings into soft narrow strips and wrapped them around David's strong wrists and fastened one wrist to each of the legs so that he was sitting on the ground with his hands lifted and outstretched and his stiff rod sticking straight up out of his crotch like a young tree. 'Can you move?' she demanded.

David twisted experimentally at his hands and frowned, a little surprised. 'No,' he admitted after a moment. 'Good,' Kate said, and she bent over and placed her lips quickly over his cock, tasting a lingering muskiness. 'I think it was very unprofessional of you to have Natalie,' she said. 'I'll make you suffer for it.' She stripped off her panties, then stood with her hips in front of David's mouth and thrust her sex towards him. 'Suck me,' she said.

Obediently David put his mouth on her and began to lick and suck at her wet sex. She put her hands behind his head and pushed herself against him, rubbing her wetness against his face. It aroused her hotly to have David at her mercy. He was very strong, with broad shoulders and thick muscles in his arms and chest, and Kate was stimulated to see him helpless before her, tied, obediently pleasuring her with his tongue. For a moment her eyes focused on the table setting and an idea struck her. She pulled one of the candles out of its holder, saying, 'Close your eyes.'

David obeyed, his tongue still busily working between her legs. Kate pulled back and with a shudder of anticipation pushed the candle between her wet pussy lips and thrust it up deep inside her. It was not as thick as David's cock, but it felt good. She withdrew it: it was wet and slippery with moisture from her body. She concealed it behind her and knelt down beside David where he sat with his eyes still shut. She lowered her lips to his straining penis and just touched the velvety glans with her tongue. David moaned and shuddered and she said, 'You'll have to lift it if you want me to suck it.'

'Oh God,' David moaned, thrusting his hips up towards her face. 'Please, Kate, please, please suck it.' Kate touched his cock again with her tongue, teasing him, making him lift his backside off the floor as hard as

31

he could. With her free hand she caught up some of her own juices and rubbed them over his balls and along the strange secret silky crease between his flat soft haunches, licking his stiff cock as she did so. He cried out and she wriggled her moistened finger deep into the crease and opened his puckered arsehole a little, coaxing, slipping her finger inside it as she allowed herself to suck gently at the tip of his cock. He writhed, enjoying the feel of her finger penetrating him, and gasped as he pushed his cock up closer to her mouth. Kate brought the slippery candle out from behind her back and without any warning pushed it up into David's hole, piercing him. He gave a great cry and she let her lips slip up and down on his cock and then lifted her head and squatted over him and guided his thick tool up between her pussy lips into her wet sex and sat down on him hard, so that as his prick penetrated her and filled her his body was pushed down and down on to the invading candle.

'Christ!' David cried out in his pleasure and pain. Kate rose and fell desperately on his surging throbbing cock, aroused beyond belief by the feeling that instead of David having her she was having him: as she rose and fell, pleasuring herself on his strong stiff prick, taking her pleasure with him, he was being opened up, helpless, unable to stop her, taken as a woman is taken, and she was controlling it, thrusting into him with her movements, spreading the cheeks of his bottom and taking him. She had never seen him take anything in his backside before and it made her shudder with delight. She wished she had a big stiff prick of her own so that she could turn him over and thrust her hardness into his virgin crack and make him feel how wonderful it was to be pierced with a thick cock, to feel something hard and hot filling him, moving inside him. He was moaning as she rode him, his head swinging helplessly from side to side, and as his orgasm approached he began to lift and lower his hips, accepting the feel of the candle sliding in and out of him, giving himself up to the sensation of being fucked by Kate as he had so often fucked her. He gave a sudden sharp series of cries and writhed against the stockings that bound him to the table. Kate felt his prick throbbing inside her as he came and she forced herself down on to him and ground her swollen clitoris against his body, feeling her own climax sweeping over her.

After a long moment she untied him and they rolled together to the floor and she very gently withdrew the candle from him and kissed his poor martyred backside.

'My God,' he whispered when he had got his breath back, 'what gave you that idea?'

Kate shrugged. 'Don't know.' She got to her feet and fetched their glasses and the bottle and returned to the floor. 'I feel so much better,' she said. 'You're good for me, David.'

They ate the remainder of their dinner on the floor, naked and flushed. When the lobster was gone and they had opened the second bottle of champagne David said, 'Are you going to tell me what was bothering you about work?'

Kate shook her head. 'I've had it. I'm going to resign. I'll come here and live with you and be your assistant.'

'Don't be silly.' He kissed her gently. 'You know you love working.'

'No, I really mean it,' Kate insisted. 'I've had it. I've got the jobs pages with me. I'm going to resign.'

David raised his sandy eyebrows. 'What's the problem? Just a bad patch?'

'Apart from the fact that my boss has got it in for me,' Kate said tiredly, 'I have to run another influencing skills course next week, and I can't face it.'

'Influencing skills,' murmured David. 'I thought you enjoyed that sort of coaching, Kate.'

'I do,' Kate said. 'You know I do. It's just that only yesterday I got the message that I shouldn't be doing them. Now I have to do another one.'

'Remind me what's in it.'

Kate sighed. 'Four-day course,' she said succinctly. 'Supposed to make the participants more aware of how they can be influential and give them a chance to practise. We cover "bridging", that's finding out what other people think, and persuasion, and assertiveness. One tutor, four participants.'

'In the office?'

'No, in a hotel. It's important that they get away from their normal environment; it makes it easier for people to try new things.' Kate jumped to her feet and went across the living area to her briefcase and rummaged in it for the envelope. 'I've got participant details in here,' she said. 'One of them is some hot shot, the director's pet. Bryony would want me to be very careful with him.'

'Look at you,' said David affectionately, joining her, 'showing yourself to London. Exhibitionist.'

Kate glanced at the window and smiled suddenly, lifting her arms above her head and turning on the spot like a dancer. She could see herself reflected in the glass. Her body was a symphony of curves, rounded and opulent, narrow-waisted, a Victorian body on a Nineties woman. When she had first slept with David she had been afraid that a photographer accustomed to beautiful slender models would find her too curvaceous for his taste, but she had been wrong. David had always adored the juicy, ripe lushness of her flesh. She stood now with her full breasts lifted and the nipples tautened by the raising of her arms, the white skin of her softly curved waist and hips reflecting the sharp spotlights. 'You're just as bad,' she said, for David was naked beside her.

'Let's shock them,' David grinned. He put his hands on her hips and pulled her close to him, lowering his mouth to kiss her. He had full sensual lips and kissed beautifully. Kate tangled her fingers in his thick curly hair and gasped with pleasure, feeling the strong muscles of his heavy body pressing against her softness.

'Now,' David said, 'who are these people?'

They sat on the rug by the big sofa and opened the

file, spreading the papers over the floor. The participant notes were at the front, accompanied by photographs.

'Three men and one woman,' commented David. 'Terrible photos; but the men look a good-looking bunch.'

'So what?' said Kate gloomily. 'I'll only see them for four days, and only to do boring business training. It would be different if I was going to train them in sexual athleticism or erotic positions.'

'Don't do it then,' said David. 'Don't turn up.'

'Don't be daft. Bryony would sack me on the spot.'

'Who cares? You were going to resign anyway.'

'If I'm going to get the sack,' Kate said, 'I might as well do it for something worth while: go out with a bang, not with a whimper.' She was going to say something else, but suddenly she stopped and sat very still, her hand pressed to her open lips.

'Thought of something?' asked David gently.

'Well,' Kate said slowly, 'yes, I have.' She lifted one of the pictures and looked at it. It showed a male face, lean and fierce-looking, with dark brows pulled down hard over bright determined eyes. 'What I am thinking,' she went on, 'is that I might as well be hung for a sheep as a lamb. Why shouldn't I teach them what I want for once? I spend all my time on these courses trying to find out what problems the participants have and sorting those out. This time I'll think about me instead: I'll be selfish. They're all good-looking. I'll teach them erotic skills.'

'But it's an influencing skills course,' said David, puzzled.

'So what? I'll relate it to sex. We'll spend the whole four days in and out of bed with each other. I'll enjoy it, even if they don't. If they complain I'll get the sack, but as you said, who cares?'

David shook his head and smiled. 'You can't make them do that if they don't want to.'

'Oh, yes, I can. The course tutor is in charge, and I do a written report on each of them at the end of it – how much they gained from the course and how much they put in to it. Oh, I can make them do what I want all right.'

'Kate, sweetheart, you can try,' David said, looking into her face. 'But I don't believe you'll manage it. You just aren't self-centred enough.'

'What? You're always telling me I'm a show off!'

'Oh, you love the spotlight, I know that. But when you used to train these courses you would come back and tell me how much all the participants learned and how pleased you were to be able to help them. I can't see you managing to manipulate them purely for your own pleasure for four whole days.'

Kate looked into David's face, her eyes alight with eagerness. 'You can't? Is that some sort of a challenge?' She stretched her hands high above her head, spreading the fingers wide. 'I can't wait!' she exclaimed. 'This can be my swan song. I'll have the time of my life. And I'll teach them influencing skills, too, don't worry.' She caught David's chin in her hand and leant forward to kiss him fiercely. 'Come on,' she said, jumping to her feet, 'Let's go to bed and talk over the details.'

Chapter Three

*A*t least the hotel was up to scratch. Kate preferred to run courses at quiet, luxurious venues, where everything was conducive to concentration, and on this occasion the administrators had done well. The hotel was an old house, comfortable and intimate, with training rooms that were almost like the sort of study you would find within a Victorian rectory. Because the rooms were quite small and there were many of them it was also very private, which suited her plans well.

The hotel manager took her finally to the health suite. 'We have spent a lot of money here,' he said. 'A large pool, as you see: jacuzzi, sauna, steam room, a fully equipped gym and aerobic studio. I'm sure there's everything that your delegates will need.'

I can think of a few things that are missing, Kate smiled to herself, but I've brought them with me. She nodded to the manager and said, 'Can you arrange for me to have exclusive use of the suite?'

'I should think so,' he agreed.

'Please book it for Thursday, that's the final day of the course. And private dining facilities throughout, if they're not already arranged.'

She left the manager and went up to her room. The

participants had all arrived and Kate had met them in reception and given them their briefing. They were due to meet in the bar at 6 p.m. for informal introductions. There was just time to do a little last minute revision before the course started.

Kate felt nervous, which surprised her. She had everything planned and she was certain, well, fairly certain, that nothing could go wrong. After a moment she realised that the quivering sensation in the pit of her stomach was not just nerves, but also excitement, sexual excitement. She went quickly across to the bed, pulling off her loose sweater and unbuttoning her combats: time to dress. Combats looked fine and gave a relaxed, informal feel, but she wanted something that would indicate that she was in authority. She already had the feeling that she would need it.

She chose a linen shirt dress in a neutral shade and sandals with a slight heel. It looked cool, comfortable and controlled. She thought of putting her hair up, tried it, considered the effect and in the end decided that she preferred it swinging loose, just brushing her shoulders. She wanted to look feminine: she wanted the men to find her attractive. After all, she had every intention of having sex with all of them before the end of the course. She looked at herself in the long mirror with approval. The dress skimmed over her breasts, just hinting at their fullness, and was belted at her narrow waist; then the skirt flared out over her ripe plump hips, giving her an hourglass silhouette. She knew that she looked attractive, excited and eager. Her skin was lightly tanned and flushed with pink and her full lips glistened appealingly. She blew herself a kiss in the mirror and whispered, 'Irresistible.'

The thought of the three men waiting for her downstairs, unaware of what she had in mind for them, made her shiver. She went quickly over to the small suitcase by the bed and opened it, looking down at the contents and breathing fast.

Over the weekend she and David had put together a 'library of training materials', things she thought she might find useful. There were clothes made of silk and lace, leather and rubber, for women and men. There was a whip with a thick handle of plaited leather and a long, soft lash, and a paddle covered with velvet. Beneath the clothes lay several pairs of cuffs and lengths of fine chain, some covered in soft fabric, some glittering metal. And at the very bottom lay a selection of books of erotica, a small glass bottle of fine scented oil and a selection of artificial phalluses, several sizes, made of smooth plastic and burnished wood and even carved and polished stone.

Kate hesitated for a moment, then picked up one of the larger phalluses and carried it across to the desk in the corner of her room, where the participants' profiles were spread out. She unbuttoned her dress and slid the smooth, cold head of the wooden phallus beneath the fabric of her panties. As she looked over each page she rubbed the silky wood very gently against her stiffening clitoris, drawing in her breath through her teeth.

The first picture was of the director's protégé, the smart alec MBA. It was the picture she had looked at in David's flat, a sharp-featured, attractive face, high cheek-boned and lean, with tanned skin and gleaming blue eyes beneath dark brows. Kate remembered that face well from a brief encounter in the hotel lobby: its owner was quite tall, slender but muscular, quick and energetic in his movements. She looked again at the picture and put the name to it: Nick. He was very attractive, so much so that she felt a warm dampness gathering between her legs. She pulled her panties down to her ankles and nudged the bulging head of the wooden phallus between the moist lips of her sex. It was thick, and she was not quite wet enough for it to enter her easily; she returned to stroking the little stiff bud of her clitoris and turned to the written comments.

'Don't get the hots for him,' she said aloud to herself.

'Look at that profile. Boy, does he need training!' She read the comments and shook her head.

Nick is very goal-orientated and a high achiever. He is intelligent and quite capable of undertaking even the most complex projects. However, he tends to be overly aggressive with both staff and clients. He has poor listening skills and is intolerant of other people's points of view. These traits will prevent him from making further progression. They have been discussed with him but he rejects them. I expect the course to make him aware of the need for improvement.

On a separate page was a note of what the participant hoped to get out of the course. The box was quite large, but it was filled with two words only in a spiky, aggressive hand: *Fuck knows.*

'Oh dear, oh dear,' murmured Kate, pressing the slippery head of the dildo against her aching vulva. Nick would clearly be a challenge to her abilities as a trainer. But he was so attractive, *so* attractive. She wondered what his body would be like: smooth or hairy, muscled or slender? Would he be a good lover? Egotistical, aggressive men were sometimes magnificent performers, always trying to prove something to themselves: but sometimes they were just plain selfish.

She moved on to the next sheet. From the photograph she saw a big man, wide-shouldered and heavily built, with short wiry hair and a subdued, shadowed face that Kate found strangely sensual. Christopher, she thought. She tried to remember him: her mind contained an image of physical size and quiet watchfulness, and a pair of deep-set, smouldering dark eyes. The whole was oddly disturbing. Reading the notes she found that Christopher's boss found him difficult to manage, opaque and unreadable. 'You never know where you are with him,' said the notes. 'A riddle inside a mystery inside an enigma.'

An enigma, Kate thought. Well, she would try to find out what he was like underneath his expensive clothes. Although he was so big he had not seemed actually threatening, but she imagined that anyone with that amount of raw physical power could be frightening on occasion. I will handle you with kid gloves, Christopher, she thought. She imagined that broad-shouldered, heavy body naked, that strange, sensual face looming above her. If a man that big took it into his mind to do something to her, anything, she would not be able to stop him. The thought made her squirm and she tried again to insert the wooden phallus into her aching vagina. She was very wet now and after a little resistance it slipped in easily, filling her deliciously. She squeezed at the slick wood with her inner muscles and leant back a little in the chair, very gently touching her clitoris with her other hand. She was imagining Christopher's big body poised over her as David had sat over Natalie, strong thighs spread on either side of her head, holding one of her wrists in each hand so that she could not struggle. She kicked with her legs and moaned in delirious protest while he thrust deeply into her helpless mouth with his taut, thick penis. The shadowy forms of the other participants loomed in her imagination, two of them stooping to lick her nipples while beautiful dark Nick took hold of her ankles and quelled her struggles and spread her thighs wide, then leant forward and pushed his eager shaft inside her. As the thick wooden phallus slid to and fro, faster and faster, Kate could almost hear Nick gasping as he drove into her and feel the skin of Christopher's abdomen tautening as he approached his climax, his cock thrusting so deep into her mouth that the velvety glans touched the back of her throat. As her orgasm brimmed up and filled her she plunged the wooden phallus deep, deep into her moist love passage, and her fingers worked busily between her legs. At the moment of climax she imagined Nick jerking and groaning as he came inside her body while Christo-

41

pher's thick stiff cock pulsed and twitched between her lips, filling her mouth with salty, delicious juice.

After a moment she withdrew the wooden phallus very gently and pulled up her panties, then sat up, shaking a little, and went on with her work. She could feel her copious juices spreading on to the silky fabric of her panties. Well, she thought, if they smell me, I'll give them the right impression. I should start as I mean to go on.

The third man was more easy to categorise than Christopher had been. His name was Edmond and he had a fair, fine-featured, aristocratic face and bright, pale eyes. His hair was soft and a little longer than average and it flopped over his high brow in a Brideshead sort of way. In the photograph he was smiling rather lopsidedly: the expression brought out a deep dimple in his left cheek, irresistibly charming. He had met Kate with smooth, quiet courtesy, talking in a clipped, quick voice that betrayed his upper-class background and a public school education. It was interesting to read what his manager said about him: 'So polite that people walk over him. He can't get his own way; he can't get acceptance for his own ideas. As for criticising his staff, forget it: he'd think it was rude.'

Well, I can deal with that, thought Kate. She looked again at the photograph of Edmond. He looks sensitive, she thought, the type who really cares what a woman wants. I bet he's good with his tongue. The thought sent a little delicious shiver running through her.

She shifted the papers and revealed the face of the one female participant. Kate's mouth twitched uncomfortably. This could be the problem one, she knew. Men were susceptible to women, manageable, but if this girl, Sophie, decided that she wanted to dig in her heels and be awkward, she could ruin Kate's most interesting ideas.

She looked at the photograph with concentration. Sophie did not look like the sort of woman who would welcome a course based around sex: she looked passive and withdrawn. Her face was pretty, heart-shaped, with big dark eyes and a cloud of curly brown hair, but her expression was timid and frightened, as if she was afraid that the camera would bite her. Reading the notes Kate found that Sophie also tended to behave in a withdrawn way at work: her manager wrote, 'She is very intelligent indeed and has excellent ideas. However, it is always necessary to tease them out of her. I have never once heard her volunteer a suggestion or say that she wants something.' A male manager, Kate noticed.

Kate sat back, looking at Sophie's photograph and shaking her head. Why do so many women find it impossible to say what they want? Why are they forced into supportive roles, sidelined, passed over, because they cannot master the art of speaking their minds in a way that gets them listened to? She felt sorry for Sophie, a good brain and a pretty face trapped by unreasonable fear, but she was more worried about the success of her course. If Sophie turned out to be a prude it could ruin everything. Kate reminded herself that on this occasion the course was running not for the benefit of the participants but for her own pleasure. She decided coldly that if Sophie looked as if she would be a dampener on the proceedings she would deal with it at once by sending her away, saying she wasn't ready for the course yet. That would leave just three men and her. The thought filled her with delicious anticipation.

Her watch said five past six: time to go down and begin. She liked being a little late, it was guaranteed to draw attention to her. She tossed back her heavy hair and smiled at herself in the mirror, then went to the door.

As she had expected, the delegates were already in the bar waiting for her. Each of them had a glass and she quickly noticed what they were drinking. Edmond, Pimm's; Christopher, gin and tonic; Nick, a bottle of some expensive lager; Sophie, something that looked suspiciously like a mineral water. No surprises there. Edmond got up politely as she came into the bar and the other men looked sheepish then did the same. They were all dressed quite formally, though not in suits. Edmond and Nick were both wearing jackets and ties, and Kate smiled to see that Edmond's tie was an old-school job, navy blue with some sort of crest, while Nick's was a loud affair that looked as if it might be by Moschino. Christopher wore a loose, well-cut turtle-neck shirt of knitted dark-grey cotton that showed off his muscular torso and gave him the look of a secret agent. Sophie had on an unobtrusive dress in a sort of olive drab colour, as if she wanted to vanish into the woodwork.

'Can I get you something?' Nick asked, just before Edmond. Kate smiled at him and said, 'No, no, there's a tab. Does anyone want anything else?' They all shook their heads: cautious, apprehensive and on their best behaviour, as participants always are at the beginning of a course. Kate went to the bar and ordered a spritzer made with dry wine and carried the glass back to the table.

The bar was quiet and unobtrusively opulent. Kate glanced around: nobody was within hearing distance of their table. 'Well,' she said brightly, 'since we're all here and there are no late arrivals, we might as well get started, if it's OK by all of you.'

They glanced at each other and Nick said cheerfully, 'Fire away, boss.'

'Not boss,' Kate said, pleased to have an opportunity to correct him at once. He was too cocky for his own good. She hoped the description was accurate in other ways as well. 'I don't tell you what to do. You're all here because you want to be.'

'I'm not,' said Nick, determined not to be put down. 'My boss sent me.'

The other participants exchanged uncomfortable glances: they had not expected direct confrontation so early on. Kate smiled a little, then asked patiently, 'Well, what do you think you're going to get out of this?'

'Bugger all,' Nick said curtly. 'Influencing? I reckon I'm already pretty influential.'

'So why didn't you persuade your boss that you didn't need to come?' asked Kate. She saw the faces of the other men move from her to Nick like spectators at Wimbledon, but Sophie was staring at her, her mouth a little open, looking astonished.

Nick hesitated. Then he said with a little more interest, 'What's persuasion got to do with it? I thought this was about getting your own way.'

'It is,' Kate grinned. 'But there's more than one way of getting your own way. If you're here and you don't want to be – then you didn't. Do you see what I mean?'

Nick's face darkened into a scowl. 'I suppose so,' he said with ill grace.

The other participants seemed to relax slightly and Kate smiled at them all. She said, 'Remember the definition of influence. You're influential when you succeed in changing someone's behaviour, but you maintain the relationship.' She looked around again at their earnest faces. 'Look, I don't want to get into details now, but I'll just set a few ground rules before we go on to the introductions; a course contract, if you like. Here's what you have to remember.' She sat up straight and used her hands for emphasis, her best model of an influential person. 'This course is a safe environment. Everything you say here is confidential, and I mean everything. Nothing goes back to your boss. I write a report on you, but it's depersonalised: it just says whether I think you put in sufficient effort, and whether I think you benefited from what I tried to show you.' She smiled into the eyes of each of them. They were gazing at her, deadly serious, and she felt a sudden rush of power. They were in her hands for the next four days. For a moment she imagined herself getting to her feet and unbuttoning her dress, revealing her body beneath it, and the four of them

45

kneeling before her, entreating her like supplicants before a queen, stretching out their hands to beg her to be kind to them. The thought filled her with a rush of arousal and she licked her lips and swallowed hard.

'But I want you all to promise too,' she went on, 'that you won't divulge anything you learn about the other participants to anyone, anyone at all, without their permission.' She paused: there was silence. She sensed that Nick was waiting to be addressed, and purposefully looked at Edmond first. 'Edmond?'

'Well, yes. Of course.' His light voice was clipped and correct.

'Sophie?'

'Yes, I promise.'

'Nick?' She wasn't going to ask him last, either.

'Well, all right,' Nick said, still grudgingly. He was behaving childishly, but that was a typical reaction of an aggressive person who finds himself not in control.

'Christopher?'

'Wouldn't dream of it.'

'Good.' Kate sat back a little and allowed her gestures to expand. 'So as I said, this is a safe environment. Anything goes. You can practise what you like. Try things that might seem really way out in the office: you might be surprised by how effective they can be. I'm going to set the tone to start with, until you get used to what we're doing, but you have to feel free to disagree with me and make suggestions if there's something you would rather do. Try to influence me. Use your imaginations.'

'You'd be amazed what I can imagine,' Nick said boldly, and he laughed. Sophie and Edmond seemed unimpressed, but Christopher also laughed, a short, cynical laugh.

'You'd have to be quite creative to surprise me, Nick,' Kate said coolly. She looked Nick in the face and raised one eyebrow and felt a sudden pulse pass between them, like an electric spark.

'That sounds like a challenge,' commented Christopher.

'Oh, it is,' Kate agreed. She took a sip of her drink. 'Now, how do we structure the course? Well, it's four days. We've split down the components of influence into three: bridging – that's finding out what others want; persuasion – that's convincing others to see your point of view; and assertion – that's making others understand your rights. Each day we'll do a little theory, then we'll practise one type of behaviour, then on day four we bring them all together. It's that simple. Lots of practice. Think about all the situations that you find difficult, and we'll practise them.'

'We were asked to bring difficult situations with us,' Sophie offered in her quiet voice. 'Things that we're really facing at the moment.'

'Quite right. It'll save you some time. But you may want to use different ones, too; I have some fairly unusual ideas for this course. I'm sure you'll all enjoy it, though.' They looked intrigued. Kate was going to say more, but one of the hotel staff came over and said, 'Excuse me, but your table is ready.'

'Over dinner,' Kate said as they sat down, 'I suggest we introduce each other. As you know, I'm Kate, from the Training and Development division. What I would like is for you to talk to your neighbour for the next five minutes or so and then tell us something about them. Not work, that's boring: about what they like to do when they're not at work.'

She sat quietly and watched for the next five minutes while the four of them tentatively began to talk. Christopher was talking to Nick and Edmond to Sophie. She was not surprised to see that Nick was monopolising his conversation, while Sophie and Edmond seemed to be doing fine, talking earnestly together in quiet voices.

'Christopher,' Kate said, 'would you like to start off?'

'Sure.' Christopher's voice was like his body, big but restrained, soft and dark-edged: a smoky voice. He

47

looked almost shy, but something about his face made Kate think that it was not shyness that held him back. He gestured with one big hand at Nick. 'This is Nick. He's a busy boy, he works like a dog but he finds time for lots of other things. He plays squash and football at weekends. He likes fast cars, he came here in a Porsche, and from what he says he likes fast women too.' Christopher's voice was dry, revealing no approval. 'If you believe him he's slept with every woman in the office and several outside it.'

Nick smirked and Kate raised her eyebrows. 'I think I can disprove that for a start,' she said, and Nick's complacent expression was replaced by one of anger. 'Thanks, Christopher; an excellent thumbnail sketch. Nick, what did you find out about Christopher?'

Nick opened his mouth, then fell silent. After a second he said, 'Er, this is Christopher. He works in the computer consultancy division. Er, that's all I found out.'

Kate raised her brows. 'I said not to tell us about work.'

'Sorry,' Nick said, scowling at her.

'Well,' said Kate, 'never mind. Sophie, would you like to tell us about Edmond?'

'Edmond,' Sophie said in a voice that was instantly attractive, soft and sweet, 'seems to have a lovely life. He lives in the country in a small house with a big garden, there's a stream in the garden, and he spends a lot of time there reading and listening to music. And he goes to the theatre a lot when he's in London.' She glanced around at the others and added shyly, 'We discovered we like some of the same things.'

'Sophie likes plays and opera too,' Edmond volunteered, 'and she likes walking in the countryside, so we had a lot in common.' He smiled at Kate and she smiled back, delighted to see that Sophie obviously found Edmond attractive and that the feeling was mutual. If they were interested in each other perhaps Sophie would be easier to draw out of her shell. 'I like this way of introducing people,' Edmond went on. 'I should add that Sophie is an experienced sky-diver.'

'What?' demanded Nick, obviously astonished.

'A sky-diver. She's been doing it for years. I was very impressed.'

Nick grinned broadly at Sophie. 'Good God,' he said, 'I'd never have guessed it. What about it, Sophie, is it really better than sex?'

Sophie flushed scarlet and looked away. She did not reply and Nick immediately launched into an anecdote of a friend of his who had tried bungee jumping and had decided it was better than sex. He was monopolising the whole table, but the story was well told and entertaining and nobody seemed prepared to interrupt him.

Am I going to let him do this? Kate wondered. What shall I do? If I let him get away with it, will he ruin everything for the rest of the group by being so bloody cocky?

But he was so attractive. He had heavy eyelids and long, thick dark lashes over eyes that looked as if they were made out of the sky, a bright clear sky early on a summer morning, and his dark hair was fine and springy and strong. It was very carefully cut, Kate noticed, and she wouldn't be surprised to find a tub of Brylcreem on Nick's bathroom shelf: he didn't look like the sort of man who would spurn artificial aids.

She stopped herself from jumping as she felt a touch on her leg. For a moment she wondered who it was, then she saw by the gleam in Nick's bright eyes that it was him. She could feel his toes caressing her naked calf: he must have pushed off his shoes. He had been wearing deck shoes, she remembered, without any socks. The touch of his bare foot on her leg made her breathe quickly and deeply.

Nick went on telling his story. It really was funny: Sophie had overcome her embarrassment and was laughing and even Edmond and Christopher were beginning to pay attention. As Nick spoke his toes climbed up

Kate's leg beneath her skirt, sliding gently over her skin. How often have you rehearsed telling that story, so you can do it without even thinking about it? Kate wondered. She could feel her nipples getting harder under her linen dress as Nick's foot advanced towards her crotch, and she let her thighs move apart.

The story ended and everybody laughed. Edmond said, 'That reminds me,' and Nick eased himself back in his chair and glanced over at Kate. His sleepy sensual eyes were very sharp under their lowered lids. His foot slipped between her thighs and very gently his toe slipped forward until it was resting on the crotch of her panties. He wriggled his toe experimentally and Kate suppressed a gasp. Nick caught his lower lip in his teeth and smiled as if in appreciation of Edmond's story and began very gently to rub his toe against Kate, massaging her engorged flesh through the tight fabric that covered it. She swallowed, trying to control her breathing. Her heavy hair was suddenly hot on the back of her neck. It was as if he could tell when his touch made her jump, made her buttocks clench with the sudden sharp pleasure of it. He put his toe on her clitoris and moved it, slowly, firmly, rubbing in little circles.

Kate could not stand it. If he went on she would come: her face and throat and shoulders would redden in a tell-tale flush and her breath would come fast and everybody would know. She pushed her chair back, pulling away from him, and said with a smile, 'Excuse me: shan't be a minute.' She headed towards the long corridor that led to the ladies', shaking her head and lifting her hair with her fingers.

The ladies' room was smart, large and thickly carpeted, with mirrors and heaps of towels and boxes of tissue and cotton wool on the tables. She sat down in front of the mirror and looked at herself, then went and splashed water on to her hot cheeks. 'That was close,' she said to herself in the mirror.

The door opened. Kate glanced up, then gasped: it

was Nick, heading towards her. His lean jaw was set with determination. 'Nick!' Kate gasped. 'You can't come in here.'

'I'm in here, aren't I?' Nick retorted. 'And you're going to come in here, too, Kate.' He caught her by the arm and pulled her after him into the cubicle at the end of the row. 'You're off your head,' she hissed, but he slammed the door of the cubicle and turned on her.

'You looked at me,' he said. 'You wanted me. Why did you run away when we were just getting somewhere?'

'Because you look like the sort of cocky bastard who would take advantage if I let you,' she retorted angrily.

'My God, you were hot,' Nick said, coming towards her. 'The crotch of your panties was soaking. Anyone would think you'd already been fucked tonight. Let me feel.' Before Kate could tell him no he had caught her by her shoulders and was kissing her. His tongue was hot and hard, exploring her mouth, and she gasped and returned the kiss. Nick's mouth tasted of wine, sweet and sharp.

He pressed her against the wall of the cubicle and scowled in concentration as he struggled with the buttons on her dress. At last it was undone to the waist and he pulled it apart to reveal her lacy bra. Without a word he pushed his hand inside the bra, cupping her breast, catching her nipple between his fingers and squeezing it hard. Exquisite pleasure flooded through her. The breath left her body all at once and she caught his head in her hands and pulled his mouth down on to hers harder. She knew that she should turn him down, refuse him; he was unbearable enough as it was; if she let him have her it would only make things worse. But she wanted him so much. She could feel his thickening penis inside his trousers, pulsing and hot, trembling in its eagerness to have her, and she could not resist it. She wanted him as much as he wanted her.

They heard the door of the ladies' open and both of

them pulled back and froze, looking anxiously towards the door of the cubicle. Footsteps crossed the floor and entered the cubicle next door; they heard the rustle of clothes and the tinkle of urine. A lazy smile crossed Nick's face; he leant forward and kissed Kate again, slowly and lasciviously, still squeezing her breast with one hand, while with the other he continued to unbutton her dress. The woman beside them sighed, flushed the loo and left the cubicle as Nick's hand slipped through Kate's skirt and ran across her thighs. Nick smiled wickedly, then lifted her panties and eased one finger inside.

'Wet,' he whispered into her ear, 'dripping wet.' His finger slid across the moist lips of her sex, stroking gently along their length, and ended up at the front, just below her dark triangle of pubic hair, caressing and stimulating the little point that was the centre of her desire. Hot arrows of sensation pierced her and her legs felt weak and shaky: she smothered a moan of need.

The door closed again. 'Oh God,' Kate burst out, 'do it, Nick.' As he dragged down his tie and pulled his collar open she fumbled for his fly and unzipped it and thrust her hand inside, feeling for his cock. There it was, hot and hard beneath her fingers, a magnificent column of flesh. She pulled herself free of his mouth and looked down at the glorious disarray: her dress half open and rucked off her shoulder, one breast bare and clutched in Nick's working hand, her skirt unbuttoned and her thighs spread apart and her panties pushed down to allow his finger deep into her aching sex, Nick's tie awry and his trousers open and his gorgeous thick hard cock held quivering and ready in her hand. She felt so aroused she could barely stand.

'Now,' she said. Nick bent quickly and stripped her panties down her legs. She stepped out of them and he moved up between her thighs, pressing her hard against the cold tiled wall. There were no preliminaries: he felt for the wet swollen lips of her sex, fitted the hot smooth

52

head of his cock between them, drew his lips back from his teeth in a snarl of pleasure and thrust.

'Oh God,' Kate whimpered, feeling the hot dry shaft entering her, 'God.' Nick groaned as the whole of him slid into her. He took hold of her breasts and squeezed the nipples harder and harder and buried his head in Kate's shoulder as he thrust and withdrew. She put her hands on his buttocks, feeling the muscles there clenching and relaxing, driving in and out of her. Simple, direct, crude sex: it was so good. He moved slowly, pushing in deeply, the hairy root of his cock rubbing hard against her shivering clitoris with every thrust, and as he pinched her nipples and bit her shoulder she felt herself beginning to come. Her head rolled helplessly and she moaned and Nick lifted his head and put his mouth on hers to keep her quiet and forced himself further and further into her and she began to convulse, her tongue quivering in her mouth, her hips jerking helplessly towards him.

'That's it,' Nick whispered into her open lips. 'That's it. Come on, come on. Feel me. I want to feel you come.'

Kate threw back her head and it cracked against the wall of the cubicle. She didn't care: her orgasm was sweeping over her, filling her with glorious, shuddering pleasure. Nick gasped and bit her throat. He began to move faster and she clutched tighter at his wonderful round arse as he plunged in and out. Every thrust was bliss, her climax seemed to go on for ever. He gripped her breasts tightly, her stiff nipples trapped between his strong fingers, and drove his stiff shaft into her as if he wanted to nail her to the wall. 'God,' he whispered, 'I'm coming, I'm coming.' He gave a long choked moan and closed his eyes and she felt him shuddering as he gave a final convulsive heave and his own orgasm gripped him.

They stood still, panting. Nick let his head fall on to her throat and she stroked his silky hair, feeling his penis stirring faintly as it lay deeply imbedded in her moist flesh. Then they jumped: a timid tap sounded on the door of the cubicle and a middle-aged voice said hesitantly, 'Are you all right, my dear?'

Kate tried not to laugh. 'I'm fine,' she called. 'Sorry for the noises: touch of constipation. I'll get something for it from the desk in a little while.'

'You poor thing,' said the voice. 'I'm a martyr to it myself. Can I fetch you anything?'

Nick was laughing, smothering the sound against Kate's shoulder. 'It's all right,' Kate called. 'I'll be fine. Thank you for asking.'

'That's all right, dear,' said the voice. The door opened and closed and Nick let out a great gust of laughter; he nearly fell over. 'Persuasiveness!' he said, gently withdrawing from Kate. 'You think fast, I'll give you that.'

'Never lose your cool,' said Kate sententiously. 'Perhaps there is something I can learn from you.' Nick stretched and pushed his hands through his hair.

'Why, what would you have said?' asked Kate as she wiped herself and began to fasten her dress.

'I'd have told her to fuck off and mind her own business,' Nick said, zipping up his trousers. He cocked his head and admitted with a wry smile, 'It might not have been so effective.'

Kate smiled at him, then stooped to retrieve her panties. 'There you are,' she said. 'There'll be more like that, I promise. Will you be a good boy, Nick?'

'As long as you deliver,' Nick said. He was still smiling, but there was a challenge in his eyes. Without waiting for an answer he opened the door of the cubicle and darted out. Kate saw him stick his head out of the door, look both ways, then saunter off as if nothing had happened. She looked down at herself: yes, flushed from throat to breasts. Oh well, she thought, it was bound to happen. Might as well start as I mean to go on.

Chapter Four

Kate missed breakfast the following morning. She wanted to arrive in the training room unexpectedly, not sit with the four participants at breakfast and listen to what they thought of her behaviour last night. She had waited in the ladies' for some time to try to make it seem that she and Nick had not been together, but she knew that she would not have been fooled and she was sure nor would Christopher, Edmond and Sophie. They must have guessed what she and Nick had done.

Well, she thought as she put her hand on the porcelain doorknob, one down, two to go. Or is it three to go? She could not decide whether she wanted one of the men to deal with Sophie, or whether she wanted to take her in hand herself.

The room was bright and warm with sunshine. It was a pleasant place to train, a pretty room, cheerfully decorated in yellows and greens: the training equipment, flip chart and overhead projector, were cunningly concealed in a corner so that you could almost think it was a comfortable sitting room. However, the people sitting in it did not look comfortable or relaxed – apart from Nick. He was sprawled all alone on a sofa, dressed in jeans and a loose shirt, his lean body flung bonelessly across the cushions, taking up nearly all the space. The others sat uncomfortably upright on chairs set here and there about the room, their restraint contrasting almost laughably with Nick's aggressive relaxation. Kate felt their eyes on her as she entered, fascinated, resentful.

'Good morning,' she said brightly, and one or two of them responded. 'How are you all? Looking forward to it?'

Nobody replied, though Nick grinned lazily at her and stretched out on the sofa. She looked him quickly up and down, realising that although she had felt his cock deep inside her she still did not know what his body looked like: he had been fully clothed, only his fly open to let him at her. A brief flare of annoyance made her dark brows draw down crossly. Whatever she had done it surely couldn't count if she didn't know what the person she had done it with looked like naked.

'This morning,' she said, in a warm, cheerful tone, 'we're going to be looking at what is called "bridging". This means the ability to find out what someone else is thinking, what they want, what their agenda is. Would any of you like to suggest what sort of style we'll use to bridge to somebody?'

There was an awkward silence. Then Edmond said hesitantly, 'When you say style, what do you mean?'

'The sort of questions you might ask,' Kate explained. 'The tone of your voice. The way you look. Your body language.'

There was another silence. Nick yawned ostentatiously and stretched, suggesting that he knew it already, that he had better things to do. Then Sophie glanced from side to side and offered nervously, 'You would sound as if you were interested.'

'Absolutely right.' Kate wrote down the suggestion on the board. Sophie sat up straighter, pleased to have got something right, and smiled at Edmond. The two of them were clearly forming an alliance. 'How would you sound interested, Sophie?'

Sophie coloured slightly and looked away, folding her hands in her lap. She was dressed so unobtrusively that you might almost have overlooked her altogether: a plain white blouse buttoned up to the throat, fawn-coloured trousers and a matching blazer which successfully concealed her slender, pleasing shape. She really would be pretty, Kate thought, if only she didn't look down all the time and dress as if she thought she was a mouse, not a woman. For a moment Sophie seemed unable to reply; then she caught Edmond's eye again and seemed to gather a little courage from it. 'Your voice would be warm,' she said, 'encouraging. And you would really listen.'

'Very good.' They discussed the voice a little more; Christopher and Edmond joined in too, though Nick looked resolutely bored. Kate wrote down *warm, soft, slow, steady, gentle* on the board and looked at it. That's how I would like a man to use his mouth on me, she thought, smiling to herself.

'You'd look interested,' Edmond offered.

'Please tell me how you'd do that,' Kate prompted him.

'Sit up,' Edmond suggested, 'and look attentive.'

'Make eye contact with the person you're talking to sometimes,' Sophie offered. 'And make little noises to show you're listening.'

'Generally,' Christopher said with a slight edge to his voice, 'don't behave the way Nick is behaving at the moment.'

Nick sat up as if stung and the other participants laughed. Kate didn't say anything, it didn't seem necessary, but she was delighted that Christopher had put Nick in his place.

'How about questions?' she went on, opening her hands. 'What about the sort of questions you would ask?'

There was another silence, then Christopher said, 'You mean questions that people can't answer yes or no. Open

57

questions.' His voice was steady and low. He had tremendous presence: when he spoke nobody interrupted and everyone looked at him. Kate found herself wondering again what he was really like, what he was hiding beneath that quiet exterior. Perhaps he is like Superman, she thought: mild mannered on top, and incredible beneath.

She made herself return to the task in hand. 'And open questions are?' she asked.

'What,' suggested Edmond. 'How.'

'Which, why,' offered Sophie.

'When,' said Nick. He seemed to feel constrained to say something.

'When is an open question,' Kate agreed, 'but it's the easiest one to answer shortly. You just have to say yesterday or tomorrow, and that's it. I would suggest that the other questions are more helpful.'

Nick looked dashed, and Sophie and Edmond seemed to glow. Kate realised that they had expected her to favour Nick, to treat him as her pet because he had made love to her. Christopher looked unsurprised and Kate was pleased that he at least had not misread her.

'You should remember,' Kate went on, 'not to ask multiple questions. One question at a time – otherwise one of them may go unanswered. What else might you do, once you've finished, to show that you've been listening?'

'Summarise,' said Edmond, as if it were obvious.

'Edmond, that's excellent,' Kate said, and saw that Edmond's pale cheekbones flushed pink with pleasure at the praise. 'You're absolutely right. If you can summarise back accurately what somebody has said, it really shows that you've been listening and paying attention. That's very flattering to the person you've been talking to, and it helps them to trust you.'

Nick yawned again, shifting his feet on the sofa's chintz cover. He clearly thought that all this soft poncy stuff was unimportant and irrelevant. 'I thought,' he said with a yawn, 'that this course was about influencing.'

'It is.' Kate raised her eyebrows at him. 'What's the problem?'

'All you've talked about so far is finding out what other people are thinking,' said Nick. 'What's that got to do with influence?'

'Remember the definition of influence,' Kate said. 'You are influential when you succeed in changing someone's behaviour, but you maintain the relationship. Nick, it sounds to me as if you're confusing influencing with winning. They're not the same.'

'They're not?' Nick sounded totally unconvinced.

'They're not. You'll discover.' She turned from him, leaving him thinking, and said to the other three, 'You seem to have understood the principles very well,' offering praise where it was due. 'I think it might be easiest if we went on by trying an example.' Her heart began to pound, because she knew what she had in mind now and she knew that this was the riskiest moment of the entire course. If it worked, she was in with a fighting chance. She lifted her head and said brightly, 'What I would like is for one of you to try bridging to me: asking me about whatever it is I would like to talk about. Remember all these things we've written down about the tone of voice and the open questions, the summarising, all the things we've discussed.' They looked a little blank, as if this were a demanding thing to ask them. 'Who'd like to try?'

She was not a bit surprised when Nick sat up on the sofa and said before anybody else could speak, 'I'll do it.' He was the sort of man who always volunteers for everything because he is unshakeably confident in his own brilliance.

The others shuffled in their chairs, looking sullen. Kate glanced at them, but nobody seemed prepared to challenge Nick. 'All right,' she said at last. 'Just for a few minutes, then, Nick, as a demonstration. Remember what we've just discussed about the sort of techniques you'll need.'

'Right.' Nick squared up to her on the sofa, grinning challengingly into her eyes. 'I'll start off with an open question, then. What would you like to talk about?'

Kate swallowed and controlled her voice: the last thing she wanted was to sound nervous. 'Sexual fantasies,' she said calmly.

Nick looked taken aback. Edmond glanced at Sophie as if he wanted to protect her from some terrible threat, and Christopher sat back a little in his chair, raising his eyebrows and smiling. After a short silence Nick cleared his throat and looked around the room, then said with an air of bravado, 'All right then, er, sexual fantasies. Do you have a lot of them?'

Kate smiled. She had known that Nick would find this hard. She answered simply, 'Yes.'

Nick made a face. 'OK, OK, sorry, closed question. I meant to say, do you have a favourite fantasy?'

'Yes,' said Kate again, unable to resist a smile, and the others looked at each other and grinned, pleased to see Nick struggling.

'Do you – ' Nick began again, then stopped himself and seemed actually to think for the first time. He took a deep breath and said at last, 'Would you like to tell me about your favourite fantasy?'

'Not really,' Kate said unkindly, and Sophie actually tittered.

Nick looked for a moment as if he would give up altogether, but he saw the others looking coolly at him and closed his lips tightly. Kate saw him consulting the list of open questions on the board. Finally he said carefully, 'Kate, what happens in your favourite fantasy?'

Kate felt as if she should congratulate him for getting it right at last, but he hardly needed encouragement. She just smiled and said, 'Well, it's fairly vague; you know, a lot of fantasies are. There's a room, a sort of prison, and three people in it, two men and a woman.'

'Do they have her?' Nick asked eagerly.

'What?' said Kate blankly, as if she were puzzled. Nick stared at her, then cursed silently and rethought his phrasing. 'Sorry,' he said quickly. 'I mean, who are they? What do they do to her?'

'Which question do you want me to answer?'

'Oh, dammit. Who are they?'

Kate took a deep breath and let her eyes focus on nothingness. 'There's a man, the villain. He's, oh, forty years old; he's strong and tall and he has dark hair going grey at the temples. His voice is like black velvet. The other two are his prisoners, a young man and a girl.'

'What do they look like?'

'The young man is – oh, I suppose he looks a bit like you, Nick.' This was true, but it was also a trap for Nick.

'Like me?' Nick leant forward eagerly, his eyes glittering. 'You mean you fantasise about someone like me?'

'He's a bit like you,' Kate repeated defensively, and fell silent.

For a moment nobody said anything. Then Nick looked shamefaced, as if he realised his mistake, and said, 'All right, I'm sorry. Please tell me what the girl looks like.'

'She's young,' said Kate. 'Fair-haired, slender as a wand, not a bit like me. The typical romantic heroine. She and the young man are in love, they're engaged. I suppose this is historical, eighteenth-century perhaps, so she's quite innocent, a virgin, and her fiancé loves her and wants her but wouldn't dream of having her before they're married, so she's still a virgin, quite untouched and pure.'

Nick shuffled on his seat. 'What happens?' he asked. 'What happens to them?'

Closing her eyes, Kate let the familiar pictures unspool before her like a silent film, feeling the warmth of arousal settling in her loins and stirring there. 'The villain has them prisoner,' she said softly. 'I don't know why he wants to torture them, but he does. He has the young man tied up and then he manhandles the girl, he pulls her clothes from her, and in the end he's holding her with her hands pinioned behind her back and she's quite naked and struggling, but there's nothing she can do, she can't escape him.' She opened her eyes and saw all the others in the room staring at her, eager and fascinated. Nick said nothing, but she continued anyway. 'He holds her in front of the young man,' she whispered, 'and she tries to pull away. She resists him, and her back arches and it makes her little sweet breasts thrust forward as he pulls her arms behind her.' She arched her back unconsciously, imagining herself pinioned and helpless, exposed before her lover's desperate eyes.

'What then?' asked Nick in a hushed, breathy tone.

'He – the villain – he puts his hands on her and runs them over her. She's afraid of him, but even so her nipples stand up proud and hard with the shame of it. He holds her breasts in his hands and weighs them, then he makes her part her thighs and tugs her shoulders back so that her legs are open and you can see between them, the soft fair curling hair and those delicate pink lips. He says to the young man, Look how lovely she is, don't you want to have her; wouldn't you like to feel yourself inside that pretty little pussy? And the young man rages and hurls himself against his bonds and calls the other man a bastard and a coward and no gentleman.'

'I don't understand,' Nick said, sounding genuinely puzzled. 'Why do you find this exciting?'

'Oh,' Kate said, 'it's any number of things. It's the girl's helplessness, the way she can't do anything when this terrible man puts his hands on her and runs them over her. And her shame. And her poor lover's struggle with himself. You see, this is what happens. The villain takes the girl and ties her down to a sort of couch; she's spreadeagled, her hands above her head and her legs apart. And then he says to the young man, What a lovely piece of women's flesh. I believe I would like to take her maidenhead. And the young man swears at him and threatens to kill him, all sorts, if he dares even to touch her.' She swallowed, seeing the scene unfolding before her eyes. 'And the villain laughs at him and says that there is only one way that he can prevent his beloved from losing her virginity to another man, and that is by taking her himself.'

Nick made a face. 'No contest, is there? He ought to get on top and – '

'You don't understand,' Kate said sharply. She should have let Nick dig his own hole, but the spell of storytelling had seized her and she wanted to finish. 'You don't understand. It's important to him that she is a virgin, it's the proper thing, he's a proper young man. Oh, he's had girls, but never girls of his own class, only whores. His fiancée is like something holy to him, something perfect. He can't bear the thought of having her before they are married. But there she is, staked out before him, helpless and bound, and he can see her breasts and the soft secret flesh between her legs and he wants her. He's hard inside his breeches, hard as a rock, and he doesn't want to admit to himself that he lusts after her because it makes her like a whore. He doesn't want to shame her, her wants to keep her pure.'

Nick swallowed hard. 'So what happens?' he asked at last.

'Oh,' said Kate, 'the villain wins. The poor young man is released and he kneels over the girl, almost weeping because he's afraid he'll hurt her and he knows that she can't possibly enjoy what he will do to her with this terrible villain looking on. He has to take her virginity even though she is frightened and ashamed. He kisses her and she can see that he's almost crying and although she is afraid and full of horror she knows that he loves her. He kisses her and he tries to be gentle. Oh,' Kate turned her head to one side, her lips parted and soft with desire, 'he's so gentle, so loving, but he can't stop: he has to have her.'

'Does she like it?' Nick asked breathlessly.

'That's the thing,' said Kate, clenching her fists. 'When she feels him touching her breasts and how warm he is when he lies on her, she feels aroused; she can't help it. It hurts her when he enters her – '

'Because he's got a big cock?' Nick suggested brutally.

Kate saw Sophie wince. 'No,' she contradicted Nick coldly. 'Because she's a virgin and she's afraid. But he's so patient, so gentle, that in the end she cries out with pleasure. It's not what the villain meant to happen at all. He's furious.'

Nick looked into her eyes and licked his lips. 'When do you come?' he said at last. His face was tense and earnest.

Kate glanced round the room, seeing every eye fixed on her, every mouth dry with sympathetic understanding of her own arousal. 'When the young man comes,' she whispered. 'He's lying on her, pushing himself into her, and she's so beautiful and helpless, tied down underneath him. He can feel her trying to move, trying to lift her hips towards him, and the thought that he is giving her pleasure overwhelms him and he comes. And then I come too,' she finished simply.

'Wow,' Nick said. There was a long silence, then he looked at the others and shrugged. 'Thanks,' he finished awkwardly.

Kate pulled herself up straight, feeling herself flushed again over throat and breast. She swallowed, then managed to say in a fairly calm voice, 'Well, thanks, Nick. Now, what do you think you would do differently if you were doing it again?'

Nick looked blank and startled that she had changed the subject so quickly from an erotic one to something businesslike. 'Well,' he said, when he realised that she really wanted an answer, 'I would, er, try to ask more open questions.'

'Any other feedback for Nick?' Kate asked, turning to the other participants.

There was a short silence. Then Sophie said, 'He didn't summarise.'

'Sophie, you should give feedback directly. You ought to tell Nick what you think he should have done differently, not me,' Kate said, gently but firmly.

'Nick, you interrupted,' said Christopher, 'and you made unwarranted assumptions.'

'Unwarranted assumptions?' repeated Nick angrily. 'You think it's easy? Jesus, you try it!'

'Perhaps you'll get a better feel for it if someone tries bridging to you, Nick,' Kate suggested gently. Nick looked briefly defensive, then slightly mollified. 'Would anyone like to try?' she asked.

'I'll try,' said Sophie quietly.

Kate was surprised, but she turned to Sophie with a pleased smile. 'Sophie, that's great,' she said warmly. 'Off you go. Why not stay on the same subject?'

Sophie looked a little disconcerted, but determined. She said after a moment, 'What's your favourite sexual fantasy, Nick?'

Nick looked defensive and angry. 'Men don't need sexual fantasies,' he said roughly. 'Women need all that stuff. Men can just get on with the job. Why bother thinking about anything?'

Sophie raised her brows, but she did not allow herself to be put off. 'Well,' she said, 'what do you think about when you're making love, then?'

'I just look at the woman I'm with,' Nick grinned. 'If she's attractive, I don't need anything else.' He looked challengingly across at Kate and grinned, making it clear to anyone who had not already guessed that he considered her to be one of his conquests.

Sophie nodded. 'I understand,' she said gently. 'I see what you mean. But what about other times? Suppose you were alone? What would you do then?'

Nick looked at her directly, trying to scare her with his aggressive frown. 'Do you mean, do I ever wank?'

Sophie shrugged. 'I don't know whether you do or not. But if you did, what would you think about then?'

Her big brown eyes looked into Nick's sharp blue ones. They were transparently sincere, interested, earnest. She was paying close attention: she looked as though she really cared. Nick suddenly seemed to forget about the other people in the room and leant towards Sophie, holding out his hands. 'There was something,' he said. 'But, but I don't think of it. I mean, I don't like to think I think of it.'

'Please tell me,' said Sophie softly, still looking into his eyes. 'What is it?'

Nick put one hand to his throat as if he were finding it hard to breathe. 'I,' he said, then stopped, then began again. 'I saw a picture when I was a boy. It was in a book my parents had about Victorian art. It was called *Brenn and his Share of the Plunder*.'

'A picture.' Sophie spoke almost in an undertone. 'What happens in the picture?'

'It's a room, a big room,' said Nick. He was looking into Sophie's eyes. 'It's in a Roman town or something, I don't know. It's dark. There's a great heap of gold in one corner, gold and marble statues and bales of silk and all sorts of stuff, and there's a black slave heaping everything up on to piles, and –' He stopped speaking and swallowed. 'And lying on top of the gold and silver there are women, four women. They're lovely, voluptuous, and half of them are naked and the other half have their clothes falling off them. Two of them have their hands tied behind their backs so their breasts stick out. They're helpless and they're terrified. And one of them is twisting round to look over her shoulder at the door, and the door has just opened. She's naked and her hands are tied behind her back and I remember she's got a gold bangle on one arm, here above the elbow. She has big dark eyes and soft lips, and her eyes are wide because she's so afraid. She's beautiful.'

'Who is in the doorway?' asked Sophie gently.

'A man. Brenn. He's a Viking, a Goth, something like that. He's got long blond hair in big plaits and he's wearing a metal-plate tunic and he's holding a spear; it's sticking up like a great long prick, and his shoes are actually dripping blood. He's been out killing the men that these women belonged to. And now he's come to see what his share is and he's laughing, he's laughing because he can see these four women and all the gold and they're his, he can do what he wants with them.'

'What does he want to do?'

Nick's eyes were very bright and his hands were clenched into fists. 'He comes into the room,' he said, speaking almost under his breath. 'He lifts his tunic and under it he's got a great huge prick, all ready, hard as a rock. The women see it and they moan with fear and writhe on the floor, they want to get away from him. And he leans down and grabs hold of the one with dark eyes and he rolls her over on to her front so her lovely round arse is sticking up into the air. She's actually lying on one of the other girls, lying across her body, so her bound hands are pushed up and her arse is pushed up and Brenn can see right between her legs; she's open to him, she can't stop him doing exactly what he wants to her. He can have her, he could have any of the others, they are all his. He holds his prick and gives it a rub, just checking that it's good and hard, and then he puts his hands on this terrified girl's white thighs, on the insides of her thighs, and she shudders and cries out with horror. He squeezes her thighs a little, just feeling how soft and silky her skin is. There's blood on his hands and where he touches her her white skin is stained with red. Then he slides his hands up to her sex. The lips are pouting at him, standing out, and he puts his thick fingers on them and parts them so that she's open to him. He can see the darkness of her tunnel, waiting for

67

him. She's struggling, but there's nothing she can do. And he pushes himself into her, right into her, up to the hilt, and she cries out as if he's stabbed her. Then he takes her, he's grunting like an animal, pushing his massive cock deep into her, over and over again. His cock is so big that he's stretching her wide open, fucking her so hard that you can hear his balls making a little soft sound every time they hit her body. And she moans and writhes under him and tries to pull away and it's so good that in just a few strokes he comes like a steam train.'

There was a long silence. Sophie's face was slightly flushed and her eyes were sparkling. She did not look at anyone else in the room. 'Nick,' she said, 'why does it arouse you to think about this picture?'

It was clear that Nick was aroused: anyone who was looking could see that inside his tight jeans his penis was massively erect, pressed up tight against his stomach and quivering as if it yearned for escape. Kate looked quickly around the room and saw that Nick's description had had an effect on the others as well. Edmond was watching Sophie and shifting his bottom uncomfortably in his chair, trying to take the pressure off his own swollen cock; Christopher was leaning forward and Kate could not see whether he had an erection, but his face was fascinated and eager and he was staring at Nick as if he wanted to eat him. Sophie herself was squirming in her seat, pressing her thighs together as if she wished she were masturbating.

'It's, it's the power, I think,' Nick said hesitantly, still looking into Sophie's face. 'And the fact that it's all so easy. He doesn't have to worry about them, he doesn't have to give them pleasure, they're just there to serve his lust. He can do what he likes. Sometimes I think that when he's got himself inside the girl he catches hold of her hair and pulls her head back so that her mouth opens. She moans and he gestures to the black slave, and the slave comes over and slides his big black tool into the girl's mouth and takes her there while Brenn takes her pussy. Or sometimes I think he wants to see the girl's face, so he rolls her onto her back and maybe he gets the slave to hold her ankles apart so that she can't struggle and then he can take her from the front and watch her face as his great big cock goes in and out of her. But he doesn't have to. He's got the power. He can do what he likes.'

There was a long silence. Sophie folded her arms across her chest, cradling her little breasts, and shivered. Then she said, 'Nick, thank you for sharing that with us. You don't often fantasise, but when you do you remember a picture of a barbarian soldier preparing to enjoy some lovely captive women and you like thinking of what he might do to them.'

'That's right,' Nick said, looking almost stunned.

After another silence Kate smiled slightly and said, 'Nick, how did it feel to have Sophie bridging to you?'

For a moment Nick did not reply. Then he said, 'She's very good at it, isn't she.'

'Yes,' Kate agreed. 'You saw how she listened, how she showed she was listening, how she looked interested, how she didn't express any opinion on what you said. How did it feel, Nick?'

'Wonderful,' Nick said suddenly. 'As if she really cared what I said.' He frowned, then before Kate could say anything else he said quickly, 'I know I didn't do it right last time. I need to practise this, I can see. Can I try again? Can I try bridging to someone else?'

Kate was very pleased that Nick seemed to recognise the importance of this skill. 'If anyone is prepared to try it, Nick, of course,' she said, looking at the other participants.

Sophie looked down, blushing again: she was clearly unprepared to share her private thoughts with Nick and the others. Christopher met Kate's eyes evenly, but his face was quite unreadable. What is he thinking? Kate wondered. She turned to look at Edmond, who smiled a little self-consciously and said, 'I don't mind, if Nick wants to try it.'

Nick nodded and sat forward on his seat, looking eager, his dark brows drawn down tight over his eyes as he concentrated. 'OK, Edmond, thank you,' he said, and Kate smiled to hear how he tried to make his voice warm and empathetic. 'Now, what would you like to tell us about your favourite fantasy?'

Edmond flushed a little. 'Well,' he began, 'it's not really very like the two we've heard. They were sort of historical, I suppose, but mine is based on real experience.'

'What experience?' asked Nick.

'About a year ago, I went to visit a friend at his parent's house. A lovely big country house, a big garden, lots of space and privacy. When I arrived I thought for a while there was nobody there, but then I heard some voices in the garden so I wandered out to find the people. My friend wasn't there, it was just his younger sister and a friend of hers playing tennis together.' Edmond looked up at Nick and Nick said nothing, only leant forward and opened his hands. 'They were just girls, nineteen maybe, and they were like something out of John Betjeman: you know, glossy hair, lovely long brown tennis legs, pretty faces, suntanned arms. They saw me coming and they both stopped for a while to watch me, but then they went back to playing tennis. I watched them for a while. They did look lovely. When they threw up the ball to serve you could see how their breasts lifted under their whites, and their knickers were moulded so close between their legs that it was almost as if they were naked. It was really turning me on and I thought that wasn't right, you know, not proper. I mean, one of them was my friend's little sister. So I wandered back to the house and went through the French windows into the drawing room. There was nobody there and I sat down on the sofa and it was so warm and comfortable and summery that I sort of half fell asleep.'

'How does this fantasy differ from what really happened?' Nick asked.

'Up to now it's all true. And what happened next is true as well. My friend's sister appeared at the French windows and came in. She was flushed, it was hot and they'd been playing for a while, and she came over to me and I could smell her warm body and see the little beads of sweat on her lips and her breastbone. And she really did lean over me as if I was Sleeping Beauty and kiss me.'

'What did you do?'

'In real life,' Edmond said with a slightly strained smile, 'I jumped up and began to witter on about the weather and how long it had taken me to drive down. She was only young, ten years younger than me, I didn't want to take advantage of her.' Nick's face revealed that he would have had no such compunctions, but he said nothing. Edmond smiled again, warmly this time. 'But in my fantasy,' he said, 'I kiss her back. My tongue goes deep into her mouth and I sit up on the sofa and reach out for her. She pulls back and puts her hands to her shirt and strips it off and she's half naked, with the most wonderful athletic young body. She has beautiful breasts and the pink circles around her nipples are already really swollen. She comes over to me and leans forward, she doesn't say a word, and I stretch up and take her nipple in my mouth. I suck at her nipple and feel it getting harder and harder and she gasps and begins to unbutton my shirt and my trousers and soon I'm completely naked and my, my prick is stiff and sticking up from my crotch. Then she kneels over me on the sofa and she gently, gently peels down her tight white tennis knickers and reveals the most beautiful little pubis I've ever seen, so sweet and tight, with light blonde hair on it and pink soft lips. She's already very wet and she smells so sweet. She still doesn't say anything, but she turns around and very gently lowers herself towards me so I'm looking right up into her pussy. I reach down her body and take her breasts in my hands and I begin to pinch and pull her nipples and at the same time I reach up and begin to lick her. She tastes wonderful, I can't get enough, and I push my tongue as far up her as I can and she gives a little cry and clutches at my tongue with her love muscles. Then I feel her mouth on me, her lips sliding down around my cock, and I stab my tongue in and out of her and flick the tip over her little love bead and she moans and pumps at me with her mouth and it's like nothing I've ever felt. She's whimpering and I pull her clitoris into my mouth and flick my tongue along the little hard shaft and fondle her breasts with my hands. I can feel her vagina start to flutter and spasm, and my balls are tight and full and I'm starting to push up in to her mouth and then suddenly we hear the French doors open and both of us gasp and sort of fall apart.'

'My God,' Nick whispered. 'Who is it?'

'It's her friend,' said Edmond. He was flushed and his high brow was gleaming with excited sweat. 'It's the girl she was playing tennis with. She sees us lying there on the sofa with our mouths deep in each other's parts and she just stares.'

Kate glanced quickly around the room. Christopher was sitting back in his chair and his big hand was stroking slowly up and down his loose trousers and Kate could see that inside the trousers his penis was engorged and that he was masturbating. He was looking not at Edmond, but at Sophie. Sophie was sitting forward on her chair, gazing at Edmond with her pretty lips parted and swollen with excitement. She had one hand pressed close against the front of her blouse, working at the tender breast beneath it, and the other between her legs: she was stroking herself through the fabric of her trousers. She looked ravishing. If I were a man, Kate thought briefly, I would like to put the head of my cock between those soft lips now.

Edmond went on, 'For a moment none of us do anything. Then the other girl comes forward. She's dark, not fair, and when she pulls up her shirt she's got big, firm breasts with long nipples. She's got her fingers on her nipples, and she's pinching them and swirling her fingers around the areola. By the time she gets to the sofa she's got nothing on. She leans forward and catches hold of her friend's blonde hair and pulls her head up and they kiss, really deeply, their tongues going in and out of each other's mouths and their hands on each other's breasts. Then they both look down at me. I'm lying there hardly able to believe this is happening, with two lovely naked girls kneeling over me and just looking down, asking me without words what I'm going to do for them.

'Then my friend's sister pulls away a little and leans forward and kisses her friend between her legs. I can see her pink tongue sliding into the dark fur, licking the crinkled lips, and she sucks at her friend's clitoris and the dark girl shudders and moans. Then the blonde one sort of lifts her friend and positions her over my cock and she holds my cock in her cool hand and guides it up into her friend's wet tunnel. She's tight, really tight, and I gasp as I feel the silken walls clutching at me. Then my friend's sister kneels over my face again and presses herself down on my mouth really hard. I lick her and suck her and thrust my tongue up inside her and I heave my hips up towards the one who's impaled on my hard cock. They're kissing each other and squeezing each other's breasts and moaning as I pleasure them with my mouth and my shaft, and we heave and sigh together and then I feel them coming, first the girl who's got my cock in her, then her friend, and then I'm coming too and it seems like a double orgasm because I gave them both pleasure first.'

He stopped speaking and put the back of his hand to his mouth, breathing unevenly. The other participants stopped stroking themselves and shuffled in their chairs, avoiding each other's eyes.

'Well,' Nick said, 'wow, thanks, Edmond.'

'That's all right,' Edmond said stiffly.

'Nick,' Kate said, pulling herself back from her own arousal to the task in hand, 'you forgot to summarise again.'

'Oh. Sorry.' Nick pulled at one ear uncomfortably, then glanced across the room at Sophie. As if he had noticed her half-hidden excitement he smiled, his blue eyes glittering at her.

'Now,' Kate said. That was enough: they were fully sensitised. When it came to the following day they would be ready for something a little more challenging. 'I think we had better get on to the business side of things.' She saw their expressions, shocked, startled, disappointed. Good, she thought: always leave them wanting more. She pushed back her hair behind her ear and enquired coolly, 'Now, let's discuss how you think this technique would be most useful in a business context.'

Chapter Five

*F*or the rest of that day they worked on business situations where bridging might be appropriate. Nick certainly seemed to have got the most benefit out of the day. He was intensely ambitious and determined, and he viewed the ability to find out what other people were thinking and feeling as just another way to achieve his own objectives in the end. He talked eagerly over dinner about the uses he would find for his new technique: dealing with staff problems, understanding why clients had issues with work he had done, neutralising conflict. 'It's been worth coming on the course just for this,' he said, grinning at the others around the table. 'Never mind that I found out some interesting things about Kate and Edmond.'

'And us about you,' Edmond put in, smiling at Nick with the friendliness that comes from shared experience.

'But we never found out about you, Christopher,' Nick grinned.

For a moment Christopher did not reply. Then he said slowly, 'No, you didn't,' and returned his attention to his dessert.

Nick looked rebuffed. For a moment Kate thought he was going to pursue it, to insist that Christopher answer him, but then he seemed to register just how big Christopher was, how broad his shoulders were and how easily he carried himself, and instead he turned his attention to Sophie. 'Well, Sophie, what about you?' he enquired. 'You asked me all about myself, but you never told us anything.'

'Oh,' Sophie said, blushing red and looking down at the tablecloth, 'I don't have anything to tell.'

Oh, Sophie, Kate thought, just tell him that you don't want to talk about it. Don't try to make it look as if you're sexless. I saw you rubbing yourself while Edmond was talking; you have fantasies all right.

'Nothing to tell?' Nick insisted. 'Oh, come on, Sophie, there must be. Even virgins have sexual fantasies. Really hot ones, I hear.'

Sophie made a little inarticulate sound of protest and turned away as if she would get up from the table. Kate said, 'Sophie, don't go,' and Edmond said sharply to Nick, 'Christ, Nick, don't bully her. Who do you think you are?'

'Hey, I'm sorry.' Nick held up his hands disarmingly. 'I didn't mean to upset anyone. Sophie, are you all right? Am I forgiven?'

'I suppose so,' said Sophie, refusing to look at him.

'Let's go and have coffee in the lounge,' Nick suggested. 'We need to relax. Kate had us all working hard this afternoon. I saw they've got bar-billiards in the lounge, it's years since I played bar-billiards. Anyone fancy a game?'

'I'll play you,' said Edmond, 'if Sophie doesn't mind.'

Sophie smiled. 'I don't mind. I'll watch. I'll score, if you like, I'm good at that.'

'Great.' Sophie and Nick and Edmond got up to leave the table. Edmond hesitated, then said courteously, 'Kate, Christopher, would you like to join us?'

Christopher said nothing. Kate looked anxiously at him and then said, 'We may come out in a moment. Otherwise don't worry, have a good time.'

The three of them left, chatting cheerfully together. Sophie seemed to have decided to forgive Nick. Kate noticed that Edmond opened the door to the lounge for Sophie and that as they went through it he put his arm behind Sophie to steer her, a gentle, almost possessive gesture. Kate sat back in her chair a little and took her napkin from her lap, crumpling it by her place. There were a few crumbs on the soft fabric of her skirt and she brushed them away. 'Well,' she said, 'I think Edmond and Sophie are forming an axis.'

Christopher leant back and raised his brows. He reached up and took off the small spectacles that he wore for work, folded them and slipped them into the top pocket of his jacket. His dark eyes were fixed on Kate, intense and deep set, and his wide, mobile mouth was set in a neutral line. He leant back further and stretched his arms above his head, pushing both hands through his short crisp hair. Kate could see the muscles on his broad chest moving beneath his loose cotton shirt. He smiled at her and she thought for a moment that the expression was condescending. 'Well,' he said at last, 'and where does that leave me?'

'I wondered that myself,' Kate said frankly. 'You were the only person today who didn't volunteer either to be bridged to or to bridge to someone else. It worries me, to be honest. I don't know what you are going to get out of the course if you aren't prepared to put yourself into it.'

Christopher was about to reply, but then a waiter came in and asked if he could clear away. Kate gestured to the table and then said, 'We really ought to talk about this, Christopher. If you have a problem with the course, or with me, we should sort it out now.'

'I'm all for dealing with problems as they arise,' Christopher said, getting to his feet. His tall body towered over Kate and for a moment she felt almost afraid of him; then she pulled herself together.

'We'd better go to my room,' she suggested. 'The others will be in the bar.'

'Your bedroom?' Christopher sounded distinctly apprehensive. 'Is that necessary?'

'All my papers are there,' Kate explained. She looked at his shadowed face and saw it tinged with reluctance. 'Look, don't worry,' she said. 'It's a suite, there's a lounge and a bedroom area. Nothing improper, I promise.' Then she frowned at the strangeness of her own words: a woman reassuring a man, and a big man at that, that he had nothing to fear from her.

He looked straight into her eyes, a searching, direct gaze that made her stomach jolt. Then he said, 'All right. I'll follow you,' and gestured with his hand that she should lead the way.

She guided him up the broad staircase towards her room, wondering what he was frightened of. What was he hiding? Why was he so reserved? With Sophie it was easy to understand – she was simply afraid of nearly everything – but someone as big and intelligent and composed as Christopher surely didn't need to be afraid of anything in the world. Could he possibly be afraid of her, afraid of women? No, that couldn't be it either, because she had seen him this morning with her own eyes, gently caressing the quivering outline of his engorged penis through his trousers as he watched Sophie rubbing between her legs with her little timid hand. Not women, then; but perhaps he had problems with women in a position of authority. Some men did, Kate knew, though she wouldn't have expected it of someone as cool as Christopher.

They reached Kate's room and she opened the door and led the way in. She gestured Christopher to one of the big chairs in the lounge area and went over to the mini bar. 'Would you like a drink?' she asked.

'All right. Thank you. Gin and tonic.' Christopher sat down on the edge of the chair, looking around him. Through the archway at the end of the room the tall four-poster in the bedroom was just visible and he raised his eyebrows, then caught his lower lip in his teeth and folded his hands between his knees, waiting for Kate to pass him his drink.

Kate mixed the drink, found ice and a sliver of lemon for it and put it into his hand. His fingers were very cool. There were fine hairs on the back of his hand, tinged with gold in the gentle light of the room. He was so strong and so subdued that Kate felt desire for him begin to pool in her loins. Like a child, she yearned for something she could not have. He seemed to be not in the least interested in her, and so she was determined that he should become interested.

'Now,' she said, pouring herself a glass of wine and sitting down comfortably in a chair opposite Christopher, 'let's talk. I'd like to know if you have any problems with this course.'

Christopher smiled slightly and looked down into his drink, turning the crystal glass around and around in his big hands so that the ice chinked. 'Any problems with it,' he said thoughtfully. 'Well, that depends, doesn't it. It depends on what you are intending to do with it. With us.'

He lifted his head and his deep eyes looked again into Kate's. His expression was cool and appraising. She said nothing, and after a moment he looked away. 'Would I be right in thinking,' he said, 'that you have been running the course in a fairly unorthodox manner up to now?'

In a moment, Kate thought, he'll ask me if it's usual to have sex with one of the participants on the first night. She replied coolly, 'This morning's session was unusual. The rest has been quite normal.'

'And I imagine,' said Christopher, still not looking at her, 'that you have other similar intentions for the rest of the course. Today was just softening us up, wasn't it?'

'You're not stupid, are you?' Kate said, with a touch of real admiration in her voice.

'No. No, I'm not stupid. I'd be very interested to know why you think you'll get away with it, though. I could call up your director tomorrow and tell him what you're up to and you would be out on your ear.'

This was more of a challenge than Kate had expected from one of the men. She sat straighter in her chair and prevented herself from licking her lips nervously. 'What makes you think I would care?' she asked carefully.

Christopher looked at her now, his wide lips parting in an easy smile. 'I understand,' he said, 'I see now. Are you by any chance using this course as a way of getting your own back?'

'More or less,' Kate admitted.

'And you mean it to be basically sexual? That's what you intend?'

His face was so emotionless. How could a man say that to her calmly, evenly, as if he were not in the least concerned? 'I wanted to have a good time, yes,' Kate said at last. A twinge of shame settled in her stomach, gnawing there.

'Fine.' Christopher looked back down into his drink, then with a quick movement lifted it to his lips and drained it. He got to his feet. 'You can count me out, then. I'll be checking out tomorrow.'

'What?' Kate exclaimed, leaping up from her chair. 'Why? Listen, you can't – '

'I have no intention of staying to be your plaything.' Christopher set the glass down on the side table. 'Sorry if it upsets your plans.'

This was the last thing Kate had expected. If Sophie had complained, threatened to run away, she would have understood and she probably wouldn't have minded. But to lose Christopher, this great quiet shadow that moved like a panther, that would be a real disaster. She hurried over to the door and stood in front of it, holding out her hands to prevent him from leaving and feeling more or less ridiculous. He was twice her size; if he wanted to he could just pick her up in his big hands and move her out of the way like a doll. 'Christopher,' she said, 'I would be really concerned if you left. I think you could learn something from the course anyway, whatever the subject matter is. You saw how much Nick benefited from today, and of all the participants you're the one that can help him the most. Edmond and Sophie are afraid of him, they can't handle aggression. Please think again about leaving.'

'I don't think you can teach me anything I want to learn,' Christopher said. He came and stood before her, looking down into her eyes. 'Please get out of my way.'

'No, no. Listen.' Kate shook her head, thinking fast. 'Christopher, tell me what the problem is. Is it me? Is there something wrong with me?'

He raised his brows and looked her up and down, appraising her as coolly as a painter. She felt herself shiver with expectation. 'No,' he said at last. 'There's nothing wrong with you. Not physically, anyway. You're very attractive, in a curvy sort of way.'

'Tell me then,' Kate said quickly, 'tell me what you would like to get out of the course. Be honest with me, Christopher. You haven't once told me what you are really thinking. Why are you so reserved?' She saw his eyes on her, wary and distrustful, and she added quickly, 'It's confidential, remember. Just between you and me.'

There was a long silence. Then Christopher turned away from her, thinning his lips. 'Confidential,' he murmured. Suddenly, with quick decision, he faced her again. 'All right,' he said, 'I'll tell you the truth. I wouldn't mind having sex with you, Kate. You're very attractive. I'd like to touch you.' His eyes were still supremely cool, and Kate could feel herself shivering and melting as his even, steady words sank in. 'But that's not as far as it goes. You see, I would just as soon have sex with Nick or Edmond, Edmond particularly, in fact. I like blond men. And I don't think they would be open minded enough to accept that sort of behaviour.'

Kate let out a long, slow sigh of comprehension. 'That's why you didn't want to talk about your fantasy,' she said softly.

'Quite right. The ones we heard were all strictly heterosexual, weren't they? A bit of violence, a bit of kinkiness, but nothing dramatic. How do you think Nick would react if I trotted out a fantasy that involved me sucking his cock? He'd blow a fuse.'

Kate's mind shuddered with a sudden vision of Christopher kneeling in front of Nick, leaning forward and opening his generous mouth to caress the glistening head of Nick's penis. She swallowed hard and said, 'I'd like to hear about it.'

'Would you? Well, women are open-minded. I think Nick wouldn't like it. In fact, I think he would hate it. I don't want to get involved in anything like this if I can't be myself. So if you'll excuse me, I think I just won't participate at all.'

Kate drew back a little, looking at Christopher with a frown. 'I'm surprised,' she said at last. 'I thought you would like a challenge. This is exactly what the course is about, after all.'

'What do you mean?' he asked suspiciously.

'It's about influencing people, changing their behaviour. You're an intelligent man, Christopher. It shouldn't be beyond you to persuade people that they should accept you the way you are. They're all here to learn something new. Look at Nick, you'd have thought he'd never change, but he's picked up something today. Why don't you use the course as your chance to teach them that you have the right to any sexuality you want? Or even that he might enjoy having his own horizons broadened?'

He did not speak, just looked at her with those deep, shadowed eyes. She paused, giving him time for her words to sink in. Then she went on, 'Tomorrow is about persuasion. Listen, Christopher, we can make you the focus of the day if you want. You could – you could try to persuade Edmond to let you do something to him, I don't know, go down on him or something. Wouldn't you like to try that? The skills training is just the same, even if it's about sex.'

Christopher's generous mouth was suddenly thin. 'I'd never get a chance,' he said tiredly. 'I can just see how Nick would react. There'd be no way.'

'Don't worry.' Kate was eager to persuade him to stay. She stepped a little closer to him and put her hands on his arms, feeling the strength of him through her fingers. 'Remember the course contract? Tomorrow morning I'll extend it. No mockery, no disapproval, and this means you, Christopher.'

'I don't need you to protect me,' he said, and there was a shade of anger in his deep voice.

'I won't if you don't want me to,' Kate said. 'It's up to you.' Her brain was whirling. 'Anyway,' she added, 'I'm sure I can think of a way to take Nick's mind off you, so he won't get the chance to disapprove. Please, Christopher, stay and give it a try. Please.'

'You sound like a child who wants something,' Christopher said, and he smiled tolerantly. 'All right. All right, Kate, I'll stay for tomorrow and see how it goes.'

'That's wonderful. I'm so relieved.' Kate was going to go back to the mini bar and pour them both another drink, but as she moved to turn away Christopher caught hold of her face in his hand and turned it back towards him. She allowed him to touch her, feeling every inch of her skin suddenly sensitised and tingling with the delicious threat of his looming presence.

'You are lovely,' Christopher said, looking down into her face. 'I like your mouth particularly. I always like full lips on women, they look promising.'

'I'd like another drink,' Kate said hesitantly. Christopher was strange, and although she desired him she would rather things went at her own pace. At present she did not feel in control. She tried to pull her head away, but his hand tightened on her chin, making her wince.

'Don't be in such a rush,' he said. 'You were planning to run this course for your own entertainment, weren't you? Well, perhaps I shall hijack it.'

'Let go,' Kate said faintly. 'You're hurting me.'

'Hurting you? I can hurt a lot more than this.'

'Don't try to frighten me,' Kate said, pulling determinedly away from him and retreating several paces. 'Christopher, I need to do some preparation for tomorrow. I think you ought to go now.'

'Preparation? Like the preparation you did with Nick last night?' Christopher came after her, covering the space between them in two quick strides. He caught her by both her arms and pulled her up towards him, dragging her almost off her feet. 'What did he do to you?' he hissed into her face. 'We all guessed, you know. It looked obvious enough. Sophie said she thought he would follow you into the Ladies. Did he?'

'Yes,' Kate whispered, looking up helplessly into Christopher's dark intense eyes. She thought he would burn her with the heat of his stare. 'Yes, he followed me.'

'And he had you there? In the Ladies?' She nodded wordlessly. 'Well, come on, what did he do?'

'He came in after me and pushed me against the wall,' Kate said breathlessly, remembering her eager arousal. 'It was very sudden. We both wanted it. He opened my dress and, and entered me, and we both came very quickly. Then it was over.'

'You slut,' Christopher said softly. But his broad mouth was smiling, he did not look as if he disapproved. 'Tell me,' he went on after a moment, 'tell me why Nick was so favoured. What would have happened if I'd come after you? Would you have told me to get lost?'

Still hanging from his hands, helpless as a scruffed kitten, Kate felt warm moist desire creeping up through her limbs and aching in her breasts. 'I shouldn't think so,' she whispered.

'But you just told me to go now. Why?'

Because I want to be in charge. Because I want to choose the times and places where I have you all. The words did not emerge: Kate just closed her eyes and shook her head. She had seen how the moment she refused him Christopher had become angry and determined, as if resistance inflamed him. If that was what it took to make him want her, then she would resist him. She said feebly, 'Please don't, Christopher.'

'Don't what? Don't touch you? Christ! You had Nick's cock in you last night, and by God you're going to have mine in you tonight.'

'No.' She tried to pull away from him, feeling his big hands gripping hard at her arms. 'No, please, no.'

'You have no choice,' he hissed, 'no choice at all. ' He pulled both of her arms together in front of her and then lifted them, holding both of her wrists tightly in one big hand, so that she stood on tiptoe with both arms high above her head, unable to move. 'That's better,' Christopher said softly, and with his other hand he reached for the buttons on her shirt.

'Don't,' Kate cried, writhing to try to loosen his grip. 'Don't.'

Christopher managed to undo one button, then seemed to lose patience. He snarled, showing his strong teeth, and caught the fabric of the shirt in his hand and jerked at it violently. Buttons flew and the shirt tore open down the front, revealing Kate's full white breasts mounded invitingly beneath the clinging fabric of a lace body. Christopher smiled slightly. 'Got yourself ready for me, did you?'

Kate no longer wasted energy in protesting: she was struggling in earnest. Every nerve in her body was tingling with arousal. His strong hands were holding her so tightly she was pinioned and helpless, like one of the captive women in Nick's fantasy. She writhed and heaved, trying to escape from him, even lifting one knee as if she would try to kick him. He laughed and held her out at arm's length, watching her body arch and twist as she struggled. 'You like fighting me,' he said softly.

Kate fell still and stared at him. Her changing eyes were suddenly brilliant green and her lips were soft and loose, full of desire. She did not deny it; her wild excitement showed in her face.

'Good,' Christopher said steadily. 'Because I like it too. So carry on. But first,' his hand suddenly tightened around her captive wrists, 'first, I want you naked.'

He jerked her swiftly towards him and released her hands, pulling the rags of her shirt violently down her arms and over her wrists. Before she could get her arms free of the sleeves and escape him he had the shirt off and on the floor and had caught her again, gripping her right wrist and twisting her arm up hard behind her back. She cursed him and reached back with her hand to scratch his face or pull his hair, something, anything, but he laughed and dodged her flailing nails and with his free hand unfastened her skirt and pulled it off her. This left her in nothing but the body, a flimsy, stretchy lace garment with a thonged back. He looked down and saw her naked buttocks and smiled with satisfaction.

'Very nice,' he said, reaching down to fondle the white orbs, squeezing and probing with his thick fingers.

'You bastard!' Kate cried, trying to catch hold of his hand and pull it away from her. 'That shirt was expensive!'

He ignored her and thrust his fingers between her legs, feeling her moist, willing wetness. 'Slut,' he hissed. 'You're all ready for me, aren't you? Well, you can wait.'

He leant over, pulling her with him, and caught up her shirt from the floor, then let her arm untwist from behind her back and held her wrist hard and pulled her struggling through the archway into the bedroom. She fought him, beating at him, trying to keep her wrists out of his grasp, but he caught her and dragged her hands up above her head and tied them to the post at the bottom of the bed with what was left of her shirt. She writhed and jerked at her hands, but the knots were tight: she could not move. She hung there, helpless, only her toes touching the ground.

'Well now,' said Christopher, stepping back, slightly breathless. He looked her up and down, seeing her erect nipples pressing eagerly through the lace of the body. He smiled and stepped forward and caught hold of the lace edge above her breasts and pushed it down so that her nipples were exposed, her breasts naked, revealed to him, thrown into sharp relief by the black lacy fabric surrounding them. Kate moaned and threw her head from side to side, her glossy hair swinging and falling across her face. Christopher stood in front of her and lifted his hands to her breasts, cupping the full swell of white flesh in his palms, kneading gently. Again Kate moaned, feeling the nipples aching to be touched, to be sucked.

Christopher stepped back, smiling to see how the hard points of her breasts swelled and thrust forward, asking for his kisses. He shook his head and Kate whimpered with frustration. 'All in good time,' he said.

He pulled off his jacket and hung it over the chair then put his hands to his belt. Kate was suddenly very still, watching with her eyes glinting through the tangled curtain of her hair as he unfastened the belt and unzipped his trousers and pulled them off. The tails of his shirt hid his groin, but his legs were as thick, as muscular as she had hoped, the thighs as strong as the trunks of trees, the calves shapely and glistening. There was only a little hair on his legs and his skin was smooth. He folded his trousers carefully, not hurrying, and hung them over the chair. As he did so he saw the little case of training materials by the bed, frowned, knelt down and opened it.

Kate heard his breath hiss through his teeth as he surveyed the contents. Presently he stood up and turned to face her. He was smiling, and in his hand he was holding a length of soft rope and a leather gag.

'Oh no,' Kate begged, 'please don't gag me. Please don't.' She wanted to be able to tell him what to do to her. If he gagged her she would be in his hands entirely, controlled by him in a way that seemed both extraordinarily arousing and terrifying.

'You have thought of everything,' Christopher said, putting the equipment down on the side table for the time being. He unbuttoned his shirt, letting it hang loosely open, then pushed down his close-fitting trunks and stepped out of them. Kate swallowed, eager for her first sight of his penis. He smiled still as he pushed off his shirt and stood before her, naked and ready.

The breath sighed out of Kate's lungs as she looked at him. His body was magnificent, splendidly muscled, smooth and glistening. He was smooth as silk except at his crotch, where the curls were light brown and crisp. Kate's eyes fastened there, staring. He had the biggest penis she had ever seen, in proportion to his big, tall body, the length of her forearm and as thick as her wrist, smooth and glossy and wonderful. The great shining glans, gleaming with excitement, twitched towards Kate as if it could not wait to enter her. She leaned back against the pillar of the bed, feeling her breasts taut and aching and her mouth dry and cold with desperate lust. She could not have guessed that he would be so wonderfully equipped. She wanted to feel that great hot shaft inside her, stretching her, filling her.

'Now, Kate,' said Christopher softly, picking up the gag and the rope and coming towards her a step at a time. With each step his rearing cock jerked towards her. He stood by her at last and she could feel the heat of his massive erection against her belly, warming her until she thought she would melt.

'No,' she whispered, and then she moaned with protest as he forced the gag into her mouth, pressing it between her teeth and fastening it tight behind her head. Then he dropped slowly to one knee before her and she felt his stiff penis brushing against the bottom of her thighs as he opened his mouth and drew in the taut nipple of her left breast, flicking it with his tongue, sucking it. She cried out, her voice changed and stifled by the gag. She wanted to beg him to do it to her, to enter her then and there with his wonderful cock, to fuck her until she begged for mercy, but she could not speak. She moaned with frustration and shuddering pleasure as his mouth sucked and sucked at her breast and his hands caressed the skin of her thighs.

He stood again after a moment and Kate thought that he would take her, but instead he reached up, tugging at the rags of her shirt until her wrists were free. She pulled down her arms, gasping with relief, and before she could move he had caught hold of her and pushed her on to the high bed. He followed her and she felt his hot strong body pressing against her, the thickness of his erection rubbing between her legs where the tight stretchy body dug into her moist, aching flesh. She tried to speak, to ask him to take her, but the gag filled her mouth and silenced her. Instead she heaved her body towards him, rubbing herself against him, arching her back so that her breasts jutted invitingly towards his mouth.

'Oh, no,' Christopher whispered. 'You said it was all right to take what I wanted, Kate. You said.' He caught her by the shoulders and her narrow waist and twisted her until she was face down on the bed. Then he dragged her arms forward and with the soft rope bound her wrists to one of the bedposts so that she was kneeling with her face just above the pillows, her bottom thrust out towards him. She whimpered and lifted her hips, feeling cool air on the insides of her thighs. The bed creaked as he got off it and she tried to crane over her shoulder to see where he had gone, but could not.

Then he was back, kneeling behind her, rubbing the length of his gorgeous hard cock up and down the quivering flesh between her legs. The lacy thong of the body was hardly any obstruction. She knew she was wet, ready and waiting for him, and every time she felt the shining head slide towards the front of her body she thought that this time, this time he would enter her, put himself inside her. But he did not. She moaned again with frustration, trying to manoeuvre herself so that he would slide up inside her aching, empty channel.

'You really think of everything,' said a voice in her ear, and she jumped as she suddenly felt a cold trickle running down the cleft between her spread buttock cheeks. Then she felt his fingers, running up and down that secret cleft and spreading the coldness gently around her puckered rear entrance, and she realised that it was the scented oil from her treasure box that he was rubbing on to her. He must have gone back for it.

Oh God. She realised with a sudden shock what he meant to do to her and she writhed and tried to shout in protest. He was too big! He would split her in two, she could never, never take that massive shaft in the narrow aperture of her arse. She moaned in protest and pulled and jerked at the bonds that tied her to the bed, trying to escape. But her wrists were firmly fettered and his big hands were on her haunches, holding her still, spreading her open to him, and she felt the great glossy head of his penis pressing, pressing at the tightly closed hole, trying to ease itself inside her.

'No, no,' she groaned, but only whimpers passed the gag. Christopher moved closer to her, arching his big body over her, and with one hand he felt between her legs, feeling for the aching peak of her clitoris. He touched her there and she gasped, unconsciously thrusting her sex towards his searching fingers, and he took his chance and pushed the engorged glans through her tight rear hole and into her anus. There was a sudden spasm of pain as he penetrated her and she cried out. Christopher gasped and began to thrust steadily, smoothly, until the whole of his throbbing thick maleness was sheathed deep in her bowels.

Then for long moments he did nothing. He did not move, he did not withdraw, just knelt there behind her, filling her, with the tip of his finger rubbing delicately against her clitoris. It was more than Kate could bear. The pain evaporated and a hot, heavy pleasure settled in her loins, filling her with shameful bliss, and she tossed back her head so that her hair spilled on to her shoulders. The tight gag bit at the corners of her mouth. She was imprisoned, helpless, penetrated, at his mercy, and more than anything she wanted to feel that wonderful shaft moving in and out of her, possessing her. Still he did not move, and at last she moaned and lowered her shoulders so that her dangling breasts rubbed against the bedcovers, scratching her engorged nipples and coaxing them into ever tighter peaks. She shifted her hips lewdly, writhing on the thick rod that pierced her, trying to encourage him to thrust.

'You like it,' he whispered in her ear. For a moment his hands left her hips and felt beneath her, caressing her dangling breasts, feeling their weight and teasing out the rigid teats that betrayed her arousal. Then he moved his hands again to her buttocks and began to slide his finger deliberately across her swollen clitoris, teasing, rubbing, while all the time his huge penis lay buried deep in her forbidden passage, motionless, driving her mad with the anticipation of pleasure.

Her loins lifted and fell helplessly, drawing out greater pleasure from his stroking finger. She could feel her orgasm building, building: soon she would come without him ever having moved. It felt strangely disgraceful to be thus stimulated, as if he did not need her, as if he were merely servicing her jaded desires. She ached to ask him to move, to take her, but the vile gag kept back all sounds apart from her moans of delight. Her body began to tighten and quiver, approaching its peak. As if he sensed it he thrust two fingers deep into her aching, hollow vagina, sliding them in and out of her while his broad thumb rubbed and rubbed against the stiff shaft of her clitoris. Pleasure flooded through her, making her heave and gasp, and as she climbed the last slope of orgasm suddenly Christopher began to move inside her, withdrawing his splendid length from her wide-stretched anus and then thrusting in again as he thrust with his fingers between the wet lips of her sex. He took her with fearful strength, slamming his body into hers and crying out, and at the second thrust she felt a shuddering of pleasure so extreme that she beat her head up and down on the pillow, biting at the gag, tears of fulfilment streaming down her cheeks. Then she lay slumped and moaning while he held her white haunches between his hands and snarled as he drove into her, fast and deep, thrusting until he reached his own anguished climax and she felt his huge cock jerking deep inside her.

He lay on her, half crushing her, and the hot shaft gradually softened within her tingling passage. Presently he withdrew and reached up to unfasten her bound hands. She gasped and fell to the bed, unable even to remove the gag for herself. He put his hands to the buckle and pulled the gag away, then drew her gently into his strong arms and held her while the aftershocks of her orgasm made her quiver and shake.

'I thought you would split me in two,' she whispered, clinging to him.

'I didn't hurt you, did I?' He sounded worried and suddenly tender.

'No, no.' She pressed closer against the smooth hard muscle of his broad chest. It felt so comforting to be held after that riot of dark passion. She shifted her head on his shoulder and he put his hand in her hair and kissed the top of her head, and as she felt his strong arms surrounding her she sighed with utter contentment. He rocked her softly from side to side as if she were a child and stroked her hair very gently and murmured soothing words. Presently her eyes closed and her clinging fingers relaxed, and she was sound asleep.

Chapter Six

When Kate woke the following morning she was alone. She stretched out on her bed, looking back on the last night's events with sleepy pleasure and wishing briefly that Christopher had been there to wake with her. It would have been wonderful to crawl down his muscular body while he lay dozing and fasten her lips on his soft cock and feel it thicken in her mouth, swelling to its full magnificence under the tender attentions of her agile tongue. But it made sense for him to have left: the others might take it wrongly if he accompanied her down to breakfast.

Outside it looked as if it was going to be hot. Kate showered and dried her hair, then dressed quickly in another clinging body and on top of it a T-shirt and light muslin skirt. Then she hurried down to the training room. There was a lot of setting up to be done that day and she wanted to be sure that everything was in order.

The main room looked as it had before, but it now contained a camcorder and a large TV screen. The camcorder was off and the screen showed another room. Kate nodded and trotted down the corridor to the next room, which had the same equipment all prepared. The camcorder in the second room was operational and the

TV screen switched off, so that people in that room could be observed without themselves seeing the observers. Closed circuit TV: an easy way to watch people interacting without actually interfering with what they were doing.

By the time she had everything set up to her own satisfaction it was time for the day's sessions to start and the others were waiting for her, sitting in their chairs and looking at her with keen attention. The men had relaxed in the way they dressed: there were no jackets or ties now, just loose comfortable trousers and open neck shirts. She noticed that Edmond and Sophie were sitting side by side on the sofa, a little closer together than strangers would, and she smiled. Sophie was wearing very similar clothes to the previous day, but the button at the neck of her blouse was undone. Nick was discussing some item of the business news earnestly with Christopher, but when Kate came in he stopped talking and looked up, his face the picture of bright obedience.

'Good morning, everyone,' Kate said. 'How are you all feeling?'

They were feeling fine, it seemed: eager, interested. Even Christopher said with a slow smile, 'I'm looking forward to the day.' Nick looked at him sidelong as if he would have nudged him, a man to man look, but in the end he said nothing.

'All right,' said Kate, 'let's get started. Today we're looking at persuading – talking somebody into accepting your viewpoint. That's going to be easier when you know where they're coming from, and that's why we started yesterday with bridging. And tomorrow, with assertiveness, we'll look at how you behave when you really don't mind what their reaction is. Today, though, it's all about taking somebody with you: convincing them.'

'Sounds useful,' Edmond said cheerfully.

'It is useful. What I'd like to propose,' said Kate, 'is that we look at a few principles first, and then jump straight in and start the practice. This is why we have the closed circuit TV set up; sometimes it's easier to practise without other people directly watching you.' She felt Christopher's eyes on her, dark and cool. 'I'd just like to start by reiterating the course contract. Remember, whatever happens on this course, it's confidential and secure. It's just between us. And I'd like to add something else; I'd like you all to try to be as open-minded as possible for the remainder of the course. No prejudging, no thoughtless disapproval. It's just something to aim for.'

A *frisson* passed through the four faces watching her. She could see them realising that what she had said must have a sexual implication, that there was going to be more of what happened the previous morning. Nick looked eager, Edmond reserved, Sophie openly apprehensive, and Christopher sat very still and showed nothing on his shadowed face.

'Here's a basic structure for persuasion for you to bear in mind when you practise,' Kate said practically, going to the flip chart. 'Before you start, plan. Think of what you are really trying to achieve, what would be a mega win; what would be really excellent, a super win; and what you would settle for, a clear win. Then you know where to start and what your fall-back position is.'

'Sounds like a military strategy,' Nick chuckled.

'Not far wrong, Nick. Once you know what your strategy is then you can begin on your task of persuasion. It looks like this.' She wrote on the board:

– Get attention!
– Make your first proposal.
– Back it up with one or two of your best reasons.
– Shut up! Don't ramble.
– Listen actively to counterarguments.

'And if someone tells you to get stuffed?' asked Christopher dryly.

'Find out why they don't like the proposal. Listen

actively to the counterarguments, as it says here. Once you know what the objections are then you can answer them. Then you've got three options.' She wrote them down on the board as she spoke. 'Repeat your original proposal; or restructure the proposal to incorporate ways round the objections; or drop the proposal altogether and think of a better one.'

'This is all pretty obvious stuff,' Nick said, flinging himself back in his chair.

Kate raised her eyebrows. 'I suppose so. But wasn't yesterday obvious when you thought about it? Even obvious things can be hard to do. Remember how you had to practise asking open questions, Nick. If you like, though, we can go straight into practice.' The four of them glanced at each other and nodded, and again Kate felt that *frisson* of excitement among them. 'Everyone agrees? All right then. This is what I have in mind. I am going to split you into two pairs; I'll be an observer. I thought we might return to a similar theme to the ones we were talking about yesterday morning.'

Sophie drew in a long breath and the men sat forward on their chairs, looking eager. Kate smiled. 'I thought you all seemed disappointed yesterday when we left the sexual theme, so I propose that we come back to it now. Does that proposal meet with everyone's agreement?'

Edmond glanced at Sophie before he nodded, but Christopher and Nick were already boldly agreeing. Sophie hesitated, looked at Edmond and at Christopher and said at last, 'I think it's all right.' Her expression was anxious. Kate noticed her discomfort, but discounted it: her mind was focused on Christopher.

'Good. All right, here's the plan. In your pairs one of you volunteers to go first. The person who's trying to lead will ask the other person to do something, anything, on a broadly sexual basis. That's all: choose your own target. It can be as extreme or as moderate as you like. Your job is to persuade the other person to do or to let you do whatever it is you want. The pair who are practising will be in Room 2 with the closed circuit TV and the rest of us will watch in here.'

At this both Nick and Edmond turned their heads and looked at Sophie with anticipation glowing in their eyes. Sophie saw Edmond's look first and she seemed to shine with a tiny gleam of confidence. Then she realised that Nick was looking at her too and she shrank back into herself, her face fixed with horror. Christopher looked steadily at Kate, his eyes never wavering.

'Sophie,' Kate said, feeling rather brutal, 'I would like you to go into the training room now with Nick.'

'With Nick?' Sophie repeated, her face as white as a sheet of paper. 'But I don't want to. Can't I go with Edmond?'

Christopher has already laid claim to Edmond, Kate thought, and paid me a rather splendid deposit. She shook her head. 'If you go with someone you want to, it hardly involves any real persuasiveness,' she said.

'But – ' Sophie said again. Nick rubbed his hands together and jumped up out of his chair, reaching down to catch Sophie by the arm and pull her up off the sofa. 'Come on,' he said, 'let's try it. Nothing to lose, eh?'

For a moment Kate thought that Edmond would jump up and try to prevent Nick leading Sophie out, but in the end he did not. The door closed and after a few moments the closed circuit TV screen showed Nick towing Sophie into the second training room. He grinned at the camera and said, 'Here we are, then.'

'He doesn't seem to have done much planning,' remarked Edmond thinly.

'You'll notice,' Kate commented, 'that Nick has assumed that he's the one who has to do the persuading. But I didn't assign any roles.'

'That's Nick for you,' said Christopher. 'He's like something out of *Top Gun*.'

'In which case,' Kate said, 'we can expect him to crash and burn.'

They watched as on the television screen Nick caught

Sophie by the hand and pulled her across the room to sit on a sofa. She sat bolt upright, her hands on her knees, not looking at him. He flopped down beside her and said with a grin, 'Well, this is easy, Sophie. All I want is for you to let me have you.'

Sophie turned her head and stared at Nick as if he had not spoken English. 'What?' she demanded, her quiet voice heavy with scorn.

'Come on.' Nick sat up and caught at her hands; she pulled them away. 'Oh, come on, Sophie, I'm great in the sack, anyone will tell you. Ask Kate, she knows.' He grinned at the camera with sudden cheerful insolence.

'We guessed,' Sophie said very coldly. She turned further away from Nick and set her jaw, the picture of silent resistance.

'Wow, it was great,' Nick enthused. 'Up against the wall of the Ladies with some silly old bat in the next stall wondering what the funny noises were. She came like a rocket, Sophie. You could too, you know. What about it?'

Sophie glanced at Nick over her shoulder. 'I thought,' she said, 'that you would rather be like your barbarian captain, and not have to worry about what the women are feeling.'

Nick was momentarily thrown, but after a couple of gaping seconds he shook his head and returned to the attack. 'Don't hold that against me,' he said. 'That's just a fantasy, isn't it? I mean, if you'd told us about your fantasies, perhaps they'd seem pretty weird too. Perhaps you'd like to be raped by someone who looks just exactly like me. Who knows? Come on, Sophie, let's do it. I promise you'll have a good time.'

He reached out for her again, catching her slender shoulders between his hands, and she actually jumped to her feet to shake him off. 'Don't touch me,' she said angrily. 'I will not let you have sex with me. You'd have to force me.'

'Do you want me to?' asked Nick eagerly, and Sophie

let out a sharp sigh of exasperation and swung away from him, folding her arms in fury.

'So you don't want to,' Nick said after a while, and Sophie shook her head fiercely from side to side so that her curls nearly covered her face. Nick made a face and raised his eyebrows ruefully at his unseen audience. 'Well,' he said after a moment, 'I guess that pushes me to the fall-back situation, huh? How about giving me a blow job?'

'Christ!' Sophie exclaimed, and she stalked straight to the door and out. After a moment she reappeared in the training room and returned to her seat on the sofa, staring straight before her, her jaw set rigid and her breath shaking.

'Crashed and burned,' Edmond said, smiling, and he leaned over a little way and touched Sophie's hand. She jumped and stared at him, her face still hot with anger, but he smiled gently into her eyes and after a second she sighed and put her hand over his.

Nick reappeared in the door, shamefaced and blustering. 'Bloody silly exercise anyway,' he said. 'Nobody could do that. Stupid.'

'Ever heard of Casanova?' asked Christopher pointedly.

'I think Sophie might be able to tell you where you went wrong, Nick,' Kate said.

'Sure. She's frigid,' Nick said with dismissive accusation.

'How dare you?' demanded Sophie, thrusting Edmond's hand aside and jumping up in her anger. 'How dare you? You didn't once ask me what I would like to do; you didn't listen to me; you didn't answer my objections; you didn't even bother to find out why I said no! Are you surprised you got nowhere? For someone who is supposed to be bright, Nick, you really can be incredibly stupid!'

Nick stared at her, astonished, as if a dove had turned

to an eagle before his eyes. 'Hey,' he said placatingly, 'calm down.'

'Thank you, Sophie,' Kate said, gesturing with her head that both of them should return to their seats. She was pleased that Sophie had stuck up for herself, but hoped it did not indicate that she would resist any further sexual ideas. Sophie's cooperation might be necessary to assure Edmond's, and Edmond was the only man whose body Kate had not yet enjoyed. 'That was a succinct summary. Nick, when someone disagrees with you, it isn't always right just to say the same thing over and over again, or make it sound as if they're stupid to disagree with you. Let alone insult someone who disagrees with you. And by the way, if I may make a comment on a purely personal basis, accusing a woman of frigidity because you've been turned down really, really stinks.'

Nick set his lips together and scowled. 'Let the other two go and try,' he said. 'Hah! Or let me try again with you, Kate.'

'Edmond, Christopher,' Kate said calmly, ignoring Nick's childishness, 'would you be prepared to go and try?'

Edmond looked suddenly uncomfortable, but he did not object. He got to his feet and as he did so Christopher heaved himself up from his chair, moving with silent precision, like a great beast. They said nothing as they left the room.

'God knows what they'll get up to,' said Nick sulkily, slumping down in his chair. Kate frowned at him, then looked at Sophie. She was sitting up straight, her arms folded across her front, cradling her little tender breasts, and her eyes were fixed on the television screen with an eagerness that Kate found quite astonishing.

The two men appeared on the screen, coughing and looking awkwardly at the camera. Edmond went to make sure the door was closed then returned uncertainly to the middle of the room, saying nervously, 'Well, I can't imagine what Kate thinks we might want to try!'

'I do have an objective, Edmond, if you wouldn't mind,' Christopher said in his deep voice. He was standing very still, his hands loose by his sides. Kate looked at the size of him and her mind filled suddenly with an image of him on the previous night, kneeling behind her and driving his massive penis deep into her anus. She shivered.

Edmond did not speak for a moment. His arms folded defensively across his chest. At last he said, 'Go on, then.'

Christopher's hands tightened at his sides. He said very steadily, 'I'd like to go down on you. I think you'd enjoy it; I've been told I'm, ah, quite skilled.'

Nick cursed beneath his breath and sat up, staring at the screen in naked disbelief. Sophie caught her lower lip in her teeth and leant forward, clutching her arms more tightly across her breasts. On the screen Edmond looked as though he couldn't believe what he had heard. He said after a moment, 'Pardon?'

'I'd like to use my mouth on you,' Christopher explained, still in that calm, steady voice.

'My God,' Nick whispered. 'I thought he was strange. He's gay!'

'He's not,' Kate said, suddenly wanting to defend Christopher.

'How the hell do you know?' Nick demanded.

Kate had not meant to tell them what had happened between her and Christopher, but she was angry with Nick and the words escaped her before she could stop them. 'He made love to me last night.'

For a moment Nick and Sophie both stared at her, speechless. Then they swung their eyes back to the screen as Christopher spoke again. 'Will you let me?' he asked.

Poor Edmond, Kate thought, remembering the profile of Edmond in her tutor brief. He hates to say no, he hates to seem impolite, but he really doesn't want to do this. What will he do?

'I think,' Edmond said very carefully, 'that I would really rather not.'

Christopher nodded his head, still standing very still. 'I understand your reaction,' he said, 'but could you tell me why?'

Edmond's eyes flew to the television camera. 'People –' he began, then broke off.

'It's secret,' said Christopher. 'No one will know. None of us would tell anyone about it. We all promised.'

Edmond took a step back, as if he was afraid. 'I just – wouldn't like it,' he said at last, turning his head away.

'Have you ever tried it?' Christopher asked him gently.

They could see Edmond blushing, the fair skin on his high cheekbones staining scarlet. It made him look very young and almost vulnerable. 'Well, no, not as such. Well, I mean – ' He hesitated, glanced again at the camera and then said, 'At school, you know, public school, there was a fair bit of that went on in the dorms, and – '

'Did you like it then?' asked Christopher, when it became apparent that Edmond had no more to say.

'Well, well, yes. But we knew it was bad, an expulsion offence, and that was before I'd ever had a girl, you see,' Edmond explained desperately, clenching his hands.

'I tell you what,' Christopher said. He still had not moved, as if he was conscious that any advance on Edmond could be seen as threatening. 'I tell you what. Why not just let me try? Just for a few minutes? If you don't like it, I'll stop. I promise. I won't be a nuisance.'

Edmond frowned apprehensively. 'I suppose – ' he said, but then he seemed to think of something else. He threw up his elegant long-fingered hands in theatrical dismay, smiling with relief. 'You can try,' he said after a moment, 'but it won't work. I mean, I like women, not men. I won't get an erection.'

'Let me worry about that,' Christopher said. His voice was dark and sleek, holding the promise of pleasure. 'Sit down there,' he suggested, indicating a chair at an angle to the camera. 'Make yourself comfortable. Close your eyes.'

Edmond hesitated, then shrugged and sat down in the chair, spreading his legs and leaning back with his eyes closed. Christopher turned and looked once at the camera, a burning glance that made Kate shiver; then he walked slowly over to where Edmond sat and knelt down beside him, on the side away from the camera so that the hidden audience would have an unrestricted view.

'My God,' Nick breathed in disbelief. 'My God, he's going to let him do it! I'd punch his teeth in before I – '

'Nick,' said Sophie's quiet voice, 'shut up and watch.' Kate looked at Sophie in surprise; every now and again she showed the determination that must allow her to jump out of aeroplanes. Sophie's eyes were fixed on the screen and she was pressing her thighs tightly together.

Christopher knelt by Edmond and for a moment did nothing. Then he put his hands to the belt of Edmond's trousers and unfastened the buckle, opened the belt, followed it with the button of the trousers. The zip whined faintly as he opened it. Edmond took a quick short breath and turned his head on the back of the chair. Christopher opened the fly of Edmond's trousers wide and gently pushed up his polo shirt to reveal his naked abdomen, white-skinned and slender, flat and tense with muscle. He put his fingers on the white skin just below Edmond's navel and ran them slowly downwards to where the blond hair began to thicken above the waistband of Edmond's briefs. Then he gently put his hand on the front of the tight cotton briefs, stroking and touching. His lips were parted and they could just hear the breath hissing through his teeth, ragged with excitement.

'Oh,' Sophie whimpered. She was leaning further

103

forward now, licking her dry lips with her pointed tongue and squirming in her chair. Kate thought of going over to her and offering to stroke her, but she decided that would be too aggressive. Nick was sitting with his hands over his face, his fingers spread so that he could look through them, like a child watching a frightening film. In a few moments, Kate thought, he'll be behind the sofa.

She heard a quick intake of breath on the screen and turned quickly to look. Christopher had pushed his fingers under Edmond's tight briefs and eased them down, revealing his groin, the soft fur of his golden pubic hair and his white-skinned, sleeping penis. Edmond had his eyes very tightly shut and he had folded his arms over his forehead as if to shut out the light. As Kate watched he moved his hips, a slow heave that could have been encouragement or could have been an attempt at escape.

Christopher leant forward and put his face very close to Edmond's crotch, breathing in the smell of his maleness, his eyes closed in ecstasy. For a moment he did nothing, just hung there, watching. Suddenly Kate realised why: in its nest of golden down Edmond's long, slender penis was beginning to stir and thicken.

Sophie had both hands pressed over her mouth, her eyes above them wide and astonished. She breathed quickly as Christopher at last parted his wide sensual lips. He extended his long, thick tongue and gently, very gently, flicked the point of it around the top of Edmond's swelling phallus. Edmond gave a little moan and the thickening rod jerked upwards in sudden excitement. The glans began to swell and assume its wonderful velvety shine, and with a sudden sigh of delight Christopher put his hand under the long shaft and lifted it and took the head into his mouth, his cheeks hollowing as he sucked.

'God Almighty,' Nick whispered, closing his fingers. 'I can't watch this.'

Edmond gasped; Christopher was caressing the now engorged stem of his cock with his lips and swirling his tongue over the purple, glistening head. His hands were gently fondling at the tautening purse of Edmond's balls and stimulating the bottom of his shaft. It seemed as if Edmond were trying not to move, but suddenly he lost the battle. He jerked his hips upwards towards Christopher's face, thrusting his now stiff and fervent phallus deep into his working mouth and moaning, 'Christ, Christ.'

'Turn it off,' Nick demanded suddenly, looking away. 'Turn it off. I don't want to watch.'

'I want to watch,' Kate said fiercely. 'Don't touch it. What's wrong with you?'

'It's disgusting,' Nick said angrily. 'I could understand it if we were watching you and Sophie getting it on, that would make some sort of sense, but watching one queer trying to turn a perfectly normal guy into another queer is just sick.'

'You are absolutely wrong, Nick,' Kate said sternly. 'What turns a person on is up to them, there's no right and wrong. Edmond wasn't forced, was he?' Nick scowled, then shook his head. 'And he's enjoying it, isn't he?'

Nick glanced again at the screen. Edmond was moaning loudly now, his head flung back and his lips parted, and he had lifted one hand and rested it on Christopher's wiry hair to keep his head still while he thrust eagerly into his open mouth. As they watched Christopher pushed his hand down between Edmond's legs and they could tell that his big fingers were stroking up and down his crease, fondling the strange secret spot behind his testicles where the skin is warm and smooth and sensitive, caressing the taut rim of his backside. Edmond groaned almost as if he were in pain and said in a voice that was thick with lust, 'Oh, God, I'm going to come.'

'He's enjoying it,' Kate said again, feeling herself warm and wet between her legs. She was desperately aroused by seeing Christopher use his mouth on Edmond. 'So what's the problem? Why should you only think about what you want?'

'I'd like to see you and Sophie together,' Nick repeated sullenly.

'Dream on,' said Sophie sharply. 'I wouldn't let Kate touch me any more than I let you, Nick.'

Is that so? Kate wondered. It sounded a lot like a challenge to her. She looked at Sophie's face: it was flushed and glistening, and the open neck of her prim white shirt showed that the pale skin of her neck was coloured with the unmistakable blush of arousal. Sophie saw her looking and for a moment stared back at her, wide-eyed. Then a gasp on the screen caught her attention and she turned away.

Nick got off his chair and came over to kneel by Kate, looking up at her. His fierce bravado had disappeared. He raked his hand through his fine dark hair and it settled gently back into place. His gleaming blue eyes with their long fringe of dark lashes were wide and anxious. 'I really don't want to watch this,' he said, and his voice was almost frightened.

'But I do,' Kate said. 'And Sophie does.'

'It can't turn you on,' Nick protested hopelessly.

For answer Kate took hold of his hand and guided it under the filmy fabric of her skirt and up between her legs, putting his fingers beneath the tight crotch of her body so that he could feel how wet she was, how her vulva was slick with juice and her clitoris was already engorged and protruding from between her swollen lips. He stroked gently over her trembling moistness and said softly, 'It really does. It really does arouse you. My God.' For a moment he sat silently at her feet, his forefinger pressing delicately on her pleasure point, looking up at her. Then he leant forward and lifted her skirt and laid his cheek against the soft bare skin of her inner thigh and closed his eyes. He had not shaved that morning and his cheek was dark with stubble: Kate shivered and let out a little gasp as she felt the roughness scraping against her tender skin.

Behind him on the screen Christopher had drawn back, lifting his mouth away from Edmond's now tautly throbbing phallus. He was holding the stiff shaft in his hand, rubbing at it gently. Edmond made a little protesting sound and stirred in the deep chair, turning his head from side to side. Then he said huskily, 'Christopher, for God's sake, don't stop.'

Nick let out a little sound that was almost of pain and buried his face between Kate's legs, breathing in deeply as if he wanted to inhale her very essence. For a moment he set his teeth to the soft flesh of her thigh, stroking gently with his tongue, and Kate clenched her jaw and arched her back. 'Kate,' Nick said very softly, kneeling there with his head buried between her legs like a child hiding from the bogeyman. 'Kate, Kate.'

Kate let her head fall back and glanced, just glanced, over to the chair where Sophie was sitting. Sophie still had her hands pressed to her mouth and she was staring first at Nick and then at the screen. Her breasts were heaving and Kate could hear the rush of her breathing. Kate said lazily, 'Do anything you like, Nick, as long as I can go on watching the screen.'

For a moment Nick did nothing, just knelt between her parted legs with his forehead resting on her thigh, breathing deeply through his nose and gazing up at the gently swelling mound beneath the tight fabric of her body. Kate could feel his breath stirring against the silky skin of her leg. She desperately wanted him to put his mouth on her, to ease her aching arousal with his tongue, but she was not going to ask him to do it. Instead she looked up at the screen and as she did so she lifted her hands to her breasts, feeling her nipples hard and proud through the silky smoothness of the body and the fabric of her T-shirt. She rubbed her fingers against her nipples, encouraging them to swell further, feeling her breasts aching with desire.

On the screen Edmond was staring at Christopher, his eyes wide, his face flushed with imminent orgasm. Christopher looked back at him and smiled, then said gently, 'Edmond, if you'd like to try something else –'

His hand moved on Edmond's engorged penis, a firm deliberate stroke that made Edmond set his teeth and gasp. 'Try what?' he asked, desperately. 'What?'

For a moment Christopher released Edmond's straining flesh. He took hold of the hem of his shirt and stripped it over his head, revealing his naked, muscled torso. He looked like a statue of Apollo, like a Michelangelo. He dipped his head swiftly forward and caught the velvety glans of Edmond's cock again between his lips, sucking with such delicate precision that Edmond cried out in a helpless agony of pleasure. Christopher lifted his head, licking his full lips, and said softly, 'I thought you might like to have me.'

'Oh, Christ,' murmured Nick, his voice almost smothered by Kate's thigh. 'Oh, Christ, Edmond, don't.'

Edmond straightened a little in his chair, staring at Christopher. His eyes were hectically bright, as if he had a fever. After a second he said in a strange tense voice, 'Have you? You mean – in your arse?'

Christopher quickly lowered his head to deliver another long, languid caress with his mouth. Then he straightened, smiling, and said, 'If you want to.'

Both rooms filled with the silence. Sophie sat up very straight and her trembling hands slipped down from her mouth to her breasts, wrapping across her, protecting herself and touching herself at the same time. Kate stared at the screen, fascinated by the way Edmond's expressions fleeted and changed, showing shock, fear, excitement, reluctance, eagerness, all in such swift succession that they were hardly distinguishable. Christopher sat still as a cat with its eyes on its prey, smiling as subtly as the Sphinx. And between Kate's legs Nick knelt with his face buried, breathing in the smell of her femininity, his head moving a little from side to side as if he was trying to deny what was happening on the television screen behind his back.

Suddenly Edmond leant forward from his chair. He said nothing, but he caught Christopher's face between his slender white hands and kissed him, a fierce possessive kiss. Sophie shuddered and gave a little cry; her pupils opened up wide, wide, so that her eyes, normally brown, looked deep and black as impenetrable pools.

Nick glanced over his shoulder and saw on the screen Christopher and Edmond in each other's arms, their mouths locked together, and his face contracted in horror. He turned on Kate, seizing her waist in his hands, shuddering with the need to prove to her, to himself, that he was a real man. 'Kate,' he said urgently, 'let me have you. I want you. Let me fuck you.'

Kate could not take her eyes from the glowing image on the screen. No words had been exchanged, but now Christopher was naked, revealing the splendid body that had pleasured her so darkly the previous night, and Edmond was stripping off his clothes as Christopher slowly turned his back. Kate fastened her eyes on Christopher's wonderful penis, remembering how it had spread her and filled her until she thought she would split in two. It was hard now, as hard as it had been last night, shining and beautiful. She said without looking at Nick, 'Do what you want. But I want to be able to see the screen.'

For a moment Nick sat in front of her clenching his fists, seemingly completely puzzled. Then he jumped up and grabbed one of the armchairs and put it a little way in front of the television facing away from the screen and flung himself down in it, holding out his hands to Kate. 'Kate,' he called, 'come on. On top of me. Come on.'

Kate got up from her chair, still watching. Now Edmond was naked too, standing behind Christopher and rubbing his hand up and down his iron-hard prick, his face taut with excitement. Kate breathed quickly as she came over to the chair where Nick sat. She pulled her T-shirt off over her head and dragged down the straps of her undergarment so that her breasts sprang free, thrusting forward. Nick gasped and reached out for her, but she stepped a little back so that he missed. 'Take your clothes off,' she said, never looking at him.

Without a word Nick grabbed at his polo shirt, wrestling it over his head, then hastily unfastened his trousers and pulled them off. Kate was still watching the screen. She could only see Nick stripping out of the corner of her eye, but even so she could see that his body was beautiful: broad-shouldered, slender, with ridges of muscle down his tanned flat stomach. Dark hair curled on his chest and ran in a line down his abdomen to the glistening triangle at his groin. She pulled her eyes from the screen long enough to register that Nick's fine, long penis was massively erect, stiff and scarlet, and she smiled. 'Nick,' she said with a laugh in her voice, 'I thought you said this didn't turn you on?'

'Christ,' Nick exclaimed angrily, 'come here.' He reached forward and grabbed Kate by the waist and thigh and pulled her towards him. She yanked open the crotch of her body and came and knelt on the soft armchair, straddling his lean thighs and slowly, slowly lowering herself towards him. He moaned with relief and closed his eyes and buried his face in her generous breasts, catching at them with his hands and pushing them together so that he could flick his tongue quickly from one nipple to the other.

Edmond was kneeling behind Christopher now. Kate could see the shining tip of his long slender phallus nudging between the tight cheeks of Christopher's backside, easing its way into the narrow entrance. She let out a little moan of excitement and allowed the head of Nick's straining cock to enter her. As Edmond penetrated Christopher and both men moaned with pleasure she slowly slid down on the gorgeous hard length of Nick's shaft, feeling the sensations surge through her as she impaled herself deeply and rubbed her swollen clitoris against the rough fur and hard flesh of Nick's thrusting body. It felt so good, so good, to have Nick deep inside her, under her control, pleasuring her. She watched eagerly as on the screen Edmond gasped and began to move, thrusting powerfully into Christopher's tight, willing hole. She timed her movements to match Edmond's, rising and falling as he thrust and withdrew, writhing with pleasure as she felt Nick's lovely hard cock sliding in and out of her. His tongue was jabbing at her breasts, flickering over her tight, sensitive nipples; with every thrust she felt the ecstasy grow, and she knew that whenever she wanted to she would be able to orgasm. It hovered there in her belly and breasts, waiting to be summoned. When Edmond comes, I will come, she thought. She let her head roll back, her shining hair swinging away from her shoulders, and her glazed eyes fastened suddenly on Sophie.

Sophie was looking from the screen to the armchair, licking her lips and moaning. Her shirt was open and her left hand was thrust inside her soft bra, squeezing hard at her small breast, and she had unfastened her trousers and pushed her other hand inside them. Kate could see the movements of her fingers, eager and desperate, rubbing at her peak of pleasure, thrusting her little fingers desperately into the soft tunnel that must be aching to feel a hard cock like Nick's filling it, filling her, fucking her. For a moment Kate wondered if Sophie was a virgin and whether one of the men on this course would have her soon. That would be exciting, to watch as a man took her virginity. It would be good if it were Christopher. Kate turned her head away from Sophie, imagining Christopher's huge, glistening penis easing its way between soft lips that had never felt a man's body before, spreading the tight walls, thrusting deep. She shuddered at the thought. Then she heard a gasp and looked back to the screen and saw Edmond flinging back his head and crying out, his buttocks lurching with the unmistakable spasms of orgasm. Christopher was groaning with pleasure and as Kate watched his massive erect cock twitched and jerked and the white sperm spurted from it into the empty air. She cried out with a sudden rush of excitement and twisted herself on Nick's cock, her climax blazing through her, heaving as she shook and groaned. Then she slumped backwards, her hair brushing against Nick's thighs, whimpering and twitching as he caught at her with his hungry hands and held her tightly and forced himself inside her with desperate, jerking thrusts, grunting like a beast until he gave a sudden violent cry and pulled her down hard on to him and shuddered as he poured himself into her.

Kate hung back from Nick's hands, limp and helpless. After a moment she opened her eyes and saw an upside-down image of Sophie trembling and moaning as she moved into the throes of orgasm. Her little hand was clutching frantically at her breast, her head was tilted back and her eyes were tight shut. The lips of her little rosebud mouth were parted, a soft, delicious triangle, and Kate could see her tongue quivering between her white teeth. Sophie caught her tight nipple between finger and thumb and was suddenly very still, her whole body shivering as she let out a little 'Oh!' of ecstasy.

After a moment Kate crawled off Nick's lap to the floor, adjusting her underwear across her swollen breasts and tugging down her skirt. Sophie gave a little whimper, then seemed to remember where she was; she sat up hastily and pulled her hands from her shirt and trousers, rebuttoning herself and trying to smooth her tousled hair. Nick sat in the chair looking stunned, then glanced at the screen and winced to see Edmond lying naked on top of Christopher, panting, his slender body gleaming with sweat. Nick shook his head ferociously and turned away, reaching out for his underpants and trousers.

Kate found her T-shirt on the floor and pulled it on, running her fingers through her hair. 'I think we'll have a short break for coffee now,' she said, her voice sounding unbelievably businesslike. 'Then we'll get Edmond and Christopher back in here and go on looking at other methods of persuasion. I think Christopher will have provided us with a useful example. Nick, do you think you grasped why he succeeded when you didn't?'

Nick shook his head again and pulled on his shirt. He looked at Sophie as if trying to enlist her help against Kate, but Sophie would not meet his eyes. He said after a moment, 'Coffee. Yeah, coffee sounds like a wonderful idea,' and slunk across to the door like a beaten dog.

Chapter Seven

Kate stood naked before the mirror in her suite, examining her body and thinking about Edmond. A summer sunset glowed outside the window. She could hear from the grounds of the hotel outside cheerful shouts and the click of wooden balls: Edmond had discovered a croquet lawn in the grounds and had offered to teach the others how to play. Nick had initially derided the idea, saying pointedly that croquet was a game for poofs, but Christopher had looked at him with a gentle smile and said, 'Do you know it's the managing director's favourite game, Nick? He played croquet for Oxford,' and Nick's expression had changed at once.

Apart from that one pointed exchange all three of the men seemed to be trying to pretend that the morning had never happened. When they met at coffee Nick had been silent and defensive for a while and then suddenly snapped back to his accustomed extrovert self, while Edmond and Christopher had behaved perfectly normally. Christopher seemed to have a glow about him, but he was so reserved that it was hard to be sure. Sophie had said hardly a word for the rest of the afternoon, but Kate had come to expect this of her and she was not concerned.

Edmond, Edmond ... the only one of the men Kate had not yet enjoyed. She thought of his slender, wiry body with pleasure and anticipation. She would make her interest clear over dinner and seduce him that night. He had long, delicate fingers, like a concert pianist; they would play her with skill, coaxing the music of her moans tenderly from her.

What would he like her to wear? A traditional young man, well brought up, aristocratic: he would like her to look feminine. Kate went through the clothes she had brought with her and pulled out a lacy Wonderbra and matching panties. She put the Wonderbra on and turned to admire herself in the mirror, running her fingers gently over the swelling twin moons of her breasts. Ignore those, Edmond, she thought with a smile, pulling on the tight lacy panties. There was a soft, floaty silk dress in her wardrobe, too smart for a course really but it would be just the thing. And high-heeled sandals to make her legs look long and appealing; and her hair up, with just one or two silken tendrils tumbling on to her shoulders. She went over to the dressing table to find the comb that she used to hold up her French plait.

There was a faint knock at the door. Kate frowned and glanced out of the window, seeing the three men still merrily playing croquet below her. She was not expecting room service. Puzzled, she caught up her cotton dressing gown and pulled it on and went through to her sitting room and answered the door.

Sophie stood there, her hands wrapped across her front in her normal defensive posture, her chin lifted nervously. 'Can I come in?' she asked.

'Sophie. Of course.' Kate stood back and gestured for Sophie to enter. 'Please.' She looked hard into Sophie's face. She looked as if she had been crying. 'Is something the matter? Would you like a drink?'

'I don't want a drink.' Sophie sat down on the chair nearest the door, then got to her feet again and paced across the room to the window. She looked out and saw the men below her at their game and turned away, a spasm of anger crossing her face. She was blinking rapidly and chewing at her lip and suddenly the tears came, blurring her dark eyes and trickling down her pale cheeks.

'Sophie,' Kate said in sudden real concern, 'what's wrong?'

She went hurriedly across the room to take Sophie's arm and comfort her. Sophie felt her touch and made an inarticulate sound of protest, flinging up her hand to shake Kate off. Kate withdrew, astonished, and Sophie stared at her wide-eyed, the tears still flowing. 'Don't you touch me,' Sophie sobbed. 'Don't try to pretend you care about me.' She drew in a deep breath and dashed her hand over her cheeks. 'I've had enough of this course,' she said after a moment. 'I've packed my bags. I'm going to go home tonight.'

Kate had not expected this. She felt her stomach close and lurch with a sudden apprehension of failure. 'Sophie,' she said softly, 'I don't understand.'

'It's simple,' said Sophie, throwing back her head defiantly. 'I'm leaving. You don't need me anyway, you're only interested in the men. I'm just in your way, you'll have a much better time without me.'

Sudden guilt caught at Kate's conscience. 'No,' she said after a moment, 'no, Sophie, that's not right.'

'I'm going,' Sophie repeated stubbornly. She scowled at Kate and turned to the door. 'I don't know why I bothered coming to tell you. I might have known you'd try your horrible persuading tricks on me. I'm just going to go, and you can – you can sod off,' she said with emphasis.

'Sophie.' Kate reached out and caught Sophie by the arm, holding her back. Sophie swung round and stared at her angrily. 'Sophie, I just don't understand. You've made a real contribution during these two days and I thought, this morning, I thought you were really enjoying yourself. Was I wrong? Why have you decided to give up?'

For a moment Sophie still seemed to be considering walking out, but then she tightened her lips in determination. 'You want to know?' she demanded. 'All right. I'll tell you.' She pulled her wrist from Kate's hand and again folded her arms tightly across her stomach as she walked over to the window. 'I've had several – relationships,' she began, looking out on to the lovely summer evening outside. 'Three relationships with men, since I left school. I was even engaged to one once. They're all the same.' Her voice was chilled with a shadow of bitterness. 'They seem different at first, but they're all the same in the end. Every one of them just wanted me to do what he wanted, to be what he wanted. None of them wanted me to be me. They manipulated me and they bullied me.'

She stopped for breath. Kate said nothing: her mind was whirling as she tried to think of a way out of this situation. It would upset everything if Sophie decided to return to her office early; she would be sure to blow the whistle.

'It's just the same at work,' Sophie went on. 'They get me to do what they want, the men do, all the time. Oh, I don't mean sexually.' She flung up one hand in an impatient gesture. 'I mean for whatever they want. Take my ideas, take my suggestions, present them as their own, take the credit. I've got twice the mind they have and they never give me the credit for it.'

'Your manager has a lot of admiration for your mind,' Kate said with simple truth. 'But he says that you never offer an opinion; he says he has to ask you for it, every time.'

'Is that what he says!' Sophie threw back her head, her thick curly hair bobbing. 'Bastard. He's the worst ideas thief of the lot. Let me do the research, let me write the report, he'll sign the covering letter. The bastard.' She swung to face Kate. 'I hoped for a lot from this course,'

117

she said. 'I can't tell you what I hoped for. A friend of mine went on it a little while ago and you tutored her and she said it was brilliant. She said it would be just what I needed. I thought, she's a woman, she'll understand, she'll be able to help me. And then when we all arrived, and Nick was so bloody minded and awful and you didn't turn a hair! You were really cool; you just dealt with him and I admired you so much. I'd give anything to be like that.' Sophie's eyes were incredibly bright, glittering with anger and unshed tears. 'But now,' she burst out, 'now I know how you do it. You've just made yourself like a man. That's all you are. You're like a man: you're manipulative and exploitative and you don't care.'

Kate was really shocked now, shocked and distressed. Sophie's accusations went too close to the bone for her to ignore them. 'Sophie,' she said with real sincerity, 'Sophie, please tell me what has made you feel this way.'

'It was today,' Sophie said, 'this morning.' She was shivering, clutching at herself with her slender arms. 'I suppose yesterday I was so surprised, I didn't know what to expect, and after all we were only talking. But today, today, you – *offered* me to Nick! You offered me to him as if I was some sort of a whore!'

Kate shook her head, but she knew that denial would only make things worse. 'I'm sorry you feel that way,' she said softly.

'I do feel that way. I do! You told me to go off into the room with him and you knew that he would want to have me. You knew it! And if I hadn't been stubborn, if I hadn't been really stubborn, he might have ended up – having sex with me, and I didn't want him to!'

'What would you rather I had done?' asked Kate.

'You could have asked me. You could have asked me beforehand what I wanted. You didn't even ask me whether I would prefer anyone else. If you just wanted to watch two people having sex on that bloody TV screen, why didn't you let me go with Edmond? At least

118

he'd have asked me nicely!' She clenched her fists in her anger. 'It was awful, it was inexcusable of you to take without asking. It was rude and vicious and I hated it.'

Kate took a deep breath. She had to meet this one head on; nothing else would work. She said, 'Sophie, I apologise. I am very sorry if what I did offended you.'

Sophie glared at her suspiciously, breathing hard. Her face was vivid and flushed with her anger and distress; she looked lovely. Kate licked her lips and then said cautiously, 'May I explain what happened?'

'If you must,' said Sophie coldly, turning her shoulder to Kate.

'Last night,' Kate said, 'Christopher came and told me he was leaving.'

Sophie spun to face her. 'Christopher?' she repeated in disbelief. 'But today he – '

'Last night he was unhappy about the whole thing,' Kate said. 'He had guessed that I – hoped for more erotic things to happen and he was afraid of what Nick would say if he admitted that he liked men as well as women. So I offered to help him. That's why I paired you up as I did today, because he wanted so much to work with Edmond. I'm sorry, Sophie, if you were upset. I didn't think of the effect that pairing you up with Nick might have. I'm sorry.'

'I mean,' Sophie said a little more calmly, 'I mean, even if it had been Christopher you wanted me to – work with, it might have been all right. He's big, but he's calm and quiet. I don't think I'd have minded quite so much. But Nick – I mean, Nick! He's so overconfident it hurts.'

'I think his confidence took a bit of a beating today,' Kate said with a smile.

Before she could help herself Sophie had smiled too. 'Oh, you're right. You know what I think? I think seeing Christopher with Edmond really turned him on. I saw how – how big and hard he was. He only wanted to have you because you're a woman and it made him feel safe.'

'You see,' Kate said earnestly, 'Sophie, you're very observant. You're very intelligent. You could draw a lot from this course; it's just that the first two days were about things you can already do. You're a natural at bridging, I never saw anyone so good at it at a first attempt; and I'm sure that anyone as bright as you can persuade. But to do both of those things you have to be able to get people to listen to you, and for that you need tomorrow's session. It's all about getting what you want, it's about assertiveness. Sophie, what can I do that will persuade you to stay?'

Sophie took a deep breath and looked at Kate, a thoughtful appraising look. 'I don't know,' she said at last. 'Assertiveness. What is it about, really?'

'Just what I said,' replied Kate. 'It's about saying what you want. It's not about aggression or anger, just stating your rights.'

'Stating my rights,' Sophie repeated, her eyes widening.

'Your rights,' Kate said. 'So you might say, I have a right to sexual pleasure as well as you. I want to have an orgasm.' She saw Sophie's face change, a sudden softening, faint colour rising in her pale cheeks. 'And then you've stated your position and everyone knows where they are. You can use it to change people's behaviour, too.'

'You can't,' Sophie said softly.

'Yes, you can, if you know how to ask. You tell them some good news first, then you tell them what you don't like about them, then you tell them what you want them to do. You keep it practical, concrete, something they can correct. So I might say to you, Sophie: I really like the way you respond to erotic influences: I think you're a very sensual woman. I don't like the fact that you won't join in our activities. I want you to tell me why that is.'

120

Sophie looked Kate in the eyes. 'Is that just an example,' she said, 'or do you really want me to?'

'I really want you to,' said Kate, and it was true.

Sophie was trembling. She came a little closer to Kate and licked her lips nervously. 'You see,' she said hesitantly, 'I really, I really haven't liked to think about sex. I mean, not even think about it, let alone do it. I always hoped I would enjoy it, but with every man it's been such a disappointment. When Nick asked me whether parachuting is better than sex I almost said yes, it is, because as far as I'm concerned it is better. The only time I ever have an orgasm is when I masturbate, and today was the first time I've done that for years. But I do have orgasms, I do! I'm not frigid!'

'I would say you're the opposite of frigid,' Kate said reassuringly. 'I saw you orgasm today. I could have broken Nick's arm for saying that to you.'

'It didn't stop you from letting him have you again, did it?' asked Sophie, with a cold edge to her voice. 'Anyway, it's always been so disappointing; I decided, I mean, I thought I just wouldn't do it. Nothing. Wouldn't have a man, not even masturbate. Just forget about the whole thing.'

'Sophie,' Kate breathed, 'that's awful.'

'It was my decision,' Sophie said firmly. 'I don't like struggling to do things. I like doing things well.'

Kate's lips parted in a soundless gasp of understanding. That was it: that hidden streak of competitiveness that was like a core of steel. That was what gave Sophie the courage to stand up for herself on occasion, like a deer brought to bay.

'But on this course,' Sophie went on, 'you've made me think about it. I couldn't not think about it. And it's been so exciting, incredibly exciting, but it's really threatened me. I'm so envious of you, Kate, truly I am, the way you get what you want and you enjoy it. You're in command. I'll never be like that.'

'Some people find it easier than others,' Kate said, 'but,

Sophie, believe me, if you learn how to assert yourself, you'll be better at getting your own way than someone like Nick who falls back on aggression. You have all the other skills too; you just need to be able to be assertive.'

Sophie looked at her for a long time without speaking. Her dark eyes were very wide and her lips were parted. At last she said, 'Kate, don't lie to me. Do you really want me to stay?'

'Yes.' It was true. Kate felt a surge of sympathy and friendship for Sophie. She was desperately sorry for anyone who had closed herself completely off from sex rather than continue to be disappointed. 'Yes, I want you to stay. I want you to learn how to be assertive. I want to see you getting your own way tomorrow.'

'I want,' Sophie repeated softly. 'It sounds all right when you say it. When I say it sounds rude, petulant, I don't know.'

'It's the way you're brought up,' Kate said reassuringly. 'It's a cultural thing. Women are supposed to be supportive and take a back seat, not come forward and say boldly what they want. But it helps so much, Sophie.'

'And I could really learn to be assertive? Even sexually?' Sophie sounded as if she could not believe it.

'Yes,' Kate said. 'What have you got to lose? The course is confidential; but if you go back to the office everyone there will know you've given up.'

Sophie looked up quickly, frowning. That touch of competitiveness had done the trick. 'All right,' she said. 'All right. I'll stay.'

'I'm so glad.' Kate was really pleased. She stepped forward and took Sophie's hands in hers and smiled at her. 'I know you won't regret it. Look, tomorrow is always hard work. Do you want to do a little preparation now?'

Sophie nodded eagerly. 'Yes. Very much. I would really like to be good at it.'

'All right. Look, let's have a drink. What would you like?' Kate went over to the mini bar and opened it.

'There's a bottle of champagne in here. How about some of that?'

'Champagne?' Sophie looked amazed. 'What for?'

'It's a great confidence builder. I'd like some. Shall we?'

After a moment Sophie shrugged helplessly. Kate found two suitable glasses, wrestled with the cork and finally poured the golden wine. She handed Sophie a glass and said, 'Your health.'

'And yours.' Sophie took a sip and giggled as the bubbles went up her nose.

'Now,' said Kate, sitting down on the sofa, 'let's think about what your objectives for tomorrow might be. A bit of planning, that's what we need.'

'*Sexual* objectives?' asked Sophie, looking apprehensive.

'Yes.'

Sophie shook her head. 'I can't. I told you, I try not to think about sex. I don't have any vocabulary, I don't have any images to fall back on.'

'Sophie,' Kate asked with sympathy, 'are you telling me that nothing has ever sexually aroused you? That you don't remember anything, that you've never seen anything that you'd like to try? What are your sexual fantasies, anyway?'

'Really, I didn't have any.' Sophie sipped her champagne, hesitating. Then she looked directly into Kate's eyes. 'But yesterday and today,' she whispered, 'I've been really aroused. I can't tell you. I mean, I never dreamed I could ever masturbate with someone else in the same room, but today I just had to. I didn't even care that you or Nick might see me. I had to touch myself.'

'What was it that aroused you so much?'

Sophie swallowed and put her hand to her throat. 'It was – it was seeing Christopher and Edmond,' she said. 'I never believed – I never knew. Did Christopher really have you last night? Or were you just saying that to defuse Nick?'

123

'He really did,' Kate confirmed. She remembered Christopher's huge strength and shivered. 'He was rough, too.'

'And today he let Edmond have him. He's so complicated. I think he's wonderful, but he scares me to death. Seeing him – touching Edmond, touching his, his penis, taking it into his mouth, it made me feel so strange. And then, when Edmond was just about to take him and you were watching and letting Nick have you at just the same time, so they were moving in and out at the same time. . . I've never been so turned on in my life. I had to touch myself. I had to.' Sophie was flushed and trembling slightly. 'I must be really weird,' she said at last.

'Weird? You're not weird, you're just broad-minded,' Kate said with a smile. She poured a little more champagne into Sophie's glass and watched her drink it. 'Look, Sophie,' she said, 'we don't really want to rerun yesterday or today; people wouldn't learn much from it. Perhaps you need some ideas. Would you like to look at some things that might give you ideas?'

Sophie's great eyes grew bigger and bigger. 'What sort of things?' she asked hesitantly.

'I've brought a sort of erotic library with me,' Kate said with a smile. 'It's in the bedroom. Would you like a look? There's books, toys, clothes, all sorts.' She got off the sofa and held out her hand and after a momentary reluctance Sophie got up too.

They walked together through to the bedroom. Sophie saw the great four-poster and said, 'Oh, what a lovely bed! What a lovely room!' She looked around like a child looking at a shop window full of toys. Then her face changed. 'Did Christopher come in here?' she asked softly.

'He dragged me in here,' Kate said, watching Sophie's face.

'Dragged you?'

'I was fighting him.'

'Fighting him? Why? Isn't he really strong?'

'Yes, he is. I didn't stand a chance. That was why it turned me on so much.' Kate felt hot as she remembered. She unfastened her dressing gown and slipped it off, leaving her in just bra and panties. 'He tied me up,' she said, standing against the bedpost and lifting her hands to show how Christopher had shackled her. 'First here, while he sorted out what he wanted from the treasure box. Then he made me kneel on the bed and tied my hands and he – he took me from behind.'

'From behind,' Sophie repeated, drawing down her brows in an anxious frown.

'I mean, in my arse.'

Sophie covered her mouth with her hand, gasping. 'But he's *huge*!' she exclaimed after a moment. 'Didn't it hurt you?'

'I thought it would,' Kate said. 'But it didn't. It was wonderful.' She gestured that Sophie should sit down on the bed and lifted up the treasure box and put it on the covers so that they could sprawl side by side and examine the contents. 'Here,' she said, opening it. 'Here we are.'

Sophie looked into the box and drew in a long breath. After a second she put her hand in and drew out a leather garment and held it out between finger and thumb. 'What's this?' she asked gingerly.

'Oh, it's marvellous,' Kate said, taking the garment from her and showing her how it should be worn. 'Look, it's like a Victorian corset. It lifts your breasts right up as if they're on a plate and it leaves your nipples bare, and it pulls your waist in, but there's nothing to get in the way between your legs. I love it.'

Sophie looked both horrified and fascinated. 'Could I wear it?' she asked after a moment. 'Would it fit me?'

'You're slenderer than me,' said Kate. 'It laces up the back. Yes, you could wear it. Do you want to try it on?'

'No . . .' Sophie turned her head away. Kate shrugged and put the corset down on the bed as Sophie put her hands again into the treasure box. When they emerged

125

they were holding the polished wooden phallus with which Kate had pleasured herself on the evening of their arrival. She said, 'Oh, my God. Look how big it is.'

'It's wonderful,' Kate said softly. 'Look at the bumps at the bottom. When you push it in deeply it rubs all the outside of your lips.'

Sophie sat for a moment in silence. Then with her arms she pressed her small breasts closer together. Her erect nipples showed through her cotton shirt. She held the phallus in her hand and pressed it gently into the crease between her breasts, shifting her hips from side to side and breathing through parted lips. Her face was beginning to colour faintly as she became aroused. She looked so fragile and vulnerable that it took Kate's breath away. It would have been easy to seduce her; Kate knew that if she leant over now and kissed her Sophie would be unable to resist. But that was not the plan; the plan was to give her what she wanted. Perhaps she wouldn't want another woman to make love to her. Well, they would find out.

Sophie looked suddenly up at Kate. She said rather breathlessly, 'Kate, it's awfully hot in here.'

'It's the afternoon sun,' Kate said. She got up and went to the window to close the curtains. Outside in the glow of the evening the men were still playing croquet; Nick had become excited and was swearing at the others, and Christopher and Edmond were looking disapproving and shaking their heads. Kate smiled and lifted her arms to draw the curtains closed.

When she turned Sophie had taken off her shirt and trousers and was sitting on the bed in her underwear. She wore a very ordinary white bra and cotton panties, but her slender figure was so nubile and delicious that she could have posed as Lolita. She was still cradling the wooden phallus between her small breasts, moving it very gently up and down against her silky skin.

'There are some books in here,' Kate said, 'look.' She dug in the box and pulled out a large, glossy book, somewhat dog-eared. 'I like this one,' she said, offering it to Sophie. 'My lover bought it for me a couple of years ago. I like nearly all the pictures. Shall we look? Something might give you some ideas.'

Sophie looked brighter, as if she felt that a book could not possibly hurt her. 'All right,' she said. 'Yes, I'd like that.' She looked down at herself and gasped, as if surprised to see the thick wooden shaft still nestling in the crease of her breasts. She put the phallus hastily aside and shifted to sit beside Kate, both of them propped comfortably against the pillows in the warmth of the room. Kate held the book open on her lap and Sophie leant over to turn the pages and look at the pictures.

The first few pages showed nineteenth-century drawings of men and women coupling. They were well executed and artistic, but also highly explicit. The women were big-hipped and small-breasted, the men muscular and superbly equipped. In every picture the act of penetration was clearly shown, a thick, stiff penis sliding deeply into a moist, willing tunnel. Sophie shivered and reached out quickly, turning and turning, as if this representation of the act of love disturbed her. Then a page of watercolour sketches, obviously drawn from life, showing a pretty, voluptuous model servicing a handsome young man with hands and mouth. The pictures were beautifully drawn and slightly impressionistic, so that Sophie had to look more closely to understand the finely realised detail: the girl's hand gripping tightly just below the engorged red glans while her other hand stroked between her lover's legs; the way her breasts hung down like ripe fruit when she leant forward to take him in her mouth; his posture and expression, abandoned and ecstatic, his head thrown back as she sucked and fondled.

'They're lovely pictures, aren't they?' said Kate softly.

Sophie looked quickly up at her, passing her small pointed tongue over her lips. 'One of my boyfriends had a book of erotica,' she said, 'and he tried to make me look at it. But it was so crude, I thought it was horrible. These pictures are beautiful.'

'They're art,' said Kate. 'Erotic, but still art, not pornography.'

The picture on the next page caught Sophie's attention. It was a line drawing, superbly vivid, showing a woman straddling a man. Her white buttocks flared out from a slender waist and her vaginal lips were stretched wide to take in his rigid, thick shaft. She was just sliding down on it and her head was flung back in the bliss of feeling herself impaled. Her pubic hair and the man's mingled in a dark mass, the centre of the picture, calling the eye to the act of penetration.

The pages turned. A blonde girl, naked, her long hair tumbling down her back, struggling against a fully clothed man who stands between her parted thighs and thrusts himself firmly into her shrinking flesh; a woman with her hands bound, flung on to a bed with such violence that her shoulders hang off it and her back is arched, her breasts jutting towards the ceiling, gasping while the shadowy figure of a man drives himself deeply into the moist cleft between her wide-spread legs; a man prostrate on a bed, his head hidden beneath the thighs of a woman squatting over his face, while another holds his massive cock pointing skywards so that a third woman can sink down upon it.

Another page. A picture of two women, Twenties flappers by their clothes and hair. One lies on a bed, sprawled naked with her legs flung shamelessly wide and her fingers stroking her erect nipples, and her friend kneels over her, her skirt lifted to show the soft mound between the cheeks of her bottom. Her hands are on the naked girl's thighs, framing the tender lips of her sex, and she stares down at the shadowed cleft and her tongue is just visible between her parted lips.

Sophie sat leaning against Kate and looked at this picture for a long time. She said nothing, but she shivered. Kate looked at her face and saw it set in an expression of yearning desire. They did not speak.

The pages turned. Another picture: three women together, all naked but for their jewels and lipstick. One kneels over another's face, thighs spread, offering the moist lips of her sex to her prostrate friend's eager, probing tongue, and another stands between the thighs of the girl who is lying down, preparing to thrust into her vagina with a massive dildo strapped securely to her slender thighs. The head of the dildo is already hidden, the rest will follow.

Another page, another picture. A young man preparing to enter his lover, a voluptuous blonde. He is crouched over her, his lips about to fasten on the tiny pink peaks of her nipples, his hand guiding the shining head of his cock just between the damp, parting lips of her sex. Her head is thrown back, her mouth open so that her cry of pleasure as he slides himself into her is almost audible. Another: two men holding a woman down, spreadeagled on the ground, her eyes closed in desperate ecstasy as one thrusts his erect member into her body and the other places her hand on his stiff cock and encourages her to feel its thickness. One of them is dragging back her head to kiss her, exposing her white throat. The other is holding her breast in his hand, sucking hard at her nipple: the fingers are denting the white flesh that they grip.

Another: a couple copulating, seen from behind, starkly engraved in black and white. The girl's legs are wrapped around her lover's waist. His tight thrusting buttocks are visible and his massive cock, huge and thick, imbedded deeply in her tender flesh. The light gleams off the hollows in his working buttocks and the round, smooth swell of her clasping thighs. All that can be seen of their faces is the girl's mouth, open, soft and gasping as he plunges into her.

Another. A beautiful girl lying on a bed, her head thrown back and her long hair sweeping against the floor. She seems to be almost fainting with pleasure. Kneeling above her is another girl; she presses against her and just flicks her tongue against the little erect cap of her breast. The recumbent girl's slender legs are spread wide and her friend is touching her between her white thighs, her fingers delicately resting on the just-visible stem of her clitoris. Although the girl is very still her head is flung back in ecstasy; the artist has chosen to paint the moment of crisis, the one split second at which she is motionless because her orgasm is just about to overwhelm her, and in a moment her back will arch and she will moan and thrust her breasts up into her friend's tormenting mouth and receive her fingers into her juicy flesh with cries of aching pleasure.

Sophie leant back into Kate's arms, closing her eyes and letting out a shuddering sigh. For a moment Kate did not move, just sat very still with her arms around Sophie as she sat in her lap like a child. Then she very gently brushed her lips against Sophie's soft curling hair and whispered, 'Sophie, Sophie, tell me what you want.'

Sophie's eyes opened and she turned her head and looked up at Kate. Her lips trembled. Beneath the thin cotton of her bra her nipples were tautly erect, asking to be touched. For a little while she seemed unable to speak. Then she said, softly but with precision, 'Kate, I want to make love with you.'

Without another word Kate leant forward and reached with her lips for Sophie's quivering mouth. Their lips met, touched, parted, touched again. Sophie relaxed against Kate's body and let her head fall back, turning up her face to Kate's caresses. Kate's mouth hovered above hers and Kate gently, gently touched Sophie's lips with her tongue, feeling their warmth and moistness, their delicious fullness. Sophie gave a shuddering moan and opened her mouth wide and Kate pressed her lips down hard and thrust her tongue deep into Sophie's mouth. Their tongues met and touched and tasted and all the time Sophie let out little trembling cries. Their kiss was so sweet, so sweet. The pictures had set Kate's juices flowing and she was already wet between her legs, but to kiss Sophie, to slide her tongue in and out between those quivering lips, filled Kate with a fierce protective tenderness, a desire to give pleasure, not to take it.

Her hands were on either side of Sophie's slender body. They kissed passionately, their mouths open to the darting thrust of their tongues, and slowly Kate's hands moved from the bedclothes on to Sophie's waist and up, feeling her ribs beneath her tender flesh and then the small subtle swell of her little breasts, cupped in cotton but tight with desire. She slipped one hand behind Sophie's narrow back and felt for the hooks of the bra, releasing it with a woman's ease. Sophie shivered as the straps slipped down her arms and the fabric peeled away, revealing her aching, distended nipples. Kate lifted her lips from Sophie's mouth for a moment to whisper, 'Your breasts are so beautiful, Sophie, so beautiful.' Then she kissed her again and put her hands on Sophie's arms and ran them up to her shoulders and then down on to the gentle roundness of those small breasts, cupping them in her hands, trapping the nipples between her fingers and squeezing them gently. The little peaks of flesh lengthened and swelled at her touch and Sophie cried out sharply into her mouth, her back arching, pressing her pelvis backwards into Kate's soft body.

It felt to Kate as if she were Sophie. She could feel the sharp pleasure, almost like a pain, arrowing down from breasts to loins as she caressed Sophie's erect nipples; she could feel the desire to be touched that made Sophie whimper and writhe in her lap. She whispered, 'Sophie, sweet Sophie, tell me what you want.'

Sophie lay with her head tilted back, her eyes closed, her tongue quivering in her open mouth as Kate touched and stroked and pinched the peaks of her small breasts. She did not open her eyes, only said softly, 'Touch me. Oh Kate, I want you to touch me.'

Obediently Kate released Sophie's breast with one hand and slipped her fingers slowly down the slender curves of Sophie's pale body, past the dimple of her navel, down to where the top of her cotton panties clung to her flesh. Her hand gently slid under the cotton, moving down and down until it felt the silky soft hair that fringed Sophie's delicate mount of Venus. She kissed Sophie again, her hot tongue filling her soft mouth, and her other hand working at her breast. Sophie moaned and lifted her hips hopelessly towards Kate's searching fingers.

So sweet, so soft, the opening flesh beneath her probing hand. Her fingers felt the beginning of the soft cleft, the tender lips, warm and moist. She sought delicately, gently, until her fingers found the little protruding morsel of flesh that was now swollen and proud with desire. She knew what she must do as clearly as if she were giving herself pleasure. Her fingers moved back a little, dipped into the slick juices that were seeping from Sophie's sex, and then returned to caress that tiny morsel of flesh with such infinite gentleness that Sophie opened her mouth wide to admit Kate's thrusting tongue and cried out as if she were being beaten.

Kate did not stop. Relentlessly her tongue probed Sophie's hot mouth, her fingers caressed her engorged nipples and the trembling bud of her clitoris. Sophie's cries became regular and her breathing came in pants and she writhed in Kate's arms, helpless, delirious with pleasure. Kate touched her more firmly now, stroking her as she liked herself to be stroked, one finger rubbing and rubbing against the peak of her pleasure while another dipped and dipped into the moist tunnel of her sex, stimulating the delicate lips. Sophie began to heave, thrusting her breasts and her loins towards Kate's working hands, and suddenly she tore her mouth away from Kate's and flung back her head, gasping, crying out, 'Oh yes, yes, Kate, I'm coming, don't stop, don't stop,' and then suddenly she stopped breathing and every muscle was rigid and quivering and her eyelids fluttered as her orgasm possessed her utterly.

After a long moment of ecstasy she slumped back into Kate's arms, trembling with the delicious echoes of her climax. She pressed her cheek against Kate's breasts, murmuring, 'That was wonderful, Kate, so wonderful. You knew exactly where I wanted to be touched.' Kate smiled and kissed her hair. Sophie sank down a little further, looking suddenly disconsolate. 'Is it because you're a woman?' she asked in a small voice.

'I wouldn't say that,' Kate said with a gentle smile. 'I have known men who had the knack.' Suddenly she thought of Edmond and without thinking she went on, 'Look at Edmond. He has such beautiful hands, long fingers. I'm sure he – '

She broke off: Sophie was looking up at her with a sad expression. She said in a little hopeless voice, 'Have you slept with him too?'

'With Edmond?' Kate smiled down into Sophie's lovely face. 'No, in fact. Why do you ask?'

'Oh,' said Sophie, wriggling uncomfortably in Kate's arms, 'it's just that I, I rather like him, and I was thinking, I was hoping, and I would rather – '

'Sophie,' Kate interrupted her gently. 'Sophie, remember to say what you want. I like, I don't like, I want.'

Sophie's dark eyes opened wide. She was silent, and then she said with a sort of timid firmness, 'Kate, I really like you, but I don't like the thought that you want to sleep with Edmond. I want you not to have sex with him unless I say so.'

'That was excellent,' Kate said, leaning forward to kiss Sophie on the lips. 'Well done. And if you want, Sophie, I won't touch Edmond without your specific order.'

'Thank you,' Sophie said earnestly, reaching up to catch Kate around the neck and pull her mouth down to kiss her again. 'Thank you.' She turned in Kate's arms and they were facing each other, kissing deeply. Sophie reached around Kate's shoulders to release the hooks of her bra and pulled it off. 'Oh,' she said, 'what lovely breasts. They're so big. I wish I had breasts like that.' And she leant forward and just touched her lips to Kate's swollen, sensitive nipple. Kate closed her eyes and gasped with pleasure and Sophie put her arms around her and held her tightly and they slid down on to the smooth covers with Sophie licking moistly at Kate's breasts, making her moan and writhe. Then she lifted her tousled head and looked into Kate's eyes and said, 'Kate, could we – I wonder if – '

'What do you want, Sophie?' Kate asked, gently and with a smile.

Sophie hesitated, but not quite so much this time. Then she said, 'I want us to – to use our mouths on each other. I want to kiss you there.'

'All right,' Kate said in a whisper. 'Yes, Sophie, please, please do it.'

Sophie did not move for a moment and Kate realised that she was waiting to be led, waiting for Kate to guide her through what she should do. Rather than tell her Kate lay back on to the covers, looking at Sophie through half-closed eyes with an expectant smile. Sophie breathed quickly, then lowered her lips again to lick and suck at Kate's distended nipples, making her moan and shiver. Gradually she kissed further and further down Kate's sun-kissed skin and as she did so she turned her slender body so that they were lying with their lips close to each other's thighs. Kate was desperate to feel Sophie's small, soft tongue exploring her hidden flesh; she moaned and spread her legs apart, lifting her hips eagerly towards Sophie's face. Sophie gave a little whimper and reached forward, setting her lips to the delicate, secret place between Kate's legs. Kate felt her tongue, soft and warm, just touching her, licking, stroking, and she cried out with pleasure and reached out to catch hold of Sophie's white thighs. She dug her fingers into the taut moons of Sophie's buttocks and pulled her until they were lying pressed closely together, their mouths buried between each other's legs, licking and sucking avidly. Kate caught hold of Sophie's thighs and spread them wide apart and lifted her head from the bed cover, stabbing with her tongue at the soft folds of flesh, parting them, thrusting her tongue deep, deep into Sophie's sex at the same time as she felt Sophie's gentle caress sweeping across her clitoris, lapping at her secret heart, filling her with unbearable pleasure. Their bodies undulated, heaving like one creature, shining hair brushing against the soft flesh of thigh and vulva, tongues flickering, tugging, probing.

Kate felt her climax approaching, sweeping up inside her like a storm. She pulled Sophie's sex down harder on to her searching mouth and caught the delicate stem of her clitoris between her lips, flickering her tongue across it, and as the pleasure seized her and carried her into orgasm she heard Sophie crying out and the moist flesh beneath her lips clenched and spasmed with delight.

For a while they lay as they were, smelling the musky, delicious scents of their womanhood. Then Sophie suddenly sat up and turned around, lowering her lips to Kate's and kissing her with an eager directness that made her gasp.

Kate opened her eyes, looking up into Sophie's shining face. 'What is it?' she asked.

'Kate,' Sophie whispered, and her voice was trembling with excitement, 'Kate, I – I want to – ' She seemed to lose her impetus and stopped, turning her head away.

Sitting up hastily, Kate put her arms around Sophie's narrow shoulders, comforting her. 'What? What do you want, Sophie?'

Sophie hesitated, then swallowed hard. For a moment she did not move; then she reached out and picked up the wooden phallus where it lay on the bed. She licked her lips and looked into Kate's eyes. 'I want to – to – ' The words were hard for her. She took a deep breath, trying to calm herself. Then she said strongly, 'I want to

135

fuck you with this, Kate. I want to push it inside your cunt and make you come.'

Those direct words, coming from Sophie's quivering lips, made Kate shiver with fulfilment. A day ago, an hour ago, Sophie could not have used those words. She leant forward and kissed Sophie deeply, touching the wooden phallus that she held, stroking it with her fingers. Then she lay back on the covers and the deep pillows and smiled up into Sophie's eyes, saying softly, 'Please, Sophie, do it to me. Put it in me. Make me come.'

Sophie knelt beside her, clutching the thick wooden shaft in her small hand, breathing quickly. At last she moved. She knelt over Kate and then lay on her, kissing her, her little tongue flickering deep into her mouth, her fingers squeezing at Kate's soft, full breasts. Kate slowly moved her legs apart and Sophie lay between them like a man, pressing her pubic bone into Kate's soft flesh so that she moaned and whimpered. Then she slowly wriggled down, down, her tongue lapping wetly over Kate's breasts and her round stomach and the soft downy curve of her abdomen, her fingers teasing and tweaking at the luxuriant curls of dark hair. Then she dug her fingers into the plump swell of Kate's thighs and pulled them apart and set the tip of the polished wooden shaft between the glistening fleshy lips that were the entrance to the silken tunnel of desire. Kate felt the cold head there, waiting, promising pleasure, and she moaned and softly lifted her hips, wanting to be filled.

Sophie lowered her dark head and licked Kate's clitoris, quickly, temptingly, just once, so that she cried out. Then she shook back her hair and looked up, teasing the broad smooth head of the phallus from side to side at the entrance. She said devilishly, 'Kate, tell me what you want me to do.'

'Oh,' Kate moaned, her head thrashing from side to

136

side in her desperate need. 'Oh Sophie, please, do it to me.'

'No,' smiled Sophie, thrusting the thick shaft in a little way and then pulling it out, so that Kate cried out and arched her back. 'No, not good enough. Tell me what you want me to do.'

'Push it up me,' Kate whimpered. 'Please. Sophie. Please.'

'Say what you want,' Sophie whispered, her eyes glittering.

'I want you to push it up my cunt,' Kate gasped at last, and as she heard the words Sophie gripped the base of the phallus firmly and thrust it deep and Kate cried out as if she were being stabbed, feeling the thick smooth cold shaft sliding all the way up inside her, touching the neck of her womb, stretching her, filling her. She cried out, 'Oh God, yes! Yes!'

'I will fuck you so hard,' Sophie hissed, and she withdrew the phallus until only its tip remained within Kate's straining body and then pushed it back and Kate gasped and squirmed on the long thick rod that impaled her tender flesh. Sophie set her teeth and thrust and withdrew the wooden shaft again and again until Kate was crying aloud, sharp cries of agonized pleasure, desperate and drained. Then as Sophie thrust, driving the thick phallus deep into Kate's heaving loins, she leant forward and gently, very gently, lapped with her pointed tongue at the quivering bud of flesh that shuddered and ached to be touched. Kate felt her caress like a tongue of fire. Filled, fucked, wild with pleasure, she writhed and moaned as she felt her orgasm lapping through her with flame and ice, freezing her and burning her with ecstasy.

Sophie drove the phallus into Kate's body as far as it would go and held it there while she stiffened and arched in the throes of her climax. Then, gently, she withdrew the long thick rod, glistening and dewed with pearly moisture. She rubbed it against her breasts and between her thighs. Then she lay again on top of Kate and kissed her, and their deep searching kisses gradually grew more and more gentle.

'Now,' Sophie whispered, 'now I want to stay here with you.'

Kate's lips parted in a smile and she reached up and put her arms around Sophie and cradled her head against her breasts. They lay still and their breathing slowed.

Presently Sophie said, 'Did I really say that?'

'What?' asked Kate sleepily.

'C – cunt. Did I really say that?'

'It's just a word.' Kate kissed Sophie's hair and held her closely, feeling her slender body soft and relaxed with the bliss of fulfilment. 'It was the right word. It was what you meant. It's not a bad thing to say.'

There was a silence. Then Sophie said with soft determination, 'Tomorrow I am going to tell the men what I want. I wonder if I dare use that word to them?'

'If you want to.' Kate ran her fingers very gently down Sophie's slender back and she arched and pushed against her hand like a cat being stroked. 'Of course you will, if you want to. Sophie, tomorrow is about giving you what you want.'

'What I want,' Sophie repeated, gazing up at the canopy of the four-poster. Her dark eyes were wide with wonder and fulfilment. 'What I want.'

Chapter Eight

'*A*ssertiveness,' said Kate, 'is about believing in yourself.'

She could feel Sophie's eyes on her, drawing strength from her. Sophie was dressed differently today, in a simple shift dress made of cream-coloured cotton jersey. It clung to her slender body, revealing unsuspected curves. They had chosen it early that morning, giggling over Kate's wardrobe like a pair of schoolgirls. The same dress on Kate looked provocative, but Sophie wore it simply. Kate knew that underneath it there was nothing but a pair of delicious, tiny white lace panties. The men did not know, but they had been startled by the change in Sophie's appearance. It was clear from their faces that they suspected Kate of having seduced her, but none of them had actually accused her. Christopher watched Kate now with a gentle, approving smile on his sensual lips, while Nick and Edmond looked from her to Sophie and back again with eager, intrigued attention.

'You can be assertive,' Kate went on, 'by knowing that you have rights. It doesn't mean that other people don't have rights or don't matter. You can recognise their rights, and still preserve your own.'

She turned to the flip-chart. 'Let's think about voice

and body language,' she suggested. 'If I intend to behave in an assertive way, how will I speak? How will I move?'

'Strongly,' Nick suggested. 'Loud voice, emphatic.'

'OK.' Kate wrote the words down. 'And the body language?'

'Direct,' said Christopher, still smiling slightly. 'Straight on. Not defensive.'

'Absolutely right.' Kate wrote down *direct, forward* on the chart and turned to face them. She stood with her feet a little apart and her body very straight, upright and relaxed. 'You have to stand firmly and feel relaxed. Tension will erode anything you try to do. And the hands should be forward, at right angles to the ground. Don't open your hands, that's submissive; and don't point.'

'Why not?' asked Nick sharply. 'It shows you mean what you say.'

'It's rude,' Edmond said, frowning at Nick. 'It's aggressive and rude to point.'

'Thank you, Edmond,' said Kate. 'You're quite right. Assertiveness is not the same as aggression. An aggressive approach tramples other people's rights and often invites an aggressive response. If you're truly assertive people will not respond aggressively to you.'

'What about the face?' Sophie asked. 'Kate, yesterday you were smiling at us a lot, and today you haven't smiled once.'

Sophie had, as usual, put her finger on the key point. 'Smiling,' Kate said, 'is what we call leakage. It's a waste of your energy. The same goes for laughing. Both of them indicate that you're uncertain and undermine what you're saying. If you want to be assertive you have to speak with a straight face.'

'Not smile at all?' asked Edmond, clearly unsettled.

'Not at all. It isn't easy; I often practise in front of a mirror.' Nick and Christopher chuckled at this and Kate looked at them coolly, not smiling; soon their faces straightened and they gave her their attention again. 'It's not easy to be assertive,' she said, 'and practice is always necessary. But if you can master it it's very powerful.'

She turned to the flip chart and lifted it on to the next page. She had written on it,

I like . . .

I don't like . . .

I want . . .

'This may look incredibly simple,' she said, frowning at Nick, who was shaking his head in wry disbelief, 'but take it from me, it works. Before you use it you really have to know what you want, and you have to keep everything very short and punchy; and it works. Shall I give you an example?'

Heads nodded. 'All right. Nick.' Nick's head swung up and he stared at her. 'Nick, I like the energy you put into what you do. I don't like the way you laugh at what you don't understand. I want you to stop playing around and try this out.'

She spoke with an absolutely straight face and in a strong, serious voice. The four of them stared at her, astonished, and Nick's face slowly suffused with a red flush. He swallowed hard and glanced at Christopher and Edmond, then set his jaw and got up. 'All right,' he said. 'What's the story?'

'We'll all try this,' she said. 'Christopher, come here, please. Nick, sit down. Now, imagine you are in a restaurant and Christopher is the waiter. He's brought you a bottle of wine and it's corked. You're going to ask him to take the wine back and bring you another bottle, and you're going to ask him assertively. Not aggressively, remember. Christopher, you don't have to say anything; when Nick's tried it I will ask you how you thought he did. The rest of you observe.'

'Is that all?' Nick demanded. Kate raised her brows at

him and he threw up his hands impatiently and said, 'Fine, fine, OK. Hey, waiter!' Christopher came over and stood, silent and impassive. 'Look, this wine's crap. It's corked. Bring me another bottle right away or there'll be trouble.'

There was a silence. Nick looked challengingly at Kate. She said after a moment, 'Christopher, would you have brought him the wine?'

'No,' said Christopher coolly. 'I might have broken the bottle he had over his head, though.'

Sophie and Edmond laughed. Kate said, 'Nick, if you're aggressive you won't help yourself. Try again; use the model. Soften him up first; tell him something you like.' Nick looked at her almost as if he did not understand and she said earnestly, 'Nick, this will work. It can help you get your own way. I want you to try it again.'

For a moment Nick was still, looking hard into her eyes. Then he said, 'Waiter!' and Christopher leant over him again, looming and quiet. 'I like this restaurant,' Nick said carefully. 'I like the atmosphere. But I don't like this wine, it's corked. I want you to bring me another bottle.'

Christopher said, 'Certainly, sir,' and took an invisible bottle from Nick's hand. Sophie and Edmond looked at each other and then at Kate.

'You see,' she said, 'that wasn't hard, Nick. You are normally aggressive, so to be assertive you actually have to do less, not more. Wasn't it easier? And didn't it work?'

Nick looked at her very hard, breathing quickly. Then he got up and said, 'Somebody else try.'

'We'll all try,' Kate said. 'Edmond, you're in the hot seat next. Come on.'

Edmond sat down, looking very uncomfortable. His first attempt was abortive: he blushed, laughed nervously and failed to get the words out. Then he said, 'I really like this restaurant, I come here all the time, I

142

think it's wonderful. But I'm afraid that this wine really isn't up to scratch, it's a bit disappointing. I wonder if you could possibly bring me another bottle?' Then he looked at Kate like a dog expecting to be sent to its basket.

'Edmond,' Kate said gently, 'this isn't about politeness. It's about being assertive. Less is more: use few words and say what you want. What you want, remember.'

'But it feels awful,' cried Edmond wretchedly.

'When you get it right,' Kate said, 'it will feel strong. Remember, sit so that you can feel strong. Sit up straight, put your feet on the floor. Don't cross your arms. Keep your hand movements vertical.'

Edmond looked for a few minutes at the flip chart as if memorising the words. Then he sat up in his chair and looked up at Christopher and said steadily, 'Waiter, I like this restaurant very much. But I don't like this wine, it's not up to scratch. I want you to bring me another bottle.' His lips moved as if he were going to add, 'Please,' but he closed his mouth firmly and said nothing else.

Sophie applauded and even Kate allowed herself to smile. 'There,' she said. 'You can do it. How did it feel?'

'I was rude,' Edmond said miserably.

'No, you weren't,' said Christopher. 'You were perfectly reasonable. You only asked for a new bottle of wine. It's not rude.'

'Sophie,' Kate said, turning to her, 'it's your turn. But we decided last night that you were going to try a different exercise, didn't we?'

The three men all looked at Sophie at once. Her pale face grew even paler and then she began to blush, colour flooding her cheeks. 'Oh,' she said, 'I really don't think that –'

'But we practised last night,' Kate said. 'And you really wanted to try it. Sophie, don't let me down.'

'I don't feel like it,' Sophie said timidly, looking at the floor.

143

'Sophie,' said Kate steadily, 'don't miss your chance. Try it.'

Sophie lifted her head and looked at Edmond, then at Kate. Her lower lip was caught in her teeth and she was chewing at it nervously and her hands opened and closed at her sides. 'I can't,' she said at last. 'I can't. I can't make someone do something they don't want to do.'

'You aren't going to,' Kate assured her. 'You're going to tell them what you want them to do, that's all. You can't make them do it. You haven't got the right to force someone or compel them to do anything. To get them to do what you want you might need to bridge to them or persuade them; you know you have those skills. But first they have to know what you want, Sophie. You have to tell them.'

For a moment Sophie said nothing. Then she lifted her head, jerking her chin up, and said, 'All right. But we agreed it could be in the other room, on the TV, didn't we.'

Kate nodded. She said to the three men, 'Sophie has a rather unusual scenario she wants to practise. I imagine none of you object to her trying it in the other room while we watch on the screen?' They all shook their heads. Their faces were tense and excited, but each of them was reacting to the situation differently. Christopher was looking at Sophie with quiet affection and an air almost of pride, like a man watching his child walking for the first time. Nick was clearly eager to redress his failure to persuade Sophie on day two. Edmond, though, looked unhappy, as if he was certain that he would be passed over and forgotten.

'Edmond,' Kate said, 'if you would go with Sophie, please.' Edmond's face brightened like the sun rising and Nick scowled in annoyance. Sophie went to the door with Edmond, and as they went out through it she took his hand.

Christopher went over to the television screen and

144

turned it on. Then he came back and stood in front of Kate, very close to her, looking down into her face. 'I think,' he said softly, 'that you have been giving little Sophie some private tuition.'

'Well, just a bit,' Kate said, smiling up at him.

'Typical,' said Nick angrily. 'I said yesterday I'd really like to see the two of you getting it on, and did you ask me to watch? No, you did not. Just let me go on playing bloody croquet.'

'I thought you didn't care about Sophie,' said Christopher, ignoring Nick. 'I was sure you wanted her to drop out. Was I wrong?'

'Not till last night,' Kate admitted. 'But when she – talked to me, I felt so sorry for her. And we decided that today would be her chance to learn what she needs.'

The television screen lit up and they saw the other training room. Sophie and Edmond stood there, face to face, a few feet apart, in front of a large sofa. Sophie glanced at the camera and giggled and Edmond said, 'You mustn't laugh, it's leakage. You have to keep a straight face.'

Sophie wiped her hand over her face as if to pull the smile off it. 'All right,' she said, 'here goes. Edmond, I really like you.' She stopped and put her hand again to her mouth as if she had only just heard her own words. Edmond stared at her, wide-eyed, his lips parted in delight and amazement. 'I really, really like you,' Sophie said again, and she took a little hesitant step towards Edmond and he came to her and caught her hands in his and kissed them.

Kate shook her head. 'This is not being assertive,' she said to the screen.

'It's like watching *Gone With the Wind*,' said Nick sourly from the depths of his armchair.

Suddenly Sophie seemed to realise what had happened. She pulled her hands away from Edmond's and wiped them on her dress, glancing apprehensively at the camera. 'Sorry,' she said, 'this wasn't what I was supposed to be practising. Sorry, I'll try again.' Edmond looked dashed and disappointed. Sophie turned to face him again and set her face into a calm, composed expression. The watchers could see her taking a deep, deep breath. 'Edmond,' she said at last, 'I really like you. What I don't like is that you haven't tried to make love to me. I want you to – ' Her voice broke off, hesitated, and then returned, strongly. 'I want you to kiss me here.' She put her hand on the front of her dress over her sex.

There was a silence. Nick sat forward in his chair, staring. Edmond said, 'I'm terribly sorry. I beg your pardon?'

Sophie glanced again at the camera as if she had not expected any resistance. 'I want you to use your mouth on me,' she said steadily.

'What, here? Now? Are you sure?' Edmond looked as if he could not believe it. He had forgotten the camera: his eyes were fixed on Sophie, on her long pale throat and her white skin and her tumbling hair. 'Are you sure?'

'Edmond, I know what I want,' Sophie said. Her voice was growing stronger at each repetition. 'I know what I want, and that's it. I want you to kiss me, to lick me. I want you to make me come.'

Suddenly Kate thought of herself in the office, leaning over Alex's shoulder, smelling the wonderful warm masculine scent of his body and hair, wanting desperately for him to do just that and unable to ask. Why, she thought, why can I teach other people to do it and not do it myself? Why?

Christopher came and stood close behind her. She felt his presence and turned to look up at him. He was smiling and he reached out and put his arms around her waist. 'I like this,' he said. 'I approve. You've done this for Sophie. I thought you were a selfish bitch at first. I'm glad I was wrong.'

Kate leant back against him, feeling his strength and warmth, his hard muscular body pressed against hers.

The sensation was exquisite. She would have liked to close her eyes and let herself flow into him, but she wanted to watch what was happening in the other room. She put her hands over Christopher's and he rested his chin on her head and they both watched with quiet attention.

Edmond was standing closer to Sophie now, looking at her. 'Sophie,' he said, 'I just want to say that I think you're beautiful, you're so attractive. I've been meaning to say so for days. I think – '

'Edmond,' Sophie interrupted him, 'I want you to use your mouth on me, not talk to me.' She bent down and caught hold of the hem of the dress and straightened, lifting it, pulling it off like a sweater. Beneath it her white body was naked but for the white V of the lace panties, just concealing the scanty dark hair of her triangle. Edmond gave a little gasp and dropped to his knees, catching hold of Sophie's narrow waist with his long hands and setting his lips to her flat belly just above her navel. They heard him murmur her name. She put her hands on his blond hair and let her head fall back, her lips parting in wonder and bliss.

'Look at that,' Nick breathed. 'Look at that.' He glanced at Kate and scowled to see her in Christopher's arms. 'Nothing for us, then?' he asked sharply.

'There's a thought,' said Christopher. He lifted his hands to touch Kate's breasts. 'You could amuse us while we watched.'

'You could amuse each other,' Kate suggested. She smiled to see Nick's expression of fear and distaste, the way he looked at Christopher as if he were some sort of noxious animal. 'That's the only option, I'm afraid,' she said at last. 'I promised Sophie I wouldn't waste any of your energies. She might need you later on. Sit quiet and watch.'

Christopher pulled her with him to a chair and down into his lap, keeping his arms around her. She relaxed into him, feeling his penis beneath his trousers thickening and swelling into a proud erection.

On the screen Edmond was still gently kissing the tender white skin of Sophie's waist and abdomen, worshipping her. His fingers caught at the sides of her panties and he began very softly to pull them down, caressing as he did so the soft flanks, the slender thighs, the delicate curves of Sophie's calves. The panties fell to the floor and Sophie was naked, standing perfectly still, her eyes closed. Edmond kissed her knees, the hollow of her thighs, the soft crease between her breasts, then stood and took hold of her shoulders, turning her to face the camera. He smiled into the lens and with one long hand he stroked down Sophie's lovely body, showing the unseen audience the soft swell of her breast, the shadowed edge of her ribs, the peak of her hip bone, the plump mound between her legs. She did not open her eyes. Her face looked like a painting of a virgin martyr, transfigured with the ecstasy of achievement, reaching the peak of her bliss even as the spear pierces her breast.

Edmond led Sophie very gently two paces back to the sofa behind them and placed her on it. He arranged her with artistic care, sideways on to the camera so that the audience might see her pleasure clearly, her shoulders on the arm of the sofa so that her head hung loosely back, her lips parted and her white throat stretched out as if inviting a vampire to come and sip her blood. The peaks of her breasts were swollen with desire, coral-pink and tight. One leg was on the sofa, slightly bent and hollowed, and the other was stretched down so that the soft pink lips of her sex were just visible, peeping through the fine dark fur that fringed them.

Christopher shifted his weight a little beneath Kate and put his hands on her breasts, squeezing them gently. She felt him move until his thickened phallus was in soft, deliberate contact with the swell of her buttocks. She moved her hips in small circles, pressing against him, stimulating him and herself at the same time,

148

gasping as he fondled her breasts. Nick was sitting back in his chair, his eyes glued to the screen, and now he opened his fly and released his hard eager penis and began to stroke it with his hand, drawing the soft foreskin away from the shining glans and breathing shakily through his teeth.

Edmond leant over Sophie and kissed her throat, her shoulders, the tiny hollow of her collarbone. She turned her head and sighed with pleasure. He knelt between her parted thighs and set his lips to the swollen tip of one breast, sucking, licking at the little hard peak. Sophie moved, her body shimmering as if a wave had passed through it, and her lips parted, but she made no sound. Edmond's lips moved on down her body until they reached the soft fleece of her mound. He hesitated there and glanced up at the camera for a moment. Then he reached down and stroked his hand along Sophie's leg, taking hold of her ankle and gently, gently moving her foot further and further from the sofa so that her thighs were parted almost as widely as they could be. The movement opened up the secret place between her legs, showing it to the onlookers, pink and glistening with moist willingness.

'Showman,' Christopher whispered in Kate's ear. She said nothing, but she smiled and pushed her breasts against his hands.

'Shut up and watch,' Nick said thickly.

Edmond kissed the inside of Sophie's knee. His tongue showed between his lips, caressing the white skin. Very slowly, very gradually his lips moved up and up, touching, soft as rose petals. Sophie took long, steady breaths, her breasts lifting and falling, her erect nipples pointing upwards, shameless and exposed. Edmond rested his face against her inner thigh and stayed motionless for a moment, gazing at the perfect, gleaming love mound before his eyes. Then he lifted his hand and gently, gently set his fingers to the outer lips, drawing them back. Sophie's neck twisted and she let out a long

149

breath as Edmond opened up her sex, revealing the little pearl of flesh that stood out just below her triangle of dark down. Then he leant forward and opened his lips and with his moist tongue he touched the little pearl, caressing it, stroking it, and Sophie opened her flushed swollen lips and let out a long 'Ah . . .' of delight.

Kate felt her breathing growing ragged with desire. She pushed her buttocks back into Christopher's lap, feeling the magnificent length of his phallus nestling between her cheeks, wishing desperately that he would lift her skirt and tear off her panties and come inside her. He was still fondling her breasts with his hands, very gently and with infinite delicacy, lifting her with each touch to a higher peak of arousal. She could feel his hot breath on her ear, his lips just brushing against the soft skin of her neck. Again and again she thrust herself back on to him, feeling the throbbing life of him beneath her buttocks. Their movements became rhythmic, almost as if he had penetrated her and was rocking her slowly, slowly towards orgasm. Her breasts ached with heavy pleasure.

For some time Edmond knelt almost motionless, his tongue lapping and lapping at the bud of Sophie's clitoris until it swelled and stood out like the stem of a fragrant fruit. She moaned beneath his touch and her limp hands came to life and lifted to her breasts, kneading and stroking the slight mounds, teasing out her nipples into eager points of pleasure. Then Edmond pressed his face closer between her thighs and the breathless onlookers saw his tongue flicker downwards, swirling through the warm folds of her vulva, seeking out the entrance to her love passage. He found it; his hands gripped tightly at Sophie's slender thighs, holding her still as he thrust his tongue deep inside her. She cried out and arched her back, frenziedly pulling at her taut nipples with finger and thumb. Edmond lifted his mouth from her sex for a moment to look up the lovely undulating sea of her body. He smiled and then returned to his labour, attending again to Sophie's bud of pleasure, drawing it into his mouth and sucking at it as if it were a nipple.

'Oh,' Sophie cried out, 'oh, God, it's so good, Edmond, it's so good. Don't stop. Oh Edmond, Edmond, I'm going to come.' Her body was writhing, her slender loins lifting towards Edmond's face, begging him to lick her harder, harder, her hands teasing and bruising the tight paps of her breasts. Edmond took one hand from her heaving thighs and as his strong, firm tongue lapped at her, faster now, he slid his middle finger into the tight entrance to her sex, penetrating her gently. Sophie's eyes snapped open, wide open, staring blindly into the air as her body stiffened with the approach of her orgasm. She gasped, 'Oh God, yes, oh, oh . . .' And then her eyes slid shut and her hands made fists and her lips parted and quivered as her body shook from head to foot with the ecstatic violence of her climax. Edmond knelt at her feet, his sensitive hands gently restraining her as she shuddered against his lips.

Presently her shaking subsided and Edmond lifted his mouth from her sex, glistening with her juices. He kissed her belly and breasts and then lay on her, setting his lips to her arched neck, white and graceful as a swan's. She put her hands around him and they lay together very still.

Nick sat back in his chair, still stroking his hard eager cock with his hand. The scarlet tip was glistening with lust. He said with difficulty, 'Kate, come here.'

Christopher's hands were still stroking Kate's breasts. Nick turned his flushed face from the screen and saw Kate sitting in Christopher's lap, rocking herself against his body, and his expression became grim with envy. 'How did you get her, Christopher?' he demanded angrily, getting to his feet. His erection thrust forward, shining and determined, its helmeted glans taut and swollen. 'Kate,' he said, coming towards her and holding out his hands.

'Look,' Christopher said quietly.

Nick scowled at him then glanced at the screen and saw Sophie sliding out from underneath Edmond's body, standing naked before the camera. Her face and her breasts were still flushed with orgasm. She smiled into the camera and said, 'Kate, I hope you think that I did that well enough. What I want to do now is come back into the main room and practise with several people. That's directly relevant to what I do at work, you see.'

Behind her Edmond sat up on the sofa, still fully clothed, his expression disconsolate. He said, 'Sophie.'

Sophie turned and went back to him. She leaned down to take his face in her hand and kiss him. Her back was to the camera and as she bent Kate and Christopher and Nick could see between her firm white buttocks the delicious pink moistness of her sex opening, wet with her juices, slippery with desire. She kissed Edmond deeply and then straightened and said, 'Edmond, that was wonderful. I can't tell you how good it was. Now I want you to come back into the main room with me.'

She bent to pick up her discarded dress from the floor and slipped it on. Then Edmond unlocked the door and Sophie turned off the camera.

'Nick,' Kate said with a slight smile as she got reluctantly up from Christopher's muscular lap, 'I think you might put that away for the time being.'

'She's coming in here for more of the same, isn't she?' Nick demanded. 'If I can't have you, Kate, I'll – '

The door opened and despite his bold words Nick turned quickly away, forcing his swollen cock back into his trousers and buttoning the fly. Sophie came in with Edmond behind her; she closed the door and turned the key in the lock.

'Did I do all right, Kate?' she asked, smiling.

'You know you did,' Kate said. 'You did very well. Now here we all are; practise with us all, if you want, Sophie.'

Sophie advanced into the middle of the room and stood looking around her. Edmond followed her, gazing at her with an expression of hopeless longing. Nick stood behind a chair, clutching at it with both hands, his fierce dark face full of savage desire; Christopher still sat where he had rocked Kate on his lap, not trying to hide the thick silhouette of his erection inside his trousers, looking up at Sophie with expectation.

Sophie licked her lips. 'I like you all very much,' she said. 'I don't like the fact that you've all got your clothes on. I want you to strip.'

'Me too, Sophie?' Kate asked.

Sophie looked a little surprised. 'If you want,' she said, but it was clear that her attention was on the men. She looked around and saw that none of them had moved; they were all staring at her. 'What's the matter?' she asked. 'Don't worry, I'll take care of everything. But I want you all to strip.'

After a little moment of stillness the men began to obey her. She stood watching as they removed their clothes, her breasts lifting and falling as her breathing quickened. She watched Nick first, admiring his lean strength, his dark colouring, tanned and smooth, muscles moving beneath his sleek skin, the thatch of black hair in his loins, the rigid column of flesh springing from it. Then she looked at Christopher and gave a little gasp as she registered the size and power of him, his height, the breadth of his shoulders, the controlled strength of his movements. She lowered her eyes briefly to rest on his phallus and her hands lifted to cover her mouth in horror and delight.

Then she turned and looked at Edmond. He was standing very still, naked already, his slender body as wiry and graceful as a greyhound's. He glanced at the other two men with an air almost of regret and then looked into Sophie's eyes. The sun through the window of the room caught in his hair, making it blaze with gold like an angel's.

Sophie smiled into Edmond's anxious eyes and reached out to touch his cheek with her hand. His face brightened and he caught hold of her hand and took it to his mouth and kissed it. Kate saw their faces softened with desire and love and she sighed, feeling her stomach jolting with a sensation that was not just lust.

All three men were naked now. Nick glanced across the room at Christopher, apprehensive and cautious, then he began to walk towards Sophie, slowly and steadily, like a stalking cat. Christopher smiled to see Nick's anxiety and he too began to approach Sophie as she stood looking into Edmond's eyes.

'Sophie,' Edmond said. Sophie jumped, then turned and saw the other two men coming towards her, their faces taut with anticipation. For a moment her nerve seemed to fail her; she took a step back and brushed against Edmond's naked arm and looked frantically behind her as if she were hunted. Edmond caught her hand and held it and she stood very still for a moment, breathing quickly. Then she turned her head and met Kate's eyes.

Kate felt a surge of something that was almost sorrow, a yearning to be as Sophie was now, on the verge of a discovery of pleasure and power that she had thought would always be beyond her. She knew that there was no place for her in the fantasy that Sophie intended to live out. She stepped back slowly and sat down in one of the deep chairs, her eyes still on Sophie's, and she lifted her right hand to her lips and very gently blew her a kiss.

Sophie's dark eyes glowed and she lifted her head as if the kiss had strengthened her. She took Edmond's hand and drew it down to the hem of her dress and said softly, 'Edmond, take my dress off.'

Edmond stood behind Sophie and lowered his head for a moment, touching his lips to her neck. Then he stooped and caught hold of the hem of the dress and very gently, very slowly, lifted it up over the delicate curves of her slender body, coaxing the sleeves along her arms, leaving her quite naked. He dropped the dress and came closer to Sophie, closing his eyes and brushing his cheek very gently against hers, his lips stirring her curly hair.

For a moment Sophie did not move. Then she looked at the two men standing before her and silently held out her hands to them. They approached her and she lifted her face so that Edmond could stoop his lips on to hers and kiss her. Edmond put his hands on her shoulders, breathing quickly as their lips met and their tongues explored each other's mouths deeply and with longing. Nick looked almost confused for a moment; it was clear that sharing a woman with other men was not within his experience. Christopher glanced at him, smiled, then in one long stride covered the distance between him and Sophie. He put his hands very gently on her breasts and she heaved beneath Edmond's lips and gave a long shuddering sigh. Christopher smoothed his big hands over the soft swell of her breasts, gently kneading the white flesh, not yet touching her engorged, tender nipples. He glanced again at Nick and said softly, 'Nick, come here. Come and touch her.'

'What?' Nick said, his voice tense and apprehensive.

Sophie detached her mouth from Edmond's and lifted her head. Her face was flushed, her lips swollen with desire, her eyes sparkling. She licked her lips and said, 'Nick, come here. I want you and Christopher to – to kiss my breasts.'

Still Nick hesitated. He looked almost as if he thought someone was trying to play a practical joke on him. 'What's in it for me?' he asked suspiciously.

'Pleasure,' Sophie said, letting her head fall back as Christopher's strong fingers flickered gently over the taut buds of her nipples. 'Pleasure.' She stopped speaking and Edmond kissed her again, his face showing his desperate desire.

'Nick,' Christopher said again, 'come on. Come on.' He moved a little to one side, making room for Nick, and as he did so he sank very slowly to his knees and reached up with his generous, sensual lips to draw the tight nipple of Sophie's left breast into his mouth, caressing it, stimulating it with his tongue.

Sophie moaned and as if her cry had summoned him Nick suddenly jumped towards her and dipped his head to draw her other nipple into his mouth, licking at it, nipping it between his sharp teeth so that Sophie's white body squirmed with delicious pleasure. Still she kissed Edmond as he stood behind her; Kate could see their twisting tongues leisurely exploring each other's mouths, searching out the sensitive insides of the lips, thrusting deeply. Nick put his dark hands on to her white skin and began gently to run them over her, feeling the softness of her flat belly, the gentle hollow where her thigh joined her body. After a moment his hand slipped between her legs and began to touch and stroke and tease and Sophie gave a little cry of delight. Christopher's big hands were running over her ribs, around to the back of her body, fondling the gentle firm roundness of her buttocks. And all the time Edmond caressed her face and neck and shoulders with his long sensitive fingers and kissed her, more and more passionately.

Kate slipped down further into her chair and watched, her face soft with an echo of Sophie's pleasure. She rested her cheek in her hand and her little finger moved between her lips; as she watched she sucked very softly at the tip of her finger, feeling with her tongue the roundness of its tip, the smooth hardness of the nail. Her thighs closed and pressed together and her breathing quickened slightly. It was so arousing to see Sophie there, her slender body explored, possessed, pleasured by three pairs of strong male hands, to see her slight breasts swelling and colouring with desire as they were stimulated by eager mouths. Kate's own breasts ached to be kissed; she drew her finger from her mouth and began gently to stroke her nipples through the fabric of her blouse.

At last Christopher leant his cheek against Sophie's soft thigh and looked up at her and said very softly, 'Sophie, what shall we do?'

As he spoke the other men all drew back a little as if waiting for her answer. She lifted her head, looking for a moment almost confused. Then she reached behind her head to stroke her fingers through Edmond's soft fair hair and with her other hand touched first Nick's face, then Christopher's, her dark eyes roaming over the beautiful male bodies kneeling at her feet, waiting to do her bidding. She took a deep breath, a gasp of utter satisfaction, and her lips curved in a smile of triumph. Then she said, 'I want you all to have me, all of you. All of you at the same time.'

'Sophie,' Edmond whispered, bending his head to bury his face in her hair. 'Sophie.'

Sophie kept her hand in his hair, stroking it gently. 'Edmond,' she said, 'you gave me such pleasure with your wonderful mouth. I want to do the same for you. Will you let me take you in my mouth, Edmond?'

Edmond said nothing, but he placed his lips on the soft hollow of Sophie's neck and kissed her. She continued to stroke his cheek, but her voice was steady and determined. 'Christopher,' she said, and Christopher lifted his head and smiled up at her. Sophie began to breathe quickly, her breasts lifting and falling. 'Christopher,' she said again, and suddenly she pulled away from Edmond's hands and dropped to her knees, looking up into Christopher's shadowed, enigmatic face. She was trembling. After a moment she reached out one hand and put it on Christopher's shoulder and slowly, very slowly ran it down his body, across the broad muscles of his chest, across the tense plane of his ribs and his strong flat stomach, down to his loins where his massive penis stood up hard and proud, inviting her to touch it. Now she was gasping, her jaw and lips shaking. She swallowed hard and then reached out and wrapped her hand around Christopher's hardness, stroking the velvety skin down very gently, drawing it away from the shining glans.

Sophie did not speak, but with her other hand she very gently pressed on Christopher's broad chest, pushing him so that he was lying on the carpet, propped up on his elbows, still smiling softly at her as she stimulated his huge member with her small white hand. Then she licked her lips and without a word straddled him, spreading her slender thighs across his strong legs. She let his penis spring up to lie along his belly and gently lowered herself on to it so that it lay flat between her legs, the glistening head showing under the soft triangle of dark fur that framed her sex. She began to slide very slowly to and fro, closing her eyes. Her nostrils flared with pleasure and her lips drew back from her teeth as she felt the hot shaft rubbing between her moist, sensitive labia.

This was too much for Nick. He had been watching with a face of burning eagerness, but Sophie had spoken to Edmond first, and then to Christopher, and he seemed to be afraid that there would be nothing left for him. He reached out and caught Sophie's face in his strong dark hand and forced his lips down on hers, thrusting his tongue into her mouth, making her gasp. After a moment he drew back and demanded, 'What about me? Damn it, Sophie, what about me?'

Kate took a quick breath, suddenly afraid that Sophie would lose her nerve. For a moment she waited, her hands clenched, and Sophie looked into Nick's blue eyes and did not speak. 'Come on, Sophie,' Kate whispered to herself beneath her breath, 'tell him, tell him what you want.'

As if she had heard Kate's whisper Sophie's swollen lips moved. 'Nick,' she said softly, 'I want you behind me. I want to take you – in my arse.'

Nick stared into Sophie's eyes, his jaw slack with amazement. When he spoke his voice was trembling. 'Sophie, are you sure?'

'I'm sure.' Sophie lifted one hand, holding it towards Edmond. 'I'm sure. Nick behind me: Christopher here, here . . . and Edmond, in my mouth.' She shook back her hair. 'Now,' she said softly. 'I want you all now.'

Without another word Nick moved around behind Sophie and knelt across Christopher's thighs, stroking his hands down the white skin of her slender back. He slipped one hand between Sophie's buttocks and she winced as his fingers explored her sex, drawing pearly juice from her wet lips and using it to moisten the tight, narrow entrance to her secret passage. Kate saw him gently slip the tip of one finger into the little puckered hole, making Sophie gasp.

'Sophie,' Nick whispered, 'has anyone ever – '

'No,' Sophie said, breathing fast. 'Nick, do it. I want you to do it.'

'Gently then,' said Nick. He put his hands on the white orbs of Sophie's buttocks and parted them, revealing the silky skin of her crease and the dark, secret entrance. He moistened his lips with his tongue and with one hand guided the glistening tip of his hard cock into the crease and placed it on the spot and began to thrust, very gently, but strongly. Sophie gasped again and rubbed herself against the hot thickness of Christopher's shaft, and as she did so Kate saw the velvety head of Nick's eager penis begin to move. Kate breathed quickly. She had hoped to see Sophie's virginity taken, and in a way her dream was coming true: Nick was about to become the first man ever to have possessed Sophie's beautiful arse. Before Kate's wondering eyes the tip of Nick's shaft began to enter Sophie's anus, penetrating her, disappearing between her buttocks until it was sheathed to the hilt. Nick gasped as he pushed himself into Sophie and clutched at her hips, his dark fingers gripping hard at her pale flesh. He hissed, 'Oh God, it's so tight. So tight. My God.'

As Nick's penis penetrated her Sophie arched her back and thrust her buttocks towards him, her lips parting widely as if she strained for air. She let out a long, low moan of pleasure. Then, feeling herself impaled on his throbbing length, she felt between her thighs and took hold of Christopher's massive shaft and slipped the huge shining head between the lips of her sex. She whispered, 'Oh, that's so good. It's filling me up. Christopher, push it into me,' and Christopher pushed his hips up towards her, thrusting himself deep inside her.

For a moment Sophie did not move. She knelt there astride Christopher's muscular thighs, savouring the feel of his long, thick cock deeply imbedded in her vagina at the same time as Nick's hard penis filled her secret passage. Then she lifted herself, very slowly, drawing herself away from the men so that both shafts appeared, gleaming with her pearly juices, slowly emerging from the silken channels of her body. She lowered herself again, sliding down on the hard rods of pleasure, closing her eyes in ecstasy as she felt herself penetrated both before and behind. Then she opened her eyes and looked up at Edmond who stood over her, holding his straining penis in his hand, aching for her to please him. She whispered, 'Edmond,' and he came quickly and knelt astride Christopher's face and Sophie leant forward and opened her mouth and very slowly took him in, savouring the taste of him, caressing his quivering shaft with her eager lips.

Unable to restrain herself, Kate pushed down her panties and slipped one hand inside, her fingers reaching eagerly for her swollen clitoris. She began to stroke herself, pushing one finger deep inside her as with another she caressed her little pleasure bud, watching wide-eyed as Sophie moaned with joy to feel herself ravished in every orifice, taking three hard penises inside her. Kate whimpered with pleasure and frustration to see the hot stiff shafts sliding in and out of Sophie's slender body, engorged and desperate, glistening with her love juices and her saliva.

The men had found Sophie's rhythm now. Christopher

held her hips firmly in his strong hands and thrust firmly up into her, and as he did so he reached up with his long tongue to lick and suck the dangling sac of Edmond's testicles so that Edmond cried out with pleasure. Nick clutched at Sophie's buttocks, gasping as his long stiff cock slid in and out of her anus, and Edmond reached down as she sucked him to caress her breasts, teasing out her nipples to straining peaks of delight. Sophie's body shuddered as they thrust in to her, possessing her, servicing her so thoroughly that she groaned with joy.

Nick's hands were shaking now as they clutched Sophie's haunches. He flung back his head, gasping, baring his teeth as his orgasm began to overcome him. He cried out, 'Oh Christ, I'm coming, I'm coming,' and suddenly he lunged forward, thrusting himself into Sophie's secret passage as far as he could, crying out as his cock jerked and pulsed inside her.

His crisis seemed to set off a chain reaction of pleasure. Sophie closed her eyes as she began to shake helplessly in the delicious spasms of orgasm. The soft flesh of her breasts and thighs quivered as she writhed desperately on Christopher's thick, hot shaft, grinding her turgid clitoris against his muscular belly and pressing her tight nipples against Edmond's tormenting hands. Her astonished, shuddering cries were smothered by the eager length of Edmond's cock as he pushed it deeper and deeper into her trembling mouth. Christopher gasped and reached up with his long tongue to sweep along the smooth secret skin behind Edmond's testicles and Edmond cried out and thrust himself into Sophie's mouth as far as he could, his buttocks tensing as he jetted his hot sperm into her waiting throat.

Sophie's mouth opened slackly as she continued to twist in the throes of her orgasm. The pearly strands of Edmond's seed trickled from her shaking lips and fell on to Christopher's face. He cried out and gripped her hips and forced himself up into her, using all his tremendous strength to ram the thick shaft of his massive cock deep,

deep into her spasming flesh, shouting with pleasure as his own climax swept over him. And in the lonely softness of her armchair Kate also reached orgasm, pushing her fingers deep inside her, overcome with the sight of Sophie's joy.

Moaning deliriously, Sophie slumped forward on to Christopher's broad chest, his twitching cock still deeply embedded in her. Edmond knelt down beside them and stroked her hair and Nick withdrew very gently from her and sat back on his haunches, fondling her delicate buttocks with his hand. Kate drew her hand away from her vulva and rested her cheek on her arm, watching with a smile as the men caressed Sophie, stroking and touching her, helping her to recover from the violence of her pleasure.

After several minutes Sophie lifted her head and looked across at Kate. She licked her lips and said in a voice that was husky with fulfilment, 'Kate, I want you to join us.'

Kate sat up, shaking her head. 'No,' she said firmly, 'I think that's enough for today, Sophie. You would all be short-changed if we didn't do some practice on your real situations now.' She got up from the chair and went over to where Sophie lay sprawled on Christopher's naked body. Taking Sophie by the arms she gently lifted her to her feet and kissed her on the lips. 'You did marvellously,' she said. 'It was wonderful to watch. But now let's take a break and then get on with business situations.'

Christopher sat up and reached out for Kate. 'It hardly seems fair on you,' he said with concern in his voice. 'We could wait a bit and then start again.'

'Oh, don't worry about me,' Kate said. 'There's still tomorrow. You all have to practise putting it all together tomorrow. I'm looking forward to that.'

Chapter Nine

'*H*ello?'
     'David? David, it's me, Kate. Can you talk?'

'I'm in the darkroom. Yes, I can talk, nothing's developing right now. What's up? Is something wrong?'

'No – nothing wrong exactly – '

'What's the matter?' David's voice changed, becoming lower and soft. 'Has something gone wrong? Has someone made trouble?'

'No, no.' Kate coiled into a ball on the bed, dressed only in her thin cotton robe, holding the telephone between her ear and her shoulder. 'No, nobody's made trouble. Is that the problem? I don't know, I'm all confused. I just wanted to talk to you about it. Have you got time?'

'Yes. I can talk all night if you want. What's going on? How many of the men have you had so far?'

'Oh – two. Nick and Christopher.'

'The dark one that you fancied and the big quiet-looking one. Any good?'

'Oh yes. Oh, very good. But David, I don't know what I've started.' Briefly Kate explained the dynamics of the course to date, the way the participants had interacted with each other: Nick's homophobic fear of Christopher and Sophie and Edmond's obvious mutual interest. 'And today,' she said, 'after my coaching, Sophie did brilliantly. She had all the men pleasuring her at once, it was marvellous for her, she seemed to be coming for hours. And then after that we did good assertiveness work too: everyone, even Edmond, and he's the archetypical English gentleman. But now I feel – odd. Lost.'

There was a short silence. Then David said gently, 'Kate, my darling, I can tell you what the problem is.'

'What?' Kate asked.

'It's called not being in the limelight. You hate it.'

'David!'

'No, it's true. The men were paying attention to Sophie today, weren't they? And there didn't seem to be much place for you?'

'I was watching.'

David laughed. 'Watching's not what you're good at, Kate. You like to be in the thick of things, if you'll excuse the pun. You're extrovert, uninhibited, an actress, you love to be admired. Taking a back seat even for a morning would be guaranteed to make you feel low. And the other thing is, Kate, you like people to need you. It's always the same on these courses. Even when you only have the participants in mind you always go through this depressed stage when you begin to feel that they've stopped needing you quite as much as they did to start with. And this time you set out meaning to have a good time yourself; I told you that you'd end up looking after the participants instead, and you have. And now you're worrying about why they're paying attention to each other and not to you. I warned you.'

For a moment Kate said nothing, only sat with the receiver on her shoulder chewing her lip. Then she said reluctantly, 'I suppose you might be right.'

'You know I'm right.' She could hear David's smile. 'I told you about it days ago, didn't I? But don't worry, Kate. I don't just diagnose problems, I know the cure.'

'What's that then?' Kate asked, sounding dispirited.

'Just talk to me a little longer,' said David, his voice soft now and caressing. 'Just a bit longer. I guarantee to cheer you up.'

'David,' murmured Kate. She knew well what he meant. When they had lived together she and David had often been separated through the pressure of work and they had perfected the art of what they liked to call long-distance loving. It had been months since they had indulged and the prospect filled Kate with pleasurable anticipation. She slipped further down the bed, uncoiling herself sinuously and stretching out on the slick surface of the cover, feeling her nipples beginning to tingle at the very thought. 'Well,' she said softly, 'all right. Cheer me up, then.'

'I'm in the darkroom,' David said. 'You remember the darkroom. Remember the time you came in to watch me developing those pictures of you and they were so hot that I had you on the floor? Do you remember?'

Kate's mind filled with an image of red light glowing over her naked limbs, making white skin look like coral and pink sexual flesh strangely pale. 'I remember,' she whispered. 'There wasn't any room, I had to hoist my legs up on to the sink. And you pulled me into your lap in the end. Oh, David, I do remember. You held my waist in your hands and you lifted me up and down on your lovely cock and you licked my breasts. Why was it so good? Why did it feel so good?'

'All those pictures of you,' David said, his voice as soft as thick dark fur. 'All those pictures I took. The first ones I took of you. They were all round us, Kate. You remember when I took them, the day we never got up, we spent the whole day in bed. I had you and then I took pictures of you lying there afterwards. I've got one here, I'm looking at it now, I still keep some of them on the walls. Do you remember when I took them? I just withdrew from you and reached over for my camera and took pictures, only a minute before I was coming inside you, only two minutes before you were coming as I pushed my cock into you. And then I took these pictures straight away. You've got a silk slip on but it looks like a rag, it's pulled down off your shoulders and pushed up above your hips so your breasts are bare and I can see right between your legs. You're totally relaxed, everything about you is so soft, your lips are soft, your eyes are just slits, soft smudgy charcoal slits, and your nipples are swollen and they're shining with my saliva. And between your legs everything is so wet, you're wet with your juice and my come, and you look so contented. You look proud of yourself.'

Kate took a long, deep breath and shifted the receiver to a more comfortable position on her shoulder, freeing both hands. She began to stroke her breasts, squeezing them as if she were trying to expel milk from her tightening nipples. She had to lick her lips before she could speak. 'Is it your favourite picture?' she whispered. 'Is that one your favourite?'

'No. I've got my favourite one here. I never take it down. It's the one of you playing with yourself.'

'What am I doing?'

'You're just lying there on the sofa. You've got your head thrown right back and your eyes are closed and your mouth is open. I like the way your lips look so soft and loose, as if you'd really like to feel someone sliding his thick shaft right into your mouth. And your hand is between your legs. It makes an amazing shape, the white skin of your hand against your dark pubic hair. You're touching your clitoris with your middle finger and all your other fingers are sort of drawn up, quite stiffly, as if you don't want them in the way. It looks odd and graceful. And you've got your other hand on your breast. You're squeezing your breast really hard, the shadows are pooling around your fingers where they're digging into your skin, and your nipple is trapped between your second and third finger and I can see how you're pinching it. You look lovely.'

'Tell me why you like it.'

'I like it because you look so abandoned. You look wanton, that's the word. You look as if you would say yes to anything, to anyone. You look like the Empress Messalina. If a dozen Roman soldiers walked in you'd open your eyes and look at them and breathe, "Come here, boys," and take them all, all of them.'

'What would they do?' Kate whispered. 'What would they do to me? Where are you?' She loved the way David's imagination ran riot.

'I'm the captain,' David said huskily. 'The centurion. It's me and my best ten men, I chose them specially, we all know what the Empress wants. We walk in and there you are, stroking yourself, your fingers working between your legs. Your legs are spread wide so we can see everything and my men take one look and they just growl with lust. They can't wait to get their hands on you. And you take your hand away from your pussy and lick your fingers and smile, then you prop yourself up on one arm and look my men up and down and say, "Who's first, then?" You point to two of them and they run forward and grab you. They don't bother to take their armour off, they just lift their tunics and under their tunics they've got big, hard cocks. They pull you up from the bed and one of them stands in front of you and pushes himself up you, all in one movement, and the other one spits on his cock and rubs it and then he stands behind you and thrusts himself up your arse and there you are, between these two sweating grunting soldiers, squirming with pleasure as they fill you up with their big cocks. The one behind you is holding your hips and the one in front is holding your breasts and you're gasping and crying out as they fuck you. They're shafting you really hard, we can hear the slap as their bodies hit yours. You were just about to come when we came in and now you're coming again and again, you're shuddering with their thrusts and your orgasm, it goes on and on. And I'm standing there and watching you and rubbing my cock with my hand just hoping that you'll take pity on me.'

'I see you,' Kate whispered. As David spoke she had let her hand slip down her body and now it rested between her legs, just touching the swelling tip of her clitoris, stroking it gently, persistently. 'I see you. I can see you're desperate. So when the first two soldiers have finished, David, tell me what I do.'

'When they've done,' David's husky voice said in her ear, 'both of them pull out of you and stagger away and you let yourself down on to your couch and look at all of us poor desperate men standing there. All of us are masturbating; we couldn't bear watching the first two screw you, but we don't dare approach you without your permission. You're the Empress, you're our Queen, you could have us all crucified if you wanted. We have to hope that you'll choose us. And you look me up and down and hold out your hand. Your arm is naked except for pearls and you crook your little finger at me and smile and lick your lips. And I walk towards you, very steadily, though I'm so excited I can hardly move, and you kneel on the couch on all fours and smile up at me as I come closer and closer. Then – '

'Then when you're standing right in front of me,' Kate said breathlessly, taking up the story, 'I flick my eyes over the others who are waiting and I choose one with a nice big cock and I jerk my head at him, telling him to go round behind me. He's going to have me while I use my mouth on you. But I'm really looking forward to taking you in my mouth. You look so eager, so earnest. David, tell me what you're doing now.'

'I've opened my jeans,' David said. 'My cock is so stiff and smooth, my balls are tight, drawn up tight under my body. My cock wants to be inside you, Kate, it wants to be in your warm soft mouth. And that's what the Empress does: she leans forward and flicks her tongue over the head of my cock, over the glans where it's so smooth and sensitive, and then she opens her beautiful red mouth and takes me in.'

'You put your hands in my hair,' Kate whispered, stroking her swollen peak of pleasure with her fingers and pinching her nipple. 'My hair's plaited and bound up with gold fillets and ropes of pearls but you don't care, you dig your strong hands into it and all the pins start to fall out and the pearls fall over your fingers, but you don't let go. You hold my head tight and you push yourself into my mouth, you're fucking my mouth. I can feel the other soldier behind me, just nudging up between my lips, and he thrusts and fills me and it's wonderful, but it's better feeling you between my lips. You slide your cock in and out of my mouth and you taste so good, you taste of salt and musk and sweetness, and as I suck you you're groaning with delight. I want to swallow you up, I want you to fill me with your hot come. David, David – ' Her voice broke off into gasps as she stroked herself faster and faster.

'I can feel your lips on me,' David muttered, 'I can feel them, rubbing around me, your tongue is flicking at that little ridge just under the head, it's driving me mad. I open my eyes and I can see the soldier behind you clutching your buttocks and ramming his big stiff shaft deep inside you. I can see him. Every time he drives into you his body hits your buttocks really hard and a sort of wave pulses up your flesh, all the way up your body, and your breasts judder and shake. It's amazing. I reach down and take hold of your breasts and pinch your nipples as you suck me and I watch the soldier fucking you. Oh God, I can feel my balls tightening. Kate, Kate, my cock's so hard, it's full of come, I'm going to come. Come now, Kate, come with me – ' David stopped speaking and groaned deep in his throat and hearing him Kate felt her own orgasm swell and seize her. She gasped and moaned and for a moment there was no sound except their heavy breathing as they recovered from their far-distant climaxes.

Then Kate sighed and said, 'David, thank you.'

'You see,' David said softly, 'I happen to think that you are the sexiest, most desirable woman in the world.' He chuckled softly. 'And I'm glad to see that we haven't lost the knack of that. Was it good for you, too, honey?'

'You know it was,' Kate breathed. 'David . . .' Her eyes fell on her little alarm clock, perched pertly on her bedside table. 'Oh, God,' she said miserably, 'I'm going to be late for dinner.' She was coming back to herself. 'And the message light's glowing on the phone. David, I'm going to have to go. I'm so sorry. Your time's not your own on one of these courses.'

'Do you feel better?' asked David's velvet voice.

'Yes.' It was true. 'I feel much better.'

'You said you wanted to run this course for you, but I knew you wouldn't keep it up. You've been looking after the participants, haven't you? It's always the same. Don't worry about it, Kate.'

'I won't worry.' Kate blew a kiss down the receiver. 'David, good-night.'

'Come and see me when you come back,' said David. 'Tomorrow night, isn't it? I've still got that rude resignation letter to your boss. Come back and see me and we'll decide whether to send it.'

'All right,' Kate said softly. 'Good night, David. Thank you.'

The phone clicked on to the cradle and Kate lay back on the bed and heaved a deep, satisfied sigh. At times like this she wondered whether she should ever have moved out of the Docklands apartment. David was certainly somebody very special. But neither of them was really suited to monogamy and she had a sneaking feeling that David was happier with things as they were: he was the best of friends and on occasion the most passionate of lovers, but without any ties. She sighed again and stretched her hands above her head, then picked up the phone and dialled 0 for reception.

'You have a message for me.'

'Oh yes,' said the receptionist. 'It's from the gentleman in Room 202. He asks if you can call him when you have a moment. Dial the room number.'

'Thank you.' Kate cut the connection and stared into space for a moment, frowning. Why should Edmond ask her to call? For a moment she smiled, imagining what he might say. Kate, I've been dying to make love to you since I saw you, may I come to your room? Would you like to go out and walk in the grounds? I wonder if –

Kate shook her head. No, she did not really expect that of Edmond. No point in trying to second-guess: if she had learnt one thing in seven years of managing and training people, it was that they would always surprise you. She dialled 202.

'Hello?' said Edmond's clipped, aristocratic voice.

'Edmond, it's Kate. You wanted me to call.'

'Oh Kate, yes.' Now Edmond sounded flustered and uncertain. 'I rang you earlier but you were engaged. I'm not interrupting anything, am I?'

'No,' Kate said with a secret smile. 'No, I've finished with that call. What's up?'

'Well, I – ' Edmond's voice faded and returned. 'Kate, could I come and have a word with you? It would be easier face to face than on the phone.'

'Of course.' Kate tried to keep surprise from her voice. 'Surely. Come round.'

'I'll be right there.'

The phone went dead. Kate looked thoughtfully into the receiver and frowned again, then gasped and jumped up, looking down at herself. She was half naked and the soft flesh between her legs was soaked with her juices. She snatched up her silky dressing gown and pulled it on and raced into the bathroom, checking that her face and throat were not too flushed. A few splashes of cold water cooled her off and she pushed her hair into some semblance of tidiness and went back through to the living room of the suite.

As she walked in there was a hesitant knock at the

171

door. Kate went over and opened it, smiling into Edmond's apprehensive face. 'Hi,' she said encouragingly, 'Come in.'

'Thanks very much.' Edmond came into the room and stood just inside the door as she shut it and turned to him. He was dressed in a pair of carefully faded jeans and a polo shirt, open at the neck to show his pale throat. He looked nervous and uncomfortable.

'Fancy a drink?'

'Well, I – ' Edmond bit his lip. 'Look, Kate, I want to come right to the point. You know what happened this morning. I – ' He seemed to run out of words and stood screwing up his face in frustration, his right hand clenched into a fist and clutched in his left.

'What's the problem?' Kate was anxious. Edmond had not concealed his feelings for Sophie; was he suffering from jealousy? She said no more, not wanting to put words into his mouth.

'I know what you did,' Edmond said with an effort. 'It was for Sophie. I thought – I thought it was marvellous, to see her taking what she wanted. I mean, she got so much pleasure from it. But now, you see, I – ' He looked into Kate's eyes and shook his head. 'This is going to sound awful.'

'Try me,' Kate said gently.

'It's just that, well, I wondered if, whether, you would help me to ask, to try to persuade Sophie to do something for – for me.'

Kate could not prevent a gentle smile from spreading over her face. 'Edmond,' she said, 'I'll help you plan it; I'll help you decide what your objectives are. But you know what this course is about. You have to do it on your own.'

'It's not just the planning,' Edmond said. 'You see, I know what I want. I know what I want to ask her. It's that you're, well, you're involved in the outcome.'

Raising one eyebrow, Kate asked, 'In what way?'

Edmond swallowed. 'You remember on the first day,'

he said after a moment. 'You remember when we were talking about fantasies. I said about how I dreamed of making love to two girls at once. I would really, really like to have that come true, and I thought that perhaps you and Sophie – '

Kate's smile broadened. 'Of course I would be prepared to take part,' she said, quite simply. 'If you can talk Sophie into it, Edmond, I'd be happy to. What do you want me to do? Do you want to do any planning?'

'No.' Edmond shook his head vigorously. 'No, honestly. I've thought about it. I know what I need to do. I'll be assertive to start with, I've planned it. *Sophie, I really like this course, but I don't like it that I've been part of everybody else's scene and not part of my own. I want you to help me realise my fantasy.* What do you think?'

'That's a fine start,' Kate said. 'My only reservation would be that if you try a full assert on Sophie she may react by withdrawing. She can be stubborn.'

'I know. I'm going to persuade her.' Edmond's face was bright and eager. Then suddenly it was as if a cloud covered the sun: his smile vanished and his eyes dropped. 'There's just one thing that bothers me, Kate. Would you tell me the truth? Honestly?'

'Of course.'

'Well ...' Edmond was looking at the floor, but suddenly his bright pale eyes flashed up. They were the colour of new leaves, a pale golden green. 'Kate, I just want to know whether you think Sophie will still be interested in me.' Kate could not prevent a look of surprise spreading over her face, and Edmond ran on hastily, 'You must see what I mean. I mean, today she had exactly what she wanted, she had all three of us doing what she wanted, and I can't help thinking that perhaps I might be a bit – I might disappoint her, just me. After ... after Christopher, I'm afraid I just won't come up to scratch.'

He looked like a worried child. Kate felt desperately sorry for him, but she could not give him the reassurance he so much wanted. 'Edmond,' she said gently, 'I can't tell you what Sophie thinks. You have to ask her yourself. There's no easy way to find out what she believes; you just have to talk to her.'

Edmond looked down again and shook his head hopelessly. 'I know I can't compete,' he said in tones of despair. 'I mean, just look at Christopher. He's – '

'Edmond,' Kate interrupted him, 'can I suggest you look at it another way?'

He lifted his eyes to hers, suspicious and hopeful. 'Go on,' he said hesitantly.

'Who did Sophie ask to go to the closed circuit TV room with her?' Kate asked simply.

'Me,' Edmond replied, warily.

'And when you were in the room, what did she say?'

There was a short silence. Edmond's face began to flush and after a moment he said, 'She said she really liked me.'

'Do you believe her?'

'Of course I believe her,' said Edmond angrily. 'She wouldn't lie to me.'

'So what are you afraid of? She chose you.'

Edmond looked into Kate's eyes, frowning and biting his lip. She could see his lack of confidence struggling with his eager desire to believe that Sophie liked him and might be prepared to listen to him. For a long time he said nothing. Then he opened his mouth, hesitated, closed it again, and spoke after another long pause. 'All right.' His voice was shaking slightly. 'All right, I will try it. I'll try.'

'Good.' Kate made her voice as warm and encouraging as she could. 'That's excellent.'

'I'll try it,' Edmond repeated, speaking more firmly now. 'Kate, will you be ready to come round to Sophie's room when I call you?'

'Of course.' Edmond was already half way out of the door. He had clearly achieved what he came for and did

174

not want any further help. 'All right, Edmond, I'll wait to hear from you.'

Edmond gave her a slightly uncertain grin and closed the door. Kate shut her eyes and leant against it, shaking her head, feeling pleased with herself. Edmond had come a long way if he was prepared not only to try some direct assertiveness with a woman he was clearly very attracted to, but also to follow it up with other techniques as required. If she had not spoken to David earlier she knew that now she would be feeling sidelined and ignored, because it was clear that the main component of Edmond's fantasy was Sophie; Kate was just the 'second woman'. But David had reassured her and her ego was not irrevocably dented. She hoped that Edmond would succeed.

There was time to kill. Kate wandered across to the easy chair by the window of her living room and sat down, staring out into the lovely golden summer evening and thinking about her resignation letter. She had determined before coming on this course that it would be the last thing she did before she left. The letter did not pull any punches: it was, frankly, rude. Would it really be sensible to send it? All the participants seemed to be learning a lot from the course and the chances of any of them complaining seemed to be insignificant. So why leave in high dudgeon?

But when she thought about it Kate couldn't face the prospect of returning to the office and taking yet another set of conflicting instructions from Bryony. Nor could she bear the thought of Alex's look of quiet sympathy when she was bawled out for yet another unintended mistake. Better to submit the resignation letter and never turn up again.

She did not know how long she had been sitting brooding when the phone rang. She crossed the room quickly and picked it up. 'Hello?'

'Kate? Kate, it's Edmond.'

'Edmond, hi!' Kate could hear from the tone of

Edmond's voice that he had been successful. 'Do you want me to come round?'

'Well, no.' Kate could faintly hear Sophie giggling in the background. 'The thing is, your room has a four poster, and it's the biggest bed, and we wondered whether we could both come round to your room, if you wouldn't mind.'

A laugh was bubbling up in Kate's throat. 'No, you can come round here. Of course you can.'

'We'll be right there.'

'OK. See you in a minute, then.' Kate put the phone down again, paused for a moment, then dialled the operator. 'Hi, could you give a message to two of the delegates on my course, please? They'll be at dinner: Nick and Christopher. Please tell them that the other delegates won't be joining them and we'll see them at nine tomorrow in the Health Suite.' The operator wrote the message down and acknowledged.

As Kate put the phone down she heard giggles and whispers outside the door. She smiled and went over to open it before Sophie and Edmond could knock. The door swung open and revealed the two of them standing there in each other's arms, kissing deeply. Sophie was wearing Kate's jersey dress and Kate could see that underneath it her breasts were bare: her little tight nipples stood up through the clinging fabric. As Kate opened the door Sophie and Edmond stopped kissing; they smiled at her and came in quickly. Kate opened her mouth to welcome them, but before she could speak Edmond closed the door and turned the key in the lock and Sophie came up to Kate and took hold of her arms and kissed her on the mouth.

Taken completely by surprise, for a moment Kate did nothing but react to the kiss. Sophie pressed her lips closely on to Kate's and her small, pointed tongue slipped into her mouth and explored gently, delicately, deeply. The kiss was possessive, direct, assertive, and Kate whimpered and turned up her face to Sophie's, feeling warm softness spreading again through limbs that had only recently shivered with the delight of orgasm.

After a moment Sophie pulled back and smiled at Kate. 'You see,' she said, 'Edmond told me he's always wanted to see two women making love together. So I thought we could start by making that dream come true for him.'

It didn't seem to be necessary to say anything. Kate smiled into Sophie's eyes and very gently placed her hands on the soft swell of Sophie's buttocks beneath the smooth knitted fabric of the dress. Sophie caught hold of Kate's face and kissed her again. Their bodies pressed together, close and tight, and Kate's arms wrapped around Sophie's slender back as their tongues touched and twined. Kate held back, allowing Sophie to kiss her, wondering what she was supposed to do. Presently it became clear that Sophie intended to provide guidance. She nudged Kate gently in the direction of the bedroom and they began to sway together towards it, locked in a tight embrace. Soon they were standing by the bed and Sophie took her hands from Kate's face and began to run them over her body, feeling her soft flesh through the silky thinness of her robe.

Sophie's hands were very small and delicate and their touch made Kate shiver. She was acutely aware of Edmond standing in the archway between the bedroom and the lounge area, his arm resting on the wall and his head resting on his arm, watching them with utter absorption. Even without looking at his face Kate could sense his excitement, a tense quivering like a leashed animal, wanting to watch but wanting also to take part. The presence of this spectator added an additional thrill to the pleasure which Kate began to feel as Sophie's deft fingers pushed the robe back from her shoulders, baring her generous breasts.

As the robe fell to the ground Edmond took a long breath and Kate realised that he had not seen her naked before. She wanted to show herself to him, she was filled with a wanton eagerness for display, and so she stepped back a little until the bedpost was behind her and reached up with both hands to take hold of the wooden post above her head as if she was tied there. The movement lifted her breasts as if she offered them to the silent watcher and she tipped back her head and thrust her breasts further forward, closing her eyes and waiting with tense anticipation for the moment when Sophie would touch her.

After a moment Kate shivered and gave a little cry. Sophie had put her hands on to her soft belly and run them up to feel the firmness and weight of her breasts, just flicking at the tightening nipples with her fingers in passing. She leant forward and whispered in Kate's ear, just loud enough for Edmond to overhear. 'Is this how Christopher tied you up?' she asked softly. 'Like this, with your hands above your head?'

Kate nodded soundlessly and she felt, rather than heard, Sophie's soft laughter close to her face. 'You look wonderful,' Sophie whispered. 'If I was Christopher I'd have left you like this. Look how your breasts stick out.' Her cool fingers traced the lines of Kate's ribs beneath the swell of her breasts, then moved softly onwards on to the flaring swell of her haunches, moving in tiny circles, pressing, touching. Kate gasped and rested her head against the bedpost, clutching tightly with both hands, hoping that soon she would feel Sophie's soft lips caressing her.

'Look, Edmond,' Sophie whispered, 'look how beautiful Kate looks. What shall I do to her?'

There was no reply. Kate opened her eyes and saw Edmond standing still in the archway, both arms wrapped across his stomach as if he were cold or afraid. His eyebrows were drawn down very tightly over his bright eyes and his lips were parted and she could see that he was trembling. His erection was visible beneath the stiff fabric of his jeans, but he made no move to touch it.

Sophie was standing now beside Kate, trailing her fingers over Kate's curves with an aerial lightness that made Kate quiver and ache to be caressed. Her nipples were swollen and hard, yearning for fingers to press them, for a tongue to soothe and moisten and torment them.

Still Edmond did not speak and after a moment Sophie smiled. 'If you won't tell me,' she said, 'I'll just have to use my imagination.' She let her hands touch Kate's flesh more firmly, but avoided her breasts and the warm mound between her thighs.

Kate whimpered and tossed her head from side to side. 'Sophie,' she moaned, 'please.'

For answer Sophie reached up and took hold of Kate's hands by the wrists and drew them down from the bedpost. She gently pushed Kate's wrists behind her and then lowered her head and set her lips to the pale golden skin of Kate's shoulder, to her neck, to her cheek, and then they were kissing, open mouth to open mouth, and Kate could feel Sophie's small breasts pressing through the fabric of her dress as they pushed together. It was blissful to kiss her: her lips were as soft as rose petals and her tongue was quick and eager, flickering like a snake's. Kate let herself relax into Sophie's embrace and gave a little sigh of pleasure as Sophie slipped one slender thigh between her legs, allowing her to rub her aching sex against the rough smoothness of her dress. Then at last Sophie let go of her wrists and with her little delicate fingers touched Kate's yearning breasts, circling her engorged nipples, encouraging the areola to swell and darken further with the rush of arousal. Kate opened her mouth wide to Sophie's passionate kisses and cried out as she felt those small sensitive fingers touching her nipples, drawing them out into tight peaks, chafing and flickering against them with quick deft strokes that left her shuddering with pleasure. Sophie held Kate's tender breasts in her palms and rubbed at the little coral-pink buds with her thumbs and all the time they kissed, deep searching kisses that made them both gasp.

Through a veil of arousal Kate realised that her hands were free. She placed them gently on Sophie's shoulders and then slowly, slowly ran them down to the soft mounds of her little firm breasts. Sophie's nipples were fiercely erect, thrusting through the thin jersey of her dress. Kate stimulated the little buds of hardness with her thumbnail and felt Sophie shudder with delight. They were entwined with each other, moaning as they pleasured each other, their tongues exploring and their hands fondling their breasts and pinching the stiff nipples.

Kate was beginning to shake with desire. Between her legs she was warm and wet, her juices flowing. She ached to be touched there, she longed to be stroked and drawn to the glittering plateau of orgasm. Briefly she wondered how long Edmond would stand silent, watching; then Sophie pinched her nipples so hard that she cried out with the delicious agony of it and her mind clouded with pleasure.

'Lie down,' Sophie whispered, pushing Kate gently backwards. Obediently Kate lay on the edge of the bed, the cover soft and slick beneath her. She opened her eyes and saw Sophie pulling off the clinging dress, revealing her beautiful slender body. Beyond her, in the doorway, Edmond was moistening his tongue with his lips and breathing quickly. Kate let her eyes rest on his flushed face, smiling at him. After a moment he looked at her and she shifted her hips on the bed, letting her thighs fall apart so that Edmond was looking straight up between her parted legs. She opened her mouth in a soft triangle of eager desire and ran her hands down her body, lifting her heavy breasts and offering them to him, showing him the soft swell of her stomach, the crinkled folds of flesh between her thighs, wet and glistening with desire. She stroked her fingers along the white skin of her loins and then laid one finger very gently on her protruding bud of pleasure, gasping as she felt the contact. Edmond set his jaw and jerked back his head as if she were tormenting him.

Sophie lowered the dress to the ground and saw this exchange. 'Kate,' she said fiercely, 'are you trying to encourage him? He's supposed to be watching us.'

'He looks lonely,' Kate replied, still smiling at Edmond.

'I think you are the one who needs attention,' Sophie said, and without another word she dropped to her knees on the floor between Kate's parted legs. Kate closed her eyes, shuddering with delight, as she felt Sophie's soft lips kissing the hollow of her knee, caressing the tender, sensitive flesh of the inside of her thigh, gradually ascending towards the warm, wet aching of her sex. Sophie's tongue was so small, so pointed, so clever. She kissed and licked all around Kate's loins, teasing, tormenting, avoiding the damp eagerness of her vulva, until Kate was crying out with frustration and misery and flinging her head from side to side; then she extended her warm tongue and pressed it gently but firmly to the quivering shaft of Kate's clitoris. Kate gave a long, '*Oh!*' of delight and began to stroke her breasts with her hands. Shimmering waves of pleasure flooded through her as Sophie began to stimulate her with her tongue, lapping and lapping, first softly, then harder, sometimes moving from Kate's engorged and trembling clitoris to push her agile tongue as deeply as she could into the moist lips that guarded the entry to her throbbing vagina. Kate cried out and her body began to heave rhythmically, lifting her hips towards Sophie's face. Sophie held her buttocks firmly in both hands, forcing her to lie still, and that strong, deft little tongue began to flicker again against the little stem of flesh that was the centre of Kate's body.

'Oh God,' Kate moaned, 'I'm coming, I'm coming, Sophie, please don't stop, please, please.' Her words tumbled over each other, muddled and desperate, and Sophie found her rhythm and with long firm strokes of her wonderful tongue lifted her slowly, inexorably to orgasm. Pleasure exploded in Kate's body and brain; she clutched at her breasts, feeling hot arrows of delight spreading from her nipples as if her breasts and her mound of love were joined with radiating wires of molten gold. Her body stiffened and arched and she hung above the covers crying out as Sophie pressed her warm open mouth over the quivering moistness of her sex.

After a moment Kate relaxed, panting, her body and limbs glistening with sweat. Sophie got to her feet and leant over her to kiss her on the mouth. Her rosebud lips were wet and salty and sweet with Kate's love-juice. Kate reached up to catch hold of Sophie's slender shoulders and pull her down, wanting to embrace her, to kiss her, to thank her for the wonderful pleasure she had given with her lips and tongue. 'Sophie,' she whispered, 'oh, Sophie.'

Sophie's slight body was as light as thistledown. As they kissed Kate rolled over until they were lying side by side and began to stroke her hand across Sophie's breasts, making her whimper with pleasure. 'Your turn?' she whispered.

'Oh yes,' Sophie murmured, writhing on the bedcovers, offering her shallow breasts and her long tight nipples to Kate's caresses. 'Oh, yes, Kate, please.'

'No.' Kate and Sophie both jumped. They had forgotten about Edmond in the spell of Kate's orgasm. Now suddenly he was beside them on the bed, dragging his shirt over his head, tugging desperately at the buttons on his jeans. 'No, I can't stand it any more,' he said fiercely as both women stared at him. 'Let me join in. I want to join in.' He became entangled in his jeans, cursed, and slid off the bed to pull them off. His body was slender and graceful, with long muscles, and his movements were fluid like a cat's. He flung away his underpants and his penis snapped out from his body, long and eager and erect, pointing towards the naked women on the bed as if it could smell their scent.

Sophie looked quickly at Kate and smiled. Then she frowned at Edmond and pouted slightly. 'But I wanted to be licked,' she said.

Edmond's narrow face was illuminated by a sudden brilliant grin. 'Your wish is my command, my lady,' he said, and he scrambled back on to the bed and reached out his hands for Sophie. She came to him willingly, her delicate body moving into his arms as if it belonged there, and he lowered his lips to hers and kissed her. As they kissed his hands explored her body, fondling her breasts, slipping between her slender thighs to touch and thrust, and Sophie began to writhe in his arms and cry out. Edmond's face was rapt, transported with desire and love.

For a moment Kate sat back on the covers. She wrapped her arms around herself and stifled a shiver, feeling left out, excluded, unwanted. She felt like a prop in a stage play: essential in its scene, but left on the table by the stage when the actors have finished with it. The rosy glow of her orgasm began to dissipate. In a moment she would be feeling really sorry for herself, so she thought back to her telephone conversation with David earlier in the evening. Because of her, because of what she had showed them, Sophie and Edmond had found each other and had gained the strength and confidence to offer each other pleasure in all sorts of ways. So what if that meant that she was sidelined? The more absorbed they were, the more intensely they concentrated on giving each other pleasure, the more successful she had been. It was a compliment, not an insult.

Kate took a deep, satisfied breath and opened her eyes. Before her Sophie and Edmond were entwined deep in each other's arms, breathing heavily as their tongues exchanged burning kisses. Edmond's fingers were buried deep between Sophie's thighs, probing and thrusting, and Sophie's little hand was wrapped around his stiff shaft, sliding up and down it with a strong, rhythmic stroke. As Kate watched Sophie let go of Edmond's cock and slipped her hand between his legs, fondling the hairy purse of his balls, and stopped kissing him for long enough to whisper in his ear.

With a smile of welcome Edmond turned to Kate. He held out his hand to her. 'Join us,' he said softly. 'Kate, please.'

Both of their faces were turned towards her, eager and loving. Kate felt a sudden surge of emotion, a mingled sense of pride and love and loss, the feeling of a teacher who knows that her pupils no longer need her. She felt her way towards them, her eyes blinded with tears, and they reached out for her with strong gentle hands and drew her into their embrace. But she did not forget the promise she had made to Sophie on the previous night. She reached out and took Sophie's hand and asked almost humbly, 'Sophie, I said I wouldn't without your permission.'

'Oh, Kate,' whispered Sophie with a tender smile, 'of course. I want to see him giving you pleasure as well as me.'

For some time they clung together, three bodies, three mouths, kissing and caressing. Then Sophie whispered, 'Edmond, please, I want your mouth so much,' and gradually the knot of naked limbs resolved itself into a pattern. Edmond lay down and drew Sophie towards him. She straddled his face with her slender legs and slowly, with a gasp of disbelieving ecstasy, lowered herself towards his waiting mouth. For a moment she hesitated, poised above him, the delicate lips of her sex just peeping through the scanty light-brown curls of fur that framed it.

Edmond looked up at the white orbs of her buttocks spread above his face and sighed with delight. 'Sophie,' he whispered, 'you're so beautiful.' His hands slid up her thighs and on to her narrow waist, enthralled by the gentle curves of her slender body. Then he opened his mouth and his hands tightened on her hips and he pulled her down to his waiting mouth, thrusting his tongue deep, deep within her.

As Sophie cried out Kate was overwhelmed with a desire to feel Edmond's body inside her. She moved quickly to sit over him and reached down to take hold of his penis where it lay on his belly, quivering with hardness. She rubbed her hand along the hot, smooth shaft and then began to stroke the velvety glans against the wet trembling lips of her sex, stimulating herself with it, making herself ready. Looking up, she saw that Sophie's dark eyes were open and she was watching with an expression of astonished excitement. Kate smiled at her and then gradually, gradually slipped herself down on to the length of Edmond's cock, feeling it slide up inside her, penetrating her so deeply that she gasped. Edmond moaned beneath Sophie's thighs and Sophie's body jerked against his restraining hands as he licked her harder and harder, stimulated beyond bearing by the feeling of his hot cock entering Kate's moist warm vagina.

'Kate,' Sophie moaned, 'kiss me.' She leant forward, her mouth open, reaching out for Kate. They kissed and Kate began to move, sliding up and down on the stiff shaft that impaled her. The sensation of having Edmond moving deep inside her and Sophie kissing her drove her out of her mind with pleasure. She began to pant and writhe, thrusting her breasts against Sophie's searching fingers, pinching Sophie's taut nipples hard, riding Edmond's cock with desperate urgency. She could feel that Sophie and Edmond were going to come soon: Sophie's body was stiffening and jerking as Edmond stimulated her clitoris with quick darting thrusts of his long, strong tongue, and Edmond was writhing and heaving beneath them, trying to thrust himself harder into Kate's wet willingness. For a moment Kate was afraid that they would come and it would all be over and she would be left behind, but then one of Sophie's little hands slipped down between her legs and a finger stroked delicately along the stiff peak of her clitoris and she gave a final agonised cry of delight as she pushed herself down deeply on to Edmond's jerking penis. A flood of pleasure filled her and she clutched wildly with her inner muscles at the shaft that filled her soft flesh, feeling it throb and explode within her as the three of them moaned and writhed and shuddered in the throes of their shared orgasm.

Presently they were all lying on the bed together, panting and smiling, a tangled heap of damp satisfied limbs. Kate lifted her head and propped it on her hand and said, 'Well, Edmond, how does reality compare with fantasy?'

'Wonderfully,' Edmond replied with a smile. He had his arm around Sophie, but he reached out to stroke Kate's face with his hand in a gesture of affection and gratitude. 'Wonderfully. You can't believe it.'

Sophie tilted back her head and closed her eyes, her body shifting languidly against Edmond's. 'I can't believe that I hardly had any fantasies at all before I came on this course. Now I keep thinking of new ones!'

'New ones?' asked Edmond with interest. 'Really?' He glanced across at Kate and smiled. 'Anything we can help with?'

Sophie opened her eyes, her pink cheeks flushing further with a charming mixture of excitement and embarrassment. 'Well, yes. Probably. Yes, of course.'

'Tell us about them,' Kate begged. She reached out and touched the warm skin of Sophie's throat and then ran her hand very gently down to her breast. 'Tell us about them, Sophie.'

With a little murmur of pleasure Sophie arched her back, thrusting her breasts towards Kate's hands. 'Oh,' she said, 'well, I would, but one of them involves Edmond, and I think he might be a little tired right now.'

'Give me a moment,' said Edmond, 'and I'll be at your service again.'

'I'd like that,' Sophie said earnestly, turning to look into Edmond's eyes with transparent sincerity. 'You see, Edmond, I haven't felt you inside me yet, and I want to so much.'

Edmond's face showed how much he was moved. Impulsively he leant forward and caught hold of Sophie's face and kissed her, pulling her close to him. 'Sophie,' he whispered when he drew back, 'I love you. I love you. You know I'll do anything for you. I will give you pleasure, I promise you. Anything you want.'

'Tell us about one of the others until then,' Kate suggested. She had to fight to reassure herself that she did not need to feel left out, that she understood why Edmond and Sophie were so absorbed in each other. If they felt safe with her, if they were prepared to involve her in their mutual discovery, it showed how much they trusted her. She was not excluded, not ignored. Thank God for David, she told herself.

'All right.' Sophie shivered a little and Edmond wrapped his arms protectively about her, holding her tightly. 'All right, Kate. It's something I'd like you to do for me – something I *want* you to do for me. You remember last night, when I – when I fucked you with that, that thing?'

Edmond looked astonished, either at Sophie's language or at the idea of what she and Kate might have done the previous night. Kate smiled and wriggled with delicious reminiscence. The thick smooth shaft of the wooden phallus had filled her up, sliding deliciously deep within her, and Sophie had just touched her with her tongue, sending her crashing over the edge into delirious orgasm. 'I remember,' she said.

'And one of those pictures,' said Sophie. 'There was a woman with a – a dildo strapped to her. That's what I want you to do to me, Kate, if you've brought one.'

'Brought one?' Edmond repeated with overtones of disbelief.

'Oh,' Sophie said breathlessly, 'you don't know about Kate's treasure box. Look, Edmond, look.' She rolled off the bed and hurried over to the little box by the window, knelt down by it and pulled it open. 'Look,' she said. 'There's books and toys and wonderful clothes, look. I want to wear this tomorrow.' She held up the corset. 'Don't you think it would make Nick look twice?'

'More than twice, I should think,' said Edmond. 'What else is in there?'

'You look at that, if you want,' said Sophie. She had found what she was looking for: a long, thick dildo made of some smooth stippled black plastic, with a framework of leather straps that would allow it to be fastened to a woman's loins. 'Look, Kate,' she whispered, in a voice that was trembling with excitement. 'Here it is. Please, will you – will you fuck me with it?'

'Yes.' Kate reached out and took the dildo from Sophie's shaking hands. She smiled as she did so. Sophie didn't know quite how inventive people could be where sexual pleasure was concerned. The implement was cunningly designed. Two of the straps met between the wearer's legs and where they joined a little pad had been sewn. It looked innocuous enough on the outside, but on the inside it was fringed with little studs which would shift from side to side as the wearer thrust with the dildo. The pad was adjustable and it could be placed to fit most carefully over the wearer's clitoris, caressing it, stimulating the sensitive flesh to an almost unbearable degree. As Kate began to strap the dildo to her thighs she felt the studs begin to rub against her, feeling like a myriad little questing fingers, pressing down on the swollen flesh of her sex lips, parting them, exploring them.

'My God,' Edmond breathed. He watched with wide eyes as Kate finished fastening the last buckle and knelt on the bed with the artificial phallus jutting proudly forward from the dark cushion of her pubic hair. 'My God, I don't believe this. Sophie, you can't want – '

His voice was thick with shock and overtones almost of horror. Kate hesitated, looking up at Edmond uncertainly. 'Edmond,' Sophie broke in, reaching out to catch hold of Edmond's narrow face between the palms of her hands. 'Edmond, listen to me.' She shook his face gently, looking straight at him. 'Listen. When else will we get a chance to try everything we dream of? When will it happen again?'

There was a silence, and Edmond gazed deep into Sophie's big dark eyes. After a moment he said very steadily, 'Sophie, tell me that you love me.'

'Oh, Edmond.' Sophie smiled at him with her face full of such sweet affection that Kate felt her own heart ache. 'You know I love you.'

'More than the others,' Edmond persisted. 'More than Kate. More than Nick or Christopher. More than anyone.' He had forgotten his inhibitions, the tyranny of his politeness; he did not even stop to think that what he said might be hurtful to Kate, to their helpless spectator. He was determined to hear what he needed to hear. Kate writhed under a conflict of emotions: pleasure that Edmond had discovered his own freedom, and a wretched, shameful spasm of miserable jealousy that he had forced Sophie to choose and to make her choice public.

'More than anyone.' Sophie echoed Edmond's words in a voice of soft rapture. She was looking into his face, her lips parted. His eyes softened in delight as he registered what she had said. He looked almost as if he could not believe his good fortune, but he did not question it. Sophie leant forward and kissed him, then let go of his face. 'But Edmond,' she said, 'whatever happens afterwards, now – today and tomorrow – I want to make the most of this. I want you to make the most of it, too.' She kissed him again, gently, then turned back to Kate. 'Kate,' she said, 'please, fuck me. Please.'

Kate wanted to make Edmond suffer now. He had forced Sophie to say how much she loved him; he had made her say that she loved him more than Kate. She wanted to make him squirm. It was not enough just to lie on Sophie and take her missionary-style: she wanted Edmond to see just how much pleasure one woman could give another – and have pleasure in doing it, too. 'Yes,' she said to Sophie. She leant forward and caught hold of Sophie's slender arms, pulling her close, finding her parted lips and slipping her tongue within them. 'I will fuck you, Sophie. Come here; kneel down. On all fours.'

Sophie gave her one wide-eyed, brilliant glance, then obediently came towards her and knelt on the bedcover on hands and knees, her little round breasts hanging downwards, darkly tipped with her erect nipples. Kate took a double handful of Sophie's soft curling brown hair and pulled back her head with it. 'Lick it,' she said, thrusting the broad shelving head of the dildo towards Sophie's trembling lips. 'Lick it as if I was a real man. Suck it, Sophie, before I fuck you.'

With a little whimper Sophie opened her mouth and took in the fat length of solid black substance. Kate held on to her handful of hair and thrust, imagining how it would feel to be a man, a master, forcing his throbbing cock between the lips of his newest female slave. Perhaps the little pale creature before him was a virgin and he was preparing to deflower her, taking the maidenhead of her mouth before he turned his attentions to the moist attractions of her tight, tender sex. The brief flare of fantasy filled Kate with shuddering arousal. The movement of Sophie's lips on the dildo caused it to stir, rubbing the little fingered pad against the burning bud of Kate's clitoris. She moaned and reached down past Sophie's working mouth, feeling under her slender shoulders to the dangling mounds of her little breasts. Sophie's nipples were tumescent with need. Kate caught the hard teats between her fingers and thumbs and

190

began to stroke them, lengthening them further, closing her eyes and imagining herself the master preparing to initiate his newest purchase into the ways of the flesh. Oh God, yes; and the helpless creature kneeling before her was not alone. There in the corner of the room stood the girl's lover, powerless and imprisoned, watching as his beloved was ravished by her owner, her tormentor. The more pleasure the master could make his slave feel, the worse it would be for that silent watcher.

'Now,' Kate whispered, thrusting the thick black shaft firmly between Sophie's lips and tweaking hard at the tight buds of her nipples, 'now, Sophie, with your right hand, reach between your legs. Stroke yourself there. I want to hear you moan.'

Sophie wanted to complain; she opened her mouth to speak and a smothered moan emerged past the gag of dildo. 'Don't talk,' Kate said sharply. 'Do it. Stroke yourself. Before I put this inside you I want you to be moaning with pleasure.'

After a moment's hesitation Sophie lifted her hand from the bed and placed it between her legs. Her shoulder moved very slightly as she began to touch herself. Kate opened her eyes, putting aside the gathering pleasure that the movement of the little pad was giving her, and looked at Edmond. Sophie had her buttocks towards him; because she was on all fours her sex was presented to his gaze, moist and open and inviting. His softened cock was already begin to rear again into life, darkening and stiffening with the rush of arousal, and his face showed his thoughts: *But this was supposed to be* my *fantasy!* As Kate watched him Sophie gave a little cry that bubbled past the moving shaft of the dildo and the slender buttocks quivered, and as if in answer Edmond's face twisted with torment. 'Harder,' Kate ordered. 'Touch yourself again,' and Sophie obeyed her and moaned as she did so.

'Good.' Kate withdrew the shining length of the dildo from Sophie's mouth. 'Turn a little towards me, Sophie.'

She arranged Sophie so that she was sideways on to Edmond, so that he would be able to see every inch of the dildo as it pushed its way inside her. For a moment she was seized with a desire to pull Sophie's hands behind her back and tie them there, to make her kneel with her face on the sheets while she received her master's thick shaft within her, but she decided against it. Sophie had come a long way, but perhaps bondage and submission might be too frightening, too threatening for her yet. She moved around and knelt behind Sophie and began to rub the smooth head of the dildo against her sex, parting the moist wanton lips, gently stimulating the protruding, glistening pearl of pleasure. Sophie moaned and threw back her head. Kate positioned the thick shaft exactly, carefully, feeling the muscles of her belly and loins tensing with excitement as she realised that she was exactly poised, that one strong thrust would fill up Sophie entirely, pierce her to the neck of her womb. Was this what it felt like to be a man? This sense of power, of possession? She closed her eyes and imagined herself again the master, kneeling behind his slave; he had stroked her, pleasured her into submission. All she wanted now was to feel him inside her, to know that she was his, to ride her way to ecstatic climax on the wings of his throbbing penis. She nudged a little closer to Sophie, feeling the soft lips making way for her; the ridged surface of the pad rubbed hard against her quivering clitoris and made her gasp. She hesitated; and then she heard Sophie's voice. 'Oh please, please. Please do it. Please – ' and with a moan of total fulfilment she thrust with her hips and felt the whole of the thick length of the dildo sink deep into Sophie's opening flesh, sliding all the way up between the silken walls of her love channel, possessing her. Sophie gave a trembling, agonised cry; and Kate began to fuck her.

She forgot about everything except the urgent desire to take Sophie. She was a man, taking a woman as a man does, thrusting deep inside her and groaning with the pleasure of it. And wonderful, wonderful control: she was Casanova, she was Don Giovanni, she was the perfect lover, the man who can go on for ever, who will thrust and thrust until his lover lies at his feet in a shuddering heap of fulfilment. The delicious friction of the pad against her flesh drove her to a plateau of pleasure until she felt that every time she pushed the thick black shaft into Sophie's wet sex she was coming, coming time after time. And Edmond was watching, watching her doing it, watching as Sophie moaned and cried and pushed her hips eagerly back to meet her avid thrusts. Kate glanced towards him, half hoping to see him writhing with misery to see Sophie so enjoying what she was doing to her. What she saw almost put her off her stroke, for Edmond had stopped huddling beside the post of the bed. He was crawling forward towards Sophie, his eyes fastened on her face, riveted, fascinated. His engorged cock, stiff with eagerness, jerked up against his naked belly as he moved.

'Sophie,' he whispered, 'Sophie, Sophie. Please come. I want to watch you come. Sophie, please.'

Kate was panting with the effort of shafting Sophie, of thrusting as hard and as deep as she could. Sophie was screaming now with pleasure, but not with orgasm: the ultimate rapture of climax had not yet seized her. Holding firmly to the smooth globes of Sophie's buttocks with one hand, with the other Kate reached round in front of her slender hips and pushed her fingers through the fine curling down of Sophie's mount of Venus. Her probing fingers found the little nut of Sophie's clitoris and stroked it, caressing it in rhythm with her strong determined thrusts. Sophie gave a wordless cry, a sound that was almost a grunt, and began to heave her hips up towards Kate, panting and shuddering, her animal cries mounting and mounting as Kate rode her. Edmond knelt before her, staring into her face, rapt, transported. And at last, at last, Sophie gave a great shout of pleasure and writhed helplessly on the thick shaft that filled her, twisting with the convulsions of orgasm until Edmond leant forward and caught hold of her slender shoulders and supported her, holding her up until the racking shudders had subsided.

After a moment of frozen stillness Kate withdrew the dildo from Sophie's streaming flesh and fell back on the covers, utterly exhausted, sweat trickling between her breasts and her shoulder blades. She began to unstrap the dildo with trembling fingers, feeling as though she were sated with pleasure, as though further stimulation would leave her helpless and unable to respond. The leather straps fell from her hands and she lay back against the pillows, opening her eyes in a sort of lazy curiosity to see what Edmond and Sophie were doing.

Sophie was half collapsed, still kneeling, her buttocks thrust obscenely up in the air as if inviting further abuse, her head cradled in Edmond's lap, his erect cock right beside her face. He was stroking her hair. When he spoke his voice was teasing. 'Here we are, then, Sophie. I'm rested and ready for you; but now it looks like you're too tired for me.'

'Try me,' Sophie said thickly, rolling on to her side and looking up at Edmond with eyes that were heavy and languid with the echoes of pleasure. 'Try me.'

For a moment Edmond hesitated. 'You said there was something else you thought of,' he said anxiously. 'If you want – '

'I'll save it till the next time,' Sophie whispered, smiling now. 'I'll keep it in reserve. You are ready, then, my lord; what shall I do?'

'Oh God,' Edmond muttered in a voice of muffled need. He put one hand gently in Sophie's soft hair and steered his aching prick towards her lips and she opened her mouth and took him in, her little quick tongue exploring the hard ridge at the edge of his glans and the tiny sensitive triangle of skin beneath it, making him moan and clench his buttocks with desperate pleasure. Kate pillowed her head on her arm and watched. She was too tired to respond with further dramatic arousal, but she felt a faint echo of Edmond's delight stirring in her as Sophie slipped her lips slowly up and down the straining length of his cock. How sweet it was to watch someone else being nurtured, pleasured, caressed; no wonder Edmond had not been able to resist the glory of Sophie's lovely face as it flushed into violent orgasm.

Edmond's knuckles whitened in Sophie's hair as she worked on him with her mouth. Then suddenly he pulled back, saying urgently. 'No. I want you, Sophie, I want you.' He caught hold of her and pulled her towards him. She did not resist and he laid her on her back, parted her slender thighs and lay between them.

'God help me,' Sophie whimpered as she felt him beginning to enter her. 'More. Oh, more. Oh Christ, help me.' She did not lift her head or raise her thighs or wrap her ankles around Edmond's waist, only lay beneath him prone and helpless, utterly defeated and conquered, her arms spread wide, crying out each time his body met hers with a soft urgent sound. Her only movement was the writhing of her head and neck as Edmond took her, but her whole body was shaking as if she was racked by repeated orgasm, one long continuous climax. Edmond lowered his head and began to lick her breasts as he thrust, his long agile tongue flickering over her erect nipples, and Sophie's cries became sharper and more piercing. 'Edmond,' she gasped as her body shuddered beneath the blows of his penetration. 'Edmond, Edmond, Edmond. Oh, God.' And then Edmond was clutching at her with both hands and driving himself as deep within her as he could and groaning with pleasure and his body quivered as he buried himself deep, deep inside her and spent himself there, overcome by the intensity of his own pleasure.

Kate realised with a sort of sleepy surprise that it was almost dark in the room: the long summer evening was drawing gently to its close. She crawled to where Edmond and Sophie lay in each other's arms and pressed close to them. Edmond lifted his head and found her lips and kissed her and Sophie caressed her with one hand, drawing her closer into their warm soft embrace. As they lay together, limbs damply enmeshed, Edmond murmured softly, 'Sophie, sweetheart, you're right, you know. About tomorrow, I mean. Do whatever you want; I'm going to.'

And Sophie smiled at him and replied, 'I'm glad you feel that way, Edmond. But I would have done what I wanted anyway, you know.'

'Assertive little madam,' Edmond whispered, and he set his lips to Sophie's slender neck.

Sophie turned to Kate and kissed her. 'Did you hear what he called me?' she murmured. 'Did you hear? I did well, didn't I, Kate?'

Without a word Kate nodded. Their bodies pressed closer and their breathing became slow and regular. They felt themselves surrounded by love and the glorious satisfaction of desire, falling together towards the black velvet cushion of sleep. Just before Kate's thoughts faded into dreams she remembered what David had said to her, practically accusing her of being a prima donna. Well, she thought with some pride, perhaps he's right: but he would be pleased if he saw what I have done this evening.

Chapter Ten

*K*ate had showered and dressed in a singlet and shorts before Edmond and Sophie woke. She came out of the bathroom to see them stirring sleepily in the bed, which had been amply big enough for all three of them. Two pairs of puzzled eyes were looking up at the canopy as if uncertain of where they were.

'Feeling all right?' Kate asked cheerfully.

Edmond, like many men, did not seem to be at his best in the morning: he groaned and rolled over and buried his face in the pillow. Sophie sat up beside him, looking like a picture with her great dark eyes half covered by the tousled mass of her hair, and stretched and yawned like a kitten. 'I'm so sleepy,' she murmured.

'It's half-past eight,' Kate said. 'We're meeting in the health suite at nine. I called room service and ordered coffee and croissants, they should be here any minute. I'm just going to look for Nick and Christopher and make sure they managed all right last night without me. Edmond, when you come down, will you bring the treasure box, please?'

Edmond grunted in assent and Kate smiled and went to the door. As she put her hand to it Sophie said from the bed, 'Kate?'

'Mm?'

'Kate, do you promise that today you'll ask us to do something that you want? Will you?'

Kate couldn't help but smile. She had intended to use this course purely to achieve her own sexual objectives, and since that first hasty sweaty encounter with Nick in the Ladies she seemed to have been following other people's agendas entirely. So much so that now one of the participants saw fit to remind her to please herself! 'I'll try,' was all she said.

As she closed the door the lift doors opened, revealing the young waiter with the room service tray. He saw Kate and frowned. 'Oh, madam, I've got your breakfast,' he said. 'I'm sorry, am I late? Are you going down already?'

'I'm going,' Kate said with a smile, 'but actually I swapped rooms with a couple of the participants last night. They fancied my four-poster bed. The breakfast is for them.'

She could see the young man's mouth opening to ask, So what were you doing in there? But he said nothing, only raised his eyebrows and went to the door and knocked. Kate got into the lift and pressed the button for the restaurant, still smiling.

One of the staff met her at the door. 'Miss, the two gentlemen asked me to tell you that they had breakfast sent to the health suite. They'll see you there.'

'Thank you,' said Kate.

The health suite was in a separate building. There was a covered walkway that led to it, but it was another beautiful morning and Kate walked instead across one of the lawns, smelling the dew and the freshness of the flowers and listening to a blackbird singing in a nearby bush. Suddenly she felt sad. This was the last day: at the end of today they would all go their separate ways, back to the jobs they did in various offices and various departments of the firm, their sudden, shocking intimacy a thing of the past. Except for Edmond and Sophie, perhaps: that had the look of a show that would run and run. And still Kate didn't know what she would be going back to. Back to her office, her desk, and Alex outside the door tempting her with his needlessly unattainable beauty? Or back to resignation and something new?

She opened the door of the health suite and went in, smelling the slightly acrid tang of chlorine from the swimming pool and the slightly deodorised scent of the jacuzzi. The suite was basically one huge room, with the swimming pool along one edge and the jacuzzi leading off it. It was a very large jacuzzi, big enough for ten or twelve people. Beside the pool was a rest area with comfortable padded loungers on wheels and beyond that was the gym. There was a multigym and a chin-up bar and a vaulting horse and a number of other bits of equipment, carefully positioned beside a range of floor-to-ceiling mirrors. The sauna and steam rooms were at the side of the gym, closed off with heatproof doors. The whole area was peppered with big potted palms and other greenery, giving it a relaxed, sensual, jungly feel.

For a moment Kate could see neither Nick nor Christopher and she felt puzzled. Then she heard the splash of water and saw a lean dark figure ploughing up and down the swimming pool. She walked a little closer. It was Nick, swimming crawl with absolute concentration, lifting his head to breathe only on every fourth stroke. He swam very well and it was wonderful to watch his beautiful body cleaving through the water, the droplets glistening on his muscled skin, his shoulders turning and turning with the regularity of a machine, his tight buttocks outlined by a small pair of black swimming trunks.

'He looks good, doesn't he,' said Christopher's dark voice. Kate jumped and turned to see Christopher himself sitting on one of the loungers with a glass of orange juice in his hand. He was wearing a white hotel dressing gown, his legs and feet bare beneath it. He had been hidden from Kate's eyes behind one of the potted palms.

'Yes, he does,' Kate agreed. She went over to sit down next to Christopher. The jug of orange juice and a tray of glasses was on the floor at his feet and she poured herself a glass and drank. The juice was sharp and refreshing in her mouth. 'How are you?' she said. 'I'm sorry about last night, but – '

'But personal tuition required for Sophie and Edmond,' Christopher finished with a smile. 'I understand. Did you have a good time?'

'Yes, but – ' No, it was not right to say the *but*. 'Yes, thank you,' Kate said, knowing that her voice sounded prim.

'Oh, professional secrets,' grinned Christopher. He looked well: his normally sombre face was smiling and relaxed. 'Well, you don't have to worry about me. I had a splendid time. I set myself a little task, a little challenge, if you like.'

'And you achieved it.'

'I did indeed.'

'Would you care to share it with me?' Kate asked, lifting one eyebrow.

'By all means,' said Christopher, with exaggerated courtesy. 'Delighted. Actually, Kate, it'll make you laugh. It was a bet.' Kate lifted both brows now, distinctly curious. 'Nick and I were having a drink before dinner. You know how cautious of me he's been since I made love to Edmond? Well, he still was last night. And after a while it began to get on my nerves rather, so to clear the air I asked him what was bothering him. I won't give you the full story, but basically I think he wanted to show that women don't like bisexual men. He betted me I wouldn't be able to, er, *score*, as he put it, with a woman that evening. This implication being that he could, of course.'

Kate found herself beginning to laugh. 'Oh, dear me,' she said. 'He lets his preconceptions run away with him rather, doesn't he?'

'He certainly does.'

'But I'm almost surprised that you agreed to a bet with him.'

'Surprised?' Christopher looked slightly suspicious. 'Surprised, why? You almost sound disapproving.'

'It just seems to be a rather, I don't know, a rather blokey thing to do: taking a bet from someone like Nick. I thought you would scorn that sort of behaviour, frankly.'

Christopher narrowed his eyes, then smiled a little. 'Come on,' he said, 'it was a simple question of risk assessment. I was confident I could win, and I managed to obtain rather attractive terms.'

'What terms?'

'A case of champagne for him if he won, and a forfeit from him if I won: no holds barred. He'd had a couple of drinks before we got on to it, or I'd never have persuaded him to accept a forfeit, but by the time we got to the betting he was so convinced he couldn't lose I didn't have a problem. He'd have agreed to a bet of prolonged anal rape by half a dozen total strangers by that stage, he was so certain he was right.'

'Oh, I see. So you had a different sort of proof in mind.' Christopher continued to smile, his secret opaque sphinx-like smile. 'Good grief.' Kate drew up her knees on to the lounger and hugged herself with burgeoning delight. 'Tell me everything, Christopher. Don't miss out a single gory detail.'

'I suppose I was in luck,' said Christopher with a little gentle smile. He let his eyes rest on Nick as he charged up and down the pool, oblivious of everything around him. 'It so happened that there was a girl in the bar who seemed to be on her own, so I wandered over and engaged her in conversation, as they say. It proved she'd been stood up by her boyfriend and she was feeling sorry for herself. So I bought her a drink and we talked and all the time I could sense Nick sitting there in the booth with his drink and fuming as he watched me chatting away.'

'What was she like?'

'She was a nice girl,' said Christopher coolly. 'I suppose I could have felt a bit of a heel, just picking her up like that for a bet. She wasn't my type really, but there wasn't anything wrong with her. Her name was Karen. She said she worked in town near here in a shop, a boutique she called it. She was a little overdressed and she had too much make-up on, but she was very pretty underneath. A figure more like yours than Sophie's: curvy. She laughed nicely, though, she had lovely lips and teeth. And she was easy to talk to.'

'She fancied you, poor girl,' Kate said, with some sympathy for the hapless Karen.

Christopher replied with a small smile, 'Well, I suppose she did, but I didn't give her any wrong ideas. I told her I was married and just away on business for a couple of nights. She knew it was a one-night stand.'

'I can't begin to imagine how Nick must have felt,' Kate said, shaking her head. 'So what happened?'

'Oh, it was straightforward,' Christopher said dismissively. 'We talked and drank for about an hour – '

'What about?' asked Kate, who was eaten up with curiosity.

'About nothing much to start with – what we did, where we lived, that sort of thing. I didn't tell her much about myself, but that didn't surprise her because she thought I was married. Then we got on to films, sex scenes in films, you know the sort of thing. I was trying to convince her that the scene in *The Piano* where Harvey Keitel puts his finger over the hole in Holly Hunter's stocking was more sexy than the whole of *Basic Instinct* and *9½ Weeks* put together.'

Kate nodded. 'Good topic.'

'And then I suggested we should go for a walk in the grounds. I wanted Nick to be able to see what happened, you see, otherwise I was sure he'd try to renege on the bet, and I couldn't figure out straight away how I could get him and Karen into my room at the same time. Well, she jumped at it: it was a lovely evening, after all. So we wandered off into the gardens and I had a hell of a job stopping myself from laughing, with Nick trundling along behind us slipping from shadow to shadow like the Man from UNCLE. It's amazing how obvious it is that you're being followed when you know where to look.'

'I shouldn't think Nick finds it easy to be the soul of discretion, either. Where did you go?'

'Almost as far from the hotel as you can get there's a little patch of grass they've allowed to grow up as a wildflower meadow. It's very pretty and the grass is long. When we got there the sun had set, I suppose it was nearly ten o'clock, but it was still half-light – you know, that lovely gold-pink light when it's really much darker than you think. And I said something totally inane about how she'd turned a dull evening into a really interesting one. Then I kissed her and she kissed me back and from then on it was plain sailing. I knew Nick was watching, I could feel it.'

'What did you do to her?' Kate asked, breathless.

'Nothing special,' Christopher said, with a sudden wicked grin. 'Nothing exciting or exotic, Kate, like the things I tried with you. She didn't want me to lie her on the grass, she was afraid it would spoil her dress, so I said that like an English gentleman I would interpose my body between her and the ground.'

'She rode you?' Kate licked her lips, enviously imagining that fortunate girl impaling herself on the magnificent pillar of Christopher's penis.

'Almost. She was very keen: had a condom out of her little purse in no time at all. And I knelt down and she straddled me and I lowered her on to me. I lifted her up and down on my cock. I would have thought they heard her in the hotel dining room, she sounded like a bitch in heat and she clutched me so hard inside I thought she was going to milk me like a cow. Quite pleasant, really.'

'You smug bastard,' Kate smiled, shaking her head in disbelief.

'That's what Nick said,' Christopher agreed sagely. 'He was furious. I put Karen into a taxi and paid for it to take her home and I thought the abuse would never stop. He tried half a dozen increasingly ingenious ways to say that the bet was off and when they all failed he leapt into his car and vanished into the night. I'm sure he thought I was going to demand to take him to bed straight away: anything to avoid that.' Christopher's smile had vanished: he looked suddenly dangerous as his eyes moved again to the swimming pool.

'What forfeit are you going to ask?'

'I don't know,' said Christopher musingly, his deep voice dark and smoky. 'I haven't decided.' Suddenly he looked directly at Kate, a challenging, fierce look with his shadowed eyes. 'I feel inclined to let myself go today,' he said. 'Nick and Sophie and Edmond have seen nothing from me yet, Kate, you know. I really mean to let myself go.'

'With me?' Kate asked, unable to prevent her voice from quivering with hope.

Unexpectedly, Christopher leant forward and touched his lips to hers. 'I let myself go with you before,' he said. 'I mean with the others. You understand me already.'

'I would like it,' Kate said hesitantly, 'if you would let yourself go with me again, some time.' As she spoke she realised that she really meant it. Christopher was fascinating, and the more she talked to him the more she found his mind attractive as well as his splendid body. She wanted to see him again.

Christopher looked at her evenly from beneath his dark brows. 'Well, if – '

Beside them Nick suddenly launched himself from the pool, the water running in delicious trickles down his lean tanned body. 'You're talking about me,' he accused Kate. He was panting and he looked absolutely furious.

'You're right,' Kate said unashamedly. 'You're absolutely right, we were. I'm almost surprised to see you this morning, Nick.' She glanced at Christopher and saw that he still wore his contained, dangerous, shadowed face, and that he was looking at Nick like a starving man at a meal. Her heart sank. It did not seem that Christopher was likely to be interested in her that day. So much for me getting what I want, she thought. But there was no point in getting depressed about it. She was fairly certain that Nick found her attractive and would be eager to engage her in a little hand to hand combat; so she took her eyes from Christopher and let them rest on Nick, admiring the way the trickles of water outlined the ridges of muscle on his chest and ribs.

'Contrary to what some people may suggest,' Nick said viciously, 'I don't renege on agreements. And I don't run away from things, ever.' He walked over to a pile of thick fluffy towels by the jacuzzi, picked one up and began to towel his body and hair.

'Christopher told me you went off for a drive last night,' Kate went on cheerfully. 'Where did you go? Anywhere interesting?'

'I went to a nightclub in the town,' Nick said. 'Where you might say I crashed and burned.'

'Really?' Kate was feasting her eyes on Nick's body. He really was exceptionally beautiful. Wet and angry, he could have modelled for a pre-Raphaelite *Hylas at the Pool*. Looking at men like Nick made Kate wish that she could paint. 'That's a shame,' she said, unable to resist turning the knife a little, 'after Christopher had shown you how it should be done.'

'I'm sure I was just trying too hard,' Nick said evenly. He was avoiding looking in Christopher's direction: since he emerged from the pool their eyes had not met once. But he would have to be blind and stupid not to feel the burning intensity of the gaze which Christopher was resting on him. He rubbed the towel vigorously over his head and tossed it away, then walked over to the jug of orange juice, combing his fingers roughly through the fine tumbled layers of hair. The muscles moved smoothly on his shoulders and arms, making Kate's throat dry. 'What about you?' Nick demanded, still ignoring Christopher. 'Edmond and Sophie both together last night, was it? Who screwed whom? Have you left them so exhausted that they overslept?'

'*Au contraire*, Nick,' said Edmond's light, drawling voice from the door. Nick's head swung up to see Edmond standing there with the treasure box in his arms and Sophie beside him and he had the grace to blush.

'Here we are, Kate,' said Sophie, riding straight over the sudden tension between Nick and Edmond, 'bright and breezy and ready for practice. What a lovely place this is.' She looked happily around at the plants and the pool. Like Kate, she was dressed just in shorts and a T-shirt, and her curly hair was pulled back off her face in a little ponytail.

'What's in the box?' Nick demanded.

Edmond came over to the poolside, set the box down and flung the lid open. He looked up at Nick with an angry, challenging glare as the contents were revealed. Nick took a quick breath and stepped closer, looking down into the box with very bright eyes. After a moment he lifted his head and grinned at Kate. 'I bet you brought this.'

'That's a bet you'd win,' Kate said pointedly. Her eyes drifted to Nick's crotch, where beneath the tight damp fabric of his swimming trunks his penis was visibly beginning to stir and thicken.

'Well, guess what?' said Nick loudly, making everyone look at him. 'Guess what? I believe that all four of you got your rocks off last night. And as it happens, I didn't. What that means is, folks, that this morning I get the first chance to decide what happens.'

'Who says?' demanded Edmond.

'I say. Christ! For three days I've been told to listen and persuade and not to be aggressive and now I'm bloody well going to have a bit of what I want. Blame

206

Kate, folks, she brought all this kit, she gave me the idea.'

In a brief moment of silence Kate felt Sophie and Edmond looking at her. She met their eyes, knowing what she would see. Yes, they were reluctant for Nick to take control, but they were afraid of him. They wanted Kate to deal with him. Sophie even mouthed, 'Please!' at her. But this was good practice too: they needed to learn how to cope with aggression. Kate shrugged at them and shook her head, indicating that she was going to leave it up to them.

Into an atmosphere that was suddenly thick with tension Nick said, 'Sophie, when I asked you before you turned me down. This time I'm not going to ask.'

He shook back his damp hair and took a fast predatorial step towards Sophie. She drew back, gasping, and in a second Edmond had leapt over to Nick and caught hold of his arm. 'Forget it, Nick,' he said fiercely.

'What are you, her keeper?' Nick demanded, throwing off Edmond's hand. 'She can talk for herself, can't she? What are you going to do, fight me for her? Challenge me to a duel?'

An angry reply sprang to Edmond's lips, but before he could speak Christopher said in his smoky voice, 'Just a moment, Nick.'

Everybody looked at Christopher. He had moved on silent, naked feet to stand beside the treasure box, and now he was smiling. Nick closed his mouth and swallowed and goosepimples came out on his back and shoulders.

'I think it's time I claimed my forfeit,' Christopher said.

Both of Nick's hands clenched into tight fists, the knuckles white with pressure. Edmond and Sophie looked at Kate and at each other, not understanding what was happening. Nick tried to moisten his lips with a suddenly dry tongue. He said nothing, but his head moved slowly from side to side in automatic denial.

'Do you want to know what the forfeit is?' Christopher's deep voice was almost caressing. 'I've only just made up my mind. I didn't realise we would have the benefit of Kate's little box of tricks here. Nick, I'm going to tie you to the frame of the chin-up bar. You are going to stand there and let Edmond and me do what we like to you.'

The breath sighed out of Nick as if someone had hit him in the gut. He took a couple of involuntary steps backwards, staring at Christopher with his blue eyes wide with horror. 'No way,' he whispered, holding up the palms of his hands in helpless self-defence. 'No way.'

'What the hell is going on?' Edmond asked the air.

'I won a bet against Nick last night,' Christopher explained simply. 'He owes me a forfeit. I thought you might help me exact it, Edmond.'

A slow grin of utter satisfaction spread across Edmond's face. He said firmly, 'I see. I should be delighted.'

Nick was standing by the edge of the pool now, unable to retreat further. He looked terribly vulnerable in his near-nakedness. For a moment it looked as though he was going to beg Christopher to change his mind, but then he seemed to register the cool determination in the big man's dark eyes. He turned instead to Kate, holding out both hands in supplication. 'Kate,' he said, his voice trembling, 'Kate, I don't want to do this. You said nobody had a right to make anyone do anything they didn't want to do. Kate, you *said*!'

'You were prepared to make us all do what you wanted a few minutes ago and the devil take the consequences,' Kate told him. 'You made the bet, Nick. You lost. Take your medicine like a good boy.'

A little sound made Nick whirl around. He saw Christopher hunting among the contents of the box and finally lifting out a couple of lengths of soft white rope. Panic began to spread over Nick's face. 'If you're trying to make me believe that I'll enjoy being like you,

Christopher, you're going the wrong way about it,' he said desperately.

This seemed to make Christopher think. He got to his feet and walked slowly towards Nick, moving more than ever like a big, prowling beast. His shadowed face showed his concentration. He stood before Nick with the ropes in his hand and after a little while said, 'Perhaps you're right.'

Enormous relief was written in every line of Nick's face and body. He jerked with shock when Christopher then continued coolly, 'Left hand, please.'

'But – ' Nick protested.

'I'll meet you half way,' Christopher offered. 'I don't have to: a forfeit is a forfeit. But I promise that unless you're – aroused, Edmond and I won't touch you.'

'What?' asked Nick, frowning in disbelief.

'You understand. If you get an erection, Edmond and I can do anything we like to you. As long as you stay soft, you're safe. Fair deal?'

Nick hesitated, then nodded vigorously. 'Yes,' he said, clearly confident that he could control himself. 'Yes, OK. What about a time limit before you let me off?'

'All right. Half an hour?'

Nick couldn't suppress a grin. 'No problem.' He flung up his head, suddenly restored to his normal cocky self. 'Where do you want me?' He stood of his own accord before the frame of the chin-up bar and held up his hands. Christopher followed him across the room and carefully lashed his wrists to the metal frame, not so tightly that the ropes would cut off circulation, but firmly enough that there was no chance of escape. Then he put his hands on to Nick's swimming trunks. Nick closed his eyes tightly as Christopher eased the tight black Lycra trunks off his buttocks and down his lean strong legs; then Christopher stepped back and Nick stood naked before them all, tied in the posture of the crucified Christ.

His pinioned body was breathtakingly beautiful. Kate

began to breathe quickly as she looked at his broad muscular shoulders, his narrow waist and hips, his long legs and the soft thick penis hanging invitingly between his thighs. She had not really looked at him before, when he had sat naked beneath her in the armchair and filled her with his eager thrusting cock; now she made up for it, scrutinising his body as though she would draw him, longing to run her fingers down the ridges of muscle that outlined the flat plane of his belly, aching to cradle the soft, full weight of his balls in her hand. Nick's head was lifted arrogantly; he stared at the ceiling above their heads, challenging them in silence.

For long moments nobody moved. Then, to Kate's surprise, Edmond spoke. 'Christopher,' he said, 'what happens now?'

Nick closed his eyes and bit his lip. His flaccid penis did not stir. Kate knew that if she was tied thus, exposed naked for the others to look at her, it would arouse her almost beyond belief. She could imagine the feel of the warm air on her bare breasts and the way her nipples would erect of themselves, begging to be licked and kissed. Perhaps Nick did not have her exhibitionist tastes; or perhaps he was too afraid of what might happen if he allowed himself to become hard.

'Well,' Christopher said slowly, 'I thought we would invite Kate and Sophie to help us out.'

Nick's eyes snapped open. 'What?' he said angrily, tugging at the ropes around his wrists. 'Kate and Sophie? That's not fair, Christopher, you bastard. You didn't say – '

'I didn't say anything about what would or would not happen,' Christopher told him. 'They might not agree. I can only ask them.' He turned and looked not at Kate, but at Sophie. 'Sophie,' he said gently, 'do you have any idea what might make Nick, er, excited?'

Since Nick approached her Sophie had been standing half hidden behind one of the big palms, looking over the top of it anxiously with her wide dark eyes. Now, though, she emerged. She was smiling an eager, feline smile and Kate remembered how she had confessed to being very aroused by watching Christopher and Edmond together. No doubt she was hoping for more of the same. 'Actually,' Sophie said in her soft voice, 'actually, I have.' Nick stared at her and she went quite close to him and looked into his face with an expression of delighted triumph. 'He's mentioned more than once,' she went on, looking into Nick's anguished blue eyes, 'that he'd like to see me and Kate *getting it on*, that's how he put it. So if Kate's willing, perhaps we should oblige him.'

'Christ!' Nick exclaimed, his eyes opening very wide as he tugged hopelessly against his bonds. Kate saw with a shudder of delight that even Sophie's words had had an effect on him: his dangling penis twitched as if it had suddenly developed a mind of its own. Nick shut his eyes tightly. 'I won't look,' he said through his teeth.

'Never mind,' Sophie said. She reached out and touched Nick's face with her little hand, just a fleeting touch, and he winced and breathed quickly and pulled away from her. 'Never mind, Nick. I'll give you a running commentary.' She turned and looked at Kate with her pale cheeks beginning to flush with excitement. 'Kate, will you help me?'

'You don't have to ask,' Kate said. She felt her breasts tingling and a slow, warm ache beginning at the base of her abdomen, a heavy sensual glow. They would arouse Nick and then he would be at Christopher's mercy. The whole situation was so creatively carnal that it made her shiver. 'What shall I do?'

'Hang on.' This was Christopher. 'Edmond, come and stand this side of Nick. You watch from that side and I'll watch from this side. A ninety degree elevation is sufficient, OK?'

'Jesus Christ,' Nick cried, struggling in earnest against the ropes now. He could not loosen them. 'You bastards!' He caught hold of the ropes and lashed out with his feet, trying to kick Christopher as he passed in front of the frame. Christopher swayed out of the way and Nick's foot missed its target, but the vicious intention had been obvious.

'Try that again, Nick, and I'll tie your feet as well,' Christopher said in tones of stern warning.

'You won't come near me,' Nick gasped, still lashing out desperately with his feet. He was strong and agile and this time nearly struck Christopher on the leg. 'I swear it, I won't let you touch me.'

'Edmond,' Christopher said, withdrawing a little, 'bring a couple more ropes, would you?'

The two men took hold of Nick, finally subduing his wild struggles and tying his ankles to the bottom of the frame, about three feet apart. Nick heaved once or twice against the ropes and at last stood still, whimpering almost inaudibly as his breath shuddered in and out of his lungs, his eyes tight shut. Any trace of an erection had now deserted him: his cock was soft and small, dangling defenceless below the nest of his balls. His spreadeagled posture made him look like Leonardo's measured man, circumscribed forever in the circle of his own strong limbs. He looked so exposed, so deliciously vulnerable that Kate's juices began to flow.

Sophie was standing beside Kate, trembling and moistening her lips with her tongue. While the men were struggling she had stood clenching her fists and occasionally letting out little cries of excitement. Now, as Christopher and Edmond took up station on either side of Nick, she glanced at Kate and pulled the ribbon from her ponytail so that her curling hair fell around her shoulders. 'Kate,' she said, 'take all your clothes off; and be ready to do whatever I tell you.' She leant forward until her lips were close to Kate's ear and whispered softly, 'Let's be really subtle. Let's do this without even touching him.'

Kate gave a quick nod and began to undress. Nick tugged against his bonds, flinging his head from side to side and groaning. Sophie looked at Edmond and gave him a sudden, quick, mischievous smile; then she removed her own clothes.

When they were both naked Sophie took Kate's hand and led her towards Nick. When they were about four feet from him she said, 'Kate, kneel down,' and Kate obeyed, wondering what Sophie had in mind. Nick's eyes were tight shut, but Christopher and Edmond were watching them both with avidity. Sophie stood above Kate, breathing quickly, her small breasts lifting and falling. She pushed back her hair with one hand. 'My lord,' she said, in a soft, submissive whisper.

Nick moaned and his lips drew back from his bared teeth. He turned his head away as if he could see the naked women before him even through the screen of his eyelids. Sophie smiled and spoke again, still in the same low, musical voice. 'My lord, my master. We are here as you ordered, both of us. Will you not look?' Nick's closed eyes tightened; his lips quivered and his nostrils flared. Kneeling before his feet, Kate looked up at his lovely body and gave a shudder of delicious arousal. She longed to reach forward and open her lips and draw his soft cock into her mouth, coaxing it to its full hardness with her tongue.

'My lord,' Sophie whispered, 'the slave master chose us as you wished. Please look, my lord, please look and have pleasure in us, or the slave master will beat us.' She dropped to her knees beside Kate; when she spoke again Kate saw that Nick's head moved, unconsciously turning as he registered the different direction from which Sophie's voice reached his ears. 'Here is my friend, master, for your pleasure. She is beautiful, her body is as lush as a ripe fruit. Her breasts are like pomegranates, my lord, her thighs yearn to please you. See, my lord, see how she offers her breasts to you.' Kate caught her cue and slipped her hands beneath her breasts, lifting the heavy globes and holding them towards Nick. He did not open his eyes, but he made a little helpless sound

213

and Sophie's lips twitched in triumph as she saw his flaccid penis beginning to stir.

'My lord,' Kate murmured, taking her part eagerly, 'my friend is as lovely as the dawn, slender as a deer, my lord, with breasts as shallow as saucers and limbs like a gazelle. I pray you to look at her, my lord; she is yours to take.'

Nick's hands gripped at the metal frame to which he was bound and his head fell forward as though he were exhausted. He was breathing fast and the muscles of his belly and loins fluttered uncontrollably as despite himself his penis continued to stir, lengthening and thickening as it hung down between his thighs. Edmond caught Sophie's eye and flashed her a fiendish grin and a thumbs-up sign.

'Oh, my lord,' Sophie whispered, 'if you will not look at us, what shall we do? We are aching for you, my lord. Have pity on us.' Nick did not raise his head. 'Then,' Sophie hissed, 'we shall have to please each other.' She came closer to Kate and lowered her head to draw one of Kate's nipples into her mouth. A thread of pleasure so sharp that it was almost like pain darted through Kate and she gave a little cry. Nick turned his head away and Sophie took her mouth from Kate's breast and crooned, 'Did you hear, my lord, how she cried out when I took her nipple in my mouth? Imagine how much more she will cry when I kiss her in that secret place, when I thrust my tongue deep within her. Imagine how she will cry, my lord.' She guided Kate gently to the ground and began to suit her actions to her words, parting Kate's thighs with her little hands and placing a line of delicate kisses down her soft belly. Kate closed her eyes and gave herself up to the wonderful sensation, sighing with pleasure as Sophie's tongue darted and thrust between her thighs. She writhed on the ground and moaned, chafing at her nipples with the palms of her hands, lifting her hips eagerly towards Sophie's face.

After a moment she whimpered in protest as Sophie's

caresses suddenly ceased. Sophie's lips brushed the inside of her thigh, a quick, firm kiss, and Kate opened her eyes and propped herself up on her elbows, wondering what refinement of torture Sophie had in mind now.

The thick rod of flesh between Nick's legs was fully extended now and beginning to creep skywards. He still had his eyes resolutely shut. But now Sophie was on her feet, moving closer and closer to Nick until their bodies were nearly touching. She lifted her heart-shaped face towards his mouth, standing on tiptoe. 'My lord,' she whispered, 'I have caressed her with my mouth, my lord. Can you not smell her love juices on my lips, my lord? She wants you so much . . .'

Nick gave a stifled curse and turned his head violently away, but the damage was done. He had caught the musky scent of Kate's arousal, carried to him on Sophie's glistening lips, and as if controlled by strings his phallus jerked upwards, suddenly full and proudly erect. The soft skin of his balls tightened and grew smooth with the swollen rigidity of his long shaft.

Sophie whispered, 'Oh, my lord,' and behind Nick Edmond's voice said, 'Nick, you've lost. You might as well open your eyes.'

'Good idea,' Christopher said. 'Kate, Sophie, keep it up: it obviously does a lot for him.'

Very slowly Nick opened his eyes. Sophie looked up at him, her dark eyes languid with sensual desire, and she lifted her lips to his and delivered a long, lingering kiss. Then she dropped back to her knees before him and reached out to Kate and they sank into each other's arms, kissing and caressing. Nick watched them with feverish eagerness, whispering, 'Oh Christ, oh fuck, oh shit,' as they touched and stroked each other. His penis was now in strong erection, thrusting skywards, its scarlet head swollen smooth with eagerness. A tear of clear fluid stood on its tip. Kate and Sophie slid towards the ground, their mouths seeking the soft haven of each other's sex, and Nick groaned aloud. He hardly seemed to notice as Christopher sank to his knees before him and gave a long sigh of pleasure as he opened his lips to take Nick's proudly swelling phallus into his mouth. When Nick felt Christopher's lips on him he stood very still for a moment, shuddering; but then he relaxed and thrust with his hips, blindly seeking his pleasure from the sensitive mouth that held him.

Both Kate and Sophie had been incredibly aroused by offering themselves before the altar of Nick's helpless, bound body. They wanted to watch Nick in the hands of the other men, but their need was urgent and the sensation of their lips and tongues flickering, probing, exploring, ignited their bodies into paroxysms of pleasure. In what seemed like seconds they were quivering and moaning as the hot fingers of orgasm reached out and gripped them, sending their tight-knotted bodies into shuddering convulsions of delight. After a little while the spasms ceased and both of them lifted their heads, curious to see what had become of Nick.

His eyes were again closed, but now it was with pleasure rather than with protest. Sophie clutched at Kate's hand, gripping it feverishly tight, as she saw how Nick's glistening cock slid deep into Christopher's mouth at the same time as Edmond, naked and shining with sweat, thrust his own stiff shaft hard and firm between the tight cheeks of Nick's arse. Nick's hands were gripping whitely at the frame that held him and he flung his head from side to side, gasping and crying out as Edmond fucked him and Christopher worshipped his straining penis with his responsive lips. He had forgotten his fear, his inhibitions: pleasure possessed him. Kate clutched Sophie's hand and they pressed together, clinging to each other, whimpering with excitement as they watched Nick overcome and conquered and subdued by unsuspected delight.

Suddenly Edmond shuddered and cried out, clutching at the smooth tanned skin of Nick's flanks as he found his surging release. Nick moaned and shook; and then

Christopher lifted his hand and drew it tenderly, delicately, along the secret hidden smoothness behind Nick's tautened balls. Nick's body jerked in its bonds and he flung back his head and shouted out in wordless ecstasy, thrusting his loins desperately towards Christopher's rapt face as his body tensed and pulsed, racked with a delirious orgasm. Then he hung limp and panting from the ropes that fastened his wrists, his body slick with sweat, whimpering as Edmond withdrew from his arse and Christopher very gently licked him clean and sat back on his haunches, smiling his enigmatic smile.

'Oh, let him go,' Sophie said, jumping to her feet, suddenly overcome by pity. 'Poor Nick. Let him go.' She reached up to fumble with the tight cords and Kate crawled to Nick's feet and worked earnestly to release him. Presently he was free and he sank to the ground in a shuddering heap, his head bowed, his breath shaking him like repeated blows. Sophie dropped to her knees behind him and put her arms round him, gently stroking his naked glistening back.

Kate caressed Nick's hair. 'Nick,' she whispered, 'it was wonderful to see you. It was so sexy.'

'And you enjoyed it,' Edmond said softly from behind Nick's huddled figure.

Nick lifted his head and looked around the faces watching him. He looked both defeated and strangely elevated. 'All right,' he said huskily. 'All right. I enjoyed it. Remember, though, you promised. This is secret.' He reached out to catch Sophie and Kate into his arms, pulling them both towards him. 'Christ,' he said in a shaking undertone, 'you two are hot. I knew if I opened my eyes . . .'

'Even with them shut,' Edmond said.

'Well,' said Christopher, 'I'm glad you all approved of that idea.' His voice sounded oddly tense to the four who knelt in post-orgasmic bliss on the floor by the chin-up frame. They all lifted their heads and looked at Christopher. He was still wearing the white hotel dress-

217

ing gown and now he pushed it back from his shoulders and stood up, revealing his magnificent, muscled body and his rampantly erect penis. He looked down on them without a smile. 'All of you seem to have come except me,' he said evenly. 'I suggest that you let me name my own pleasure now. Any objections?'

The four of them looked at each other and then up again at Christopher, shrugging and shaking their heads. Christopher's shadowed face lightened briefly with the hint of a smile and Kate felt her stomach lurch with desire for him. But it would not be her, she knew: he had his imagination set on the others today. She was not surprised when he held out his hand and said, 'Sophie.'

As if spellbound, Sophie got to her feet and walked towards Christopher. Edmond stiffened briefly as if he would get up, but Kate put her hand gently on his thigh and he shivered and settled again to the floor, watching. Sophie took Christopher's extended hand and looked up into his face.

'I think you really enjoyed seeing Nick tied up, Sophie,' Christopher said gently. 'Am I right?'

Sophie said nothing, but she nodded. Christopher's lips parted in a smile of creamy, cat-like satisfaction. 'I wonder,' he murmured, 'how you would like it if I were to tie you up?'

A long, lascivious shudder passed through Sophie's body. She took a quick, deep breath, and the deep pink points of her shallow breasts tautened. She lowered her head as if she were ashamed and whispered, 'I don't know.'

'Then I think I will find out,' Christopher said in her ear. He moved quickly to the treasure box and drew out a pair of manacles, bracelets covered in velvet and joined by a long chain. Sophie fastened her eyes on the restraints and shivered again, catching her lip in her teeth.

The huge head of Christopher's scarlet cock jerked up towards his flat belly as he came slowly towards Sophie.

218

Her slender body looked incredibly fragile beside his tall, muscular torso. He pressed one bracelet closed around her right wrist and she gasped and shuddered; then he pulled her beneath the bar and dragged up her left arm, tossed the chain across the bar and fastened the final bracelet. Now she was held there, her arms pulled high above her head, her shallow breasts lifted by the raising of her arms, the rosy points of her nipples swollen and distended with excitement. Her body swung a little from side to side, almost suspended from the sturdy chains that gripped her delicate wrists.

Beside Kate Nick raised himself to his knees, swallowing thickly as he stared at Sophie's lovely body so shamelessly displayed to him. His cock, which had been soft and flaccid after its feverish climax, began to twitch and thicken again and Kate quickly reached out and put her hand on it, coaxing it back towards a full erection.

Christopher stood very still, looking at Sophie. She met his eyes for a moment. Her face was flushed with exhilaration and her lips were full and moist. Then she let her head fall back so that her curling hair tumbled across her slender shoulders. Christopher smiled at her, then returned to the treasure box and stooped and drew out the whip.

Again Edmond began to get to his feet, a protest on his lips, but this time both Kate and Nick caught hold of him and held him down. He did not fight them, but he called out, 'Sophie, Sophie, if you don't want it, say so!'

Startled, Sophie lifted her head. She saw Christopher approaching her like a panther on his silent feet with the whip in his hand and her dark eyes opened very wide and her lips parted. She caught the chains between her hands as though trying to pull away. 'Please,' she whispered.

It might have been protest or supplication. Christopher unfurled the long, soft lash of the whip and shook it out, watching Sophie all the time. 'You said that the slave master would beat you,' he told her softly. 'Are you ready for your punishment?'

Sophie closed her eyes and gasped for breath as Christopher reached out and trailed the lash of the whip across her shoulders, down the swell of her breasts. He wrapped the lash around her taut left nipple and pulled it tight and Sophie cried out and shook as if he had struck her.

But this is what I didn't dare do last night, Kate thought. I thought Sophie wasn't ready for it. How did he guess? How did he know? She loves it. For Sophie was crying out and writhing as Christopher squeezed her nipple with the thong of the whip, and when he shook it loose and stood back from her she gasped in a deep breath of mingled fear and anticipation and twisted as she hung from her chains so that her snow-white, slender buttocks were presented to Christopher and her enraptured audience. 'Master,' she whispered, 'I am ready.'

'My God,' Edmond hissed beneath his breath. He crawled a little way across the floor and pressed himself close to Kate so that she was sandwiched between his body and Nick's. All three of them were trembling. It was not that they really believed that Christopher would hurt Sophie, but the contrast between his height and strength and the utter helplessness of Sophie's slender body was infinitely tantalising and erotic. Kate was still gently stroking Nick's hard cock with her right hand, and now with her left she felt down the smooth skin of Edmond's belly. She pushed her fingers through the golden-brown fur of his pubic hair, weighed and stroked the soft globes of his balls, and at last wrapped her hand around his stiffening penis and began a gentle, rhythmic rubbing. Edmond shuddered and his buttocks clenched in involuntary reaction, but he never once glanced at Kate. Three pairs of eyes were fastened firmly on Christopher and Sophie.

Moving with slow animal deliberation, Christopher

took another step back from Sophie. He coiled the lash of the whip between his hands and then experimentally struck it against his muscular calf. His face twitched as the blow landed and he leant down a little to examine the red mark on his skin. Then he shook out the lash again and drew back his arm, ready to strike. Edmond whimpered and the muscles of his belly gave a sudden, delirious quake, and Nick and Kate both drew in deep breaths of delighted horror.

The lash sang in the air and landed with an audible crack. The blow was artistically placed at the very top of Sophie's white slender thighs, just below the swell of her taut buttocks. Sophie cried out and writhed in her chains, swinging away from the blow: a sharp red line glowed on her pale skin. Christopher moved swiftly around and struck her again. This time the lash landed on her ribcage just below her breasts, curling lasciviously around her sides, and her whole body jolted as if she had received an electric shock. Another blow, this time directly across Sophie's soft flat abdomen, and her head fell back and she let out another cry in which the overtones of pleasure were unmistakable.

Christopher struck her three times more on her back and buttocks and she moaned and twisted as she dangled before him. Her arching back thrust forward her small round breasts and her thighs parted and closed, alternately hiding her moist sex and revealing it. The soft pink flesh of her hidden lips was gleaming with juice and the pink bead of her clitoris protruded eagerly from its hood, begging for release.

At last Christopher caught back the lash of the whip and walked slowly over to Sophie, his huge cock so fiercely erect that it brushed against his belly with each step. She hung slackly from the manacles, her head dangling to one side as if she had fainted. Christopher reached out delicately and with his right hand traced the scarlet lines that the lash had drawn on her flesh, making her shiver and whimper. Then he took hold of her chin and turned her face up to his. Sophie did not open her eyes, but her lips parted and trembled as if she expected a kiss. But Christopher only looked down at her with his dark steady eyes, and the tension mounted.

After a few moments Sophie opened her eyes. They were drowned and glittering with unshed tears. She looked up into Christopher's face and swallowed and her breasts lifted and fell as she drew in deep, quick breaths.

'Do you know what I'm going to do to you now, slave?' Christopher said softly. He was holding her very firmly: his strong fingers were digging into the soft skin of her face. 'Can you guess what your next punishment will be?'

Sophie tried to shake her head, but he held it still. With his left hand he put the long, thick handle of the whip against her body and drew it slowly down towards her triangle, watching her face. Her eyes closed and tightened as the hard thickness of the handle pressed against her belly, her loins, pushed its way into the fine dark fur of her mound. Christopher still held her face turned up to his, his eyes narrowed and his brows drawn down into a dark bar as he watched her expression. The handle of the whip nudged at her closed thighs and Sophie whimpered and tightened her legs together.

'Don't resist me,' Christopher said softly. He tried again to push the thick leather handle between Sophie's closed thighs and she flinched away from him. Moving with breathtaking quickness he stepped back, caught the whip back into his hand and landed a sharp, stinging blow across Sophie's white flank. She jerked and gasped with pain, her hands clutching at the chains from which she hung.

'Open your legs,' Christopher ordered her, replacing the handle of the whip against her thighs. Sophie moaned and shivered and the muscles on her back and shoulders tightened as she pulled herself a little more upright to allow her legs to part. A little cold smile appeared on Christopher's face and he very, very slowly pushed the leather handle between Sophie's legs and began to slide it gently to and fro along the glistening lips.

An undulating, shimmering wave passed through Sophie's body from her chained hands to her shoulders and breasts and down through her loins and her slender legs. She let out her breath in a long, hesitant sigh of ecstasy. Christopher looked steadily at her drowned helpless face and then with a jerk withdrew the stiff leather and held it up before his eyes.

It gleamed with a coating of pearly juice. A smile twitched on Christopher's mobile mouth. He held the handle towards his nose and luxuriously drew in its scent, then rubbed at it with his fingers and began slowly to transfer the moisture to his rigid, avid penis. Sophie moaned with disappointment and lifted her head, whispering, 'Please.'

Both of Kate's hands now encircled a throbbing, swollen cock, and beside her Nick and Edmond were trembling with arousal. Kate had the heel of one foot clamped between her thighs and was rubbing herself against it. She was wet and ready and when Edmond caught hold of her waist and pulled her towards him she complied eagerly. Edmond pushed her forward and spread the cheeks of her bottom apart, probing with the hot head of his penis for the entrance to her sex. She moaned as he found the notch and thrust strongly, sliding up inside her so that the velvety coarse sac of his balls pressed and rubbed against her aching clitoris. Then he stopped moving and knelt behind her, filling her, his hands resting on her white haunches. Kate understood: Edmond was so excited that if he moved he would come, and he wanted to delay the pleasure. She pushed back against him, closing her eyes briefly as the pressure of his testicles against her engorged clitoris sent a rush of sexual pleasure through her. Nick came close to her and knelt by her shoulders, his cock red and eager and thrusting upwards towards her face. She thought that he would demand that she satisfy him at once with her mouth and was trying to frame a way to tell him that she was determined to watch Christopher and Sophie, but Nick said nothing. He reached beneath her body for the heavy globes of her dangling breasts, cupping them in his hands and stroking the nipples gently with his thumb. A shivering gasp trembled in Kate's throat and she lowered her shoulders, pressing her breasts harder into Nick's palms and shuddering.

Christopher had finished transferring the dampness of Sophie's sex from the whip handle to his massive phallus. He did not seem satisfied and he went to the little bottle of oil which stood by the frame where Edmond had left it. As he bent to pick it up Edmond laughed a little, making his penis stir and shiver as it lay deeply embedded in Kate's moist flesh, and reached out to stroke his hand gently down Nick's lean tanned flank. Nick flinched briefly, then relaxed and moved a little closer to Kate's haunches so that Edmond could reach across to his groin and take hold of his hard cock and gently masturbate him.

'Please,' Sophie whispered again, her eyes fastened on Christopher's body. It gleamed now with oil at his loins and the tops of his thighs and the stiff column of his penis. 'Please.'

With a quick feline movement Christopher was behind her, pulling her head back by the hair. He thrust the handle of the whip beneath the swell of her small breasts and lifted it roughly so that it jerked the slight mounds upwards, catching sharply against the tight peaks of Sophie's nipples. 'A slave doesn't ask,' he hissed into her wide-open eyes. 'A slave accepts what is done to her, or she is punished.' Sophie's eyes slid shut and she let out a little moan. Her body arced, pressing her nipples harder against the tormenting leather of the whip.

For the first time Christopher seemed to register how much taller he was than Sophie. He frowned, then glanced around the room. His face cleared as he saw what he needed and he went quickly to fetch it: an aerobic step, a yard long and about eight inches high. He put it on the ground behind Sophie and caught hold of her arms, lifting her bodily so that her toes dangled in midair, then kicked the step forward and lowered her on to it. This brought her buttocks in line with his groin: his thick erect penis brushed against the red and white flesh. Sophie lowered her arms a little, twisting to try to see Christopher behind her, and he stepped back and snarled and flicked out the lash of the whip again, catching her on her ribcage and around the swell of one breast. 'Keep still,' he ordered her.

He lifted the bottle of oil again and began to pour a thin stream of it on to the gentle white swell of Sophie's buttocks. The transparent fluid trickled down the delicate cleft and Sophie gave a little squeal of shock and surprise. Then her eyes opened very wide and she swung round, catching hold of the chains to help her and saying urgently, 'No, Christopher, no, no, I didn't want you there, I wanted you – '

Instantly Christopher's big hand was over her mouth. Her wide-stretched eyes stared into his over the smothering hand. 'Understand me,' he said softly into her face. 'Slaves don't ask for what they want.' He swivelled Sophie around and with the hand that held the whip bent her forward as far as he could, presenting her lovely bottom to him like a beast. She shivered and clamped her cheeks tightly together, resisting him. Christopher prodded with the broad scarlet head of his cock at the dark crevice, but it was closed against him.

'Relax,' he commanded her, and pushed again. Sophie whimpered and her bottom cheeks clenched even more tightly. Christopher took a step back and slapped the white cheeks hard with the flat of his hand; a red hand-shape appeared, staining the pale skin, and Sophie cried out. 'Open to me,' he commanded again. Sophie's back arched and she tightened her cheeks even further. Christopher landed another ringing slap. Then he pushed his hand between her legs and rubbed the edge of it along the wet lips of her sex, just flicking with his finger at the protruding bead at the front of her cleft. Sophie moaned and gasped and forgot to clench her buttocks and the huge shining head of Christopher's magnificent penis pressed against her oiled rear entrance and very slowly slid inside her.

Sophie opened her lips and let out a long, wavering cry as Christopher's massive shaft very slowly pressed into her tight rear passage, spreading the puckered lips, filling her up. The soft flesh of her haunches was quivering as her inner muscles spasmed, shuddering with the confusion between pain and pleasure. The act of penetration seemed to take for ever, but at last Christopher's gleaming body was pressed tightly against her slender buttocks, the whole of his splendid length sheathed within her. Sophie's breath came in quick short pants; her helpless fingers opened and closed on the empty air.

Reaching round in front of her, Christopher chafed her nipples with his hand and the shaft of the whip. She shivered and moaned. 'You wanted to be fucked,' he said softly in her ear. 'This is how I fuck my slaves.' His muscular buttocks hollowed as he withdrew a little way and then thrust again, deep and firm. 'I like to take my slaves in their arses,' Christopher hissed in Sophie's ear. 'It's so tight, it's like a velvet fist holding me. Feel how tight it is, slave.' Again he withdrew, this time almost entirely, and with one long thrust embedded himself again to the hilt in the clutching grip of Sophie's anus. Sophie's eyes were closed and her lips were quaking with a mixture of horror and delight. Christopher moved again, beginning a slow steady rhythm, and after a moment Sophie let out a little whimpering cry of frustration.

'What?' Christopher stopped moving and leant a little forward. 'Not enough for you, you whore?'

'Please,' Sophie moaned helplessly, twisting in her chains and writhing on the thick shaft that impaled her so shamefully, 'please, master, please, my lord, touch me there. Please, please. I beg you. Master, master.'

'Touch you?' Christopher repeated. He lowered his head and kissed Sophie's shoulder and she shuddered. Then, very slowly, he let the handle of the whip trickle down between Sophie's breasts, down her belly, between her legs. She lifted her head and took in a deep breath of anticipation and he waited, waited, and then without warning thrust the thick handle home into the wet tunnel of Sophie's sex. Sophie gave a surprised, animal sound and her body shuddered. Then she opened her mouth and let out a full-throated yell of pleasure, for Christopher had begun to move again, thrusting into her with his splendid penis and at the same time driving the whip shaft deep into her vagina. The shock of his thrusts made her body shake and her breasts jerk and quiver. She held on tightly to the manacles and cried out desperately, 'Oh yes, yes! Master, my lord!' and then her cries became inarticulate shouts and her body began to spasm as a cataclysmic orgasm swept through her. Christopher continued to thrust with the whip until Sophie hung from the chains twitching and whimpering in the aftermath of her pleasure. Then he withdrew it and dropped it and took hold of her slender haunches with both hands and began to pull her back on to him to meet his thrusts. His body was shining with sweat and he let out sharp animal cries as he shafted her mercilessly.

Edmond could bear no more. He let go of Nick's penis and began to move within Kate's body, sliding in and out of her with quick urgent thrusts. Kate gasped and pushed her bottom up towards him to allow his body to press even harder against her aching clitoris as he moved inside her. She whimpered, 'Nick, Nick, let me – '

Without a word Nick came to her and knelt before her, his eager cock sticking up out of the dark curling hair of his groin. Kate opened her mouth and he pushed the hot smooth glans between her full lips and gasped as she took him in, circling the thick shaft with her lips and flickering her tongue over the shining head. He tasted wonderful, still with a tang of chlorine from his swim cutting sharply through the musky masculine savour of his skin and his recent orgasm. She could no longer see Christopher and Sophie but she could hear Christopher's cries growing louder and more desperate as he approached his peak. Closing her eyes, she let herself be surrounded and filled and overcome by the delight of having two men within her, one in her vagina and one in her mouth, just as she had foreseen.

In only a few moments Edmond began to pant and his thrusts became uneven as he neared his climax. He gasped and pushed himself into Kate as if he meant to bury his whole body inside her. She rubbed herself against him and moaned and Nick leant forward over her and again caught hold of her dangling breasts, and as he pinched her dark nipples she gave a cry of surprise and delight as her orgasm rose up within her as if from nowhere and swept through her, making her hot tunnel spasm and clutch at Edmond's faintly twitching cock, making her lips loosen and soften on Nick's working penis so that he grunted and pushed himself even deeper within her mouth. He caught hold of her hair and shouted as his balls tightened and the hot seed pulsed through his jerking cock and flooded her hungry throat.

After a moment Nick withdrew from Kate's mouth, wincing with the shock of the cold air after the warm wetness. Kate's head felt as heavy as lead, but she lifted it and through the curtain of her hair saw Christopher still clutching Sophie tightly against him, his head thrown back and his teeth bared in a ferocious animal snarl of satisfied lust. Sophie's body was totally limp, dangling from the chains around her wrists and Christopher's strong hands, and her soft hair hung forward, concealing her face. Christopher's clutching, clawlike fingers gradually relaxed their grip and he set his teeth and withdrew from Sophie's body. As he moved she moaned and her limp head swayed a little. Christopher held her up with one hand and with the other reached up to unfasten the manacles. One snapped open, then another, and suddenly Sophie was leaning against him, still totally limp. He lifted her and caught her into his arms, small and fragile as a doll, her head hanging brokenly backwards from her white shoulders.

Edmond jumped to his feet and took a couple of quick steps across the room as if he would take Sophie from Christopher. 'Sophie,' he said urgently, and then to Christopher, 'Christ, is she all right?'

As if his voice had awakened her Sophie stirred in Christopher's arms and whimpered. Christopher looked down into her face and smiled and said to Edmond, 'I think she's just a little overcome, Edmond.'

'Let me take her,' Edmond said, holding out his hands. There was a little silence: then Christopher held Sophie out like a child and Edmond hurried to him and drew her gently into his arms, burying his head in her soft hair and whispering endearments below his breath.

Nick stretched out on the floor like a cat before a fire. 'God,' he said, 'I ache everywhere. Jacuzzi for me, folks. Sound like a good idea?'

'Jacuzzi,' Sophie said in a little slurred voice, sounding almost drunken. Nick laughed and went over to help Edmond carry Sophie to the jacuzzi. He stepped on the button and the water began to roar and spin; Nick got into the pool and held up his hands and Edmond lowered Sophie very carefully into them, then got into the foaming water too. Kate heard Sophie say in the same stunned, astonished voice, 'I thought I was dead,' and Nick replying with a laugh, 'So did we, Soph.'

Kate lifted her head and looked up from the floor to where Christopher stood very still. She shivered when she saw that he, too, was watching her, his dark eyes fixed on her, unreadable and tantalising. For a moment she was afraid. Then she got to her feet and took a deep breath. Goosepimples came out on her spine as if someone had walked on her grave. She walked very deliberately over to Christopher and looked into his face. 'I didn't dare try anything like that yesterday,' she said. 'How did you know she would like it?'

Christopher gave a little shrug. 'I told you,' he said. 'I'm pleasing myself today. I truly didn't care very much whether she did or not. If she'd been really unhappy I would have stopped. That's all.'

Standing close beside him, feeling the warmth of his naked body, Kate was rocked by a sudden wave of desperate desire. But as she felt the moist flesh between her legs clench uncontrollably with needing him she recognised that there was more to her feelings than simple lust. He fascinated her, he enthralled her, she had seen no facet of him that she did not like and want to know more about; and after four days she still hardly knew him.

Suddenly Kate's heart hurt her, as if a fist had gripped it and squeezed it so that it jumped and laboured in her chest. She opened her mouth to say *Christopher, I love you*. Then she stopped herself, thinking that she must be crazy. She hardly knew him. Instead she said, 'You came up by train, didn't you.' Christopher nodded. 'And you live in London. Listen, let me give you a lift home tonight.'

'Well,' said Christopher slowly. Kate raised her brows as if this were just a casual, no problems question, just the sort of offer anyone would make, nothing special in it at all. She tried to conceal the eagerness that made her want to tremble like a greyhound on a leash. Say yes, she begged to herself, say yes.

'I'll think about it,' Christopher said, looking at her with level eyes.

Kate smiled and shrugged and said, 'OK,' trying to sound casual, trying not to show her shocked disappointment and rejection.

'Come on,' he went on at once, 'that jacuzzi looks

good.' He reached out and took Kate's hand and smiled, a sincere confiding smile that made her stomach jump.

She was completely puzzled. Why coldly put off her approach and then show affection? Why was he giving out such conflicting messages? 'Christopher,' she said softly, 'now I know why your boss finds you hard to manage. My God, I don't understand you.'

His smile broadened. 'I know,' he said cheerfully. 'Drives you mad, doesn't it?'

Chapter Eleven

They sat in the jacuzzi and recovered and talked about how they would use their new skills at work. Kate asked each of the participants to commit to one thing that they were definitely going to do when they got back to the office, something they could all follow up for each other by telephone calls and electronic messages.

'I'm going to be assertive on my very first day back in the office,' Sophie said at once. 'I'm going to tell Mike my boss that I like the fact that he trusts me but I don't like the way that reports always go out in his name, and I want the next report I write to go out with my name on it.'

'Mine's an assertiveness one, too,' Edmond said. 'I'm going to say to one of my staff that I really like working with her but I don't like the way she always leaves things half finished and dashes on to the next thing, and I want her to make sure that the next job I give her she gives back to me properly completed.'

'We can practise with each other,' Sophie explained eagerly. 'We can role play it. It'll be really useful.'

Nick and Christopher were silent. After a little while Kate prompted, 'What about you, Nick?'

There was a long pause. Then Nick said, 'I'm going to

tell Bob, that's my boss, that he's been right to criticise me in the past. I'm going to ask him how he wants me to change and I'm really going to listen to what he says to me. I'm going to bridge to him.'

'It won't be easy,' Kate warned him.

'I think I've realised that,' Nick said, with a surprisingly kind smile.

All eyes turned to Christopher. For a moment he did not speak, only lay back in the jacuzzi with his head resting on the rim and his eyes closed. Then he could no longer ignore the expectant silence and he sat up a little. 'I really don't like the thought of changing myself,' he said in a quiet, guarded voice.

'I'm not asking you to change *yourself*, Christopher,' Kate said as gently as she could. 'You know I don't want to change you. I just want you to identify one thing that you will try to do differently when you get back to work. A behavioural change, not a change to you personally.'

After another long pause Christopher said, 'But I don't know what I can change that would, how shall I say, benefit me. I do my work well. What else is there?'

Kate resisted the urge to tell him what she would change and waited. As she expected, after only a little while Nick glanced uncomfortably at Edmond and Sophie and then said diffidently, 'The thing is, Christopher, over these four days I think we've all decided that we like you, but the thing is, you never show what you're thinking. And you don't say it. And it makes you hard to deal with.'

'You kept on surprising us,' Sophie said. 'Because we didn't know what to expect. Do you think you could try to be a little – a little more upfront? More open?'

'More open,' Christopher repeated, his voice utterly toneless. He hesitated, obviously thinking hard. Then he said, 'But what difference does it make whether I show what I'm thinking or not? Why should you care?'

Looks were exchanged. Then Edmond said very slowly, 'You see, Christopher, we think we like you, but

I for one have absolutely no idea as to whether you like us.' He paused. Beside him Sophie was nodding earnestly. Christopher still seemed unconvinced, and after a moment Edmond explained, 'You see, it *matters* to me whether you like me or not. That's why I should care.'

'If you show us nothing, you cut us off,' Nick said unexpectedly. 'We can't talk to you. That can't be good for you.'

'*No man is an island, entire of himself,*' Sophie quoted gently. '*Every man is a piece of the continent, a part of the main.*' Edmond smiled and pushed closer to her and laid his head very gently on her shoulder.

There was a long silence. Then Christopher got to his feet and hauled himself out of the jacuzzi and walked away from it, his hands folded behind his head and his elbows pulled forward to shield his face. Kate and the others stared at his wet naked back, breathing shallowly, afraid of what he would do. The silence drew out and out. Kate wanted to break it, to offer the simple, straightforward, obvious solution that the tutor can see which nobody else has grasped, but she could not see it, let alone say it. She knew if she opened her mouth she would cry out that she loved Christopher and beg him not to turn his back on her. Absurd, she told herself, absurd, ridiculous. You only want him because you can't have him. Don't be a fool.

At last Christopher turned and looked at them. He looked utterly puzzled. When he spoke his voice was uncertain, almost timid, quite unlike himself. 'You mean,' he said hesitantly, 'you mean it really matters to you what I think?'

'Yes,' Sophie replied, speaking for them all. 'It really matters.'

'Well,' Christopher said, making the words with difficulty. 'Well, in that case, I don't suppose it hurts if I say that at the beginning of the course I thought you were all pretty ordinary, but since then I – I have changed my mind.'

'You mean you like us now,' Nick prompted hope-fully, smiling up at Christopher. He did not reply, but nodded, looking at the ground.

What has happened to you, Christopher? Kate wondered. What became of you in the past that has made you so closed, so defensive? It can't be just a question of ambiguous sexuality, there must be more than that. I wonder if I will ever find out?

Christopher was climbing back into the jacuzzi now, silent and clearly moved as the others reached out their hands to him, encouraging and affectionate. He said nothing and made a business of splashing his face and neck with water. Kate realised that it was time to change the tone slightly, before things got too intense, and so she said cheerfully, 'I always feel lucky at this point that as the tutor I don't have to make any commitments to changing myself.'

'You?' exclaimed Sophie, clearly surprised. 'But, Kate, you can do it all. You can do everything! I wouldn't have any problems if I were like you.'

Kate laughed hollowly. 'That's what you think,' she said. 'Listen to this.' She outlined briefly the Alex situation, his beauty and her unsatisfied desire. 'There's no reason why I haven't said anything,' she shrugged. 'It just never seems to happen. I think about it; I don't do it.'

'I think you ought to make a commitment too,' Nick said with a grin. 'I suppose we could stretch a point and call it work related. I'll send you an email next week to check up on whether you've asked him to bed yet.'

'Me, too,' offered Edmond.

Kate smiled ruefully. 'Nice try, Nick; thanks, Edmond. But I probably won't be there to get the email in the first place.'

'Why?' asked Sophie. 'Are you going away?'

'I'm going to resign,' Kate said baldly.

'Resign?' they chorused. Even Christopher seemed

shocked, startled. 'Whatever for?' Sophie asked. She looked deeply upset. 'Why?'

'Listen,' said Nick, 'it says in the course instructions that there should be a follow up course in a couple of months. I was thinking about that, I was looking forward to it. What sort of a time will we have if we get another tutor, not you?'

'Have you got a better offer?' asked Edmond.

Kate shook her head. 'I haven't got an offer. I haven't even made any applications. I've just had enough. My boss is a pain. One day she asks me one thing, the next day she tells me to do the opposite. I'm only here because Bob' – she nodded at Nick, who raised his eyebrows in surprise – 'is the senior director of our division and he pulled strings with Bryony to get me to do the tuition. I had client commitments for this week. She told me about it last Friday and I was furious.'

'That explains your decision to make it a little unorthodox,' Christopher said evenly. 'Taking it out on us, were you?'

Kate was going to deny it, but before she could speak Edmond repeated, 'A little unorthodox!' with a laugh, pulling Sophie into his arms in the swirling water. 'That's a bit of an understatement, Christopher. Look at us!'

'It's worked, though, hasn't it?' Sophie told him, arching her back. Her little breasts bobbed among the bubbles.

'It's worked,' Nick agreed. 'Kate, you remember what I wrote on my *Objectives for the course* box.'

'I certainly do,' Kate grinned at him. Seeing questioning glances thrown to her by the others she explained, 'Just two little words indicating that he didn't think he'd get much benefit from the course.'

'And you've really turned me round,' Nick said. 'I mean, I know I'll find it hard not to revert to type when I get back to the office, but I'm going to make the effort. I mean it.'

'We'll get in touch with you and ask how it's going,' offered Sophie generously.

'Kate, don't resign,' said Edmond. 'There's always some way away from a bad boss. Can't you talk to her?'

Kate shook her head. 'She isn't the world's greatest listener. She sits and watches you while you say something, but nothing ever goes in. And she's only interested in her own political future. Onward and upward on my own, that seems to be her motto.'

'But – ' Sophie began.

'If you got Alex into bed, that might make you feel better,' Nick interrupted.

'Look, I'll think about it,' Kate said. 'And if I decide to go I promise I'll write to you all and let you know where I am. There's no reason why we shouldn't get together again anyway, even if it's not on the follow-up course. I'd like to.' She could not prevent herself from glancing at Christopher with an expression of barely concealed hope.

The others seemed to sense that she did not want to discuss it any further and they drew back a little, talking about more general things. Presently the jacuzzi threatened to turn them all into human prunes and they got out and dressed and by agreement decided to spend the rest of the time before lunch practising office situations.

Lunch was in a private dining area just off the main dining room. Waiters seemed always to shuttle in and out just as the conversation turned to sex, causing giggles and blushes. After a while when the main course had arrived and they were left alone, Kate said, 'I vote we play a game.'

'What sort of game?' demanded Sophie, who had already drunk a glass of wine.

'Nick gave me the idea on the first evening,' Kate said, smiling at Nick. 'It's called, Anything Goes Beneath the Tablecloth. We all sit here having a normal business lunch and making business conversation, but under the tablecloth we're all going to do really lewd things to

237

each other. If you moan or go red or whatever you're out. What about it?'

'I like the sound of that,' said Nick. 'Makes lunches much more interesting.'

'Why, what were you doing to Kate on the first night?' asked Sophie. 'I never guessed. Is that why you followed her to the Ladies? What were you doing?'

'We're supposed to be talking about business,' Nick reproached her. She looked chastened and returned her attention to her food. Then she looked up again at Nick, who was sitting opposite her, and her dark eyes opened very wide. Kate smiled, guessing that Nick's toes were already creeping up Sophie's slender calf. Nick was sitting beside her and she wondered if she could put him off his stroke. Her hand rested lightly on his thigh and began to inch slowly upwards.

By the time they returned to the health suite after lunch they were all thoroughly aroused, stimulated almost beyond bearing by fingers and toes and thighs. Nobody had actually climaxed, though Sophie had almost been 'out' at one stage, but she had managed to escape by turning what had clearly begun as a little yelp of sexual pleasure into a sneeze.

As Christopher closed the door of the suite Nick held out his hands and said, 'I'd like to propose that you let me choreograph the action for a bit. I've got an idea I've always wanted to try and I think you'll all enjoy it too.'

'Don't you think it's Kate's turn to say what we should do?' Edmond argued. 'We've all been pleasing ourselves one way or another and she gets to play second fiddle. I don't think that's fair.'

'Let's ask Kate,' Nick said, quite calmly.

They all turned to Kate with questioning expressions. She lifted one shoulder in a careless shrug. 'I don't mind,' she said. 'I can't complain so far, can I? I think we ought to give Nick's idea a try.' She knew that if she were asked what she wanted at this moment she would say, Christopher. All she could think about was how much she wanted to feel him lying on top of her, entering her aching sex with his massive cock, punishing her with his weight and strength. This would not necessarily be entertaining to the other three and she worried about her growing fixation.

Nobody else seemed to have any objections. 'OK, then, if everyone's happy,' Nick said eagerly. He pulled his shirt off over his head and flung it away, revealing his lovely lean torso. 'Let me explain. Look, come on over here.' He led them over to the lounging area by the pool. They sat down around him like children waiting to hear a story, surrounded by the potted palms and warm steamy air. Kate found herself sitting at Christopher's feet and she pressed against his leg like a dog asking for attention, using all her control to prevent herself from looking up at him with pleading eyes.

'Now then,' Nick explained. His brilliant blue eyes were glittering with eagerness. 'It's just something I've always, sort of, hankered after. I suppose you'd call it a human chain. You know, everyone doing something to somebody else? If you'd all like to try it, I, er, I have an arrangement in mind.'

'No surprises there,' Christopher said. He sounded slightly cutting, but when Nick looked at him anxiously he smiled and said, 'No problems, Nick. Let's hear it.'

A slow smile spread over Nick's hard narrow features. 'No,' he said slowly, 'no, I think it would be easier if I showed you. You see, I'm not exactly sure how we'll all fit together.' He put his hands to the buttons of his jeans. 'So,' he added, 'I think we should strip for action.' He unfastened his jeans and pushed them off, then kicked them into a corner out of the way. The muscles on his broad-shouldered, narrow-waisted body flexed as he bent to pull a couple of the low, padded loungers more closely together. His long penis was already lifting, swelling to full rigidity, and he moved with a contained excitement.

The others exchanged glances. Then Kate said, 'Well,

we have our instructions,' and put her hands to her singlet to pull it off. As she stripped it over her head, momentarily blinded, she felt a hand brushing against the points of her breasts, shooting a sudden sharp pleasure through her. She yanked off the singlet and looked up into Christopher's deep eyes. He was bending over her, smiling, and she let out a long breath of avid desire. Murmuring his name, she reached up and began hastily to unbutton his shirt, sliding her hands under the crisp cotton to feel the strong, broad muscles of his chest, the delicious hard ladder of his ribs, the tightly knitted plane of his belly. The shirt was open and she pushed it off, guiding the sleeves down his strong arms, stirring the delicate dark hairs on his forearms with her fingers.

Suddenly she realised that in the whole of that evening of dark passion she had never kissed him, never tasted that wonderful, wide, mobile mouth, and with a little cry of urgent need she stretched up towards him, her lips parting.

He hung above her, looking down into her face. Kate knelt perfectly still, her sharp breathing lifting her breasts, stretching out to him with the fingers of her mind, yearning for him. She felt like a teenager racked by the first pangs of hopeless love, obsessed, driven, desperate. Behind her Nick and Edmond were undressing Sophie, caressing her so that she giggled and whimpered with anticipation, but Kate could not hear the sounds. All her soul rested in Christopher's shadowed face. What use was it to demand? If she took his kiss, it would be worthless. A forced gift is not a gift.

She thought of Karen, the girl from the boutique who had lost Nick his bet. Christopher had kissed her, he had told her so; kissed her and seduced her and pulled her down on to him, impaled her and made her scream with pleasure. A sharp pang of jealousy caught at Kate's breathing and she sensed that it showed on her face.

Perhaps Christopher saw her eyes tighten, or perhaps her emotion was so strong that although she did not move he felt it radiating from her like heat and light. He stooped his head very slightly, leaning towards her. Kate saw him move and her throat tightened with a rush of unbelieving gratitude and desperate longing. He was, he was going to kiss her! Her eyes closed and a little sound escaped her, a tiny whimper of bliss, and then she felt Christopher's lips on hers.

At first he simply placed his mouth on hers and remained motionless, breathing steadily. She felt the warmth of his lips, the hardness of his teeth hidden behind them. His breath was sweet, tinged with overtones of the coffee and wine he had drunk over lunch. For what seemed like long minutes he did not move. Then one of his big, powerful hands touched her bare back, moving upwards to the nape of her neck, and she shivered and leant back, abandoning herself to his strength. His fingers dug into her hair and held her head still and she gasped helplessly, opening her mouth to him, and he pressed his lips more closely on to hers. His warm, strong tongue entered her at last, tasting and probing, and the pleasure was intense, exquisite, subtle music of the senses, like a single thread of sound, a pleasure more refined and delicate and heightened even than the sweetest and most gentle coupling. Tears sprang to Kate's closed eyes. She lifted her arms and wrapped them around Christopher's naked shoulders and pressed herself to him. Her tight nipples rubbed against his chest, adding their own shrill counterpoint of sensation to the complex single theme of their kiss. Part of her was wholly absorbed in the smell and feel and taste of him, but part of her mind was already leaping ahead, imagining how he would place her softly on the ground and lie on her, still kissing her, and how her knees would move apart for him as his strong fingers stroked her breasts.

But he was drawing back from her, lifting his head, loosening his hands from her hair. She whimpered in protest and tried to catch him back, but he shook his head, smiling gently. 'Kate,' he whispered, 'follow the choreographer.'

Kate wanted to answer angrily, 'Fuck the choreographer, Christopher, I want you,' but she bit back the words and closed her eyes, fighting against a feeling of loss so strong that it threatened to overwhelm her. She might never have another chance. Her eyelids trembled and she lifted her hand quickly to brush away a tear that escaped and began to trickle down her cheek.

Then she felt his hand on her face. She opened her eyes quickly, not caring that they were full of tears, and looked at him. The corners of his beautiful, firm mouth were lifted very slightly. 'That lift tonight,' he said. 'I accept.'

'Oh,' Kate managed to reply, smiling, 'great. OK.' She was filled with delight and excitement. She wanted to say that she loved him, but she knew she must hold herself back until she understood his feelings better. She resisted the urge to jump to her feet and punch her hand into the air in delighted victory.

'Kate, Christopher,' Nick's voice called. 'Over here.'

He had pushed two of the loungers together lengthways and now stood by them, grinning broadly. 'You look as though you're getting on well,' he said. 'Let me start with you. Kate, lie down here, at the head end. That's right.'

'I'm back to front,' Kate complained, but she obeyed.

'There's method in my madness,' Nick reassured her. He let her settle and lie comfortably, then reached beneath the lounger and adjusted it so that its head end was lifted in the air. Kate's hips were lifted too, tilted upwards so that the dark mound of her sex was raised and opened between her softened thighs.

'My God,' Kate said, almost embarrassed despite herself, 'this is a lewd position.'

'Isn't it,' Nick agreed. He turned to Christopher. 'If you would be so kind,' he said, 'kneel over Kate's head and, ah, let her use her mouth on you. There are more

242

men than women, you see, but I have to be even-handed. That means every woman gets two men and Edmond gets to enjoy his dream again and have two women.'

Kate breathed quickly with delight. She turned her head on the smooth surface of the lounger and watched as Christopher slowly removed his trousers, revealing his wonderful nakedness. He made a move as if he would come over to her, then stopped. 'So what's the rest of the arrangement?' he enquired coolly.

Nick grinned. 'Edmond will kiss Kate where she wants it most,' he said. Kate smiled gently to herself, thinking, that's what you think. I'd give up this whole business to be back in Christopher's arms and feel his lips on mine. 'And Sophie will look after him with her mouth. And I get to have Sophie, which as you know is something I've been angling for for days.'

Christopher's lips twitched and he chuckled. 'Sounds fair,' he said. Without another word he came and stood over Kate. His cock was not yet fully erect: the soft skin still half covered its half-grown head. He looked down at Kate's prone body and smiled. 'Shall we dance?' he asked her.

A thick clutch of anticipation prevented Kate from answering, but she reached out with both hands and caught hold of Christopher's strong thighs, drawing him towards her. God bless Nick, she thought. How had he guessed that she had not yet tasted Christopher's body with her mouth? She steered Christopher to kneel over her, his legs straddled on either side of her head, the coarse skin of his testicles brushing against her forehead. The smell of him surrounded her, musky and masculine, warm and wonderful, melting her into arousal. She opened her mouth and licked the underside of his penis. Before her eyes it twitched and thickened, growing visibly as the blood pumped into it. She gave a little moan of pleasure and reached up to draw the tip between her lips, closing softly around it and sucking, licking, gently easing back the tensing foreskin with her tongue. The sensation of power as Christopher's cock grew within her mouth was delicious. She forgot everything but the need to give him pleasure, to make her soft lips the perfect receptacle for his lust and desire. Unconsciously her body shifted on the lounger, ripples of motion passing down it so that her jutting breasts lifted and fell.

In her mouth Christopher's phallus had attained its full magnificence. She could harbour only the gleaming head and a few inches of the long shaft, and she lifted her hands to caress the base of his thick stem and the taut sac of his balls. Thoughts of her own pleasure were far from her mind, but then his strong fingers touched her breasts, flickering against their dark peaks. The little buds lengthened and tautened instantly and Kate cried out, her voice muffled by the smooth hot gag of Christopher's pulsing flesh. A shudder of ecstasy rolled over her and her thighs lifted and parted, and as if by magic a mouth was there, there between her legs, stirring deep dark pleasures as it gently brushed against the soft skin that edged her loins. Edmond's lips, Edmond's sensitive tongue, adding to her pleasure.

The duet was now a trio and vaguely, through the sound of her own moans of delight, Kate heard Sophie's voice crying out in ecstasy as a quartet became a quintet. She imagined what she could not see, Edmond arched above her licking and lapping at her with his tongue while his stiff phallus slipped in and out of Sophie's rosebud mouth: and Sophie lying there with her slender thighs parted to allow Nick to possess her. Kate tilted her head back to allow Christopher's splendid penis to thrust even deeper into her mouth and pictured Nick with Sophie. He would slide his arms under her thighs and lift them so that her sex was open to him, so that he could enter her as deeply as he could and shaft her properly. He could not help but be competitive, and he would want to show Sophie what he was made of. Edmond's deft tongue curled around the quivering stem

244

of Kate's clitoris, pressing against it, and she lifted her round hips towards his face as she listened to Sophie cry out and imagined Nick's hot stiff cock sliding in and out of the tight pouting lips of her sex.

Gradually ecstasy mounted inside her. She could sense Christopher too approaching his climax and she worked on him even more earnestly with her tongue and lips, drawing him with her towards the peak of pleasure. Her lips ached with the effort of accommodating his massive phallus, but she did not want to stop. Edmond lapped and sucked between her thighs, moaning as he did so. She felt her orgasm gathering, coiled in the base of her abdomen like a beast ready to spring, preparing to fall upon her and drag her down.

Then, without warning, the door of the health suite swung open with a crash. Startled and surprised, the human chain began to disintegrate, falling apart as its links let go of each other and rolled upright, astonished, flushed with interrupted pleasure, shocked and angry. Kate was the last to sit up. She looked towards the door and her hand unconsciously lifted to cover her mouth as she saw who stood there.

'What the *fuck* is going on here?' demanded the little figure at the door. Bryony took a few steps forward, literally shaking with astonishment and indignation. She was dressed for work in a close-fitting, sharply tailored suit and looked fierce and angry. Before the force of her personality the participants withdrew a little; Edmond drew Sophie protectively into his arms and even Nick looked abashed.

'Kate,' Bryony hissed, coming closer to Kate where she sat naked and defenceless on the lounger. 'Kate, you stagger me. I got a feeling you were planning something, but what the hell is this? What do you think you're doing?' She flung back her red-gold head and shook her hair angrily. 'Get out,' she said. 'Don't dare to show your face in the office again. I'll send your stuff after you. And don't expect a reference, either. As far as I am concerned you are finished with this business. You'll never work again.'

Kate could not speak. Her mind was still fogged with the shock of her interrupted orgasm and the unexpectedness of Bryony's arrival. She took a deep breath and blinked. There seemed to be nothing she could do, and she began to get slowly to her feet.

Instantly one of Christopher's big hands was on her shoulder, holding her down. 'Kate,' he said steadily, 'who is this person? Introduce us.'

'I am Bryony Griffith,' said Bryony coldly, 'head of Training Services and Human Resources. Kate works for me, or should I say she *worked* for me.'

'And you're an expert in this type of course, are you?' Christopher demanded.

Bryony's head jerked up, sensing challenge. 'I can tell abuse and impropriety when I see it,' she said angrily. 'And who are you?' She kept her eyes fixed on Christopher's face, ignoring the fact that he was naked and massively erect, his huge cock thrusting out towards her and glistening with Kate's saliva.

'A participant who has found the course very valuable,' Christopher told her.

Scowling, Bryony turned away from him to look at the other participants. She registered Edmond and Sophie clinging to each other and her lip curled with scorn; then she set her eyes on Nick. They flickered once over his naked body, then returned to his face. 'I've seen you in the office,' she said, the angry tones of her voice slightly tempered by consciousness of Nick's influential position. 'You're Bob's PA.'

'Right,' said Nick. 'And I'd like to know what the hell you think you're doing, interrupting this course.'

Bryony took a step back as if she had been stung. 'My God!' she exclaimed. 'Look around you! Is this what you came to learn? How much is this course costing us? It's bloody disgusting!'

'What gives you the right to interfere?' Sophie said

unexpectedly, bristling like a small cat protecting its kittens. 'You don't know anything that's been going on. We've all learnt what we came here for.'

'Do you think we're puppets?' demanded Edmond. 'You think Kate forced us to do something we didn't want to do?'

'Look,' Kate said, 'I don't want to cause you all trouble. I'll just – '

'Kate,' Christopher said softly, 'stay where you are.' He had both hands on her shoulders, holding her down, and he moved up close behind her so that she could feel the heat of his big body through her naked skin. She leant back against him slightly, trembling, hardly believing the way that all four of them were springing to her defence.

For a moment Bryony looked thrown. Then she turned her attention from Edmond and Sophie to Nick. 'I know how much Bob wanted you to come on this course,' she said. 'He asked me particularly for Kate to tutor you. I don't think he had in mind that she would *screw* you.'

'I suggest that you ask him in a week or so's time whether he thinks the course has had the desired effect,' Nick said. He was speaking very evenly and he began to walk towards Bryony, one steady step at a time. For a little while she stood with her head lifted fiercely, challenging him; then it seemed that his gradually increasing physical closeness was disturbing her. Her eyes shifted and Kate saw her swallow hard. Nick sensed her discomfort and a wolfish smile began to spread over his face. 'I'd be quite happy to sit in on your discussions,' he said, 'and explain just how Kate's unorthodox methods manage to work.'

'Bullshit,' Bryony said, setting her jaw. 'I don't believe a word of it. She's finished. I'll go and call Bob now and tell him just what you've all been getting up to.' She turned to go, barely hiding her relief at escaping Nick's blue stare.

Hardly seeming to move, Nick reached out and

snagged Bryony's arm. 'You're not going anywhere,' he told her.

'Let go of me!' Bryony shouted at him, trying to pull away. She seemed utterly astonished that he should lay hands on her. 'How dare you?'

'I'm just going to give you a personal demonstration,' Nick said. He caught hold of Bryony by both her upper arms and pulled her quickly towards him. The jerk made her head fall back and Nick stooped his mouth on to hers and kissed her, smothering her protests. Kate put her hands over her mouth, amazed and anxious: Bryony was not the right sort of woman to try this approach with. It was easy to imagine her getting Nick sacked for impropriety, suing him for assault. She waited quivering for Nick to draw back, for the torrent of abuse which would descend on him.

But it did not seem to be happening. At first Bryony protested vigorously, writhing and wriggling in Nick's hands, trying to pull away. But he held her fast and kissed her harder, his strong tongue digging deep into her mouth. After a moment her stifled cries of protest changed to whimpers and her pinioned hands opened, the fingers parting stiffly into tense claws. Nick pulled her even closer to him and pressed against her; his hard, erect penis, shining with Sophie's juices, brushed against the fabric of her skirt. Bryony shuddered and suddenly relaxed into his hands, limp and moaning.

At once he drew back, still holding Bryony securely by the arms. 'You see how persuasive this is?' he said. 'Now guess what. We're all going to join in the demonstration.' He glanced around and as if he had summoned them Edmond and Sophie and Christopher came forward, their eyes bright with excitement. Bryony twisted in Nick's hands, protesting, but it did her no good. She opened her mouth to scream and Nick at once kissed her again, gagging her with his lips. As he held her still the others laid hands on her, pulling off her smart jacket and her tight skirt so that she stood before them clad only in a tight body and lace-topped stockings. She struggled and fought, but to no avail. Christopher picked her up bodily, one big hand clamped over her mouth, and carried her over to one of the loungers. Sophie was already waiting there with a handful of scarves and ropes and they stripped off the body and pulled down the lacy scrap of her knickers and fastened her down, spreadeagled, one of the scarves bound securely over her mouth.

Kate got slowly to her feet and walked across to stand over Bryony, looking down at her. She writhed against her bonds, heaving and protesting through the gag, naked except for her stockings. Her body was very small and slight, white-skinned and starred with golden freckles, but her breasts were surprisingly full, with wide, dark areolae. Above the gag her green eyes were furious. Kate could hardly believe that Bryony was pinioned there, utterly captive, at her mercy. She shook her head and smiled. 'Good grief,' she said softly. 'I don't know what to suggest.'

'Make her come,' Edmond said thinly. 'Show her the sort of thing you've been showing us. We should all make her come.'

Nick was standing by Bryony's head. Now he put his hand on her cheek. She pulled fiercely away from him and he gave a little quick smile and slowly ran his hand down her neck and on to her body. 'She's beautiful,' he said softly. He glanced up at the others. 'Is it still my show?' he asked in a tense, hushed voice.

'If you want, Nick,' Sophie said. 'She's put us all off. See if you can't get us started again.'

Nick licked his lips. 'Christ,' he whispered, 'I'd like to have her.'

A smothered squeal of protest passed the gag and Bryony's tethered body burst into desperate struggles. Nick leant forward and brushed his hand down her breasts, frowning with concentration as he teased one dark nipple into taut readiness. 'Hush,' he said softly, 'you'll enjoy it, I promise.' He looked quickly up at the others. 'Edmond, Sophie,' he said, 'come here, come and suck her tits. Please.'

Edmond and Sophie came forward to obey. They knelt down on either side of the lounger and leant forward, lips opening, and began to lap with moist gentle mouths at Bryony's jutting breasts. Bryony's body tensed and arched and she gave a shrill cry that was half stifled by the tight scarf; her bound hands opened and closed spasmodically. Nick caught his lip in his teeth and ran his hand down her body, exploring the soft white skin, testing the flat resilience of her stomach and twisting his finger in the red-gold curls of hair in her groin. Then he too knelt down and put his hands on the delicate flesh of the insides of her thighs just above the dark stocking tops, stroking upwards towards her exposed sex. Bryony writhed and moaned. Nick stretched forward and began to kiss the white skin he had touched, lapping with long strokes of his tongue towards the quivering, moist lips and the little pink pearl of flesh that protruded just below her shining triangle.

Kate felt Christopher's big body behind her, pressing close to her again. She jumped and turned to face him, looking up at him. 'Let them,' he said softly, 'let them. We had some unfinished business.'

'Oh, yes,' Kate whimpered. She moved into his arms, reaching up for him, stretching her lips up to his, feeling herself completed and surrounded by his strong, possessive closeness.

Their lips met. Kate surrendered herself to the kiss and the ecstatic clutch of desire seized her again, making her shudder with delight. Slowly they sank to the floor, exchanging burning kisses, their hands exploring and caressing their eager bodies. Christopher was still fully erect and Kate bent her head to draw him again into her mouth, wanting to savour the wonderful taste of him, to smell his closeness and feel the wonderful, hard silkiness of his engorged flesh. He remained still for some time, breathing hard as she tenderly serviced him with her soft mouth, his big hand resting in her hair. Then he caught hold of her and pulled her up.

'Look,' he whispered. Kate pressed against him and turned in the circle of his arms to watch what he pointed out to her.

Sophie and Edmond had stopped their caressing of Bryony's breasts. They were lying on their sides on a pile of the thick white towels, head to tail, moaning as they pleasured each other with their mouths. Their bodies were pressed so close together that they seemed almost to be two halves of one creature. As Kate watched Sophie began to quiver with the onset of orgasm; she rolled on to her back, whimpering and shaking as Edmond clutched her white hips hard in his hands and drove his tongue deep into her sensitive flesh. As her shuddering ceased he positioned himself over her and thrust his taut cock between her lips, gasping with pleasure as he pushed hard into her mouth, taking himself inexorably towards his own climax.

And Nick was poised over Bryony on the lounger. He had unfastened her legs and untied the gag and now he was positioning himself at the entrance to her sex, just making ready for the moment when he would possess her. She had given herself up to him utterly: her slender ankles were locked around his back and her head was thrown back between her bound wrists. As Nick penetrated her with his long, stiff cock she gave a high, shuddering cry of joy, and he began to move rhythmically within her, sliding his thick shaft in and out of her and panting with effort and ecstasy.

'It seems to me,' Christopher whispered in Kate's ear, 'that we could be similarly occupied.' He got suddenly to his feet, pulling Kate up after him, and without effort swept her up into his arms. She lay unresisting, wondering where he would take her. Moving quickly, he carried her over to one of the gleaming metal weights machines. It was positioned directly before the floor-to-ceiling mirror. He put Kate gently down and sat down on one of the padded benches and leant back against the body of the machine, his huge erect penis sticking up from his loins. 'Look,' he whispered, 'you can see yourself. Kate, I'm waiting for you.'

It was time. It was really going to happen. Kate stood over Christopher, looking down at his magnificent body. Every nerve in her was tingling with arousal and the knowledge that soon, soon, she would be able to take that wonderful penis within her, feel him moving inside her, bring him to his climax with the clutching fingers of her moist willing sex. She straddled him quickly and leant forward so that he could draw one of her aching nipples into his mouth and suck on it. He closed his teeth on the little pink bud and Kate flung back her head in a sudden spasm of pain and pleasure. Then she lowered herself towards him.

The massive glistening head of his cock parted the wet lips of her vulva. She hesitated, revelling in the antici-pation. He sucked again at her nipple and a shooting star of pleasure flew from her breasts to her loins, shuddering in her engorged clitoris. Very, very slowly she began to slide down on to his massive shaft, feeling it spreading her, filling her so tightly that she thought she would burst. The sensation was unbelievable, the warmth of her sex flaring into sudden hot desire as the cold fingers of ecstasy from her breasts darted through her. She half fell the rest of the way and then Christopher was inside her, sheathed to the hilt, filling her utterly.

There was no rush. This pleasure would last as long as she wanted. Kate moved her hips in a little lascivious circle, pressing her throbbing clitoris against the hard root of Christopher's cock. She leant forward and kissed him feverishly, pushing her breasts into his hands, inviting his tormenting caresses. For long moments she remained as she was, impaled upon him, the pleasure mounting within her as their tongues touched and twined and his strong fingers flickered against her nipples. Then, with a moan of pure ecstasy, she began to move.

She was so wet with desire that his thick shaft slipped easily through her aching tunnel. She writhed upwards and then sank down again, gasping to feel his hot phallus sliding back up inside her. She opened her eyes for a moment and saw him looking over her shoulder; turning her head she saw that he was watching in the mirror as she rose and fell on him, watching as his shining cock appeared between the full white cheeks of her bottom and then disappeared again as she lowered herself on to him and took him inch by straining inch into her hot mound. He squeezed her breasts with his strong hands and set his teeth to her neck, biting at her soft skin. Conflicting desire filled her. She wanted to take him into her again and again, riding him to urgent climax, and she wanted it never, never to end. She twisted now as she rose and fell, surging up and down on his throbbing penis, taking her pleasure from his wonderful body. Christopher gasped and began to heave his hips up towards her, pumping into her, his face locked in concentration as he watched himself in the mirror sliding again and again into Kate's willing sex.

A cry from the poolside caught their attention and made them glance briefly across to where Bryony lay beneath Nick's thrusting body. He was forcing himself into her now, panting as he shafted her with all his strength. His body was shining with sweat and his eager cock gleamed as it appeared and disappeared from the red-gold cushion of her sex. Bryony was flinging her head from side to side and screaming, 'Oh, that's so good. Fuck me, Nick, fuck me. Harder, deeper, don't stop.' And then her heels drummed against his back as she shuddered with the onset of her climax. Her body twisted and bucked under Nick's urgent thrusts. He gasped and caught hold of her hips and drove himself into her, once, twice, and on the third massive lunge he yelled with pleasure and began to shake as he spent himself inside her.

'Kate,' Christopher whispered, 'now.' He sat up a little straighter and pulled her close to him, holding her haunches in his strong hands and thrusting himself up into her. Kate began to pant as her climax mounted inside her and she leant forward, blindly seeking Christopher's mouth with hers. They began to move in unison, moaning as his body slid in and out of hers, and Kate twisted her hands together behind Christopher's strong neck and drove herself against him. He shuddered as he moved, his shadowed face darkening with the rush of his pleasure. His nails rubbed delicately against the jutting teats of her breasts and an instant, electric thrill rushed through her. She felt her orgasm coming, coiling in her bowels and then spiralling outwards up her spine until it burst and exploded in her head and filled her body with jolts of ecstasy. She called out Christopher's name as the pleasure possessed her and clutched at him with her hands. He took his fingers from her breasts and held instead her hips, clutching her tightly to him. Then, slowly, he got up, lifting Kate with him. She hung down from his hands, limp with exhaustion, his thick cock imbedded deep in the still faintly twitching flesh of her shimmering body. Christopher turned and laid her down on the padded bench, never withdrawing from her. He took hold of her hands by the wrists and stretched them above her head, holding her still. Then he began to thrust into her, letting out sharp animal cries of effort. Kate's head rolled from side to side. She could hardly utter a sound for the pureness of the pleasure; he pushed his massive cock into her, over and over again, while she still trembled with the aftershocks of her orgasm, borne up on a plateau of ecstasy. Her body spasmed around him and she clutched at him feverishly with her inner muscles and after only a few more ferocious, rutting lunges Christopher cried out and bared his teeth as he found his own fierce release within her, sating his lust in her shuddering flesh.

He lay on her, panting, and when he let go of her wrists she lifted her heavy hands and wrapped them around his shoulders, feeling his lungs filling and emptying, his heart pounding in his broad chest. Her heart was full of satisfied love, but she said nothing. Tonight she would drive him home and then, perhaps, if everything went well, perhaps she would be able to tell him. Briefly she wondered how she would cope with Christopher's liking for men as well as women. Well, there was no knowing until she tried it. She pushed the thought away.

At last Christopher withdrew from her, kissing her gently as he did so. He put his arm around her and lifted her and she clung to him, shivering.

'Well,' said Nick's voice, 'what do you say, Bryony? Keep quiet about it, and perhaps Kate might let you join us on the follow-up course. If you criticise Kate, I'll tell Bob just how much you enjoyed yourself just now.'

Kate and Christopher both looked up. Nick had untied Bryony's wrists and was carrying her across to the jacuzzi. She lay in his arms utterly relaxed, her thick hair hanging down heavily from her limp head. Her lips parted and she smiled as he lowered her into the swirling water. She said huskily, 'That sounds like blackmail.'

Christopher shook himself, then scooped Kate up into his arms and carried her across the room towards the jacuzzi. 'Not far wrong,' he said, as he stepped carefully down into the warmth and the gentle, stinging caress of the bubbles. Kate, still stunned with pleasure, whimpered in protest as the water rushed against her sensitised skin.

'Kate was saying earlier,' Nick commented, 'that she was thinking of resigning. We didn't like the sound of that.'

Bryony seemed genuinely surprised. 'Resigning?' She struggled to lift her head, pushing her wet hand through her red-gold hair. 'Resigning? Kate, is that right? Why, for God's sake?'

There was no way that Kate could come up with a reasoned reply. She was nestled against Christopher's broad chest, concentrating more on listening to his heartbeat than on what Bryony was saying to her. She shook her head and said nothing.

'I don't think Bob would like it,' Nick mused, 'if I told him that one of our best tutors was resigning. He might want to find out why.'

'Look.' Bryony was straining against the water and Nick's arms. 'Look, Nick, are you saying this has something to do with me? Don't get me wrong. I'm don't want Kate to resign; she's a valuable member of the team, we need her. I'm as surprised as you are.'

Sophie and Edmond had got to their feet now and came down into the jacuzzi hand in hand. Sophie looked at Bryony without sympathy and said, 'Perhaps you ought to pay more attention to what your people are thinking.'

'Have you been on this course?' Edmond asked pointedly. 'I think you'd find it very useful.'

Kate buried her head against Christopher's chest, waiting for the bomb to drop. She had never heard Bryony accept criticism quietly. But moments passed and there was silence. Eventually Kate looked up and saw Bryony lying in Nick's arms, her head tilted back against his shoulder. Her lips were quivering with pleasure. Nick had placed her body across the jets of water so that they were swirling and bubbling over her breasts and between her legs, caressing her with a thousand soft fingers.

Very softly, Nick whispered in Bryony's ear, 'There's a follow-up course in a couple of months. I bet you'd find it as useful as I did. Wouldn't you like to come?'

Bryony jerked in Nick's hands, trying to thrust her sex harder against the jet of water. 'Yes,' she whimpered, 'I want to come. Please.'

'Ask Kate nicely, then,' hissed Nick.

After a moment Bryony lifted her head. Kate had never seen her as she now looked, her face softened and slack with pleasure, her hard eyes moist and her lips loose and full. She said softly, 'Kate, would you let me come on the follow-up course?'

At that second Bryony changed in Kate's eyes from a boss and a dragon to a participant, someone who needed her and could be made happier and stronger through her intervention. Her dislike evaporated. 'Of course you can,' she said warmly, 'if you want to.'

Nick's face lit up. 'Well,' he said eagerly, 'if that means there's another person joining our team, it seems to me I've got a lot more scope for my next arrangement. Three men and three women – wow, I'll have fun with this.' He caught Bryony's wet, tousled head on to his arm. 'Bryony,' he said, 'it's time you met the rest of us. You're going to be getting to know us all pretty intimately in the next few hours.'

Epilogue

The first day back in the office after a spell away is always likely to prove a nightmare, and Kate arrived at her desk at 7.15 to give herself a chance of coping with the deluge. Things could have been worse: it seemed that Bryony had been as good as her word and arranged for the urgent cases to be passed to somebody else. Kate reflected on how easy it is to misjudge a person; easy and dangerous.

She dealt for a while with post and email. There were no messages yet from the course participants, though they had all promised to correspond. After half an hour or so she felt the need for a caffeine jolt and she went around to the coffee point in the open-plan area.

Nobody had started the coffee so far that morning and Kate spent a little while setting up the filters. Presently coffee began to drip through into the first jug. Kate leant against the wall and closed her eyes, smelling the wonderful aroma of the freshly brewing coffee, and let her mind roam back to yesterday.

Nick had surpassed himself . . . All afternoon he arranged people in different ways, keeping them aroused and amazed by his creativity. Time passed in a flash until he said with a reluctant face, 'We'll all have to hit the road pretty soon. I've been saving something up. Kate, it's for you: it's a thank-you arrangement.'

They laid Kate on one of the loungers by the pool. She was sitting almost upright, relaxed against the soft cushions. 'Now,' Nick said, adjusting the lounger so that Kate's body was positioned a little further back, 'now, here goes. Bryony, Sophie, come here and kneel down by her.' He guided their mouths to Kate's breasts and they began to lap, their tongues wet and warm and delicious against her naked skin. The tips of her breasts tightened, the coral-pink flesh crinkling and stiffening with pleasure. Kate gave a long, luxurious sigh and closed her eyes.

'Edmond,' said Nick's voice, 'I know what you'd like to finish up with. Go ahead. Christopher, if I could leave Kate to you . . .'

Kate heard Sophie give a little cry, and for a moment her mouth left Kate's nipple. Kate turned her head to one side and opened her eyes and saw Edmond kneeling behind Sophie, running his hands down her slender back and on to her white buttocks. He kneaded the soft flesh between his hands, bent forward and just for a moment pressed his tongue into Sophie's crevice, teasing the delicate skin around the anus so that she shivered. Then his hands slid on, down between her thighs, easing her legs apart and tracing the soft edge of her mound. Sophie whimpered and thrust her buttocks towards him and closed her lips tighter on the erect tip of Kate's breast. Edmond smiled and placed the head of his cock at the entrance to her sex and thrust until he was sheathed inside her.

The wet flesh between Kate's legs clenched unconsciously as she watched Edmond beginning to move, slipping his long, hard penis in and out of Sophie's body. She arched her back, pushing her aching breasts eagerly up towards the two soft mouths that suckled on them so deliciously, and her head rolled with pleasure. There on the other side of her knelt Bryony with Nick behind her;

the skin of his hands looked very dark as he gripped her snowy haunches with his hard fingers. He too was ramming her from behind, but he had chosen to take her in her arse and she was groaning with disbelief and ecstasy as his shaft plunged into her secret passage. Nick had turned Bryony's back a little towards Kate so that she would have an unrestricted view of what he did to her, and now as she watched he reached down with one hand and pushed two fingers into the moist mound between Bryony's legs, stroking with the pad of his thumb at the pink pearl of flesh that protruded just below her pubic triangle. Bryony's body jolted and she began to push back towards Nick, forcing herself down further on to his invading fingers and welcoming the ardent thrusts of his hard phallus, but she never hesitated in her diligent caressing of Kate's tight nipple.

The aching emptiness between Kate's legs suddenly metamorphosed into a tightening fist of desire as Christopher moved up between her wide spread thighs and nudged with the head of his wonderful cock against the moist, pouting lips. Kate's head turned slowly, as if it were very heavy, and she gazed deep into his eyes as he took hold of her buttocks in his big hands and began to enter her. He moved with unbearable, delicious slowness, savouring every moment as he penetrated her and the thick shaft forced its way up between her tight, warm walls. Sophie and Bryony sucked harder at her breasts and she flung back her head, gasping for breath. Christopher pushed himself into her, inch by inch, until at last the massive head of his penis touched the neck of her womb and the warm, hairy purse of his balls nestled against her buttocks and he lay still, filling her.

He lay within her, motionless. Kate could not bear it, she could not help herself: she began to writhe her hips from side to side, twisting herself on the thick rod that was buried in her, grinding her engorged clitoris harder and harder against the hot root of Christopher's beautiful phallus. Her arching back offered her erect nipples to the eager, suckling mouths that surrounded them. She cried out with desperate pleasure and frustration and above her Christopher suddenly laughed and began to move, withdrawing from her almost completely and then plunging back into her with all his strength: long, slow, juicy thrusts that made her yell in an uncontrollable howl of delight. He went on and on, pushing himself remorselessly into her so that his balls bounced against her loins. Kate abandoned herself to the sensation, her body jerking and surging upwards, ripples of rapture pulsing through her. At the moment of orgasm she froze, unable to move or breathe or cry out, her heart momentarily stopped, all her life suspended as she hung silent in an unending moment of ecstasy. Then she collapsed and lay panting as on either side of her Nick and Edmond urged Bryony and Sophie to their own gasping crises and Christopher drove himself furiously to climax within her still spasming sex.

'Penny for your thoughts,' said a voice. Kate almost jumped out of her skin and flushed scarlet before she saw that it was Bryony beside her.

'I'll give you three guesses,' she replied, smiling. The coffee had finished dripping and she opened a new pack of paper cups and poured a cup for herself and one for Bryony.

'If I had known how much fun you have on these courses,' Bryony said as she accepted the coffee, 'I would have understood why you like running them so much.'

'That's not – ' Kate began defensively.

'Not fair, yes, I know. Don't worry, Kate.' Bryony sipped her coffee and looked narrowly at Kate over the rim of the cup. 'Listen, were they being straight with me? Were you really intending to resign?'

'Well, yes,' Kate admitted.

'I'm glad I came, then. I mean, apart from the obvious reasons. Perhaps I haven't made it clear how much you're valued.'

'Thank you,' Kate said, a little stiffly.

'I wonder,' said Bryony, 'whether perhaps we could have lunch some time next week. I'd like it if you could explain what I missed on the first three days of the course; if I'm going on the follow-up day I ought to understand the course material, don't you think?'

'It'll take more than a lunchtime,' Kate said.

'Well, we can book the time in. Whatever you think it'll take: a crash course, if you like. I regret rather that I never went on any of these courses. I ought to understand them if I'm going to run this department. I'd still like to have lunch, though. Can I ask my secretary to arrange it?'

Kate hesitated. Then she said, 'Yes, Bryony, that would be good. I'd like it.' And she meant it. Bryony's attitude was suddenly so different that Kate believed she was even looking forward to it.

There was a beat of silence. Then Bryony said, 'Did you get Christopher home safely?'

Kate's head jerked up in surprise. Bryony had never, once, asked her about her personal life: she had always seemed totally uninterested. Now her small, bright face was enquiring, warm, open. Kate looked down and took a sip of her coffee, wondering briefly whether she should answer. Of course she should: not to would be an unmerited rebuff. 'Well, yes, I did,' she said eventually.

'And?' Bryony prompted.

'And nothing. I took him home; he took his bag out of the car and thanked me very much and then he went to the door.'

'Oh, Kate.' Bryony sounded as though she couldn't believe it. Her expression was sad and sympathetic. 'After all that business on the course! Didn't he ask you in?' Kate shook her head, looking rueful. 'I am sorry.'

Kate lifted one shoulder in a delicate shrug. 'I'm not worried,' she said, rather more boldly than she really felt. 'He's shy. The course was one thing, his life is another. I don't mind; I'm going to the theatre with him next week. It's all arranged. I think we're sort of starting from scratch.'

'But I saw him making love to you,' Bryony hissed, dropping her voice. 'Why hold back now? I don't understand.'

'The thing about influencing,' Kate explained, 'is that sometimes you have to go at the other person's pace, you have to follow their agenda, if you want to influence them. If I push Christopher he'll run away, he'll switch off. So I won't push.'

'Well,' Bryony shook her head, 'you've got more patience than me. I'm seeing Nick tonight and if I don't get what I want there'll be trouble.'

Kate laughed. 'The two of you together!' she exclaimed. 'I'll be able to see the fireworks from my balcony. He's not exactly easy to handle, you know, Bryony.'

'That's your opinion,' Bryony began with a smile. Then another figure appeared at the coffee point and she instantly switched back into assertive businesswoman mode. 'Well,' she said, 'lots to do. See you, Kate.'

Alex turned to watch Bryony striding away down the corridor. 'You're very friendly with Mrs T. all of a sudden,' he said to Kate, raising his dark brows.

The old sensation of desire and helplessness caught at Kate's throat. Despite all her resolutions she felt suddenly that it was useless, that something very deep blocked her from telling Alex how she felt. Perhaps it was because she was his boss: he might feel that he didn't have any choice, he might feel compelled. She couldn't bear the thought that he might say yes and not mean it. It was impossible, no point in trying. Anyway, she consoled herself, there was always Christopher. She could think about him instead for the time being. 'Coffee?' she asked Alex.

'Thanks.'

'You're in early,' Kate said as she poured the coffee.

'Yeah, well.'

She realised that Alex looked uncomfortable, awkward, almost like a bashful boy. He seemed tired, she noticed suddenly, and unhappy. 'Alex,' she said, frowning, 'is everything all right?'

'Look,' Alex said quickly, 'can I come into your office and have a word? I got in early because I thought you might be here.'

Oh God, Kate thought, he's going to resign. Shit, shit, shit. 'Yes, of course. Come on,' she said, and led the way.

They went into her office and she closed the door. 'What's the problem?' she asked him.

For a moment Alex said nothing, only stood looking down into his coffee cup and twisting his toe on the carpet. Then he said, 'I wanted you to hear from me rather than from one of the team. Ah, I broke up with Tina at the weekend and she moved out on Monday. I wanted you to know.'

'Oh,' Kate said in a small voice, 'I'm sorry.' She never knew what to say under these circumstances. The most selfish part of her was pleased because now Alex was alone, but Alex looked so weary it was impossible not to feel sorry for him.

'Oh, don't worry about me,' said Alex with an air of bravura. 'It was an accident waiting to happen: we've been on the rocks for ages. I, I'm not too cut up about it; not at all, really. I just wanted you to know.' He licked his lips and looked up. 'There was something else as well. I got some joining instructions through yesterday, I'm being sent on one of these influencing courses, and I know you run them. I just wondered if you might be running the one I'm going on.'

Kate shook her head regretfully. 'Afraid not,' she said. 'We avoid people tutoring their own staff, it can be awkward back in the office.' She looked up into those bright, bright eyes under their sparkling lashes and thought, I wonder if I can wangle it this time, though? Possibly?

'Oh.' Alex looked dashed. 'Well, look, Kate, do I really

have to go? I mean, I'm pretty influential already, all the guys say so. Why do I need to go on this course?'

'It's a good course,' Kate told him earnestly. 'In my view, everyone could benefit from it. That's what I was discussing with Bryony, actually.'

'Really? *Really?*' Alex looked amazed. 'Well, if you say so . . .' His voice faded out. 'It says in the instructions,' he said, 'that I need to discuss it with my line manager before I attend. Would that be you?'

'Yes, that's me. You can talk about it any time.' You can do anything to me any time, said Kate's hopeless desire.

Alex turned as if to leave Kate's office. Then he seemed to catch himself back and stopped, drawing his shoulders up. 'Kate,' he said to the door, 'there was something else.'

Kate felt a lump lurch in her throat and her heart began to beat faster. 'What?' she asked, trying to keep her voice even.

Alex swung suddenly to face her. 'I wanted to ask you – ' His voice broke and faded and he gave a soundless curse. 'Look,' he said at last, 'would you like to come for a drink tonight?'

The breath sighed out of Kate's lungs. For a moment she did not believe what she had heard. She frowned and licked her lips and said, 'Sorry, Alex, what did you say?'

'Forget it,' Alex said fiercely, flinging his hand in the air and turning away. 'I mean, it doesn't matter. Don't worry about it.'

'No,' Kate said urgently. She jumped after him as he reached for the door handle and caught his arm, swinging him to face her. 'No, Alex, I – '

He was staring down into her eyes, his breath coming quickly. She found herself trembling, still hardly able to believe what he had said to her. 'Please,' she managed to say after a moment, 'please, don't go. Tell me what you said. I just, I just didn't hear it.'

Alex licked his lips. As she had remembered, his tongue was long and sharply pointed. For some time he did not speak and Kate found thoughts spiralling through her mind. Suppose everything went well with Christopher? What then? Could she really begin seeing Alex now? Did he want to see her, or did he just want to have a chat to his boss? She was shaking with consciousness of his closeness, but she still did not know what he wanted or what she should do.

'I asked you if you would like to go for a drink this evening,' Alex said at last, very steadily.

He really had asked her, he really had. She was his boss; it must have taken a vast amount of nerve. Kate stifled a shiver and made herself smile. She still didn't know what sort of drink he meant. 'Yes, sure,' she said cheerfully. 'Why not, it's Friday, isn't it? Where do you want to go, the wine bar downstairs?'

'No.' He was shaking his head quickly. 'No, I don't mean after work. Kate, I – ' He bit his lip. 'I mean a real drink, Kate. Just us.'

Triumph rushed through Kate's veins. A real drink! 'Sure,' she said without another thought. 'I'd love to. What do you want to do?'

Alex's pale face flushed from cheek to brow as if he could not believe his success. He looked young and naïve and infinitely, tantalisingly desirable. 'We can meet in town,' he suggested. 'Or I, I could come to your place and pick you up. If you'd like it,' he added hastily.

'I'd like it,' Kate said, letting her voice become warm and husky. 'What time?'

'How about eight?' Alex said casually, trying hard to sound cool.

'Sure. That would be great.'

They stood looking into each other's eyes. Alex made a sudden, quick movement as if he was going to lean forward and kiss her, but then he withdrew just as quickly. 'Well,' he said, 'er, see you then. 'Bye.' He flashed her a quick, bright smile, then opened the door and slithered through it.

Kate stood very still in the middle of the room, staring at the closed door. It was beyond belief, but it was true. He wanted to see her. Her mind leapt forward to that night. Would they get out for a drink, or would she invite him in for one? What would he do to her?

But – Christopher. How could she accept Alex's offer, with a date fixed with Christopher for next week? She frowned and pushed her hand through her hair, starting the inevitable process of teasing it out of its comb. Then, out of the blue, a thought struck her. Christopher liked men as well as women. Why not seduce Alex, and then, and then bring both the men she most desired together into her bed? The thought of the two of them giving pleasure to her and to each other made her shudder with lust and excitement.

She had no idea of Alex's sexual tastes, but when she thought about it more it seemed relatively unlikely that he would be happy about jumping into bed with another man, no matter how attractive he found Kate. Resistance was almost inevitable. Kate walked slowly round to her desk and sat down in it, leaning back and stretching her arms above her head with a satisfied, feline smile. Wasn't she an expert in influencing? This could be her next test of skill: Alex and Christopher in the same bed with her. That would be worth the Influencer of the Year award. The prize shone in her mind, an extremity of pleasure. Her brain flamed with searingly sharp pictures. She imagined the sensation of Christopher's wonderful, massive cock in her sex, the musky taste of Alex in her mouth. She saw herself sprawled on her bed with her thighs flung wide, Alex crouching over her, his pointed tongue stabbing and lapping between her legs and his hard penis sliding in and out of her mouth. She looked up at his taut testicles and the firm white arches of his buttocks, darkly split with hair. And there, kneeling over him, Christopher, preparing to enter him before her eyes.

The bright morning sun glittered on the office opposite her window. It was a modern building, made of reflective glass, and bright shards of light shattered from its surface and showered coruscating reflections on to Kate's face. She shivered luxuriously, allowing the mental images free rein. 'Oh, Alex,' she whispered to herself, 'I hope you're looking forward to this as much as I am.'